SEQUENCE

ADRIAN DAWSON

"Genius is not about concocting
hair-brained schemes. Genius is
about making them work."

Alison Bond. August 16th 2043.

Published by Last Passage. www.lastpassage.com

First Published in Great Britain in 2011 by
LAST PASSAGE
www.lastpassage.com

Sequence is a work of fiction inspired in part by documented science.

Cataloguing in Publication Data is available from the British Library.

ISBN: 978-0-9565770-1-6

Typeset in Bembo and Arial by Last Passage Studios, Nottingham UK.
Cover Design and Illustration by www.d3-design.com.
Printed and bound by CPI Group (UK) Limited, Croydon, CR0 4YY.

'Dirty Love' and 'History in the Making'
written by Luke Morley and performed by Thunder.
Reproduced with thanks to Luke and the boys for the great music.

Last Passage Publications,
Nottingham, UK.

Also available by Adrian Dawson:
CODEX

Follow Adrian Dawson on Twitter: @adeydawson
More information: www.adriandawson.co.uk

GET THE BEST OF BOTH WORLDS!

By purchasing this novel from new in paperback format,
you are automatically entitled to a **FREE** high quality
ePub file which you can sync with your eReader of choice.

To claim your file, simply scan and email your receipt for
this paperback purchase to hello@lastpassage.com.

For Jo and John
Timeless Companions

Author's Note:

Sequence is a little different to many novels in that two very different typefaces are used throughout. Whenever you see **this** typeface, you are dealing with events past or present.

However, whenever you see **this** typeface, you are dealing with a parallel story which starts at the same point in time, but then runs quickly ahead into the future.

Note the dates included at the head of each chapter, my friend. Therein lies many a key.

St. Anthony and St. Paul - David Teniers the Younger - c.1645
Showing overlaid map geometry.

PROLOGUE
AUGUST 3RD 1132.
SERRES, PERPIGNAN, FRANCE.

In a time that Davies could barely recall or – truth be told – held no grasping desire to, his father had been a stonemason. Man and boy. It seemed so far away from him now that it could almost have been another life; another man.

The scent of the stone today, carried through the stale air with that of oil and dust, brought back unwanted memories of that life; of that man who had yet to be classed as such. These were dark scents, the kind that Davies had long since chosen to forget. Shit seeping through the lats from the barn; the fetor of freshly oiled leather and stale tobacco on the old man's breath; the metallic aroma of warm blood as it mixed with the tears and sweat which ran to earth from a pale twelve year old body.

Short of favours and a steady trickle of cash sidelines, his father's main business almost always came from the dead; carving their final message to the world – their epitaph. He etched a great deal of unfulfilled legacies into the kind of materials that would outlast their own deteriorating flesh many times over. For many years he had tried unsuccessfully to teach Davies that craft, one that his own father had handed down to him, along with a number of articles of clothing and a pair of never used cufflinks.

7

To Davies, that had summed the profession up perfectly. It was something that could be handed down because it was free and shit; there was precious little money to train family offspring for anything else. Besides, *'you don't get yourself a trade, boy, you ain't nevah gonna be able 'take care o'me. Your ma fuckin' off like she did'*. At that point his Pa would always point a grub-like finger up toward the blue of the Nebraska sky, like perhaps the boy's mother had *chosen* to let the cancer steal her away. Davies pondered that one often. He sure as hell wouldn't have blamed her if she had. The only words he remembered hearing from the husky old man in the days after she was gone were; *'S'pose I gonna have to carve her some nice words now. Damned if I can think some up. And who's d'yuh think's paying for that?'*

(I am Pa. Ev'ry god-damn day 'my life.)

As an emergent teenager, however, Davies had placed himself as squarely as he might on the road to becoming a man. A big man, mind, more than his father had ever been, and he had started to see just how ill-fitting the hand-me-downs had become and he wasn't about to slim down his ambitions to slide into them. Still, it had somehow become - though he felt loathed to admit it even now - exactly what his father had said it might one day be; a trade to fall back on.

(Another one.)

Even Davies himself, having failed at 'most everything else he tried, had been unable to miss the irony that the trade he had initially chosen to fall back on - that of 'stealin' and (where necessary) 'a spot o' killin' - was also the one that kept his father, and those like him, scraping a meagre living.

The only other skill Davies ever seemed to have developed, apparently, was fucking women; pretty much whether they wanted him to or not. Robbery, murder and rape, however, were not only his *favoured* career options, but also the ones that had been denied him for over five long years. He was looking forward to arriving back in the workplace, refreshed and ready after an enforced absence; pulling up his chair and getting back to business as it were. It was swimming so close to him now that he could almost taste it on his deformed tongue, the cause of his subtle impediment. '*That boy talk funny,*' they'd say. Not all his life of course, but certainly from the day of his fourteenth; the day his father had belted him that little bit too hard and sunk his bottom teeth clean through his tongue, leaving him spitting blood and a slice.

Perhaps, given the fact that he had never fulfilled so much as one of his father's expectations, low as they might have been, this was why Davies had somehow felt that he had needed to do this one job right. To carve the symbol – *his* symbol – so perfectly. So crisp, sharp and, yes – so very *beautiful* – that even a father who had yet to be born would look on him with the pride he had been denied throughout his shitty juvenile existence.

It went without saying that Davies chose, where possible, to forget what he could of his family, and yet he remembered every harsh lesson he had ever been taught. How could he not? Memory, after all, walked hand in hand with pain. It was something that, once burned in, could be suppressed but never fully erased. It waited like a painful itch; lingering until the day it felt that some benefit could be drawn from pulling itself to the fore, requested or not.

So he knew now, as he had heard way back when, that stone had 'grain' – like wood – and that its structure needed to be worked to a mason's advantage. He was also aware that (like thievin', rapin', killin') swift decisive strokes, hard and fast, were far more effective and true than the slow cautionary tap-tapping demonstrated so often by the painfully inexperienced.

He never held stock with the shorter chisels, either. *'Dem ain't worth shit, Boy.'* 'Short' did not carry the weight required for the job in hand and the only way to correct it would be to make the tool unusably thick and clumsy. No, Davies used a very slim chisel, almost two feet in length and forged from the toughest metals available at the time; bearing a sharpened tip that would have put many of the swords he saw daily to shame. In the wrong hands, such a lengthy item would probably be unwieldy. And the hammer? Big, blunt and impossibly heavy for some, but not a man of Davies' stature. Now it seemed, many years after his father's insistent and insulting instruction, he finally had the strength needed to wield both tools as precisely as if he were carving butter with a heated knife.

When the design was complete he checked the symbol against his own; the one he had worn for the four years since his conviction, and smiled when he saw that it was nigh-on perfect. The dark edges of the stone, weathered by age, gave way to the sharp light of the freshly exposed interior in smooth curves and strong, unwavering lines. He knew that his father would, just this once, have been proud, though he doubted (no, scrap that – he knew *damn well*) that he would never have made any such emotion visible.

But his father was not around was he? And why should Davies try to prove himself to him now anyway when he was almost thirty-eight years old and he hadn't seen hide nor hair of the man for half that life? Why had he even felt the need to try?

The old man hadn't even bothered attending the trial or seen the death sentence delivered to his son like a final demand.

(Why try?)

No, there was no-one around to be proud for Davies now but Davies himself, and wasn't *that* always the way?

(Why keep tryin'?)

With a sigh, breath and spittle whistling like leaves around his tongue, he removed a tapered sliver of fine pumice from an untreated leather belt and, using it as though sandpaper, began to smooth the bevels of the design. Carefully he blew away the fine dust and added a few drops of patina until the facets collected the cold hues streaming through the window and shone them back to his even colder eyes like angled mirrors.

He took a deep swig of water from his skin-flask, removed the two tables from individual leather purses, gently, and placed them into the circular recesses he had carved already.

They fitted perfectly.

(Look at them.)

He had known they would.

(Pa? See? Look at them.)

Another brief pause and one last look of admiration for his work then he took a deep, rasping breath and heaved the stone away from the floor like a dead-lifter. His already huge biceps bulged yet further and glistened with sweat from the heat of a fading late-summer day. With the stone at waist height, he leaned forward until it caught in the hole and rested a moment. Then, using almost the last of his strength he pushed forward, the ridges of his taut stomach acting as a press until his handiwork disappeared into the altar like a fox sliding backward into its lair. It rumbled as if in echo to the thunder which had begun to build steadily in the world outside.

It would be many hundreds of years before his skills, those his father had told him he would never - *evah* - perfect, would be seen again.

His primary task complete, he lifted a crude broom fashioned from dried grasses and twine and swept the floor of the church as best he could. *'Always tidy your shit up afterwa', boy'.* For some reason, even now, the older Davies felt it imperative to clean up his shit. His task would not be truly complete until it was done.

Within ten minutes the floor was cleared and he had done everything that had been asked of him. The tables were locked away - secure - and Davies, in stark contrast, was as free a man as he had long struggled to be. No one without the other. That, so they said, was the way it worked.

(It had better.)

He was all but ready to walk from the church and bathe in this new freedom when he felt another compulsion, one he didn't really understand. He sensed, somewhere within him, that he should kneel before the altar, just for a moment, and offer thanks. His family had been Baptists, probably for as many generations as Baptists had existed, but this was yet another hand-me-down that he had been so unwilling to accept. Davies had chosen not to believe in God, but rather to believe in Davies. After all, what was destiny if it was yet another thing you were unable to call your own?

Still, here was a man who could not deny that some really strange shit had sneaked into his life of late. The kind of freaky goings-on that might make a lesser man bow down and offer eternal loyalty to a deity that had very probably ceased to exist a good long time ago. And yet here he was now, facing a stone of God. Carving it, for Christ's sake.

Michael Davies was a man who was not even supposed to have been born and yet, at the same time, was already supposed to have been killed, sentenced to death, months ago. What could it harm to say thanks? Just in case? Cover all the bases.

He knelt on one knee, just like he'd seen the family do and crossed himself as a gentle blast of cold air curled from behind his shoulders. He probably did it wrong, but if God *did* exist, would he care? How petty were supreme beings anyway? He lowered his head and recited a prayer he once heard. It started 'Our Father, who art in Heaven…' and he pretty much ad-libbed it from there, his voice respectfully lowered.

Then he felt it. As surely as he had felt the rush of air that he had so foolishly chosen to ignore. Right in the nape of his neck; cold and sharp. No glory of God flowing into his body, but the razor-sharp tip of a blade that was all-but ready to. He hadn't even heard the bastard's footsteps; didn't even know what it was until he heard the voice.

"Où sont les tables?"

Davies lifted his head and creased his eyes at the polished marble of the altar. He saw the reflection of a large man, a bright red cross adorning the front of his tunic. Just one man, sword held firmly to his neck. *Geoffrey de fucking Beaujoulais* or whatever his name was. Always the spanner in Davies' plan. He had wanted to kill him three days ago, along with the others, but the prick had declined sleep and ridden on ahead to ensure that 'their passage would be safe' or some such shit. Davies had known that he could not risk waiting until the man returned, they might ride out again immediately, and so Geoffrey had escaped his

13

fate. Temporarily, it would seem.

He had known that this man would come looking for him one day, and that he might even possess the intelligence to find him. What he had been totally unprepared for was that he had been intelligent enough to have found him so soon. What Geoffrey had been unprepared for, on the other hand, was that he had been so goddamned stupid as to have come alone.

But then, hadn't that always been this guy's problem? He was always the one raising that polished sword of his high in the air and carping on about 'glory' and 'honour' whilst singularly failing to realise that he and his people – like Davies himself – were little more than thieves anyway. What was it they said about 'honour' and 'thieves'? Davies couldn't remember, not exactly, but it had something to do with there not actually being any.

He closed his eyes and took a deep long breath, determined not to fail now when he had come so far. He was desperately unprotected and felt it, having only a flimsy breastplate over his sleeveless coarse green tunic. Without warning, he clenched his yellowed teeth, twisted his head down and to the right, his thick neck breaking contact with the blade, then rose and swung his huge wrist and forearm with as much force as he could muster.

He caught the knight across the side of his helmet, knocking him sideways. Awkward. The man stumbled on the uneven floor, the flailing blade catching Davies' upper arm and cutting deep into the flesh. Then it fell loose in his armoured glove and Davies turned swiftly, kicking it hard across the church until it clattered against the western wall, the sound echoing like breaking glass. Then Davies punched. Hard. He could feel the knuckles break in his hand against the metal visor, but didn't care. They would heal far faster than any blade wound he might suffer. Then, as Geoffrey reeled backward, Davies lifted his leg and caught him full in the balls. Don't protect those puppies when you're riding a horse, do you big fella?

The knight fell to his knees, leaning forward and Davies sealed the deal with a swift upward kick to the face. The hardest he'd ever given, despite painfully thin leather moccasins. Between two lesser men the blow would probably have been both a foot and a neck-breaker.

The man was thrown backward like a failing acrobat, his chain-mail crunching loudly on the cold stone floor despite the thin muslin tunic of Cistercian white and red that he wore with such unwarranted pride.

Davies looked to the sword but decided, wisely, that to waste time retrieving it would be a very bad move indeed. So instead he took a step back, pondering his options, until he felt his heel catch something. Something cold, metallic and heavy. Something like divine inspiration. Perhaps a 'thank you' for the 'thank you', as it were. He looked down through the knight's visor, saw the first hint of fear in the man's eyes and smiled.

He stooped, reached behind and picked up the hammer and chisel. He flipped the hammer a full three-sixty in his left, unbroken hand, catching it by the handle once more and smiled. His eyes became wild and he screamed loudly, maniacally, as he became Davies once more and brought the hammer down with full force across one of the knight's knees. The man wore armour, sure, but at the joints it was at its thinnest and it crumpled like paper, allowing the heavy lump to strike bone with most of its delivered power. Then he repeated the process three more times, one for each limb. Each time the hammer made contact the knight screamed and Davies, eyes wide, screamed even louder, desperate not to be outdone.

With the knight unable to move, short of a maggot-like writhing from the pain, Davies whirled around the church, spinning and laughing. It lasted almost two minutes. When he had exhausted himself he collapsed to his knees, falling astride the crippled man's stomach and glancing seductively – perhaps as a lover might - at the blood red cross emblazoned on his chest.

"I'll take 'Dead of Knight' for ten points, Geoffrey," he said with a twisted smile as he used his broken hand, his thumb at an awkward angle, to line up the chisel in the centre of the cross.

How thoughtful, he mused, for his victim to have provided him with so clear a target. He could see those eyes again, staring from their dark recess and widening toward the inevitable. The man tried to struggle and mumbled something incomprehensible in French but Davies' weight, coupled with an inability to gain upward leverage with shattered limbs, made it little more than a futile gesture.

"Je monte avec mon Dieu." The man's voice was resigned now, ready.

Davies lifted the hammer high, smiling the kind of smile he hadn't managed to smear across his hardened face since he'd watched the old lady he'd doused in petrol sear like the witch he had always liked to think she was.

"Yeah? Well, you can ride *to* him now. Shithead."

He brought the crude block down on the chisel with the weight of all the anger he had ever known. The chain mail the man wore over his sideless linen undertunic, whilst enough to withstand a flimsy arrow carried on the air, stood little chance against the weight of the sharpened iron or the weight of injustice guiding his adversary's arm. It tore apart like an old dish-rag, the kind Davies' father had used to oil the stones. The tiny steel links crunched loudly and joined the chisel on a swift, bloody journey into the man's chest. The force momentarily lifted his extremities away from the floor and his breastplate, his *internal* breastplate, popped like a firecracker.

The hammer came down again, and a third time, stopping only when Davies felt the man's spine crumble through the metal and heard the sharp strike as the tip pierced the cold slabs beneath him.

Davies smiled again, gently lifted the man's hinged visor so that he could see the blood as it started to bubble from his mouth, then just sat and watched, admiringly, as the man fought for breath that would no longer come.

"Écoutez et répétez," he said, tilting his head. "*Boudine!* Translation? *Bullseye.*"

He leaned back, upright, and smiled again as another thought entered his head. It had taken three full days for him to reach Serres on foot, hard stones biting through leather the whole way, and the sound of the rain outside was growing stronger by the minute. Suddenly that didn't matter any more. Not when he had transport, courtesy of his soon-to-be-dead friend here.

"Hope you left the keys in your horse, dipshit," he said, eyebrows flicking upward. "'Cos I think I'm gonna need to borrow it."

There was no understanding in the man's eyes. Not for the language of the words Davies had spoken or for the fact that he had met his death so swiftly and unexpectedly, having spent the last five years fighting one of the bloodiest campaigns in the history of mankind. Slowly but surely, as his killer stared down at him with the warm, gentle smile of a mother admiring a new-born child, there was nothing left in those eyes at all. They

17

did not close, but the life was gone and the bubbling stopped.

With a shrug Davies climbed to his feet. These things never seemed to last quite as long as he wanted them to. He pulled the chisel from the man's chest with sword-from-the-stone pride, then returned to the altar and gathered his other tools. The tools of his trade - if he ever needed one.

It felt good to kill again. Not like Narbonne, that was all too remote, but actual hands on. He liked to feel the warmth of the blood and see the life drain from the body in true close up. He would probably have to do it again real soon. First he wanted to fuck a woman, though. Any woman, but preferably one who had no desire whatsoever to be fucked.

Always more fun that way.

Besides, wasn't that where the word 'fuck' came from anyhow? That's what he'd heard. In the nineteen hundreds it had been the term for rape, given that suspects were tried 'For Unlawful Carnal Knowledge'.

Shit, he thought, he was gonna do something to a woman, maybe even *plenty* of women, that hadn't even been invented yet and he was gonna make them love it. You just try to get your crazy head around that.

"Tell you what-dere, Mikey-boy," he said to himself, the words struggling to fight around his tongue as he rubbed his shattered hand and ambled from the church toward the elongated future which awaited him. Blood was running the length of his left arm, but no tears diluted its rich colour. Not any more.

"This really is some crazy shit you got going on here."

He stepped over the body without sparing another glance.

"Ain't no fucking doubt about *that*."

ONE

CALIFORNIA. TODAY.

It's a damn sight colder than I expected.

Which is why my hands, for now at least, are pushed as deep into my overcoat pockets as they will go, searching for the kind of warmth that might keep my fingers from locking solid. I curse to myself. Why am I here now? What did I think I would have to gain? What was it that made me come so early when the cold is biting at my skin with the kind of teeth that should only appear inside the mouth of a small rodent? I know that this won't do me any good whatsoever.

Come to think, what would?

It's coming to an end. All of it. Soon it might actually be over. And then, just as suddenly, I realise that what I am feeling now must be excitement. It's been a stranger to me for so long that I barely recognise it when it calls. It is that which has made me sit alone in the cold for the better part of an hour now, freezing my bony ass off. I'll tell you something for free: it feels good. Really it does.

I can't help myself. I just have to take one more look at the letter. I have to make that childish smile of mine grow even wider as I read the words one last time, though by now I know every last one of them by heart.

They've travelled with me for countless years and they'll probably travel with me to my grave.

Which is kind of ironic, really.

So I pull the blue envelope from my inside pocket and open the flap again. Always the best quality, always lined. This is both the latest and the last of those envelopes, the letter having made its home within it just six months ago. There have been many others, of course, each ravaged by the passage of something that I know for a fact cannot be altered and replaced when their condition deteriorated to such a degree that they could offer protection no more.

I carefully slide out the ivory sheets, allowing the elements to take one more bite, and open them to see the stark near-black script flowing across the surface of the paper. And I smile, just as I always do. I'm not trying to sound overtly romantic when I say that just to see the words is like watching a friend beckoning you into the warmth of their home each and every time. I feel compelled to read them to you. So that you might know....

* * * * *

Nick,

I'm so very sorry. I never was very good at goodbyes, but I hope you understand why I had to do this - to leave you to finish this alone.

I'm sure you felt that this was the beginning, but perhaps you realise now that we share very different perceptions of where the beginning actually belongs. For me, if you're interested, it always starts on the day of my twelfth birthday.

I am in a graveyard, kneeling in thick grass. My uniform has a line of thick mud around the hem and torn pleats are riding over my knees.

My shoes, normally so clean, are almost unrecognisable under the dirt which covers them and sharp stones bite into my legs.

I am alone in time, begging in a way I never thought possible and I feel as if the world is somehow punishing me.

I am begging for my dead mother's forgiveness. Why? For being able to beg at all. The cold truth is that I am alive and she is not.

Today, I come to put things right.

Five long days have passed since I discovered the truth - that the woman whose death had delivered me into this world, who had spent a lifetime lost and alone in ways I will never fully comprehend, had been raped. I am the product of the worst pain a woman could be forced to endure; the product of a rapist's longings, not a mother's. I am left wondering if perhaps my mother chose to die, simply because she could not bear to open her eyes and look at me.

I am twelve years old. I shouldn't have to carry a burden like this.

This is not my mother's grave, even I am wise enough to understand that. I adopted it two years ago when I came to the cemetery with my friend Gemma and it has become my personal altar ever since. Whenever she visited the grave of her mother, so did I, as best I could. It is as far away from the neatly tended plots and marble statues as it can possibly be. It is alone and left fighting for itself against the world, a twenty-dollar miss-spelled stone crumbling at the edges whilst year after year the inscription fades beneath yet another layer of dirt.

Hear Lies, God's special gift to us all.
Those who care are those who need to know.
Until He crosses our paths again.
Be at peace.

No name and no date. And, yes, those words could have been written specifically for me. It is because I cared that I needed to know and even now, when that knowledge is burning like coals in my stomach, I remain resolute in the decision I made to ask the questions. The who, the what, the why and the when. It was not until I was given the answers that I actually felt shame invade my body. In that instant, I knew that I had to return here. I had to seek forgiveness from whatever lame excuse for parenthood I had created for myself.

Later that night, wide awake and tearful, I began to realise something else; something darker than I had ever imagined. I realised that this would be my last visit. A debt was hanging unpaid and I should give up what was not rightfully mine; my right to life itself.

So I ease the razor from my pocket and take a deep breath, my heart pressing against my ribs as I prepare to make the cut…

Then a warm voice; behind me.

ScaryBob; the name we've given this creepy guy who's been hanging around the school. Teachers have told us to stay well away, but he never comes close. He just sits on a bench and stares at us as we play.

"I asked if you were alright, young lady?" he says, and though gravelly, his voice is unexpectedly soft, "I saw you crying…"

As he crouches beside me he catches sight of a glint. He takes my hand firmly in his own and his eyes widen. The blade has made a mark on my wrist but little more. Not yet.

He sighs. A world of weight in one breath. "I think you and I need to have ourselves a talk."

I'm reluctant, of course, but I feel lost. Eventually, we talk about my mother, and my life, and for the first time I begin to accept. I don't feel better or worse, I just… understand. He has already taken the blade and now he tries to extract something else, something I do not want him to have. Promises I am reluctant to give, even to myself.

And then, as the tyres of Sheriff Coulson's blue and white Dodge grind dirt in the distance, he places a broad hand into his coat pocket and pulls out a silver locket attached to a simple chain.

Inside is a watch - face white as snow, numerals black as coal. And, whilst the casing is already decaying on the outside, the inside is showroom condition; the glass as smooth as the day it was ground.

"It looks old."

"It is," he replies with a smile. "And I'd like for you to have it."

"I can't…"

"I was given this watch many years ago by somebody very special," he says, calmly, "and I will tell you a secret - it never stops. Ever."

Seeing the look on my face he laughs. "There's no special trickery involved. It's self-winding, that's all." He pauses, staring first at the face of the watch, and then at mine. "But I always figured that for as long as I had it in my possession I should check this watch regularly. I guess I decided that if the seconds ever stopped counting then maybe - just maybe - so would those of the world around us."

"I have a terrible disease," he says quietly. He looks dead ahead, as though talking to himself. "For years it has been eating me alive and now its feast is coming to an end. My time, it seems, is over."

He looks back to me and shakes his head. "But not yours. Not yet. You are alive because of what God has given you and His gifts should not be handed back. This isn't Sears & Roebuck. This is life - God's special gift to us all."

He laughs gently. "See? I can read headstones too."

Coulson and his deputy are holding wide-brimmed hats against the wind as they start up the path toward me. I stand up and straighten my uniform, ready to hand myself back to Cedar Ridge.

"Will I see you again?" I ask.

He looks up with a smile. "It sure would be something to look forward to, wouldn't it?"

It was clear that the meal would soon be at an end. I never said goodbye. Perhaps there was no need.

For me, this is where it all began. And despite it seeming like a strange dream, I know that it was not. I know because it is now 6:58pm. Precisely. And if this watch is real, how can the things that happened that day not be the same?

Not only does it sit here with me and record the seconds as I write, but I also know with a certainty you will not share - yet - that it will continue when you and I are both long gone. It will outlive us both many times over and will never stop because it can never stop; not when there is no end to the things we do. I look through my window to the streets below. All is calm - but not for long. Here's where a battered old Ford will soon arrive to kick some of my dust into cloud.

Understand as I leave you, Nick, that I am happy with my life. Happier than I have been in any other chapter of it. The only hurt stems from the knowledge that I promised myself two things in the days that followed my acceptance of possession. The first was that if I ever met the man who raped my mother I would kill him without a thought. The second was that I would never again try to take my own life. This special gift.

It is only now, writing a note to a man I've never met, that I realise I lied on both counts.

Goodbye and good luck, Nick.

I know you'll take good care of me.

★ ★ ★ ★ ★

It's just a suicide note. A goodbye. Isn't it?

To you perhaps, but not to me. To me it's not *just* anything.

These sheets of paper are actually the most precious document this shit-bag world has ever thrown my way. More important than my acceptance into the declining fold of the Los Angeles Police Department, more important than the deeds to my apartment and far more important than my marriage certificate. Christ, I've had junk mail that was more important than my marriage certificate. And yes (though I know you will probably come down hard on me for this now) it is even more important than Vicki's birth certificate.

Vicki, blonde and all grown up, having changed faster than I can track from pig-tailed cherub to beautiful young object of man's desires, is my daughter. Not that I actually get to see her much these days; too busy for the old man it seems, but I see her more than I did in those dark days way back when. Not just the days, either. The months and the years that followed after Katherine, her mother, moved to Seattle with the man who used to criticise my oral hygiene and make me gargle with pink toilet cleaner before charging me more money than I could ever afford. I never realised that the guy had been giving my wife oral as well. Not until I came home one night to a note.

I should have known the instant I saw the envelope. Brown. And no good news ever came in a brown envelope, now did it?

In a blinding instant my home became a house again; somewhere to exist, not somewhere to live.

I never chased. What was the point? She was reasonable about access to Vicki, far more than I ever took advantage of and far more than I would have been granted from a judge with knowledge of the state of my life at that point.

That was eleven years ago and I see Vicki maybe once a month now, if she's free. In her youth I was lucky – and she wasn't – if I made it to see her once a year. I'm sorry to admit to that, but I have enough lame excuses to bore you for a week.

ADRIAN DAWSON

I've read this letter far more times than I can count or would care to try. *Just in case.* In case of what I have absolutely no idea because, like I say, I know every last word; every damn syllable and every careful stroke of the pen as if I had written the damn thing myself (even that slight smudge on the capital 'D' of Sheriff Coulson's Dodge). But still I have that fear. That inane fear that involves the forgetting of some small but *imperative* detail, when my time comes.

What if? can be one hell of a powerful stimulant to irrational action. If you can bear the ramblings of a tired old man, you'll see why it's been so for me. You'll see so much else as well, and you'll learn some things *you really ought to know*.

Now I guess I would say that, wouldn't I? After all, this is my story and I want you to listen to every word, but it's honestly no advertising gimmick. I hold no store with the 'finest beer in the world' claims. Whether it is or it isn't comes down to buying a bottle and throwing the stuff down your throat. If it tastes like piss then the guy with the smile can repeat the line until he's blue and it won't make you buy another bottle. Unless you have a penchant for drinking piss, of course.

So if you want to listen, please do. If not, then feel free to swirl around your own ocean with your eyes and ears searching the depths for other things. It won't change anything about your future (which is the real beauty, I have to tell you), but then history is an important subject and that can't be changed either. I want to give you a history lesson about things which have yet to happen. Things that *will* happen, come what may.

I read *those three words* again; the ones I adore, and my anticipation mounts. Hell, I've waited a long time for this day to arrive and so you can't just expect me to sit here thinking about which

26

meal for one I should nuke when I get home, or whether that fella with the limp on Ev'ry Daze will find out about his wife and the doctor.

Three words. Three very simple, carefully chosen words.

It always starts...

And within them lies the crucial word; *always*. Until I received this letter I would never have dreamed it possible to envy the use of just one word of English language quite as much as I do now. It must happen, must *have* happened, so many times. Over and over and... well, you know. List goes on.

But not for me. So much has happened; so much has *yet to happen*, but still mine is and always will be a one-shot deal. It sneaked into my extraordinarily dull life on a very bleak Thursday, unremarkable in every way save for the fact that I'd just started smoking.

Again.

TWO

It was already shaping up to be a pretty shitty day. Sure, I'd had worse – the lines on my face should tell you that much - but I'd never yet found a situation where that actually seemed to offer any form of compensation. None whatsoever.

I'd got two low-life dealers in court at nine, both wearing suits I couldn't afford. By twelve I'd got the same two low-life dealers back on the street, flanked by attorneys with ties I couldn't afford. I'd no idea of the exact time that one of their late-teen clients next chased the dragon right into its dirty lair and left another set of kids (always more than one) without heat, light, or food – 'til the neighbours started to wonder, I suppose - *'til the smell of mommy rotting got bad.*

It was probably within the hour.

I cut my way through the blackest rain I remember, arriving at Jack's Shack by twelve-ten and counting up change in my pocket for a pack of twenty. Barry (the Jack of Jack's Shack) smiled a broad Jamaican smile as I walked in and gave me that disappointed look he gives so well as I walked out. I said nothing. This time I'd gone four days, three hours and twenty-six minutes (approximately, you understand) and that, my friend, is a record. By about four days, I think.

I took my usual seat at Cody's, my coat dripping like I'd got ice in the pockets, and looked up through the deluge just in time to catch my low-lifes sliding like fish into a car they couldn't afford. A few seconds later it disappeared with a gentle squeal along I-101.

It's at this point that you probably expect to hear the words: 'never to be seen again', but I can't tell you that. I knew it would be back. Just you see if it wouldn't.

Tomorrow, maybe the day after, I'd be buying another pack and watching that same car scoop up more of the dirty fingernails who'd sensibly never skimmed from the guy with the clean hands. He'd send them the benefit of another expensive tie to uncover technicalities on a 'per' basis, then he'd send them the car. Finally, when they'd all shared another laugh at my expense, he'd send his little suckerfish out to swim through the schools again.

Fish is what they were to me. Slimy little fish. You caught 'em, hauled 'em in, kept 'em long enough to get some snaps and then you let 'em go. It always surprised me that I never took mugshots down to Cody's of an evening to pass round over a beer. *Hey, everyone… check out the one that got away from me today!*

Like there would have been any point. As I've said, these were little fish. You don't mount these on inch-thick mahogany and hang them over a lodge fire. Shit, most days I couldn't even stop judges tipping rudder fish back into my murky pond. Back into an undercurrent that always seemed to travel in circles.

Meantime, I had three full sets of paperwork to write up, so I'd have to go fishing again the following day; first light. I downed the last of the whisky and slammed the money on the bar.

Cody said nothing, but his face spoke volumes. It seemed that whatever had caused Barry's disdainful smile was now running a serious risk of becoming an epidemic.

I so desperately needed another cigarette, but figured I'd exercise patience and finish the one I was smoking first.

★ ★ ★ ★

All three files were still on my desk, along with a new pile of unopeneds which I placed on the 'To-Do' pile I had been carefully constructing on the floor. A handwritten Post-It was wavering in the air-con against the picture of Katherine and Vicki (I never did get around to digging out a shot of Vicki alone) which I chose not only to ignore, but also to peel off, scrunch up and throw as close to the bin as I could manage. Not because it was handwritten, you understand, but because one glance told me it was in Deacon's handwriting and Deacon could wait. I took the ashtray from my top drawer. Four days since I'd seen it and far longer than that since I'd actually bothered emptying it. I added one more spent butt to the pile, sighed, and started attacking the papers.

From one of many desks behind me, I heard the hiss of Wells and the slap of a high-five; Rodriguez no doubt handing over at least a twenty on a lost bet. I don't know who'd gambled on me breathing clean air the longest, and I didn't bother to turn and find out. I just did what I always did. Kept to myself and did what I had to do. Which right now was typing out shitty reports.

All the while Deacon's crumpled handwriting was prompting me from stage left: *My office…*

When I'd written report number two, the note got the better of me and I retrieved it, opening it out to reveal the words *before you do anything else.*

I noted that he'd creatively underlined the word 'before'. Which was just peachy.

Another half-smoked, my fourth within the hour, created the summit of Mount Marlboro as I opened my bottom-right drawer, my special drawer, and leaned down to take a swig of Jack. Figured I might just be needing it.

I grabbed my jacket and headed up to the third. Not that one needed a jacket to gain entry to the third you understand, it wasn't that exclusive a club, but Deacon's personal invitations usually left precious little time to stop back on two on your way out. Best to take what you need.

He was on the phone when I entered and was looking - as ever - like his ma had dressed him for a job interview he wouldn't get. He also looked unnaturally flustered. Okay, so the room was hot even with the blinds down, but I got the distinct impression that it was the voice on the other end that was causing his hairline to develop this particular line of diamanté saltwater.

And I liked it - Deacon on the back foot, I mean. Now that just *had* to be the wife. Or one of his three annoyingly precocious daughters. He was sure apologising to somebody, and where Deacon was concerned that was something you couldn't help wishing you'd caught on camera. Every glance upward was telling me I should have knocked, whilst a manicured hand smoothed the sweat in with the gel, a monogrammed cufflink exposed in the process.

A cap 'D'; Roman face. Deacon all over.

Now, believe it or not, I'd always been a fair guy and I had this unspoken rule. If and when Deacon achieved the physical impossibility of eight years longer on the force than I had, then

I'd knock. Until then he'd just have to keep his family apologies and his handwritten Post-Its that little bit further apart from each other.

I guess I was smiling that odd smile I'd perfected so well at the time he'd hung up. The one just guaranteed to piss him off. Why not? Ten bucks told me I was there so he could piss me off and I believe that shit like that should work both ways. I'm a firm believer, when it suits my needs, of equality in the workplace.

"If you've got somewhere you need to be tonight, Lambert, then I heartily suggest you cancel."

He turned disinterestedly away and pulled a Diet Coke from a wood-effect mini-fridge by the window. Coke would have been bad enough, but Diet Coke? Where had all the whisky drinking stereotypes gone? It took a second, but then I realised. The only one left was standing in front of Deacon's desk smiling an odd smile. The desk onto which a painfully thin Manila file had just been slapped.

"Oakdene," he said bluntly, easing back into his chair and pulling the ring on the can (carefully, though, those nails cost money). "Take a drive. I need you to check out one of the patients. A girl."

'Fan-*tastic*," I said, with slow pain. And yes, I know it was only one word, but this really was the All-Juice of sarcastic answers. I mean, you just couldn't have squeezed any more in if you'd tried. You see, in this precinct (as I'm sure it goes in so many others) the phrase 'a girl' in the context of a major investigation had its own time-honoured definition. It referred, for the most part, to one particular breed of girl, the kind who are known to spread 'em and co-operate far more readily for the bad guys than for the good.

With this in mind, you'll forgive me if I took a while to getting to the 'pleased and delighted' stage of my assignment acceptance speech She'd tell me jack shit then tell me to jack off.

I opened the file and saw three piss-poor copies of piss-poor originals. Eight paragraphs of Latin scribbled onto a scrap of dirty paper, with the words: ITINERIS HAUD TEMTATIO, circled and asterisked. It'll come as no surprise, I'm sure, but short of offering a future way of cheating at scrabble it all meant shit to me. The other photocopies were two of the autopsy shots. The first was a close-up of a tattoo on a dead man's ankle; the second a close-up of a dead man's face. He didn't look especially happy, I have to say, but then he was dead. I mean, given those circumstances, who the hell would?

"The guy you're looking at had three to the chest, one to the arm and one that took a rather generous slice out of his ear," Deacon said, without looking at me. "City Refuse found him lying in a pool of his own behind Mister Yang's. And it would appear that those aren't the first bullets he's taken either; they're just the first to kill him. He also has two rather nasty lower-back shots maybe four or five years old and at least five knife wounds of varying ages. One has tissue that isn't fully repaired so we're talking eight weeks old at best. That alone would have put him in County but he isn't on file at any L.A. facility. I'm guessing he isn't from around here."

He lowered himself into his black leather high-back. When it came to leather chairs, bosses had high-backs. The more dead cows you sat on, the more authority you wielded. It was some kind of law. Deacon wouldn't be happy, I always figured, until the day I entered to find him astride a still-snorting steer and waving his hat in the air.

"He isn't talking because he isn't breathing," he offered blandly, "and I'd like to know why."

"And nobody saw or heard a thing, right?"

Rhetorical question.

Mister Yang's was a decent Chinese supermarket, the kind with some foods you'd never tried and some you'd never realised you'd never tried. It had been there as long as I could remember. It was just unfortunate that 'there' was on fifth which, over a good many years, had descended from its already lowly status to become the shittiest part of the shittiest part of town. Missions, single room occupancies, soup kitchens. Drugs, rapes, stabbings, shootings. Had 'em all. I only ever went to Yang's when the till had been emptied and/or the new assistant had met the same fate as his or her predecessor. Every time I'd hear the same line; nobody saw nothin'.

Least of all the irony of double negative.

It's no longer there (in case you fancied getting mugged Szechwan style). It got torched about two years after they found the stiff and all the food got cooked in one big street-side barbecue. Now I know it's a crying shame when such a long standing institution as Yang's is lost to us forever but trust me, I was there. The smell was fantastic.

Deacon pulled a ten by eight from one of his own files and laid it down. I picked it up to see a full-colour, full-body of the naked stiff, eyes and mouth wide open. Nothing unusual there. Even those who expect to die don't actually expect it to hurt quite the way it does. Our guy was mid- to late-thirties with close-cropped hair and a goatee. A single line of bad stitching from abdomen to breastplate indicated that he'd already had his majors 'thrown and sewn' by a senior, leaving a clumsy junior to button him up against the morgue's permanent winter.

"You'll notice that on the fragment of Latin you have there are two handwritten additions. One says Teniers - 1645, which is apparently a reference to an artist working around that time, so this could be art theft, or maybe a fraud. But the other note says: Tina Fiddes - 113."

"And...?"

"And it's taken some digging but eventually we've discovered it's the name and room number of a patient up at Oakdene. What she knows about art we don't know. Yet. That's pretty much where you come in..."

"Fuck you, Deacon." The photo landed back on the desk, my open hand still trying to push it deeper into the veneer. I almost couldn't believe he was doing this. Again. I say almost, because this is Deacon we're talking about. "Who's the we? Who's really on this?"

No reply.

I laboured the words. "Who's on it, Deacon?"

Deacon took a deep swig of Coke - correction *Diet* Coke - wiped his mouth and smiled. It curled down the sides, which told me that I wouldn't like what he was going to say. It also told me this was the reason he was going to say it. Now the thing is, I knew a lot about suits, shirts, ties, watches, cufflinks; all that stuff. All the stuff that Deacon wore. I'd put more people away than I'd care to mention for stealing or shifting any or all of the above and that was how I knew that fish wore 'good suits / bad shirts' and attorneys went two-for-two. Deacon, on the other hand, was always none-for-none.

Sure, the suits and the shirts looked like they were cut good, but that was good shopping, not good tailoring. The guys I put away wouldn't have been seen dead hawking the kind of stuff he wore around. I always gave him credit for trying on a meagre salary such as his, though. More than mine, sure, but a lot less than the J. Edgars he had once been so eager to join.

And every penny would be going straight into those nagging and precocious mouths. The kind of mouths that need feeding with new handbags and shoes to match and then a new dress because the shoes are a different shade of primrose to the dress they already have and now they have the new dress does this handbag really go with it, or should they get a clutch bag as well just to be safe? Spend, spend, spend.

All except for Emma, the youngest and most brattish of the Deacon clan, of course. She cared little for clothes as I understood it. Her mouth just needed more school fees and another fat-assed pony she'd never ride.

Oh yeah, and let's throw Braxton the St. Bernard puppy into this happy mix – because I doubt he was cheap to feed either.

So why do I bring this up now? Because the shirts and suits tell me that Deacon has very little left in his Italian leather wallet once the ladies are all looking gorgeous and the monthly livery fees are paid to keep Braxton's next tin of food in hay and oats. Which meant that those perfect ice-white teeth of his, the ones that glinted and sparkled in that annoying way that they did whenever he was addressing a young female officer or handing out shitty details to an older, more masculine one like myself, were bought on credit.

And if a man didn't own his own teeth just yet, then I sure as hell didn't want him smiling at me like that with them.

"Ellis and Dean," he said. So matter-of-fact. So very glint. So painfully sparkle.

"Double fuck you," I feel I was very clear about that. "Since when did I become library clerk for Ellis and Dean? What? They've got the legs, but they don't like the legwork, is that it?"

Deacon leaned forward, looked me right in the eye and tried to paint a sense of intrigue across his fake-tan, his chin resting on his hands. "Would you maybe like to know what this guy was wearing when we found him?"

I tried to laugh it off. "Like to know or want to care?"

Deacon wasn't stupid, though. That I did know. He was annoying, sure, and not as sharp as his elevated position might demand of him, but he wasn't stupid. He knew damn well he had me on both.

He smiled one of those 'have I got a story to tell you' smiles; the kind I really dislike. "Well, let's just say he wasn't wearing the same suit he isn't wearing now. Add to that the fact that his fingertips have been burned off, professionally it seems, and what we have here is a naked stiff with no fingerprints, nowhere to keep his loose change and nothing that bears even a passing resemblance to a clue as to why he's been shot five times."

"Except we have the Latin," I offered. "And the girl."

"Not at the scene, we don't,." Now the eyes were as wide as the smile. "They come later."

He pulled out another picture and laid it down. It showed a small yellow rubber parcel, the same size and shape as a half-smoked cigar. One of the wide, expensive ones. I just knew I was not going to like what it was.

"Those beauties don't show up until your friend Doctor Jessie opens his back doors to see what he's been eating of late and finds this. It seems somebody doesn't like what he's carrying and has told him he can quite literally stick it up his ass."

He smiled at his own joke. Had it been amusing, I might have joined in.

"Now stories about dead guys with rubber bungs containing foreign texts stuffed up their rear-end soon get around. I mean, this isn't anything normal like coke or horse. Nobody ever got swung for smuggling Fourth Century Latin through customs, which that is by the way. So at five o'clock this morning, much to Jennifer's eternal delight, I'm dragged out of bed because the Feds want to take a look at the case. My case. And look at it they do. For the full fifteen minutes it takes them to box up every one of the damn files and take them away."

My case. The Feds. And now we were getting somewhere. Because if there was one thing Deacon hated more than me screwing up one of his cases it was the Feds coming along and stealing one, thereby denying me the chance. Would've been so different if he had actually passed their medical last year, I suppose, but there you go.

"And these pictures?" I pointed to the copies.

"Fortunately for us these were already on the circuit, so we've taken copies for each team. Ellis and Dean lead and get the stiff, the scene and associated forensics. Rodriguez and Wells are deciphering the Latin and checking out the Teniers link and you - in true movie fashion - get…," two annoying rabbits with the fingers, "…the girl."

I'm shaking my head even before he even breeds the rabbits. "And anything I find I hand to Ellis and Dean, yeah?" I laughed quietly. "Just how many 'Fuck you's' am I up to?"

"Anything you find comes to me," he said sternly. Like he meant it. "Now you know I hate to level with you, us sharing this mutual dislike thing as we do, but I really, really and - dare I say it? - really don't like the suits taking my cases away. Stiff turns up in our neighbourhood, we find out which of our neighbours did it. That's our job. It's what we get paid to do. Leave it to the Feds and my guess is we'll never see or hear of this again." He downed the last of the Coke, scrunched the can and basket-pitched it into the trash.

"And it's three, by the way."

He leaned back in his chair. Still looked serious. In the same way a five year old does when they are about to explain why Barbie must drink from the green mug and not the pink. "Listen, Nick, I've got a stiff here and I really wanna find out why. I wanna know why he's buck naked, I wanna know why he's got Latin stuffed up his ass and, yeah, I wanna know why he's so very interested in Tina Fiddes - 113. It would also be nice to know where the bullets came from that killed him and why, despite the fact that all blood patterns point to him being killed in the alley, the two bullets which passed clean through him are nowhere to be found."

Where the bullets came from; interesting. Possibly. "So the bullets aren't standard?"

"Custom made," he said, eyebrows raised like it was something that genuinely surprised him. "Slightly different alloy to any we can find on the market. Instead of straight copper/nickel these have about seven percent zinc and three magnesium as well. Ballistics are still trying to work out... well, why? Now, the fact that these bullets are probably home-made or manufactured to order is good because if we trace them, we might just trace the buyer or the maker. And if we do that....?"

"We trace the killer," I said stoically.

"That's the idea." He looked at me straight.

"Do I have a choice?"

Deacon sighed. "Listen... you and I both know you're a mess. You've been dying on your feet out there since…" Fortunately for me, and far more fortunately for he and his own wellbeing, he thought better of it. "Well, let's just say you're damn lucky I let you loose on your own. Which reminds me… you didn't stay for the press gathering this morning, did you?"

"The two dumb-ass punks?" I said. "They'll be in front of a judge again before too long, you wait and see if they aren't."

"Oh, you've got that right," he said knowingly. "Sooner than you might think, in fact."

I had no idea where he was going with this. "Meaning?"

"Meaning that 'dumb-ass' as they are, their lawyers aren't. Their lawyers have been reading dictionaries of late and they've come back with some really big words. Words like 'brutality', 'counter-action' and 'compensation'."

I could feel my jaw dropping, like I was unwisely sucking on a lead weight. "You have got to be kidding. It was justifiable, for Christ's sakes. They were armed and they resisted arrest." I thought for a moment. "And they were scum as well."

Deacon feigned a smile and shook his head. "Which any civil jury might buy, had you exercised the good sense not to administer your 'justifiable' rearranging of their facial features whilst one of them was not only totally unarmed, but also cuffed to a railing." He raised his right eyebrow. His deathly serious one. "They have reliable witnesses on that, by the way."

"We'll ride it."

Deacon shrugged. "We might. On your own, however, you're looking at an Armani.... Know what I'm saying...?"

Unfortunately, I knew full well what he was saying. Armani - a very expensive suit. One I really couldn't afford and I doubted that was meant on a purely fiscal level.

"What are you saying, Deacon? You hanging me out to dry?"

He shook his head. "Not my style. Not unless it's... how shall I phrase this....? Justifiable. What I am saying though is 'yes, I can offer you a choice'." He said that bit with a look. "I just can't guarantee that you'll like it, that's all. I want you right out of harm's way and if that means you only handle the really low-level stuff for a while then I'll even chip in for the spade. Either way, the only thing you're rearranging until this has blown over is paperwork. Ellis'... Dean's... Anyone's. Christ, you can make them coffee if it keeps you out of the way, but I'm guessing that even if I chained you to the god-damned machine you'd somehow manage to blow up a Starbucks." He took a deep breath and looked at me straight. "To put it bluntly, Nick, I'm reigning you in."

So I looked at him straight. "You know what, Deacon, you only ever call me Nick when you want something."

"I want something," he said without humour. "I want you to stop being an ass and play as part of a team for once in your goddamned life. That way we might just get to beat the Feds on the naked stiff and you might just get all the help and support Santa promised you when the time comes."

With the best impersonation of feigned reluctance I could manage, I retrieved the photo. I pretended I was glancing, but I wasn't and I think he knew it. I was looking. For what I

41

didn't yet know, probably just something – anything – that might place me a square step ahead of 'I've got a Masters in psychological profiling' Ellis and his techno-whizz sidekick. Deacon's trace smile told me he knew I was back to being a cop and also that he knew why – because (loathed as I would be if he asked me to admit to such a thing) it was not just the threat, it was also genuine intrigue. And it was genuine intrigue that usually set a good cop on the road to solving a case. In my experience, nothing niggles a person into action quite like it.

The threat helped, of course.

I could also tell, from the diamond-like glint in Deacon's eye, that he knew I was pissed at getting the shitty detail. Sure, knowing might be heading to the same place as caring, but it was travelling in a much faster car. It would get there long before its six-letter friend.

The picture of the stiff looked, well, like a picture of a stiff; a dead guy on a slab. Sometimes things didn't need to get any more complex than that.

I guessed at some kind of fully-automatic for the reason he had ended up there though. None of the entries had the star formations of blown flesh or powder burns that suggested point blank, and yet all five had hit his upper body whilst he was still standing. Could've been five gunmen, of course (indicating a serious hit) but somehow I didn't think so. The wounds were almost in a line and that was winking at me and mouthing words like 'one smooth sweep of the arm'. Some of the deductions came without the winking, like the way I figured that by the time the return sweep came along the guy was already falling on his ass. That's when they pierced his ear for him.

By blowing two thirds of it off is what I mean.

Deacon looked at me with his 'are you still here' expression. And yes, I was. Just for one more minute. Because what I was looking at now, seeing as I had little else to play with on this case, was the tattoo. Normally a detail such as that, short of demonstrating definitive gang links, wouldn't even have raised an eyebrow. And this was neither. After all, it was little more than a neat design - something that nearly every kid under twenty-five had at least two of etched indelibly about his (or her) person.

Yet this particular mark of allegiance, if that's what it was (or had been), was on his ankle, his left. So now I was winking back at my instinct by sensing it was more than just a neat design. I felt that this particular design meant something to someone. Not that the 'someone' was me, of course.

Deacon was still looking. So now I was wondering just how far could I push it before I heard the words 'this ain't your case, Lambert.'

"So what's with the tattoo?" I asked. Strike one.

"No idea."

Short and sweet, so I held up the full body picture. "And can I keep this?" Strike two.

"No."

A little shorter but no less sugary.

"And can I get a run-down on...." And I don't even finish strike three, which can only mean...

"This isn't your case, Lambert. You're strictly support." Contact. Home run.

"So, I'll...just... go check out the girl then?" I smiled that odd smile again.

His head was down; already reading through another file on his desk. "That's the plan." Then he looked up again and smiled his own little smile – one of those 'right back atchya' affairs. Down went the corners.

"Round about now would be nice."

Which is why you always have to remember to take your jacket with you to the third.

THREE

There was no reason for me to have known, or have cared I don't suppose, but it was that very same Thursday that Issue 2817 of *New Scientist* magazine hit the stands. It led with a story detailing how man could well be in a position to land on Mars by the year 2025.

Now call me cynical, because I am, but I've studied one too many photographs in a little too much detail and listened to at least three or four too many bar-room debates. Consequently I'm still of the opinion that it might have aided the cause if mankind could plant his feet on the god-damned moon first. Sorry Neil, but I can't even say that it was a performance worthy of an Oscar nomination, given that you only had one real killer line in the whole charade and you somehow managed to screw that up on live TV.

My apologies to Buzz as well, although I have to say that I reserve my sincerest condolences for Michael Collins (the man who had to remain in the capsule). In the hangar. In Nevada (or somewhere boringly similar). Bummer. Imagine travelling all that way – by Jeep I suspect, as opposed to a space-craft possessing less raw computing power than the TV remote control I use whenever the charade comes on TV – only to become the man who never even got to pretend to set foot on the earth's only – and resolutely unattainable – satellite. Just so that we could piss off those of a more communist persuasion.

Personally, I never read the article and it was another year and a half before I even got around to ordering a back copy of the issue. Page forty-seven was what interested me, and it was pretty much given over to just one story which detailed a weird – for which read 'inexplicable' - discovery made during an oil drilling expedition in Russia:

Diamonds Aren't Agerill's Best Friend

Agerill Manson, the US-based contract drilling company who have been operating for almost a year in the West Varyegan and Tagrinsk oil fields, 1500km north-east of Moscow, have run into problems during exploratory digs near Chasel'ka.

After drilling successfully to a depth of 1827m they hit what they at first took to be an extremely dense rock layer which blunt the drilling head. After removing the drill string in 10m sections, engineers decided to use a diamond studded bit. Remarkably, they still could not break the 1827 barrier and a further retrieval of the drill head revealed that this too had become blunt. Another diamond bit was added but to no avail. The bit, unlike the 1827 barrier, was soon broken.

Gareth Swales, Agerill Manson's Head of Russian Exploration, admitted that he and his fellow engineers were baffled. "I've worked on over 200 drill sites," he said, "achieving depths of up to 6000 metres and consider myself fairly experienced in this field. Never have we had a problem that could not be overcome when it came to achieving the required drill depth, but here we seem to have found truly impenetrable rock. The area appears to be localised, however, as we have three RA-D (Rig Automation Drilling) derrick's in the area and the other two have hit depth (and oil) accordingly. Breaking the 1827 on RA-DB has now become a matter of principle. They just don't want to give up."

This is the first time that Agerill Manson have used the RA-D system in their Siberian fields. The system, which removes most of the drudgery of the operation and removes workers from the danger around the head of the well, uses a robot gantry crane to lift the required complement of tubes to and from the derrick. "The system is proving exceptionally reliable," Swales said, "as the sections are only 10m each, instead of the usual 30m, they

SEQUENCE

can be transported and stored much easier as well as resulting in a smaller, more manageable derrick. The RA-D system has hydraulically powered handling devices and computer-controlled operation which means it can pull a complete drill string, up to 6000m, out of the well and stack the pipes without human intervention. The only problem is that, whilst this system both increases safety and reduces manpower, the added number of shorter-length tubes increase the overall time it takes for the drill string to be removed. Ordinarily this is not a problem, but RA-DB at Chasel'ka looks like it could need replacing more than most to get the job done."

When questioned as to what he felt the obstruction to his drill string might be, Swales remained philosophical. "I have no idea," he said, "but even though our two previous bits appear on the face of it to have failed to gain even a centimetre in depth, I am sure that whatever it is will become weakened and give way to the power of my team in the very near future." Scientists are already speculating that they may have discovered some kind of 'super-rock', one far more compressed than uncovered before. If this is the case, then when the team do break through, samples of this rock brought to the surface may prove of huge scientific interest.

And it's to be hoped that Swales and his team do succeed; Agerill Manson's Siberian dig is being funded by a US$ 12.5 million (ECU 9.8 million) European Bank for Reconstruction and Development (EBRD) loan which has financed the construction and operation of the three RA-D rigs after seismic tests indicated that good yields were on the cards. Tom Agerill, AM's 58 year-old CEO and a long time oil veteran, has indicated that RA-DA and RA-DC are between them producing 25,000 barrels a day. This, however, is a long way from the 120,000 barrels a day indicated to the EBRD. On the face of it, these targets cannot possibly be met unless RA-DB succeeds in breaking through.

So what's down there? As ever, we'll let you know when we do.

47

And whilst, by publication date, the story was already six weeks old, that was the last that was heard of RA-DB's diamond-studded drill heads being perpetually blunted at Chasel'ka. Ever. There was no follow-up story, no revisit and no answers. Like moon exploration (and that of Mars I suspect) it just... petered into history.

No-one outside of Siberia or Agerill Manson ever found out whether or not they ever broke through to a rich seam of the black stuff on which we all drive to work and soon the story was forgotten. Which is exactly what 'they' wanted. Not Agerill Manson, of course. They were delighted (and relieved) when RA-DB finally struck a rich well (which, it transpired, only required them to move their rig a matter of feet - they had simply been unlucky in initial siting). But Agerill Manson did not, as promised, share news of their ultimate success with the world at large. Which, to the thinking man, would tend to suggest only one thing; somebody somewhere blocked the story. Somebody who had the resources required to do that kind of thing. Makes you think, doesn't it?

On a seemingly unrelated matter at the bottom of page forty-seven (and occupying just four-by-one column inches) was posed the following question and where one might reasonably purchase the answer:

Telepathy, telekinesis, psychokinesis, clairvoyance and out-of-body experiences...
Fraud and bunkum or worthy of detailed scientific study?

In "*Intelligence Behind the Universe*" (State University Press, $23.50, ISBN 0 6879 2413 2), leading scientist Victoria Bovey argues the latter and claims that the mechanistic world view of most scientists is nothing more than an article of blind faith which prevents deeper investigation into the paranormal.

This was not an advertisement placed by the book's publishers, rather it was *New Scientist* magazine's nod to the comedy T-shirt wearing weirdos out there who might not be the readership they craved, but still had the $5.95 cover price burning a hole in the pocket of their Hawaiian shorts and no haircut on which to spend it.

SEQUENCE

The reason that New Scientist ran the book-link was in a fruitless quest to look a little bit hip. The reason they allocated it so little space, however, was because they weren't really as hip as they liked to think they were and it wasn't, in their eyes, referring to anything even vaguely approaching true science.

Except that it was. It was referring to the most real science that man had ever tried and failed to fully comprehend. More real than quantum physics, genetic re-structuring, cloning, liquid computing and artificial intelligence all put together. It would not arrive with us for a long time, but it was there all along, waiting to be uncovered like an old heirloom in a dusty loft.

When this science did come to light it did so because of a train of thought developed from the discovery of a single object; one that had perpetually blunted a series of diamond drilling heads 100km south of Chasel'ka. On the day the two stories ran nobody saw the link. Nobody could even have dreamed that there could be a link.

How ironic is it then that both stories appeared on the same page.

It's true. God really does work in extremely mysterious ways.

Sometimes.

FOUR

THURSDAY, JUNE 9, 2011.
LENWOOD, CALIFORNIA.

There were a number of extremely distasteful reasons why I hated the prospect of travelling out to Oakdene. As it had been almost three fun-packed years since that had last happened, those reasons had clean gone out of my head. Some I'm sure I'll stumble over later, but once the heavy wooden door creaked open one of them - just one - came floating right back with a vengeance. It filled my face and moved fast up my nose.

It was the Goddamned *smell*.

I mean Christ, we had cells at the precinct and, yes indeed, sometimes a freaked out first-timer literally shit himself waiting to be 'bailed and beaten' by dear old dad or a hard-liner deliberately gave you a little present to clean up after he'd gone, but *Jeez*... This wasn't just in the walls, it was mixed in with the goddamned mortar. Oakdene had its contingent of auxiliaries, sure, and they cleaned up regularly, but it was a fight they were seemingly destined to lose. Shit had, quite literally, become the very essence of this building.

At the time of this particular visit, Oakdene was the largest 'privately-run institutions' of its kind in the state - *profit-making asylum* to you and I - located on cheap land no more than a stone's throw from Lenwood, eighty miles along I-15 from L.A. itself. It was, I don't mind telling you, one mother of a nasty drive up there, not least when you were proving that L.A.'s rush hour lasts a lot longer than its name might suggest and then heading out toward the desert in a twelve year-old Taurus with a broken air-con unit and a driver's side window that jams four inches down.

The building was old, although because it lacked the carved numerals over the doors of some, I had no idea exactly how old. What I did know is that its design was what some might call 'Gothic'; all towers and spires and dark stones. The building was crumbling from the ground up, though even I was aware that it hadn't always been like that. Once it had been a school; a pretty good one I'd been told. And I can bet in those days, maybe thirty years back, when the corridors were tended and running to the sound of around three hundred mixed-sex brats, it was a whole different place to the empty shell it had become. Now the high ceilings were little more than an inconvenience to the semi-retired caretaker and the carved plasterwork had become little more than intricate shelving on which one might reasonably store a large collection of dust until it was needed.

The high entrance hall, once a pretty impressive introduction to the place, was now just a dim and dirty cavern, as though it had been carved by the sea to create a refuge from which one could hide from the light of day. And not only did it have that stench (and how) but every surface above the height of average human reach had a semi-opaque layer of dirt that took the paintwork down a few shades toward sombre. Even at the lower levels, where the choice of colour had been 'that brown' that supposedly 'shows nothing', dark smears ran along the walls. Some were no doubt where the gurneys had caught whilst the others I could only wince and hazard a guess at. Each would stay there until the next tin of paint came out. Many more years I suspected.

At the furthest reach of this cave, however, my spirits always struck it rich in the form of a pot of black - *African-American* - gold.

Maggie; still guarding the desk. Truth be told I very much doubt she'd left the building since I'd been there last. Huge, round, reliable Maggie. The same Maggie who could always look so innocent whenever she said, '*Now what smell would that be?*' Smiled through it all and helped when she could; as long as you knew where the line was and names didn't get mentioned either side of it.

After working Support Services at County ER for ten years, Maggie had ultimately decided she'd had enough of the bureaucratic shit and opted instead for the real thing; subsequently becoming one of the more delightful columns supporting the Oakdene building. If I remember correctly, and I think I do, I found this out in the three hours and sixteen minutes it took for her to poker-shark me out of forty-eight-fifty, and for an ex-inmate to shit out a diamond.

The guy I'm referring to, in case you're interested, travelled by the name of James 'Jamie' Coulson. He had been declared low-risk; which indeed he was. He was just one of those guys who hated his boss so much that one day in the summer of ninety-five, the day the boss in question declined the young Mr. Coulson's request to 'have a sit' in his new 320CLK, he spent his entire pay cheque at the twenty-four hour hardware store down on Fremont. The only possible reasons I can think of to create a twenty-four hour hardware store are either to give the night-time muggers somewhere handy to buy reasonably priced knives, or to furnish pissed off insomniac employees who might get an unrelenting two-in-the-morning urge to buy fifty-seven cans of expanding filler foam. Which is exactly what Jamie did. It was the kind you buy to fill in holes where the wife hurled a plate at you and missed, if you're me. The kind that sets like a kind of spongy concrete.

Our Jamie not only bought every damn can he could afford, he then perpetuated his craving by spending four hours of the following afternoon quite literally solidifying the two day old Mercedes from the inside. Just so his boss couldn't 'have a sit' in it either. Apparently, it had taken six hours to carefully carve a route behind the passenger seat and retrieve the guy's laptop.

Let's not forget that I've got Deacon for a boss. Translation? I really liked this Jamie guy.

Now Jamie would have gotten away with no more than a fine and damages had it not been for his behaviour in court. That, which I was privileged enough to witness for myself, ranged from answering all questions in a series of high-pitched beeps he called 'slow-modem' to urinating on the stenographer's wig. That stunt alone got him referred to Oakdene for psychiatric reports, but it was grabbing and eating the fifteen-hundred dollar earring of his 'court-appointed' that meant I not only got the privilege of driving him up there, but also stayed long enough to lose at cards to Maggie.

With the likeable reprobate cuffed awkwardly to the headrest, he and I talked pretty much all the way. And here, as I recall, was a perfectly rational and coherent young man who shared my passion for the Dodgers and butter-cream pies. Because he asked me nicely, though, I never let on. He said he'd needed a break from the wife, the job and the sheer stress and hell of being him, that was all. I knew how he felt. Looking back now I think Jamie Coulson was probably one of the sanest people I've ever met.

I flashed a smile at Maggie. She flashed an 'I bought a new watch with your money' smile back and nodded in the direction of the Director's office. 'Director of Care' to use the full title, if you can believe that. And therein lies the most distasteful of the reasons I hated going to Oakdene: Creed.

I shoved into the pseudo-Dickensian office; hard as I could with no worry over formal introductions. There was no point. Creed and I were already acquainted.

Seated like the intolerant mill-baron he was born one hundred and fifty years too late to be, Creed was every reason one should be dissuaded from allowing any sense of autonomy in an institution that's supposed to care. A small, skulking individual with beady-eyes enlarged by glasses four decades out of date, he had a bad comb-over, an arrogant tone and a unique ability to sweat regardless of ambient temperature. These, of course, were not the reasons I disliked him as intensely as I did, I've never been a book and cover man, but they didn't exactly endear me to him either.

No, I disliked Creed because of stories I'd heard and things I felt, and I am a smoke and fire man. There were other things I learned later, and I'm sure I'll get around to telling you all about them in due course. Then maybe you can take the burden of lying awake at night dreaming up ways to prove them.

Just not now.

"Detective Lambert, how very nice to see you again," he said, trying and failing to look unaffected. "It's been what... two...

three years?"

Green leather creaked over walnut as he squeezed himself free of $900 of relative's money, his pudgy hand outstretched. His eyes told me he remembered our last meeting all too well. The fact that I didn't clasp his neatly scrubbed, ever-sweaty palm in mine told him so did I.

"February two thousand," I said. "Jennifer Sanchez." A name I'll never forget. And one that Creed is no doubt trying to, though I doubt it keeps him up nights.

"Ah, yes," he said. Like we were reminiscing. "A terrible time. Terrible. She was such a lovely girl. Lovely, lovely girl. Anyway, that's not what brings you here today now is it?" His face was praying really hard that it wasn't.

I noticed the brass football trophy on his shelf and my eyes narrowed. I reached out, picked it up and winced. It was even heavier than I recalled. "You still have this?" I said, deliberately sounding surprised.

"Of course," Creed replied, moving swiftly around his desk and pulling it roughly from my hand before replacing it, millimetre-perfect, where it had been moments before. "It is a trophy very dear to my heart."

"Oh, I'll bet it is," I said under my breath, and left it at that. "Anyway, Tina Fiddes," I added bluntly. "She one of yours?"

"By which you mean a patient...?" he said, glancing down at something and nothing with a carefully timed delay. "She is indeed one of ours, Detective. Why? Do you need to speak with her?" He smiled and I didn't like it. I didn't like anything that Creed did, you understand, but I really didn't like this. "If you do, then I feel you may have had a wasted journey."

"Meaning what?" I asked, hard-edged. "She here or not?"

"Oh yes, Detective, she's here alright. Here... this way." He shrugged, picked up a large set of power-keys from a reproduction bureau and brushed past me out of the door. "But you'll not find it easy speaking with her."

I followed along the intermittent light of the corridor. Every second or third bulb was out. Not only out, but high. The kind of high that makes them a pig to replace; at least until it got so bad you needed a torch. "And why's that exactly?"

"Because our Tina is mute." His moleskins creaked an awkward pace on the tattered chessboard vinyl. A pace designed to keep him comfortably ahead of me.

"So she doesn't speak?"

"I believe that's what 'mute' means, Detective."

Mute was not a word I'd expected to hear and, for a brief moment, I have to admit to being thrown. Where it left me in the great scheme of things I really didn't know. Screwed probably, but that was hardly a first in any sense. "Does she listen?" I asked.

Creed laughed weakly. "Sometimes."

"Then perhaps I'll just talk to her."

"So am I to presume you came here completely unaware of her condition…?"

Oh boy, Creed had the bit now. One up and he knew it. Worse than that, he loved it. As he talked I vowed to make it my personal mission to ensure that such a situation never arose again.

I played it like I didn't see it. "By which you mean her inability to speak?"

"By which I mean her autism, Detective," he said, his voice slowed by sarcasm. Still walking, he turned his head just long enough to satisfy himself that I had absolutely no idea what autism was. I'd heard of it, sure, but then I'd also heard of a metastatic bronchogenic carcinoma. I'd still have needed the lovely Doctor Jessica Morris at County to explain it to me, though. Probably as she slid her scalpel into the flesh of a guy who'd just croaked from one.

"It's a severe disorder of communication and behaviour that develops before the age of three," he continued. "Autistic individuals are rarely able to use language meaningfully or to process information from their environment. About half are able to speak, although this rarely extends further than a mechanical repetition of the things they hear." He turned to face me with a superior look. "Although Tina, it seems, can't even manage that."

He flicked back and quickened the pace. Unable to hear my stride over the squeaking of his own goddamned shoes, I don't think he'd expected to find me quite so close behind him. As we started up the stairs, his tone became very so on and so forth. The way it often does when disinterested people quote lengthy passages they read once.

"Some autistics have precocious ability such as excessive numeric or mathematical skills. They may have uneven patterns of development, a fascination with mechanical objects, a ritualistic response to environmental stimuli and a resistance to any change in their environment. Now resistance to change..." He pondered that one for a moment. "Now that is something our Tina is very good at."

So Creed could read. Hope shows its face even in the arse-end of our universe. "You mentioned certain skills," I said. "Does Tina possess any? Above and beyond what you might expect I mean?"

I knew I was clutching at straws with that but I still wasn't seeing the link between a mute, some Latin text and a naked guy with five more holes in his body than the national average.

Creed's squeaky feet had stopped and he was peering over his lenses through the toughened glass embedded into dented brown panelling of one-one-three. Satisfied with what he saw, he slid his key into the lock and gave it a half twist.

"We really don't concern ourselves with such things here, Detective," he said, and the door swung open. "We're far more concerned with administering treatment and keeping them in a safe environment than seeing whether or not they are capable of balancing balls on their noses and clapping for a fish."

We stepped inside.

On the first floor, in the furthest corner of a desperately featureless room, the woman whose name I'd seen scrawled on a scrap of paper stuffed where the sun refuses to shine was sitting where it did its best to redress the balance. The only furniture comprised a well-made bed, a pine table, two matching chairs, one shelf and a bookcase, though I didn't note its contents.

Tina was perched on the wide, flaking sill of a large arched window and leaning her head against mesh-reinforced glass which, if you strained through the etched-in grime, might just overlook the badly tended lawns to the rear. She was staring, her legs drawn up to her chest and rocking gently. Back and forth, her timing seemingly taken from a tune she was gently humming to herself.

In every respect save one, she was your perfect asylum cliché.

Except that Tina Fiddes, and you'll forgive me if it seems like I'm romanticising again here, was probably one of the most beautiful women I have ever seen in my entire life. In the flesh, at any rate. Not that I'd ever mixed with supermodels, but you get my point?

She was illuminated by the warmth of the yellow-stained glass, accentuated by what would very soon become a sunset and her hair, straight at first, fell into golden ringlets at the shoulder. Loose fitting blue-grey jogging pants hugged the top of white Reebok hi-tops and a figure-caressing white vest was being pulled upward by her posture, revealing just a few inches of the small of her back. Her shape was perfect and her face was perfect. Shit, at this point I was betting even her hands were perfect.

And just maybe I know what you're thinking, but it wasn't like that. First off, my next big one was in August and it was fifty; this girl had a way to go to see thirty. I'm guessing she was twenty five at most. And second, this was not a sexual beauty. This was a cover of fifties Vogue beauty. A Monroe, Mansfield and Russell beauty, and I just didn't expect to be confronted by such a thing in an under-funded backwoods shitheap that looked and smelled like Oakdene, that was all.

Creed's tone turned sickly. "Tina, poppet, you have a visitor. He's a Detective. With the Police Department."

Tina, held in the only square of radiance the room had to offer, turned her head and looked idly back through the kind of mock haze that seems to infest darkened rooms. Immediately I wondered if her reaction had been aimed at sound alone. I wondered that because it was at that moment that I saw her eyes. A rich and piercing ochre; willemite set in ivory. I'm sure artists have searched for years to find models with eyes like these, only to subsequently be condemned for exaggeration but, real as they were, those eyes didn't see me. Or Creed. They didn't seem to see anything. If they did, then her brain was making no attempt to register it.

After perhaps three seconds of looking straight through us both she turned away and started her tune from the first bar. It was as though she'd heard a sound and had then realised that it had been nothing more than the wind. What she looked at afterward I don't know, but whatever it was, I very much doubted it was outside that window.

I got a split feeling and neither segment felt good. One half told me I'd be taking Deacon much, much less than he'd hoped for, and the other that Creed – and I so hated this bit – might just have been right all along. His self-righteous voice was still sticking pins in my head. Wasted journey.

"You can leave us alone now," I said, casually picking up an origami dove, beautifully crafted, from the shelf and admiring the delicacy of its construction. I was guessing that it was Tina's handiwork because let's face it, there was jack-all else to do in this room and if origami was your thing, my guess is you'd have the spare time required to get rather good at it. Meanwhile, my delivery of textbook indifference was designed to show Creed that I actually knew what I was doing.

Which I wished were true. At least as true as I'd somehow made it sound.

Creed turned with an angry look in his eyes.

Given his stature, he came across like a fat little squirrel threatening to bite the ass of a pissed off grizzly.

"I'm sorry, Detective, but I simply can-*not* allow that."

The thing is, I was on official business. Very official and very confidential police business, if you please. And Creed, though he hated it and had hoped to somehow skirt around it, damn well knew it.

I placed the dove back on the shelf, carefully as I could, then turned slowly and stared through those thick lenses of his; right into his beady little eyes, comically enlarged. I wondered just how magnified the angry look in mine was to him.

"Yes you can, Creed. Now get the hell out."

FIVE

Klein looked out across the drilling rigs as the helicopter passed low over the Chasel'ka exploration site and watched as a group of gorilla-like, oblivious crewman went about their business in the distance. There was no snow falling from the milky sky today but the landscape was a subtle white, indicating that even the afternoon sun had yet to clear the frost.

The pilot pulled sharply to climb a low hill and warned through his headphones that they would be landing in a few minutes. Klein had been in the same seat for five straight hours now and could not think of a single bone in his body that wasn't making him aware of its displeasure. He calmly pulled on padded gloves, stretched his fingers inside and clipped the cuffs to the sleeves of his matching jacket.

Beyond Chasel'ka, as the ground descended toward another endless plain, he could see the hauling rig still in place at the Ratta site, just under one and a half kilometres from the main dig, and the various members of the team awaiting his arrival. To the right of the camp, standing behind red and white striped tape held by steel poles, were a group of the 'locals', all quasi-oriental in appearance and wearing traditional attire.

Each had their own style of tan or brown jacket, all possessed the ubiquitous fur-lined hoods and cuffs, and each wore a brightly coloured patchwork hat. There were perhaps fifteen or twenty in total, presumably gathered to observe the events unfolding in their normally tranquil and less-than-exciting midst.

The pilot hovered twenty feet above a specially cleared and flattened area of land, excess soil still piled to the sides, and turned ninety degrees before gently lowering the skids. Alun Monroe was already approaching through the swirling white frost, head lowered, and opening the doors as the rotors cut. The high pitched whine that Klein had become so accustomed to on his journey began to lower, leaving a hollow feeling in his crudely thin head as though the condenser had just cut on his fridge.

"Good afternoon, sir," Monroe offered, dutifully closing the door behind his guest.

"Where is she?" Klein asked bluntly.

"Under cover, sir." He indicated the direction in which they should walk.

As they moved through the camp one of the watching locals, a man perhaps in his late fifties or sixties with a thick jet-black moustache and matching hair, started to shout aggressively from the head of the gathered crowd. He waved his hands and stomped his feet like he was standing on burning coals, his deep set eyes curled angrily at Klein and Monroe. In the silence of the wilderness, his voice was booming. The rest of the group, whilst not joining him vocally, nevertheless shared his look of gnarled contempt.

Klein, having spent three years working in Moscow following his graduation from the Massachusetts Institute of Technology, spoke perfect Russian but could not translate a single word the man was saying, suggesting that, unlike many indigenous people of the Siberian plain, he was still conversant only in his own tribal language. Whoever and whatever he was, he was certainly pissed at somebody and for now, it seemed, the arrival of Klein made for an expedient focus.

Only one in the group did not look angry: To the man's right a woman held a baby protectively in her arms, his hood three times larger than his face, and looked desperately worried, her eyes almost pleading. Unlike the others, it was almost as though this woman feared something; something she felt might even harm her growing family. All the while, the elder's rants rippled across the flat earth toward Klein like a stampede, his low voice spilling the continuous tirade of indecipherable abuse.

"Who's that?" Klein said coldly, stopping only so that he could turn sneeringly toward the crowd.

"Name's Yaloki," Monroe replied wearily. "Chief fucking reindeer herder or something, I don't know. Very protective of 'the Evenki lands and the traditional way of life'. Every time anyone so much as sneezes on a map of this area, let alone comes and digs for oil, he's screaming and writing a stream of letters to Moscow."

"But we're not digging for oil," Klein said bluntly, "Agerill's are. So why doesn't he just go away and bark at them?"

"Because this time he thinks you're unearthing something far more important than oil," Monroe offered, watching, listening and translating, though it quite obviously bored him rigid to do so.

"He's saying that his grandfather bore witness to the... 'Lord of Thunder'... as he threw his fiery spear into the land and sprinkled the sky with lights to claim this area of land for his people - very handy for Yaloki - And before he threw his spear he roared with a great ferocity. Now we are not only stealing the land but also removing the spear and that will make this 'Lord of Thunder' wreak savage revenge. He says that we should go now."

Klein sighed. "Lord of Thunder? Right. Presumably every celestial event they ever witness has something to do with vengeful gods and fiery damnation spreading across the land."

Klein tired of such people. Uneducated. Blind. Why should he, or even the oil-drillers, care what some rag-tag group of uneducated Russian Eskimos felt? What did they know about progress? If it had been left to them Captain Birdseye would still be catching his fish with hand-whittled spears for Christ's sake.

"Well, at least we know from his very eloquent analogy that it dragged a trail and threw enough particles into the air to light the sky." He looked back at Monroe. "And the roar I like, that's gonna help us a lot."

"Sonic boom, surely?" Monroe offered.

Klein shook his head. "No. A sonic wouldn't be audible until after the meteor had disappeared. It would have attained supersonic speed long before entry, so a sonic wouldn't even start to travel until heights of thirty kilometres. But he said that the roar came *before* the spear. That, to me, suggests something altogether different."

Monroe narrowed his eyes. "Such as..?"

Klein smiled knowingly. "Electrophonic."

"Which would account for the magnetic properties of the ball," Monroe agreed, finally nodding in understanding.

Klein smiled. It had been well documented that certain explosive sounds were heard simultaneously with, or even preceding, the appearance of meteors, even though this was a clear contradiction of the physical laws of sound propagation. Earlier scientists had placed the phenomena down to a purely psychological side effect of seeing a unique celestial event such as a meteor but much research, including Klein's own, had deemed that unlikely.

The scientific community at large had ultimately concluded that any sound which could travel at such high speed would have to be produced by direct conversion of electromagnetic radiation into audible sound. Which would mean that the meteor was producing very low frequency radio waves on entry. Those waves, after travelling far faster than raw sound alone, would then strike any ordinary object within the vicinity of the observer and only then be converted into something audible.

Klein was starting to realise that he was about to meet a very special lady indeed.

With a knowing smile, he turned away from the Evenki and followed Monroe across the camp, passing the coarse tents which had been temporary home to the eight team members for the past five weeks.

"Do we have composition analysis yet?" he asked.

"Not yet, but she's very heavy. Heaviest yet. Here, I'll show you where she hit the deck..." He veered to the right and headed in the direction of the immense hauling rig.

The pyramid-shaped structure was a little over thirty feet high, constructed from an 18" diameter toughened steel framework and possessed five huge winches formed in a circle near its peak. To the right of the rig were five powerful generators arranged in a line, each one serving their respective winch. Klein looked up. From one of those winches and blowing in the wind which whipped across the plain, hung less than four feet of the sixteen-times-half-inch-wrapped supporting cable, the end sections now splayed apart like an open hand.

"It broke a cable?" he asked, his surprise evident.

"Yes, Sir," Monroe replied. "Damn near brought the whole rig down at one point." He moved to one leg of the pyramid and stared down into the huge hole than ran diagonally away into the darkness of the earth.

Klein also looked in, then looked up and around, into the far distance. "How far are we from the Chasel'ka dig?"

"Two thousand five hundred metres," Monroe replied. Knowing Klein as he did he then anticipated, and answered, the ensuing question. "Which, given that she was 1827 metres down, gives us an angle of entry of approximately thirty-six degrees. So yes, we're about as sure as we can be that this is an off-shoot from the 1908 big one."

"I don't think she's just an off-shoot," Klein corrected, still wading knee-deep through a blurred sea of thoughts he wasn't sharing. "I think what we might have here is a core."

He looked deep into the rich black hole, perhaps twenty-five feet in diameter at point of impact, and thought to himself. Whilst this fragment could have impacted here a darn sight further back in time, the distance from the 'big one' in Tunguska on June 30 1908, and the angle of entry, made far too much sense to avoid. Tunguska was 400km to the east and the angle showed this fragment to be travelling in an westerly direction at the point of impact.

Klein was aware of many theories put forward for Tunguska. Not all of them involved meteorites, it seemed, because no fragments had been found at the site itself. Unlike most who had voiced an opinion, however, he understood that this was not as surprising a result as it might initially seem. Meteors, he knew, rubbed against air particles as they entered earth's atmosphere, typically heating their structure to more than 3000 degrees Fahrenheit. This kind of intense heat vaporises most meteors, leaving only a stream of particles shown as shooting stars. Others, however, had been known to 'splatter' and create a huge fireball and explosions, some of which had been heard up to 30 miles away.

Except for Tunguska, of course. The explosion there had been heard almost one hundred miles away, which would tend to suggest not only that the meteor had indeed splattered and, given the immense swathe cut into the Tunguska forest, this would appear to have been at some great height – but also that it had done so with frightening speed. Klein also knew that meteors made of iron withstood the stresses better than those made of stone, but even iron meteors would tend to disintegrate as the atmosphere became denser, usually at around six miles up.

If that had been the case here, then a strong core may well have survived the splatter and had its angle of entry altered sufficiently for it to have deviated the 400km needed to impact the Ratta plain. And this core, even if not iron, was certainly metallic. That was how they had managed, despite its incredible weight, to pull it free.

"So you used her magnetic properties to bring her up?" Klein asked, looking up to the broken winch.

"Indeed we did," Monroe replied. "Pulled her out the way she went in. We knew that, given Agerill Manson's problems we'd have little or no chance of drilling her and lifting her straight. There was no way they could dig a hole wide enough to that kind of depth anyhow, so we did some geological flyby's, a few seismic tests and eventually discovered the entry hole right the way over here. The vegetation had really taken hold again by that point, so it's no surprise that nobody's happened across it. It just looked like an overgrown cave."

"And then...?"

"Then we sent some test probes down, which recorded exceptional magnetic levels and decided that if we were going to pull her out this way, given the distance, then we'd probably be better using the electromagnetic heads."

"Just how heavy is she?"

Monroe laughed quietly. "How heavy do you want her to be? She broke one of the damn winches didn't she? And over three days it took all four of the others, full charge I might add, to finally get her up. Based on that alone I'd be putting her in the region of eighty, maybe ninety tons."

Klein exhaled in surprise, then looked dubiously back to his colleague. "And she's only eight feet in diameter?"

Monroe nodded. "Give or take."

"Then she sure as hell isn't iron."

"No way, not at that weight. I think the densest we've seen so far was Nebraska - 1948. She was ninety percent iron, eight and a half nickel. Some cobalt and magnesium. But this....? Christ, I can't think of a material on earth that weighs what she does at that volume."

Klein smiled at Monroe's choice of words. "Neither can I," he said, the smile becoming a sneer. "So I think I'd very much like to meet her now."

They continued to the furthest side of the small camp; a solitary soldier wearing white and grey snow-camouflage stood guard at the tent, rifle held at an angle across his chest. In addition to the tapes around the compound, a second temporary barrier had been erected to keep the uninitiated at bay. The soldier saluted and stood to one side without question, allowing Monroe and his guest unhindered access inside.

Monroe looked expectantly to his superior.

Klein smiled. "Hello, beautiful."

His eyes were wide for a time, then became ingrained with curiosity as he approached the ball. At first glance it held the appearance of an immense steel bearing, terra-cotta in colour. Except it did not possess so smooth a surface and nor was it perfectly spherical.

The surface of the object was roughened, which hinted to Klein at it having been created as opposed to made, and large chunks of blackened rock were fused randomly to its surface from the temperatures inherent as it ploughed into the earth. Through the gaps in the molten rock, Klein could see that the temperatures on atmospheric entry had also succeeded in melting the metallic surface of the ball itself, though not to any great depth. Smooth, reflective ridges now flowed across its surface like gentle waves. Because the ball had been spinning on descent these ridges had formed into a complex series of swirling patterns. Beautiful patterns which grabbed hold of his image and threw it back at him like abstract art.

"Radioactivity?" he said without glancing up.

"No worse than your cell," Monroe replied with a shrug. "She's quite safe."

Klein unclipped his right hand glove and left it to hang limply from his padded sleeve, then crouched low and gently reached out his hand to tentatively trace the ridges with wide fingertips.

With an inquisitive lilt, he then placed his palm, slowly and carefully, flat on the metallic surface.

"How long has she been in the open?" he asked suspiciously.

"Eighteen, nineteen hours," Monroe replied.

Klein narrowed his eyes. "She should be a lot colder...?"

Monroe nodded. "She should be, but she isn't. Of course, there's latent heat from the depth she was buried but she doesn't appear to be a conductor, so it'll take longer to adapt to environmental changes."

Even so, Klein thought, she should be colder. She really, really should. Even the worst metallic conductor of heat would have been freezing in a sub-zero environment such as this by now. Simply, by touching the sphere he should have run a definitive risk of his hand literally sticking to the surface.

He smiled to himself. Since he had been twelve years old and had first realised that it was the scientists and not the priests who held the secrets of this world, he had waited for a find like this. Something new; something quite literally 'out of this world' and something that would lead him toward a greater understanding of the world in which both 'buyers' and 'consumers' lived.

But then no, he figured, screw understanding. That was only base camp on the mountain he was so very eager to conquer. The summit was control, and that was always where Klein had wanted to be. It had been a forty-four year wait for this day. Now he had to ensure that he kept a firm hold of the dream that was rightfully his.

"Have the Committee been informed?" he asked, his fingers back to caressing the metallic rock.

Monroe shook his head. "Just yourself, sir," he said. "I'm working on a report which should be complete and emailable after one or two more days of in-situ study. Then they can decide what we should do with it."

Klein was losing himself in his own distorted reflection, touching the curled image of his features like one might caress the only surviving photograph of a missing relative.

"Let me finish that report for you," he said quietly. "I have one or two suggestions I'd like to put forward myself."

Monroe smiled. Having worked for Klein for over fifteen years, he was acutely aware of what his boss wanted now and how he would go about getting it. Being a Presidential Scientific Advisor, and being trusted, usually gave him the power to suggest and gain approval on just about every course of action he desired. Right or wrong.

"You want her for yourself, don't you?"

Klein lifted to his feet and pulled his glove back into position. Snow or no snow he was guessing it was at least minus fifteen outside with the addition of wind-chill.

"Of course I want her," he said defiantly, deliberately squinting his eyes toward a statement of the obvious, "and between us, Alun, we're going to make damn sure that she pricks up her ears when I call."

SIX

THURSDAY, JUNE 9, 2011.
LENWOOD, CALIFORNIA.

Maggie, wearing white plastic over light blue, was preparing for the evening pill run by the time I returned along the corridor. Every colour under the sun and every synthetic emotion under the skin was laid out in neat little rows, each tagged according to needy recipient. She glanced over her glasses as I approached, but didn't stop what she was doing. Nobody here, least of all the ever-caring Maggie, wanted the responsibility of confusing Benzedrine with Benzodiazepine and placing a red-hot poker up the backsides of those who couldn't relax enough to fall asleep in the first place.

Only once the pills were laid out neatly did she look up fully and offer her usual welcoming smile. Then she turned back toward her desk to place the last few ticks on the relevant paperwork.

"Don't need to ask if you got anything…?" she said idly.

I shook my head as I approached the desk, pulling the facial of the stiff from my file as I walked. "You ever seen this guy, Maggie? I mean, has he ever been up here to visit?" I held it out.

Maggie lifted her half-rims up from her nose as she leaned over to look. She strained in the gloom so she pulled the picture from

71

my hand and held it under her desklamp, the way checkout girls in supermarkets do to see if your twenty's the real deal. The curl of her mouth to form a pouting bottom lip gave me her answer before she spoke. "Visit Tina, you mean? Nope, never seen him." She glanced over the top of the lenses again with a smile. "Doubt I ever will the way he's looking, either. How'd he come to look so dead?"

"Shot," I said. "Five times."

She curled thick lips into a fake wince, but I knew she'd seen and heard of far worse. "And you think he was a friend of our Tina?"

"Either that or he just knew *of* her," I replied, the hopeful edge gone from my voice. "He had her name and room number scrawled..." I searched for the right words, "about his person... when we found him."

"So he might have been on his way over here," she suggested, "but simply never made it?"

"It's a possibility," I said. Maggie was no fool. "So does this Tina girl have any visitors at all? Any family or friends?"

"Just the one; older sister. Lives downtown, I think. We have an address somewhere. You want it?"

I nodded, figuring I might as well.

She turned and opened a chipped wooden drawer-cabinet to rummage through a series of files. All of which, despite the state of the rest of the building, were in perfect alphanumerical order. But then, this area was twenty square feet of Maggie's domain and she tended it well. Good old Maggie.

"Farmer... Fickle... Fiddes. Here we go." She pulled the file and closed the drawer. "Ah yes, Sarah Fiddes, 1180 Seventh,

South Central, that's it."

She wrote the details in a neat script on the back of an envelope bearing the institution's insipid green and yellow logo. "Thanks," I said; politely. I doubted the address would do any good, but at least I had it if any whistles got blown and my playing field changed. "So what about this girl. This… Tina? What's she like? Any trouble."

Maggie threw me a corrective look. "Nick, I'll tell you. Of all the patients I have ever had to administer to, and there's been a few over the years I can tell you, I don't think I've ever met one who's less trouble than Tina. I mean sure, some days you might be coaxing her out of that little world she's in before you can help her get dressed, but she's never a bother. Good as gold." She looked back to the picture in my hand. "And whoever he is… or whoever he was… I'm just glad he never made it here. Has a look about him that suggests a whole sackful of upset, and… well, she's just too nice a girl to be having to deal with any upset, that's all."

Upset. That was what Maggie euphemistically called severe trouble.

She handed over the completed envelope and returned to push the steel pill wagon, wheels squeaking softly along the vinyl and clunking through the odd torn patch that revealed the pitted grey concrete below.

"You wanna keep talkin', you betta start walkin'," she said. So I followed.

We talked about nothing in particular. Oakdene, Maggie's three boys (she loved 'em), Maggie's ex-husband (she hated him), Creed (shit, everyone hated Creed), and I asked about some of the other patients I saw on her route. I asked about those who wept, those who screamed and those who just slept; the ones who'd obviously decided that bad dreams pretty well kicked the crap out of bad reality. It was mainly polite small-talk.

I asked how long Tina had been here: five years or so, Maggie reckoned, but the sister had been working in Chicago for a few years and only found out a couple of years ago. Parents dead, apparently. No visitors at all prior to that. I asked if she could read (she could - five languages) and write (same five - impressive) and whether or not she was always calm (ooh, DON'T you get her angry, Nick - shatters illusions when she gets mad that girl). So I asked how often she'd gotten mad during Maggie's tenure. Twice - both with Creed, like that came as any surprise.

As we walked I figured that, as Maggie was on the verge of being left alone for the night, save for the odd scream she'd no doubt have to attend to, and I had nowhere in particular to be, I could spare to kill an hour and keep her company. In the absence of anything we could use from the girl, there would be little point in whatever report I could staple together hitting Deacon's desk before morning anyway. That said, I'd be out like a shot if I saw her getting a deck of cards out.

We reached one-one-three and Maggie peered through the glass in much the same way as Creed had done.

Checking.

"We give Tina fenfluramine in small doses, but it's only experimental," she explained gently. "You ask me it's a crying shame. I mean, she's so intelligent really, you just can't get it out of her that often, that's all. She deserves better than this, that's for sure."

She leaned close and spoke quietly, as though her superior's foreboding presence lingered like yet another bad smell in the corridors long after his overweight body had vacated the building. "Creed doesn't approve, but I've been known to have a game of chess with her on occasion and that young lady could give some of the big-leaguers a run for their money. It's not just that she wins, Nick, it's the sheer *speed* with which she does it. You make your move and bang she makes hers. Genius every time. Don't know where she learned to play but mercy me did she learn to play"

I looked through the glass and saw Tina sitting exactly where I had left her; exactly where she had remained throughout the full half hour I had been with her. I had shown her the picture of the stiff and she had looked. Or she *might* have, I don't know. Either way she'd just turned away again. It had been the same with the tattoo and the Latin. Nothing. Not even the smallest glimmer of recognition in those beautiful brown eyes.

Her head was resting on her arms now and she was looking out toward the last of the daylight. Dreaming perhaps. I wondered if she knew all about us, the world around her and was sitting waiting for some miracle to give her the means through which she could become a part of it. Perhaps she looked beyond the crumbling walls and across those endless fields. And maybe she thought *one day I'll have myself a run through those.*

Or maybe not.

Maybe Tina Fiddes' world extended no further than the walls of her imagination. For her sake, I hoped so. Whilst I knew little of what it must be like for her to be trapped inside herself, I could only imagine that it would be easier to cope with if she was never made aware of what it was she was missing.

Besides, who was to say that Tina Fiddes' world wasn't a far better one to inhabit anyway? To tell you the truth, some of the things I learned in the days and weeks that followed this particular visit make me wonder to this day if we should all be searching for the miracle that would enable us to become a part of *hers*.

"So how often does her sister come over?" I asked. "Now she's resident in California?"

"Three, maybe four times a week," Maggie said. "Nice girl. Early thirties, real pleasant sort, if you know what I mean." Her voice took on a sense of amazement, "And to look at them together... well, they were sketched with the same pencil, I can tell you. She'll come around noon, smarten her up some; you know... run a brush through her hair and make her up a little. Then, if the weather's holding up, she'll maybe take her into the grounds for a walk. The usual stuff. After that they might take a look at some of Sarah's work; see if Tina can help out. Then it's 'Snickertime'."

She laughed. "Always brings Tina a Snickers bar. And her face lights up like.... Well, you just have to see it. It really is a sight. Fact, should you come back for any reason and you want to get her attention with your pictures, you could do worse than bring her one along. I can't guarantee she'll visit our world for you, but I bet it'd be worth fifty cents of your hard-earned to try...?"

Suddenly, though not altogether unexpectedly, my interest was aroused. Not by the Snickers thing, of course, but by the *other* thing. "Exactly what kind of work does her sister do?" I asked. Ergo: *why in God's name does she bring it along?*

"Oh I don't really know," Maggie said, shrugging hefty shoulders. "Some kind of archaeology I think. I don't pretend to understand. But she brings her maps and her parchments and her secret notes that tell of *buried treasure*. And they pore over them a while." She laughed at the very thought. "Still I think it's good for Tina to have something worthwhile to do, you know? Something to exercise that powerful mind of hers. I mean I do my best, but I'm not that good a chess-player, so I don't think I'm exactly stretching her imagin..."

"What kind of maps?" I said, interrupting. "Local? U.S.?"

Maggie's face told me she was not best pleased at being interrupted, but she answered all the same.

"Well, I don't know really," she said. "A map's a map where I'm from and I really don't pry too close. I mean, it could be China for all I know. It's their business, not mine."

Unfortunately, because Maggie just oozed honesty, I knew she had meant every word of it. Right at that particular moment, however, honesty was not what I needed. I'd have paid very good money for an intern who *did* pry. Just a little.

Just enough.

"And what about these '*parchments*'." I used the word advisedly as I rummaged for the photocopy of the note we'd found wedged in the stiff. "Were they like th…"

I needn't have bothered looking, because long before I'd even located it in the file Maggie had unwittingly given me my answer. The answer that had stopped me driving straight home to San Marino that night and made me follow I-105 right into Inglewood where I could make the turn to the less-than-pleasant area of Los Angeles known as South Central.

A place where, with a bit of luck, I might rake through the junk and find the home of Tina Fiddes' older sister.

"And don't you go asking me what was on them either, Nick," she had said, dismissive. "Lord knows I don't read English that well some days, let alone *Latin*."

SEVEN
MONDAY, JULY 4, 2011.
WASHINGTON D.C.

Eleven members of the President's Committee of Advisors on Science and Technology (PCAST) were already seated in deep mahogany leather when the twelfth, Klein, entered the room. He was ten minutes late but, as ever, that did not concern him too deeply. He despised the fact that he was required to attend such sessions at all, having to spend time arguing his cause, so he saw no reason to actually arrive early as well.

It would be true to say that each of those gathered here today was both highly intelligent and an expert in their given field, but the problems almost always arose from the fact that none of their fields seemed to share a common boundary or even overlap. Klein had often mused that the minutes of such gatherings should have been recorded on elastane, given they had an uncanny knack of stretching unnecessarily into the evening. It would probably take PCAST four or five hours just to decide that the best shape for a cartwheel involved the use of curves.

With the merest nod of recognition to the Chair, Neil Grainger, also charged with overseeing the President's Office of Science and Technology Policy (OSTP), Klein took his seat at the table, flicked the clasps on his case in unison and removed the required papers, a tablet computer and a sleek chrome remote control unit from his case.

"Glad you could join us, Joe," Grainger said, adding only the slightest hint of sarcasm.

Klein smiled back, lips condescendingly carving ridges into his cheeks.

"Thanks, Neil. May I...?"

The overweight Grainger did not want today's meeting to stretch any further than it absolutely needed to do. He had discovered on leaving the house that morning that his daughter was pregnant. Not a problem unless one took a look both at the reputation of Grainger himself, and at her birth certificate (she had another month to go before she turned sixteen). He could not remember the last time that the phrase 'we'll talk tonight' had played on his mind so much. How the hell could the daughter of the man who set the scientific framework for the entire United States of America reach the age of fifteen without learning what the hell a rubber was?

He made a dismissive flick of his thick wrist. "Go right ahead."

Klein pressed a button on the remote and the lights dimmed, leaving a square of deep blue on the furthest wall where his tablet screen was now being projected. He beckoned for one of the assistants and handed over the SD Card to be inserted into the tablet, Klein himself moving to the front and passing the briefing notes he had prepared to each of the attendees. He pressed a button on the remote. Almost immediately, an image of the Ratta site appeared on the wall.

"This, as you are all aware," Klein began, "is the impact site of the 'Siberian Sphere' as it is now being termed. It appears to have entered the earth's atmosphere as part of the larger meteor at approximately 4.15pm on June 30th 1908, breaking up a few miles above Tunguska, four hundred kilometres east of this site. The explosion caused considerable damage to the environment there, however... no fragments were ever found."

"Excuse me?" Eric Gilliard interrupted, somewhat predictably.

As Chairman and CEO of Gill Semiconductor, Eric was, at thirty-three, one of the wealthiest men in the United States. With his position came substantial power and quite often, it seemed, he liked to exert it by showing others that they were making mistakes. "What is this exactly? Is this a meteor or a meteorite?" He looked to the other members for approval. "I mean, you appear to be calling it both." He looked more than pleased with himself.

Klein sighed. This was precisely why he did not feel he should have to justify himself to jumped-up computer millionaires who foresaw no consequence of decisions they would be allowed to make here today.

"If you knew anything about cosmology," he said with a deliberate hint of disgust. "Then you would know that it is a mete*or*."

"So why not just call it a..."

"Until it hits the earth," Klein interrupted. "Any meteor which makes contact with land instantly becomes.. a mete*orite*. May I continue?"

Gilliard did not reply. He tried not to look embarrassed, but Klein could see that he'd wished now he'd kept his big mouth shut. Which he probably would now. For a while. Until the next chance to play one-up came a-knocking.

"As I was saying," Klein continued, "no fragments whatsoever were found at Tunguska. So, having been alerted by Agerill Manson to the presence of something hard enough to perpetually blunt a series of diamond-tipped drilling heads, we sent a team to investigate and discovered this entry hole. Now, this hole is almost two and a half kilometres from Agerill's site and the sphere itself was buried just under one-point-eight kilometres down. So, those of us of a mathematical bent..."

He shared a nod with Barbara Scalise.

Barbara was fifty-one, hair and make-up of a TV anchor half her age and also President of the Massachusetts Institute of Technology. She was renowned for her almost prodigious mathematical ability.

".. will realise," Klein continued, "that this means that the sphere hit the earth with enough force to travel almost three-point-one kilometres through some of the hardest landscape on the planet; composed of both permafrost and solid rock."

He smiled. "And it did this without any disintegration whatsoever."

"So what of composition?" Grainger asked. Placed as he was at the head of the elongated table, he was closest to Klein and appeared to be

81

genuinely intrigued.

Klein pressed another button on the remote and the image changed to one of the sphere set against the barren landscape, still covered in blackened molten rock, the terra-cotta breaking through in uneven patches.

"Well," he said, "this was the state in which it was found. The composition of the black coating you see here is extremely typical of meteor composition at ninety-one iron, eight-point-two nickel and point-eight cobalt. This was removed very carefully and kept for further analysis, but its removal subsequently revealed the inner core."

Another button press changed the slide to one of the uneven metallic sphere alone in a lab environment, the ridges catching the spotlight under which it had been placed and stretching it into a series of long undulating yellow-orange streaks,

"The composition of which has... yet to be identified."

And this caused precisely the kind of reaction Klein had anticipated. Eyes widened, heads turned and brows furrowed. It was increasingly rare in a PCAST congregation to hear the words 'yet to be identified'.

There were some at the table, not least Ralph Healy, former CEO of the Lockheed Corporation, who believed there was little, if anything, of which mankind was not already aware. His train of thought was always 'how do we use what we have?' as opposed to 'how do we uncover new things?' Of course, it was Gilliard who spoke up first. It was almost *always* Gilliard with his obscenely expensive suits and paid-for-tan that spoke up first. "So you don't actually know *what* it is?"

Klein saw the subtle implication. The hint of a vengeful dig. "It's Siberium," he offered bluntly.

Gilliard pulled an expression of fake puzzlement and glanced around the table, seeking that same approval someone seeks when they have just told a joke and they want to see who's laughing. "What? Siberium? What the hell's that? You've just made that up."

Klein smiled. "Of course I have," he said calmly. "That is precisely what one does when one needs to name an element which has not, as yet, been known to exist."

More subtle gasps from those gathered. Did Klein just insinuate what most had just realised he'd insinuated?

"So this is not a compound? It's a completely new... *element?*" Barbara Scalise asked, lifting half moon glasses on the string around her neck and holding them to her eyes so that she could examine the papers Klein had handed her at the start of the meeting.

"Yes it is," Klein said proudly. "It's definitely *not* a compound."

"Maybe so," Gilliard offered, the freshening of his brow beneath wavy blonde hair demonstrating both his embarrassment at being completely out of his depth and, conversely, shown up at every opportunity. "But you can't call it Siberium, for God's sake. It sounds ridiculous."

"More so than, say, Berkelium? Or Lawrencium? Or even Einsteinium?" He could see that Gilliard was about to say something, to criticise him once again, but a glance around the table had shut him up. Klein hadn't just made these up, they *existed*. It was just that, as there was no mention of silicon, he hadn't actually got a clue what they were talking about. So he remained quiet, fumbling awkwardly with his ridiculously loud silk tie.

Even the look in Grainger's eyes showed that he saw the funny side; Gilliard could be a pain in the ass on occasion, but that wasn't the point. Grainger was here to keep order. "Gentlemen," he said, "I think we have more important things to discuss than the naming of such an element. Josef, I believe you're looking to have this sphere, this Siberium if you will,..." he glanced at Gilliard who looked like he'd choked on an olive. If Grainger had said the name out loud, then he'd all but approved it, "...forwarded to your own laboratories for analysis. Could you tell us why you propose such an action?"

"Certainly," Klein said, pressing another button until the image on the wall became one of a bright star. "As you will all be aware, when massive stars reach the end of their life, they explode as supernova, then they are bound by physics to contract until they ultimately become black holes, phenomena so dense and gravitationally powerful in composition that beyond a certain point even light itself cannot escape. We believe that the arrival of the sphere would be consistent with the after-effects of some immense object striking such a black hole with almost unimaginable force in some corner of our galaxy or universe, ultimately shattering the super dense core. This may have travelled for hundreds, possibly even thousands of years until it eventually collided with our own planet. As such, we believe that this Siberium is a fragment of... the matter that comprises black holes."

"And do you have any evidence to back this theory up?" Grainger asked.

"As yet... no," Klein offered, "but we do know that this is an entirely new element, possibly... indeed *probably*... the result of the kind of fusion present in contracting helium nuclei. In addition, this sphere - at only eight feet across - weighs almost fifty times an equivalent sphere of lead and is *extremely* magnetic. In truth, it would appear to demonstrate a disproportionate gravitational pull of its own not dissimilar to those we now associate with black holes."

Barbara Scalise leaned forward, the glasses down again and dangling across the front of her blouse; her pencil thin eyebrows were raised with interest. "And just how strong is this pull?"

"Very weak in truth," Klein said, "but definitely measurable. And, given that this new element is so dense as to have made a mockery of even diamond cutting technology, it seems we are stuck with just the one piece. As KleinWork Research Technologies are the world leaders when it comes to the kind of equipment and expertise required to perform the necessary tests on this element, we feel that we should, temporarily of course," he looked to Grainger, "take possession."

"Why not laser it?" asked Healy, head down reading the notes.

"Sorry?" Klein asked, although he knew in an instant that Healy, having extensive knowledge of, amongst other things, spacecraft re-entry, had instantly noticed the flaw in his argument. Now he was going to share it with the entire committee and blow the deal.

Healy, fifty-five and built like a savage footballer, was not a man to be messed with. He'd had run-ins with everyone from the unions to the mob and eaten them all for breakfast. Scientists were like mini-snacks to him now. He looked up, and straight at Klein. "Can we see the image of the sphere alone again?"

Klein smiled and reluctantly pressed the remote, the sphere appearing on screen once more; the ridges catching the light. *Shit.*

"It appears that certain temperatures have melted the surface of this sphere into clearly evident ridges," Healy said, "And, adding the requirement of friction to create such a flow of molten matter, those ridges could not have been caused in the perfect vacuum of space. So one can only assume that they are a result of temperatures involving the entering of our atmosphere. Which would, at most, be no more than around three or four thousand degrees Celsius; something easily attainable with our laser cutters. So why not simply cut the rock?"

All eyes turned to Klein. He could feel them cutting into him more powerfully than any laser his lab possessed.

"That's correct, Ralph," he said, trying to remain oblivious whilst smiling through gritted teeth. He pushed his glasses up his long thin nose, "and ultimately, of course, that's what we intend to do. However we must be aware of two things; firstly the effects, especially magnetic and gravitational, of the sphere as a whole before we start to diminish its inherent structure; and secondly, the effects of melting such an unquantized element. There may be toxins or indeed explosive reactions that we cannot even begin to be ready for without a great deal of detailed study. Obviously if laser-cutting becomes a possibility in the near future then, once again, KleinWork are best suited to perform such a delicate operation." Bullshit, bullshit and double bullshit with cheese.

"Wait a minute," Gilliard interrupted. Again. "If this is a new element, metallic in nature and possessing measurable magnetic properties, then surely we should all have a slice of the pie. I mean, in the right hands, this discovery could lead to unimaginable technological leaps."

And profits, Klein thought, and the implication that KleinWork's hands

ADRIAN DAWSON

were not 'the right hands' hadn't been lost on him for an instant. All Gilliard really wanted to know was how well the damn thing conducted electrical impulses.

Gill Semiconductor had been working unsuccessfully on 'liquid computing' technology for many years now, at great and fruitless expense. Of course, year upon year, Gilliard himself had stated that advances in such technology were 'imminent', but 'imminent', like 'tomorrow', was a period of time that seemed destined to never actually arrive.

In the liquid computer system Gill Semiconductor were hoping to overcome the problems of taking conventional silicon and either depositing or etching it from a surface which, on a nanometer scale, created roughened surfaces and imperfections. So, instead of silicon, they had been attempting instead to create nanowires using a biological liquid catalyst that favoured growth in only one direction in an alcohol solution. Charged proteins within these solutions would then be used to biologically or chemically switch a transistor.

The speed benefits offered to computer processors, if this system could be perfected, would be enormous, placing Gill Semiconductor only one small step away from a true Quantum age. But, if he was consistently failing with liquid computers, then maybe the time was ripe for him to search in a new direction; or indeed, to look for a completely new element. Such as Siberium. Perhaps this new element would be more stable than silicon on a nanometer scale?

Not a chance, Klein thought. Not whilst he still had breath in his body.

Fortunately. Grainger was already shaking his head. He knew just as well as Klein where Gilliard was heading. "I would have to agree with Josef here. KleinWork definitely possess the resources a find of this magnitude warrants and, once the initial research is done, which will be....?" He looked to Klein.

"Two years," Klein lied. "Three at most."

"Then, let's say two shall we?" Grainger said sharply. He turned to the others. "After which, the research will be shared, the committee can

86

reconvene and decisions can be made regarding the appropriate steps forward."

"That seems more than reasonable, Neil," Klein said with a smile and, with a click, the image on the wall was gone. He knew that there was to be a Presidential election soon enough, and that would mean that this PCAST team would struggle to survive its current structure.

As he took his seat back at the table, Klein leaned back and relaxed, knowing that he now had exclusive access to the Siberium and any results it might throw his way. From there on he'd easily be batting successive permutations of the committee out of the park for years with Gill Semiconductor-esque 'near results', just to ensure it stayed that way.

"Right then," Grainger continued, still wrestling the knowledge - far sooner than he would have hoped, and far more publicly than he would have liked - that he was going to become a grandfather. He was still trying to work out which day it might have been that he had kissed his daughter goodbye at the same time as he had kissed goodbye to his ambitions of one day running for Senate. "Item two," he said without looking up. "Revisions to the OMB Circular regarding Public Data Access."

Typically Klein wasn't listening. He also had his mind on other things.

EIGHT

Something fell off the Taurus as I bumped from the South Central exit ramp of I-10 and onto Central itself. Something loud and metallic. Something expensive. Something else. I didn't bother stopping to see what it was; there wasn't much point the way I saw it. Firstly, because you don't get out of your car on Central unless you really have to or you want to lose it; and second because hate the car as I did, I was simply left to admire its tenacity. The damn thing just didn't want to die on me completely. Not yet at any rate.

I passed the streamlined fifties homage that was the Coca Cola building and continued through increasing deprivation until I hit the Seventh crossway. I drove along until I saw 1195 (close enough), near the junction with San Pedro and pulled over between a battered old truck and what could best be described as a 'pimp-mobile'; a long wheel soft-top Cadillac in deep maroon with white wall tyres and cream leather. As I emerged from the car three Hispanic youths, all under sixteen, one of whom was bouncing a ball against the wall and catching it in a black fingerless glove, glanced up with narrowed eyes.

Bouncy-ball kid kept it going in a 'Great Escape' three-stage movement, his eyes on me and his mouth forming wide circles as he chewed gum. Multi-talented, I figured. He and his pals were checking me out rather then the car, I figured, given that they'd have been able to joy-ride a tractor to better effect.

Even so, I take no chances. Not any more; I still have to get this fat ass of mine back home somehow or other so I turned and stretched as though it had been a real long journey. Which it had, but that wasn't the real reason. As I turned I made sure they all caught a good look at the Smith and Wesson I keep nestled under my arm. They quickly glanced down again. The car would be safe.

1180 formed one upright thin strip of a much longer block down a tall, dimly-lit alley at the head of which a blind hobo sat on the floor playing harmonica. Badly. He wasn't actually begging I don't think, just chancing his arm. And whether he was actually blind or the shades were a ruse I didn't know, but I threw him a dollar anyway. The smell that drifted from his clothes told me that whilst there were few people in this city more deserving of my hard-earned than I, he just about qualified. The note floated in front of him and he caught it before it hit the floor, quick as a flash. Blind my ass.

These were L.A.'s real old buildings, the kind you see cops breaking the doors down on when you watch reality TV; a poor hybrid of tenement and warehouse style that landlords seem so keen to snap up in their seemingly endless pursuit of fleecing the less fortunate inhabitants of the neighbourhood with low quality 'space' (as opposed to 'housing').

The door to the building was set back from the street far enough for the escapes to drop on those no doubt numerous occasions when the fires of hell stopped by for coffee and, below it, worn steps led to the basement apartment, rentable only to those who couldn't afford light or a positive digit. The stone fascia was dark, almost black and the windows painted a deep olive green that was cracking and flaking to reveal the rotting woodwork beneath. Of the windows that were open on the alley side, most had washing hanging over the escape, though I doubted that sun or breeze ever managed to permeate such a thinned out environment.

And I could already see 'Sarah Fiddes' in my mind. Nothing like her sister. She was early thirties, so Maggie had told me, so I was guessing '2-3-0' on the 'marriages, kids and kids who shared the same dad' stakes. Lank hair, cigarette glued to her bottom lip through every syllable and the youngest and loudest in her arms. Real bad, but comfortable, shoes over which the ankles had started to spread. And she'd have that city-famous 'Downtown' attitude. A hard to penetrate combination of 'fuck you' and 'what's in it for me'. Where the interest Latin texts figured in this little picture I'd painted I couldn't even begin to imagine.

I sighed and rang the buzzer to Apartment Five; Sarah's place, then wiped the crap off my finger. And waited. Nothing. Zilch.

I rang again and stepped back, looking upward. The washing twitched on three but the scent I got was much closer to that of nosy-neighbour than fabric softener.

"Who you lookin' for?" A voice behind me; deeply Hispanic.

I turned slowly to see a young kid, maybe eighteen or nineteen with a spiky crew-cut. He wore a 'Qué-Mart' security uniform which was clean and well pressed, his tie perfect and the bright green arm of a pair of surf-dude Oakley's hanging over his breast pocket. Kid rated his job, you could tell that much. In his arms he carried a bag of groceries, presumably from the place he had just spent the day looking out for.

"Apartment 5, Sarah Fiddes," I said. "Know where she is?"

Which I realised as soon as I'd said it was probably a dumb question. Most times it seemed, the closer you put people together the further apart they were. Stand their homes on top of each other and they barely even speak.

West of the city, in towns like Lenwood and Barstow, where they had a local sheriff and the nearest neighbour could be three miles away, everyone knew everything. Who did what, when and how, and what they had for breakfast that morning. Here I'd be lucky if the kid even knew what Sarah Fiddes looked like.

As it happened, I was lucky.

"You a relative?' he asked, his face curling into forced defiance. "Friend?"

He was twitchy; head moving all the time. Left, right, left again. I figured he was as new to playing tough guy as he was to security work. They probably both came along about the same time. And now he was trying to be cocky *and* intimidating – two looks that just didn't suit his age or his build.

"Nope," I said quietly. And, because I hate 'cocky' I left it there, deliberately looking everywhere but at his face until the silence became too lengthy and he could bear it no more.

"Bringing trouble?" he asked. Twitching again. "Cos if you are you can turn your ass right around."

"You know her then?"

"Maybe I do," he said, moving back and forth on his legs. "Maybe I don't?"

"Know where she is?" I asked. Ve-ry slow-ly.

"Maybe," he said again, his eyes almost closed in defiance, "but that don't mean I gotta tell you, do it?"

I reached under my overcoat, into my jacket pocket, and pulled out my badge. Exposed the gun again as well, just to be sure.

"Nope," I said, pushing the badge in his face and looking elsewhere, "but this does."

The kid's head moved back slightly as if he'd been hit and he shot me a look. "She in trouble?" he asked, his voice suddenly changing into something that belonged more to the mouse I figured he really was. I was guessing that he might not be the sharpest pencil in the case. The kind that was easily led, influenced, if you know what I mean.

"Not as much as you if you know something you're not telling me," I said. And I said it very quietly and very slowly, turning to lock eyes with him.

Whilst his eyes looked shocked, mine threw daggers and then narrowed just enough to twist them. Just to show the kid that when intimidation does its job properly, 'cocky' understands that it pretty much blows the deal unless it keeps itself out of my face and shuts the hell up.

His face changed straight away, but not how I'd expected. Now he was all 'big wide-eyed smile', which was a million miles from the usual. Normally you'd flash a badge downtown, the smile would disappear and the door would slam, if only metaphorically. Not this kid; he actually seemed pleased to see the LAPD knocking on his neighbour's door. "O-kay," he said, nodding his head. "See, I didn't know you was a cop. I mean, if I'd've know I'd've..."

"So where is she then?" I asked again, and I made sure my tone was that little bit firmer than before.

He took a deep breath and thought. "See...? Thursday...?" He looked down the alley. No answers there, my friend. He snapped back. "Thursday you'd find her at Freex."

"Who's Freak?" I said. "Friend of hers?"

He laughed like I was stupid. Bright white teeth. "Nah, man... *Freex*. You know, like, with an 'X'." He looked like I should know what that meant. I looked back like I didn't. "It's a club," he said. "In Ladera. She hangs out there most Thursday and Friday nights."

I'd heard of just about every club in Ladera, but never 'Freex'. "Does she come back late?" I asked. In other words, do you watch for her coming back?

"Later than you want to be hanging around these parts," he said, raising his thick black eyebrows. "If you know what I mean?"

And yeah, I knew exactly what he meant. "So where do I find this club?"

"You know the drug store on Jefferson?" he asked. I nodded. "Right behind. Big old building. She took me there once." He smiled proudly. Our Sarah had taken him out. Once.

"Billy, que pasa?" A voice from the first floor. We both glanced up and I noticed that the washing hanging over the escape near apartment one included a shirt just like our Billy was wearing right now. One with a 'Qué-Mart' logo stitched on the breast pocket.

He smiled; embarrassed. "My ma," he said, almost like an apology. "She ain't so good."

I nodded and took out a card. I'd had them printed on one of those arcade machines for four dollars when I'd got tired of writing out my direct line over and over. "Well, Billy," I glanced up with a smile. "I'm gonna go find this 'Freex' place in Ladera, but if I don't find Sarah, I'd really like you to let her know that I need to speak with her. Will you do that?" The card was poor, and I mean really poor – low grade paper and ink smudged so bad you could only just read the thing, but the kid took it and stared at it as if it said Universal Studios Star Search Division thermographed in gold letters.

"Yeah, sure," he said. Nodding and smiling. "Hey, I only work part time at the mart, you know. I'm studying law really."

"That's great," I said, only just trying to hide my sarcasm. The last thing I needed now was a life story.

"Yeah," he said, his proud face back on. "Gonna get myself educated, join the LAPD myself, or maybe even the FBI." He nodded confidently, like it was a given. "I got friends, you see? They gonna help me out; I do them favours and they gonna put in a word. I mean, you know, when I got my diploma and shit."

"Hey, Billy? Where you at?" Ma again. Her voice sounded painfully weak, as though she'd dredged everything she'd got and fired it out all at once. It wasn't an angry voice, just one that had heard the only company she kept wasting time outside and was kinda wondering why it hadn't yet walked through her door. It reeked of loneliness. "You know my dinner ain't gonna cook itself."

Kid smiled, embarrassed and pointed to the groceries with his free hand. "Ma. I'd better.... Well, you know?"

I nodded and smiled back. The more I saw of Billy Roberts the more I liked him, because unlike so many of his friends no doubt, the kind who spend their days bouncing balls against walls and looking out for cars to jack, this kid wanted more. He was studying and he'd got a shitty job to take care of two things;

Ma and the bills. Blunt pencil or not, he might just take himself and his Ma someplace better one day.

Anywhere was better than here.

What he also understood, I sensed, was that the thing that weighs you down sometimes is not the ambition, but the hefty bag of respect you have to drag around with it. That was why he'd changed so quick; launched into 'good citizen' when he'd seen my badge. And if that sounds like hypocrisy, given my complete lack of respect for the likes of Deacon, then you could do worse than bear in mind that in those days my ambitions extended little further than starting the day alive and doing all in my power to end it the same way.

And I should have seen it then. Impressionable young kid like that, not too bright and always looking after his Ma wouldn't have had too many 'friends'. So I should have asked about the ones he had; the ones who were helping him out.

But I didn't.

Which is why, whilst I'm sure that amongst other far loftier goals, the kid shared that self-same survival ambition of mine, only the day after he told me where I might find Sarah Fiddes, the poor little bastard singularly failed to pull it off.

NINE
Thursday, June 9, 2011.
Ladera Heights, Los Angeles, California.

The only thing behind the drugstore on Jefferson, short of a square of sheer desolation that had been threatened with redevelopment for as long as I could remember, was boarded warehousing. Probably a cool place for an 'underground' club, I figured, and certainly an ideal place for an unregistered one. Which would only serve to make it that much harder to find. Having taken a walk and seen or heard jack, I parked up in the shadow of a flickering lamp near the drugstore trash and pulled out a cigarette. I wasn't exactly hiding, just watching and hoping. I didn't have to watch, or hope, for very long.

Two guys and a girl, all leather and chains. Whatever kissed their puppy I suppose. They sure looked like freaks, the irony not being lost even on a guy my age and I could have got out then - asked them outright - but I figured it better to just watch and learn. The guys were both real big, one bald. Both wore patent leather pants and big screw-you boots. They strode with purpose, dragging the girl whose long bleach-white hair was tied back into some kind of baked Alaska affair. She stumbled at regular intervals, sharp heels not designed for rubble. All three took turns in dragging heftily on something that very probably wasn't sold in packs of twenty at Jack's Shack.

When they reached the far end of this self-styled 'exclusive development opportunity' they went straight to the fifth door along on the warehousing. Like the others, it was little more than a rusting steel plate. Unlike the others; it was unlocked. In a blink they were gone. I looked up and saw that all the windows above were broken, the last of the daylight glinting charcoal blue through a series of cracked panes. Which would explain the lack of noise, I guessed. This wasn't just an underground club; it really was an *underground* club, if you get my drift.

I climbed out of the car, into the cooler and only marginally cleaner air, then crossed the flattened square. I arrived at the door and curled my fingers around the side of the steel plate, there being no real handle to speak of. It opened with a deep low creak, like a heart tearing. A steel staircase, similarly corroded, disappeared into some depths of depravity I didn't even want to ponder. I could hear pounding music seeping upward so I slowed the door's closure and edged my way down. Thank the Lord for soft-soled, comfortable shoes.

At the foot of these stairs was another bald guy. Now he really was a big mother; made the other guy look like a porg. The kind of eyes you don't mess with and the kind of eyes which are employed watching doors because they're the kind of eyes you don't mess with. Beside him was a steel tin, wide open; plenty of notes inside and one or two other things. Like bags. Bags of tablets and little bags of powder. I was guessing they weren't sold to help the instant diarrhoea of those who were stupid enough to mix it with the eyes.

"Help you?" His voice was calm, polite even, but still sharp gravel. Somehow I don't think he wanted to help. Not really.

"No thanks," I said, and I kept moving toward the second door. Like that was ever going to work.

In an instant he twisted so that he filled the doorway - and then some - one hand firing forward like a coin-press and grabbing my collar together. He lifted his arm slowly and, though I ain't a small guy, he pulled me right to my toes.

I smiled like I didn't give a shit, reached under his grip and pulled the badge again, then held it right where he could see it. "Listen..." I glanced down at the hand, "... Jake," If it wasn't his name then it was a damn stupid thing to have tattooed across his knuckles, unless Jake was his bitch. "I'm looking for a girl. Now if you let me go and find what I need, I might just forget that I ever found some other things. Like this place. Which means that when we're next doing a drugs bust and I have to put forward some ideas, I'll probably have forgotten that Freex ever existed... know what I mean?"

"What girl?" he asked. His head tilted on a neck that barely existed and brought tattooed stitches closer together.

"Did I say 'ask me a question and let me go', or did I just say 'let me go'?" S-mooth.

He thought for a moment, or something similar. Then, reluctantly, he lowered his arm and let go. I straightened my coat and smiled. "Thanks, Jake, that's real..." I searched for the words, "...community spirited of you."

He pulled the door open like some kind of thuggish concierge and I caught something along the lines of 'any trouble and...' before the wall of bass hit me like a truck. Christ, I was getting old. Way too old for this kind of volume, anyhow.

The place was packed full of, well, freaks. Some like the three I'd already seen, some like biker-types and some like nothing you have ever seen in your entire life. Real S&M shit with pierced tongues, nipples and probably the bits you only get to see if your sharing waffles come breakfast. And yes, the nipples were exposed - how else would they have chained themselves to each other? Masks, leather, PVC (in more colours than I ever knew were available), and thigh-high leather boots with more chrome than a Harley.

Three types of dancer hung from the high ceiling in tweety-style cages. The girls, the guys and the not entirely sure's; all lit by pulsing coloured lights and pin sharp green lasers. In the centre a guy (I was guessing) in a head-to-toe red PVC suit was strapped to a golden crucifix; false nails of the 'through the palms' variety and strands of red material giving the full blood-drip effect. He didn't dance, rather he just writhed. *I don't want your dirty love, I don't want you touching me...* pumping loud.

My sentiments exactly.

A series of metal gantries criss-crossed above, no doubt original features from the warehousing days. I'd been in a similar club once before near Venice beach. That one, however, had been 'pseudo' - a trendy spot for the rich and famous brats who were desperate to show how weird they really were, just before they went home to their rich-kid version of normality.

Freex wasn't. Freex was full of people who were just plain should-be-at-Oakdene barking. I'm betting there were more sets of handcuffs kicking around that one room than in the whole of LAPD Central.

I squeezed through some of the crowd, heading toward a neon-lit bar at the furthest side, and apologised as I pushed hard against a teenage redhead in a metallic blue catsuit. It wasn't until after I'd reached the bar that I realised she wasn't actually wearing a catsuit at all. She wasn't actually wearing anything. Except for some rather ingeniously applied metallic blue paint.

I shook away the thought, leaned over and beckoned the barman/woman/thing. Now I know it's always safest to wear latex in food and drink preparation, but it's also safest to know where to stop. The guy was head-to-toe Bridgestone, like some kind of rubber bullet. And Christ... hot? I was sweating. This guy? I didn't even want to think about it.

"Sarah Fiddes...?" I asked. I had to repeat it three times. Each one that bit closer to the bulging area of black rubber which I took to be an ear. In the end he pointed toward the end of the bar where a girl with black hair - and I mean raven in a coal mine at night with the lights out hair - was talking to a home-grown homage to Hellraiser's 'pin-head'. Technically, I was still on duty so I ordered a coke with shitloads of ice and when it arrived I squeezed myself her way.

I stopped right behind the girl, just close enough to her three-pierced ear, and repeated the name, "Sarah Fiddes?"

She turned and looked me up and down, singularly unimpressed. Ragged hair hung over her eyes, she had matching black lipstick with accented edges, and hand-painted black shapes completely surrounding her eyes, like bat-wings with sharp points curving down her cheeks. She looked more like eighteen than the mid-thirties I already knew her to be. "Who's asking?" she said; the South Central attitude back with a vengeance.

"Detective Lambert, LAPD," I said, flashing the badge. Again. "I'm here about your sister."

She blinked slowly, completing the black shape, then shrugged and said, "Then you got the wrong girl; I don't have a sister." She turned away and continued her discussion with the human pincushion.

But she did have a sister. I knew damn well she did, and not just because Maggie had told me where she lived, or because Billy had told me where she was hanging out tonight. Not even because rubber bullet had pointed her out to me directly. I knew because in the few seconds she had faced me I had seen something unmistakable in the midst of the bat shapes; her eyes. Same piercing brown and almond shaping as her sister's. Slap all the make-up you like around them, sweetheart, you can't disguise 'em.

And though she had done a pretty good job of trying to hide it, those eyes had possessed a little something embedded within them that shone like tiny diamonds. A little something that might even have looked like concern. Now, I'm no psychologist of course, but why would someone be concerned over the welfare of a sister they didn't actually have?

"I've been to see your sister," I said, shouting over whatever it was they were playing. She didn't turn around. "Never seen eyes like hers." I let a couple of bars fill the void. "Not until today."

Then she did turn, only this time she was angry and she wasn't about to hide it. "Why the *hell* have you been to see my sister?"

"I thought you didn't have a sister?" I shouted.

"I don't," she said nonchalantly. She sighed, resigned. "So... why have you been to see her?"

I reached into my pocket and retrieved the page bearing the bad photocopy of the Latin note and turned it to face her. "I need to know what you can tell me about this."

She read for a moment, turned and excused herself from the conversation with pincushion, then faced me directly. "Where did you get this?" she asked. She looked concerned again now. Very concerned. *Worried*.

"Can't tell you," I said, "But you *did* notice the note on the top?"

Tina's name and room number. She'd seen it alright. "Who wrote it?"

"I was kind of hoping you could tell me that."

Her only answer was to purse her lips, her eyes back on the text. "You do know what this is?"

I shook my head. "Not yet. But you do?"

"Oh, yes," she said, nodding like the Taco-Bell dog. "At least... I *think* I do."

I leaned closer so I could lower my voice to a scream. "And what do you *think* it is?"

"Trouble," she said, so quietly that I had almost lip-read the word. She looked up, staring me right in the eyes. "And the fact that you don't *know* it's trouble, means that you're probably in a damn sight more than you think." She thought for a moment, closed her eyes and took a deep breath. Then she looked slowly around the bar, scrutinised every face. Whilst theirs were all smiling, or looking deliberately moody, hers was looking pretty freaked out, no pun intended. When she found nothing she turned back to me. "We'd better get out of here," she said, grabbing my arm. "'Like now."

So we did.

★ ★ ★ ★ ★

"What kind of trouble?" I asked as we climbed into the Taurus.

She didn't answer. Not immediately. She pulled a pack of gum from her bag and offered one over. I declined. As she placed a piece in her mouth, she looked back at the Latin and said, "How many people know you have this, Detective?"

"My Section Chief, a few more guys in the precinct. Enough."

"Then you really are so very screwed."

"And why is that exactly?" I asked, emotionless. I've been screwed too many times to count. In that sense anyhow.

"Because, what you have here is something that is not supposed to exist. I mean, I know it does, and so do quite a few others, but that doesn't mean it actually does. Officially, I mean."

"So what is it? And, conversely, why does it not officially exist?"

"It's a map," she said knowingly. "And... *conversely*... a very important one."

We were quiet for a moment, only the clattering of the car over the rubble and deep breaths punctuating the air, then I found a thought. "Why did you lie to me?" I asked. We pulled onto Jefferson from behind the drugstore. "Why tell me you had no sister?"

Somewhere in the distance a dog, probably chained and pissed about it, barked like a kerosine explosion at perfect one-second intervals. I heard it clearly through Sarah's desperately elongated and rather annoying silence.

"I have my reasons," she said eventually. "Tell me... how long have you been a detective, Detective?"

I nearly always let people run with changing the subject. It's usually a different road, sure, but it's very rarely a dead-end. "Since I was twenty-four," I said. "Too long."

"Do you like it?"

"Hate it."

"So why do it?"

I smiled. "I thought I was asking the questions."

"You were wrong, get over it."

The smile widened. "I don't know how to do anything else."

"And do you ever clean this car?" She was looking at the pile of crap gathered in the passenger footwell.

"No." It was the truth.

She turned away, looked out of the window and carried on chewing the gum like a teenage kid.

"So where does the map lead?" I asked.

"It's more a case of 'to what' does the map lead," she said. "It leads... or rather it's *supposed* to lead... to something that's been missing for a very long time. Something very important indeed."

"And that is....?"

"Tell me," she said, ignoring my question. "Of all the detectives, why did they put you on this case?"

"That's not what I asked."

"Objection noted. Question stands."

I was starting to like this girl. "They didn't."

"But you went to see Tina?"

"Yes, but only because, and I mean no offence to your sister, I always seem to land the shitty jobs."

"None taken," she said, intrigued. "So how come?"

"How come I get the shit? Probably because it doesn't matter quite as much when I screw things up."

"You screw things up?"

Under my breath I said, "So Deacon would have you believe."

"Who's Deacon?"

"My boss."

"Do you like him?"

"Hate him."

"Do you like yourself?"

She took me by surprise with that one. Clever girl. "Sorry?"

"Do you like yourself?" she asked again, this time turning to face me so that she could stress the words.

I thought for a moment and shrugged. "More than I like Deacon."

"So you're a detective who, despite being unable to do anything else, can't even do being a detective very well?"

"That's about the size of it. Thanks for clearing that up."

"You're very honest," she said. She had a lot to learn.

"And now it's your turn... 'to what' does the map lead?"

She smiled at me, thin black lips stretching even thinner. "It tells you," she said, "Here." As though maybe I should have known this already. She leaned toward me and ran her finger along one line of the Latin. "*Latito Fus Deus Et hominis* – the Divine Laws of God and Man."

"Which are what?"

She smiled again; thinking. Then... very, very sarcastically... she said: "Oh, don't bother to have it translated before you come looking, will you?" I threw her a look. "They're sacred, Detective. Very sacred indeed."

She glanced through the text again, to herself, and with each scoured line her mouth and eyes flicked further into a new expression: one of realisation, shock and wonder. Previously, I had only ever seen that look on the faces of dead people. For them it meant that instant when they had not only met with God, but had also realised just a little too late that they had needed to die in order to achieve it. I didn't know what it meant for Sarah. Not yet.

"Many people, myself included," she said, "have waited a very long time both to prove this document's actual existence and then to hold it in their hands."

"And now that you are...?" I asked. "Holding it in your hands, I mean."

She laughed gently through her nose. It completed the look of resignation that was already creeping across her face. "Now I'm just as screwed as you are, Detective."

"I wouldn't worry," I said. "Nobody knows I tracked you down."

She looked across the top of her eyes. "Oh great, so you're a naive detective as well. Marvellous."

I remembered then what Maggie had said; that Sarah had brought work up to Oakdene. Stuff that she was working on. "Tell me... what is it that you do for a living?" I asked. Being honest, given the jet black clothing, matching hair and really weird ideas on make-up, I have to say that Sarah Fiddes didn't actually look like she did anything for a living.

"Am I part of your case?" she asked, her head lowered. I couldn't tell if she was still edgy or not, but a question to a question told me she just might be. "I'm sorry Detective, that was rude of me," she said suddenly, saving me the task of answering. "I'm a freelance archaeologist."

I pulled up at the junction of Westwood, waiting for the lights to change. The streets were much quieter now that darkness had fallen. "And what does a freelance archaeologist do exactly?"

"It varies. Personally, I deal solely with religious artefacts," she explained. "I locate misplaced items of spiritual significance on behalf of my clients and I... well, dig them up."

"And who commissions you? The church? Religious nuts?" Is there really that big a difference?

"Nope." She smiled, pulled that jet-black hair of hers over her right ear and glanced out of the window again, "Just people who want to get a little closer to God without the help of such a worthless institution, that's all."

"And these would be valuable artefacts?" I asked with a knowing smile.

She tilted her head both ways, causing her necklace to jangle. It was only then that I realised that, along with her black clothing she also, in spite of her comment, was wearing a large black crucifix. "Spiritually perhaps," she said. "My clients do place a certain value on the items I locate, of course, but I doubt that it's measured in quite the way you might think."

"But they do pay you? I mean true spiritual fulfilment can't be a cheap deal. Can it?"

"*So shall the knowledge of wisdom be unto thy soul: and when thou hast found it, then there shall be a reward.*" she quoted with a wry smile. "Yes, Detective, for what I do I get paid well enough."

"And where does your sister fit into all this?" I asked. "Maggie tells me that you sometimes take files up to Oakdene and show them to Tina. Why would you do that?"

Sarah hadn't expected that question, I could tell that much. She sure as hell hadn't suspected that I knew she took work out there. She looked at me as if her mind had taken a momentary time-out then snapped back like a bow and took a deep breath.

"Tina... is a very special person," she said, pulling a wisp of hair away from her eye. Her voice lowered and her sentences became fragmented, as though she had to search for them in a jumble of rejected alternatives. "She's one of a kind. Sometimes you'd swear she sees nothing at all but it's quite the opposite really. She sees *everything*. Things you and I will *never* see." She shrugged. "She just doesn't show it, that's all. She sees structure in things you'd swear were random and order where you'd bet your soul there was chaos. Sometimes that gift has helped me to... locate things."

And now I was really intrigued. I glanced toward her. "Locate things how?"

"Because she sees *patterns*, Detective. You see, the objects I seek are not lost, like car keys. Any idiot could have stumbled over something that was lost and in the case of my objects they would have had many centuries in which to do it. No, the items I seek haven't been found for the simple reason that they have been hidden. Very, very carefully. There are clues to their whereabouts, of course, but these are often so diverse that they appear to hold no connection at all. Unless, of course, you can see the pattern and make the link. Some were compiled by men of genius you'll never see in your lifetime; men who would be way ahead of their time even today."

She leaned back and smiled. "And when *I* can't see how they play together... Tina can."

"So why would someone who'd very carefully hidden an item hundreds of years ago go to the trouble of leaving any clues at all to pinpoint its location?"

"In case they *died*, Detective. Which, given the times in which

108

they lived, was far closer to probability than possibility, let me tell you. Remember... these objects are deeply spiritual - prized not only to man, but also to history itself. They were - are - far more important than a single human existence. They were hidden, sure, but only for short-term protection. There should have been no risk of them remaining hidden forever. They were always meant to be unearthed, just as soon as the danger of them falling into the wrong hands had passed. So the keepers always made sure that if anything went wrong, *if anything happened to them*, then there was a way for somebody they trusted, or somebody who understood, to locate them and give them back to the world. It's kind of like putting a fail-safe, or a 'back door', into a piece of computer software."

"And Tina's what... your hacker?"

"That, Detective, is exactly what she is." She smiled a contemplative smile. "In more ways than you can know."

"So why not use a computer to find the links?"

Sarah shook her head.

"No good, see? Computers are quick, but they think like computers - i.e. they *don't* think. At all. They're blessed with logic and geometry but even the most powerful software has no concept of *abstract* or *insinuation*. The human mind does, however, and nobody's is faster than Tina's. She's pretty much one of a kind."

I thought again about Maggie, and what she had told me of Tina's chess playing abilities. That it wasn't just the moves she made, but also how fast she made them. That it wasn't just about *intelligence*, but also about the speed with which it was used. And I guessed now that if somebody, somewhere was searching for a religious artefact, a *valuable* religious artefact, and following clues laid down by a man who could formulate strange links, then they wouldn't want to be poring through pages and pages trying to find and interpret those links. They'd seek out someone who could help them find the answers they needed fast.

I pulled the car back up on Seventh, taking the same space behind the same truck. The street was quiet save for the odd car heading nowhere in particular and a blue and white from one of the downtown precincts doing the kind of drive-by that's supposed to stop the hoods doing the same.

"So, if somebody had *all* the clues, the things that you would normally collate, then Tina would be the person to take them to. I mean, if you wanted to make sense of them?"

Sarah unclipped her belt. "Oh yeah," she said, "she'd be the person alright." She sighed and handed back the sheet. "So tell me, what does the terribly honest Detective Lambert drink when he's not drinking coke with ice?"

I glanced at my watch. My shift was more than over now.

"Jack Daniels with ice," I said. "And it's Nick."

"Well then, Nick," she said, still smiling as she climbed out of the car, "seeing as we're both so very screwed I'll make it a large one. Then you can tell me what else you've got to show me. And, more importantly, where the hell you got it."

TEN

In the six years since Josef Klein had successfully negotiated unequivocal access to the Siberium sphere, pretty much nothing of commercial use had been gleaned from it. Which, in matters scientific, is so very often the way. True to his word, although a full two years late, he had reluctantly had his team laser desperately small chunks from the surface, eight in total, and had them shipped in secure transit to seven laboratories across the United States and one in Germany. Klein himself had retained most of the new element, including two spheres - each precisely two feet in diameter - and some smaller fragments that had been distributed within the group.

Sub-scientists came to pretty much the same conclusions as the big guys; those at KleinWork. Whilst Siberium was indeed a completely new element, unique in every way, it was extremely stable and possessed nothing intrinsically usable. Certainly its molecular structure offered exceptionally high resistance to changes in ambient temperature and strong magnetic properties, but it was simply too dense in composition to make it effective in any kind of manufacturing environment. The crippling costs involved in gleaning any advances of note would, in the first instance, have had shareholders baying like wolves for resignations and then been further outweighed by the extremely limited quantities of the material available; approximately four hundred cubic feet in total.

Even Klein, for all his hopes of huge overnight leaps in technology, had

111

effectively shelved the project, systematically firing or sidelining those team members whose research had been so fruitless along the way.

Which was not to say that the various project management teams at KleinWork Research Technology had been standing still; far from it. They had, over that same period of time, patented three new fibre-optic technologies and developed 'polymex-memory'; a system whereby digital information could be photographically printed onto a light-sensitive chip no larger than a credit card, yet be capable of storing up to 10,000 high quality movies complete with seven-channel audio tracks. KRT had also been instrumental, in partnership, in developing 'waveless' cellular technology which had resulted in the globalisation of the wireless internet (or CentraNet™ as it was known by this point), running at almost thirty-three thousand kilobytes per second. It had been installed into even the lowest-priced laptop computer within two years, along with KRT's super-long-life lithium-screen batteries.

Klein, whilst perhaps not the richest man on the face of the planet, certainly had no worries about where his next billion might be coming from. Even so, he was still searching for one more technological leap, one that KleinWork Research would again not only pioneer, but also own.

And it was one member of the team responsible for the fibre-optic technologies, David Sherman, who, in early 2016, had accidentally hit on the idea that would ultimately lead to phase one of that leap.

Dave, twenty-three years old and still a junior scientist within KRT's Fibre Optics Division, was sitting at home, being forced by his wife of eighteen months to watch a paranormal special on National Geographic called 'Sense and Sense Ability'. For the first fifteen minutes he pretty much complained the whole time. Mainly that he was missing the Lakers' game. Then, through a series of systematic threats to his civil liberties (wives can do that) he was forced to 'shut the hell up and watch'. So, instead of watching and short of any paint whose drying process required his vigilance, he let his mind drift onto more important matters. Such as wave particle duality. Which is the kind of things scientists are thinking about when they look blank. Good ones at any rate.

Wave particle Duality, or WPD, had been a major stumbler for Dave and the fibre optics team from day one of their research concerning, as it did, the inherent behaviour of light itself. In simplistic (non-Dave) terms it referred specifically to the difference between light acting as waves and light acting as particles, and was centred around an experiment performed in a German laboratory as far back as 1985. The problem was not what happened as a result of the German experiment, rather it was the fact that even now - some thirty-one years later - nobody had offered a truly feasible (or rational) explanation as to *why* it had happened.

Imagine a very dark room. Black. Inside this room is nothing more than one light source and only two other elements. The first is a screen onto which the light is projected and the second is a piece of card placed directly between the light and the screen. This card has two slits cut into it. For the purposes of this explanation they are vertical slits, but it really makes no difference, because light spreads. What you see on the screen is not two slits of light that have shone through the card, but rather a series of vertical light and dark bands.

Why? Because light travels in waves. And waves interfere with each other; they create a series of peaks and troughs and whilst peak/peak combinations give higher peaks, peak/trough combinations simply cancel each other out. When this experiment is repeated in a tank, with water replacing light, then the results are exactly the same; peaks and troughs. So that's that then. Light, even though it is constructed of a series of individual particles called photons, travels in waves.

At least, that was the *theory*.

One that the Germans blew out of the water, if you'll pardon the pun. Because in 1985 they repeated this experiment. But there was an inherent difference in their methods. This time, instead of a 'room', they created a perfect vacuum environment, so that not even particles comprising the air itself could interfere with the results. They had the same card with the same two slits, but now, instead of a 'screen' the Germans used a very, very sensitive photon detector.

Then came the crunch; instead of a 'light' they used a 'light particle

113

generator', a device so advanced as to be able to fire only one photon of light at a time. It would wait until long after the initial particle had passed through the slits and struck the screen before it would even consider firing another.

Once this repetitive process had run for a little over five hours, Die Wissenschaftler checked their results, expecting to see a perfectly even distribution of particles on the screen, given that there could not possibly have been the kind of interference that would have caused the previous pattern of banding.

They were wrong. And shocked. Shocked, perhaps, that they were wrong. Because what the photon detector registered was, in fact, an identical result to the ordinary screen; the same pattern of bands. But how could it, they wondered? How could light possibly interfere when there was nothing - absolutely nothing - for it to interfere with?

And that was when those in the scientific world who were known - and those who wanted to be - started to put forth a whole series of desperately improbable answers. One of which - indeed the most widely accepted - was Wave Particle Duality. In this theory light, they claimed, acted in two ways. It acted as waves until it was detected, and then it acted as particles. As if it somehow 'knew' that it was suddenly being detected, like a startled deer suddenly looking up from its casual grazing.

In Dave's eyes, such a theory had always been one thing; a crock, but not quite as much as some of the others put forward, such as multiverses. In the multiverse theory, for every point the particle appeared on its way to the photo-detector, numerous other universes sprang up in its wake, each offering a differing result for the particle's direction of travel. What happened then, of course, was that each one of these new universes now faced the same problem. So numerous further universes then sprang up by way of a solution. So on and so on until there were billions upon billions of universes springing up in billionths of a second. It was the particles in *these* universes, some claimed, that the initial particle was 'aware of' and consequently interfering with.

That was why the unique patterning continued to form.

So if multiverses were not the answer, in Dave's eyes, then what was? How was it that a single particle of light could interfere with itself as if it was part of some huge non-existent wave? Dave thought it through as he watched an elderly Japanese man levitating on grainy 8mm film shot in the sixties, his wife chomping her way through a bag of Doritos to his right. And he had one of those crazy thoughts that scientists have from time to time; one of those they usually subdue, simply to avoid the ensuing embarrassment that involves their work colleagues making them a paper hat. Dave didn't. He worked on it and worked on it yet further in his head until it all made sense.

And that was the key. It all made sense.

What if God actually existed?

Which, it's worth bearing in mind, is pretty much like a scientist appearing on TV and saying 'Hey, perhaps the world really is flat after all'. Even Dave knew that the basis of most scientific discoveries was to disprove God's intervention in this world, if not his very existence. To say that he might actually exist and shape our world would, for Dave, be commercial suicide of the highest order. But Dave didn't mean God, not in the archetypal 'bless me for I have sinned' sense, he merely meant the *scientific equivalent* of God.

Because we, as man, had uncovered the laws. $E=MC^2$, $M=F/A$, $P=MxV$, bread always lands butter side down and so on. But we didn't *write* the laws, we just found them. So who wrote them? Because, if 'somebody' or 'something' had created laws then it, or they, would have put rules in place, rules that told every particle on our planet to obey those laws. So, Dave wondered, was something forcing a particle to follow rules even if the other rules surrounding that particle had been changed? In other words, would a particle of light be *told* to travel along the route it was destined to take, even if the other factors - the ones which would have forced that course - had been removed?

So Dave had leaned back on the sofa and thought as he listened to his wife munching chips. He realised just how stupid he might sound if he ever voiced this theory back at the lab. Unless, of course, he could offer

115

some kind of back-up to his theory, something to give it genuine weight. Phase two.

How would it work, he thought? *Really* work? Well... every particle would have to *know* where it could and could not be at any point in time, as laid down by the laws. And for that to work, every point at which it could be - as well as those it couldn't - would have to be catalogued; numbered, like points on some immense sheet of three-dimensional graph paper.

Which worked for Dave. So far.

Simply, if there's another particle already resident on co-ordinate 2345326597741953423563 then you, my friend, cannot reside there unless you move it. But you *can* be on point 2345326597741953423564, because there's nothing else resident there. Although, Dave surmised, it would be much bigger numbers and there would be a lot more of them.

So if this were true, Dave wondered, how would he, as a scientist, explain living, breathing entities? Things which interact and change and alter the environment which surrounds them? And he smiled when he formulated his answer. His wife asked what was so funny and he said 'nothing'; she really wouldn't understand. She was a hairdresser; a damn good one with over thirty movie stars currently on her books, but a hairdresser all the same.

Okay Dave, he told himself, so the world is made up of zillions upon zillions of co-ordinates, like the most intricate three-dimensional grid imaginable. And it is onto these grid co-ordinates that particles can and cannot fall. That they are *allowed* to fall. And the decision is made by the 'law-maker', hereafter known as 'God'. So God, therefore, would be little more than a number cruncher. Which is not to undermine his task, because these were an almost unimaginable series of numbers Dave was talking about. To himself.

But God, essentially, was a computer. Not some IBM tower crashing Windows Panorama every five minutes, or even anything that possessed circuits and transistors, but the most impossibly huge number crunching system imaginable. Like a brain, Dave thought. Yeah, just like a brain.

SEQUENCE

After all, a brain's also a computer.

Which would make us, and animals to a slightly lesser degree, merely pieces of software. Interactive software. Hacking software. Ones that, in effect, hacked into the computer and made alterations. We make our own decisions about where we go, how we move and what we move. But, hack as we do, we too are constrained by the laws of 'God'. We can't walk through walls, bend steel with our bare hands or breathe underwater. And we can't bend strips of metal that are ten feet away without any mechanical help, can we? Which was an odd thought for Dave to have really, because there was an eight year old Indian girl on the TV screen as he pondered, and she was seemingly doing exactly that. If this footage was genuine - which was pretty much up in the air at this point - then how in God's name could she do that?

Then Dave realised, according to his new theory of a Computational God (as he had just named it in his own little computer), exactly what the girl was doing. She was merely hacking deeper, that was all. Not much deeper, granted, but deeper than you or I or even Dave ever could. Perhaps her mind was open just a fraction more than most. Maybe she could even see, or at least sense, the hidden co-ordinates in her head. And then maybe, just maybe, she could actually change the sequence.

Which, if it were true, explained quite a lot of things that Dave's wife had forced him to watch on TV of late. It would explain why a labrador-cross puppy could get uncontrollably agitated at precisely the same moment as his beloved owner died in a car accident some fifty miles away (America's Strangest - 10/05/15). It could *see* the sequence. It would explain how a French student could, quite literally, read the minds of a studio audience (Inexplicable - 01/02/16). He could *see* the sequence. Even more intriguingly to Dave, it would also explain how a woman in New Jersey had suffered bad dreams about a plane that had ultimately crashed (Believe It! - 05/02/16). She could *see* the sequence *before it had even run*.

Which brought into play that other great nemesis of science; fate. If the New Jersey woman could see things *before* they happened, then surely

117

that would mean that they were *going to happen* no matter what. They were *destined* to happen. The sequence was already out there, just waiting to be seen. Which was how the woman had seen it in her dreams - and Dave no longer thought it a coincidence that it is during sleep that the human brain is in its most open and 'receptive' state. So the computer was running a program, living things were interacting with it and some, like Mrs. New Jersey, could even see the results of those interactions well in advance.

All of which made perfect sense to Dave. At least, he *wanted* it to, but how would the others react when he walked in and declared that God, in his opinion, not only existed but was worthy of detailed scientific study? Would he really be laughed out of the room? Out of a job? So, for a few moments he threw all the possibilities back into the ring, and for a long time it was a close fight. Computational God versus billions and billions of parallel universes springing up each and every time any particle on this earth decided to move its scrawny little ass.

Computational God won by a knockout in the eighth.

Two months later, after drafting and (perhaps, foolishly) submitting an eighty-seven page thesis, Dave Sherman found himself sitting in the opulence that was Josef Klein's Los Angeles office situated on the ninety-fifth floor of the KleinWork Tower - an imposing glass and chrome edifice built on reclaimed land at the corner of 5th and Alameda. There, seated in a very corporate red leather chair, they spoke at length. Initially Dave had expected both the ridicule and the firing, but neither came a-knocking. Josef Klein had actually read and understood Dave's report and, whilst he could not pretend to agree with it all, he felt that it had 'merits'. Ones that were indeed worthy of further investigation.

"You're not serious."

"But I am. That's the problem."

"They'll laugh at you the world over. And when they're finished laughing at you, Dave, they'll start on me."

"Maybe they will. But for how long, if I'm right?"

"And this is all because a girl bent steel on your TV?"

"No, Josef, this is because of wave particle duality."

"I'm not convinced."

"We fire light. It travels in waves and therefore it forms patterns. It's interfering. And that's what's *supposed* to happen. But then we fire one particle of light at a time. Particle, Josef, not wave. Nothing to interfere, but still the same pattern every god-damn time. And currently there's not one scientist on the face of this planet who can adequately explain that."

"And yet your little Kashmiri girl has cracked it?"

"No, but she can help us to *understand* it. You see, I think that the light forms patterns because there is a route for it to follow... a route that it's been *told* to follow, and that it continues to do so even if we break the rules... Rules that should never, ever have been broken."

"Like firing one photon at a time?"

"Exactly. There's a sequence. Like a program running in a computer, perhaps even controlled by some sort of computer. Not of the kind we understand but some huge.. brain... Controlling the numbers. Setting the sequence.."

"And the girl...?"

"Can see that sequence. Can alter it at will."

"She can hack the computer?"

"Why not?"

"And, in your opinion, that proves that God exists?"

"It proves that *something* exists. You want to give it a name, fine, we'll call it God."

"Scientists aren't supposed to prove that God exists, Dave. In case you've forgotten, we're supposed to prove that he *doesn't*."

"But I'm right."

"No, Dave, you're crazy."

"But I might be right?"

"Okay, okay. We have good profits from the fibre-optics and the waveless technologies so there's plenty of research money in the pot. But tell me...? If I were to let you run with this... temporarily, I might add... where would that money go? What do we do to get the answers?"

"The key, Josef... the *only* key... is the understanding. If we, as humans, can understand how the true purveyors of ESP, telekinesis, telepathy and psychokinesis might... possibly... attain certain abilities, then we might be able to understand not only how they manage to see the sequence, but also how they harness it."

"And we do that by...?"

"Studying them. Twenty-four-seven. We run tests, change patterns, check genetic patterns, control diet and so on. In a way that no research facility has ever done before, we find out what makes them *them*."

"I don't know. We'd have to disguise it. Give it some gloss."

"We've done it before."

Klein thought for a moment. "Yes, I suppose we have."

Dave was astounded that his employer had been so easy to convince. He might not have been, had he known just where it was that Josef Klein had been in the few months before he was flown to Chasel'ka in 2011, but for now he was working blind.

So it was that in October 2016, three months after his first meeting with Dave Sherman - the first of many - Josef Klein appeared on no less than three prime-time talk shows announcing his company's latest venture. The time was right for giving back, he said, just as his writers had scripted. KleinWork Research Technology, and Josef himself, having been appalled to hear the plight of some of the world's children, were going to do what they could to help. In January 2017, he declared, KleinWork Research Technology would launch 'The NorthStar Foundation', so named because it would act as 'a guiding light' to the underprivileged. And he said it like he meant it.

The NorthStar Foundation would be responsible for the complete funding and ongoing financial support of thirty-eight live-in centres across the

USA to help children between the ages of three and sixteen. Of course it would be difficult to differentiate the coulds from the could-nots, but there would be a series of criteria that would have to be met, including poverty level, nutritional and special educational needs. In a nutshell, those children who needed help most, with over 300 new acceptees per year, would get it first.

What wasn't stated, of course, or indeed edged toward by any one of the three sycophantic interviewers, was that one of the primary criteria for acceptance, indeed the most important one, would be the results of the aptitude tests. KRT, unbeknown to the world at large, would be targeting children who either directly demonstrated, or whose closest relatives had demonstrated, even the slightest hint of paranormal ability. Then, along with the aforementioned levels of care, these children would be studied and encouraged. Firstly to see if they really could change the sequence, and secondly find out how.

Which was how, on March 28th 2017 - just over a year after Dave Sherman's wife had systematically shushed him through the first part of 'Sense and Sense Ability' - a five year old girl by the name of Alison Bond became one of the first children to be accepted by The NorthStar Foundation.

A very special girl indeed.

ELEVEN

Sarah opened the main door and we stepped in from the street. The hallway was gloomy, narrow and dirty. Papers and unforwarded mail were scattered everywhere and grime was etched deep into the black and white flooring. Almost immediately, the door to apartment one flew open and Billy was in the frame: jogging pants, T-shirt and big toothy smile.

"Oh, hi Sarah," he said, faking surprise. The smile said that he liked Sarah. Liked her a lot. "You got in okay?"

Sarah smiled. "Yes. Thanks, Billy," she replied. "That's really sweet."

"Billy? Where's that damn TV Guide?" Ma again, shouting from inside the apartment.

Billy looked embarrassed. "Gotta go," he said. "Ma."

She gave him a wink. Once the door was closed she rolled her eyes at me and shook her head with a 'bless him' smile. "There is a lift," she said as we started climbing the bare wooden stairs, "but it hasn't worked the entire time I've been here."

"And just how long is that?" I asked. Subtle.

"About two years," she replied without turning. "Landlord

keeps saying he'll get it looked at, but the landlord's a lying bastard on far more levels than that, so I'm not gonna get into breath-holding competitions."

We reached the top floor, apartment five marked by half a plastic digit, and she unlocked the door. Inside was cleaner than I'd expected, but it sure as hell wasn't the Ritz. "Lose the coat and I'll get you that Jack," she said, throwing her own onto a rack and heading off through a grimy doorway to the right.

I stepped forward. Inside. The furniture was old and almost certainly second hand, the kind of junk that finds itself sitting outside cheaper stores rather than inside decent ones. A lime green sofa dominated, fraying at every seam, and a three-legged pine coffee table supported by books filled the tiny space between that and an ugly electric fire. The TV was one of the old wooden-sided affairs with a huge grey convex screen and there was no sign of a VCR or any kind of cable box.

The room itself was bare floorboards and cracked plaster, some of which was old enough to have been repainted, only to have cracked again and the air smelled of dust and stale mould.

I moved toward the window, thin white strips of material hanging limply at either side and saw that the apartment did at least have one redeeming feature. The view.

At a loss for anything else to compliment, I stuck with the obvious.

"You can see right across the city from here," I said, sounding genuinely impressed and looking over to the close-knit expanse of coloured halogen in the distance, red lights flashing on and off at the top of the Bank of America.

Sarah's voice was distant in every sense. "Sorry?"

123

"You can see..." and then I turned and looked straight through the door where Sarah had disappeared. And, just for a moment, I had to catch myself. Because what I saw, as I'm sure you've figured out for yourself, was not for one second anything like I had expected to see.

The 'second' room was immaculate. It was big, lit with modern uplighters and had a mezzanine design that positioned the bedroom above, pure white bedding with built-in robes to the right, and the kitchen below. To the right of the robes was a door, presumably to the bathroom and beneath it was Sarah, illuminated by recessed lighting and pouring a glass of Jack for me whilst simultaneously removing the cap from a bottle of Bud for herself. The kitchen possessed spotless white units with chrome doors, chrome fridge, a cooker unit set into the wall and an array of chrome utensils hanging from a grid. It was very smart. The kind of smart that my salary would never afford me.

I stepped into this room, more than twice the size of the other and stared, open mouthed.

The wooden floor in here was so deeply polished that I could almost see my own reflection looking gob-smackedly back at me. It was decorated in what could only be described as 'minimalist chic'. Abstract paintings in bright colours, the kind done with five flicks of one mother of a brush, hung on two walls facing the windows which, unlike the other room, possessed pale grey vertical blinds. A curved leather sofa and green-glass coffee table occupied the central area and faced a widescreen TV, Blu-Ray and Surround system near the window. This was class. Real executive class.

Sarah smiled as she handed over the Jack.

"You can close your mouth now," she said. "Train coming."

She took a swig of the Bud, placed it on a chrome mat on the coffee table and headed back to the kitchen to fix some food.

I moved around the room, picking up ornaments and admiring the pictures. "This isn't *quite* what I expected," I said.

Sarah was tipping nacho-style crisps into a bowl. "I guess not, but I like to keep a low profile," she said.

I looked around this apartment within an apartment. At one side of the door through which I now felt I had followed Alice was a steel-frame bookcase bursting with out-of-place volumes and to the right a glass topped desk with two computer systems sitting on top; a wireless printer suspended underneath. Two computers. I didn't even have *one*. Both were made from clear plastic with flat matrix screens embedded. One also had what appeared to be some kind of speaker system placed at either side; tall glass cigar shapes angled on grey doughnut bases with four mini-speakers embedded into their length.

I nudged one of the clear plastic mice and the left hand screen came to life, with the screen now showing a long list of bands and albums, like some kind of mega-jukebox.

Sarah had been watching me as she prepared the chips and dips. "So what tunes do Detectives like?" she asked, already on her way back, heels clicking.

I thought for a moment. "All sorts, I guess. Though I've always had a soft spot for Nina Simone. No voice quite like it... in my humble...'

She leaned over my shoulder, clicked into a search function on-screen and keyed in 'Nina'. The full list disappeared, to be replaced by only two items; 'Canta Nina - Latino for the Soul' and 'Nina Simone - The Greatest Hits'. A double click on the latter and the piercing piano and pure velvet opening of

'Here Comes the Sun' emerged like syrup from the glass sticks. Sarah smiled and retrieved her Bud. "I have something for most tastes."

"So," I said, sceptically, "care to tell me about this 'low profile'?"

"Not a lot to say," she said, and took a deep swig. "The things I search for can be valuable, if indeed someone wants them badly enough. Some could even be classed as priceless, I suppose. I just find it helps if I look like the last kind of person who'd be uncovering and selling those kinds of things, that's all."

I'd seen a similar thing with middle-weight dealers. "So if anyone comes knocking and you open the door...?"

"They only see the other room," she said proudly.

Worrying, but clever. Indeed, worryingly clever. "So, given that you like to 'uncover' things; where does this 'map' as you call it, fit in?" I removed the page of Latin from my pocket and handed it over.

Sarah's mouth curled upward, accentuating the black lines, and she shook her head in admiration, as though she still could not fully believe that she was actually holding this scrap of badly-photocopied paper in her hand.

"It's actually a fairly common system," she said, handing back the sheet and nudging the mouse on the other computer so that it's screen also burst into life. "You see, in the Middle Ages people hid things all the time, and for a whole host of very different reasons. Any clues they would leave would be targeted purely at others who shared their understanding of a particular method. One of those methods was to encode the information within paintings."

She moved to a stack of pen drives from behind the screen and selected one called 'Paintings'. She plugged it in and moved back to the screen. When the disk image appeared on screen she opened a folder called 'Teniers' and then, from a selection of folders listed by year, selected '1645'.

"But this is just a note," I said, skeptical.

"Indeed it is," she replied, "but it can still be a map. A written map, as in 'go here, turn there'. And it was also - once - attached to a painting. In fact, I can tell you exactly which painting, and that's not just from the date that someone has very kindly added to the top of your copy, either."

"Teniers, 1645?"

She nodded confidently, then opened a file from those listed. It was obvious, even to a technophobe like myself, that it was some kind of scanned photo but showed only a beige rectangle with a much smaller rectangle positioned bottom right.

"Yours is a slightly reduced copy of the original parchment," she said, taking another deep swig of the Bud. "But this is a photo of the back of one of Tenier's works. It's been computer enhanced to the degree where you can now see that something was, for a time, attached there. Forensic tests have also shown traces of Gum Arabic, which would back that theory up."

She traced the shape with her finger. "Now, because the discolouration of the surrounding area is so slight, hence the need for computer enhancement, that would tend to suggest that the original parchment did not stay on the back of the painting for very long. Which is why it's been so hard to trace. Based on calculations I've done, I estimate the original to be a little bigger; around ten percent larger than the copy you have here. The important thing, however, is not the size; it's the proportions, the height and the width, and they're spot on."

She closed the image of the reverse. "And the painting onto which your parchment was originally attached is the almost infamous..." she double-clicked again and it appeared on-screen, "*Temptation of St. Anthony and St. Paul in the Desert.*"

She looked at me like... voilà.

"Infamous?"

She smiled. Cats and cream. "Oh, yes indeed."

"Why?"

"Because this painting has something that just reeks of embedded meaning...."

"Which is?"

"Very carefully constructed and highly unnecessary geometry."

I'm sure I looked puzzled. "Explain....?"

She thought for a moment. The way tired parents might think of ways to explain nuclear fusion or bed-time on a date night to eight year olds. The accentuated jet of the eyebrows started to curl down toward the middle.

"Well, all paintings have geometry," she said eventually. "You know? Defined structure that follows aesthetic rules. The golden section is the most famous method...?"

In the instant that she looked up she suddenly understood that I had no idea what she was talking about. "It's complex," she shrugged, "but if you were to draw a line either from the top, the bottom, the left or the right of a given picture at almost sixty-two percent of the distance, and place your focal object on that line, it... well, it looks good. It balances. Things in the middle look odd, they really do. Sixty two percent across, up or down - that's the ideal, and lots of artists knew this formula and used it. Renaissance artists believed this dimension to be so perfect that they called it the Divine Proportion."

"So it's just a way of deciding where best to put things?" I asked. Layman's terms.

"Exactly," she said. "And when you paint, that's what you do. You decide where best to put things. Sometimes it's because it looks good, and sometimes it's because it has meaning. Writing has its subtle implications and so does art. When you see things in a painting that follow a geometry that serves no aesthetic purpose, you can bet your ass there's a hidden meaning."

I looked at the painting on the screen. "And this has... hidden meaning?" I asked.

"Lots of it," she said. "For years this painting has been studied by every art expert you've ever heard of, plus a good few you probably haven't. Eventually a group in England uncovered what is now referred to as 'the Teniers Square', although the fact that it's not a perfect square, when it could so easily have been, demonstrates that there's probably more to it. I think what you've got in your hand there... is the more."

"Here, I'll show you," she said with almost childish enthusiasm. "Study the painting, tell me what you see."

"I know less than nothing about art," I said, shaking my head. Actually I did know one thing about art, and that was that I knew absolutely nothing about....?

You get the idea.

She smiled. "We'll soon fix that, I assure you. So...go on, Detective ...look at it closely."

A flick of the eyebrows. "Tell me what you *see*."

TWELVE

Thursday, June 9, 2011.
Los Angeles, California.

I did my best to talk around the painting; the way I might if I'd seen it once and was describing it back as part of a case. It showed a semi-desert scene, the kind you'd expect to see in some Middle Eastern country. For obvious reasons, it was composed primarily of yellows, oranges and shades of ochre. Left of centre were two bearded men, seated and wearing robes, the one closest bearing a capital 'T' on his right shoulder. His friend held a staff in his right hand and was talking to him whilst he, it seemed, tried to ignore him and read a book.

The man with the 'T' also had a staff, but rather than hold it - he had the book, remember - it was leaning against a small rock formation fashioned into a rough hexagonal altar. Placed on top of this altar, in the very centre of the painting, was a statuette with a wooden base depicting Christ's crucifixion, a green-glass bottle, a sand-timer and the upper half of a human skull. Why these guys carried half a human skull on long desert trips didn't seem worthy of time or effort. In addition to the book being read by the one of the guys, three more leaned against the altar. A wicker-bound gourd and a cracked bowl had been painted in the bottom corner.

Because the men were seated at the base of a cliff face - one which occupied the entire left hand side of the painting - and the desert stretched into the distance to the right, only the upper-right of the image showed sky, but within the pale blue were two birds. One was distant, no more than a few swift brush strokes, but the other was designed to stand out. Jet black; some kind of raven or crow, it carried a large circular loaf of bread in its beak. A very large loaf; which was impressive for such a tiny bird. The impossible size/weight ratio brought to mind Monty Python's Holy Grail and migrating swallows bearing coconuts.

One of the seated men was pointing skyward toward the bird, presumably amazed at its ability to attain flight at all whilst carrying enough food to feed its offspring for a month. In the distance a solitary figure strolled disinterestedly away from view on the flat plain beneath a church. Either he'd not seen the bird at all, had seen it all before or wouldn't be impressed unless he saw it coming home with one of the smaller Burger King outlets in its mouth. Sarah listened to everything I said. She frowned in places and laughed in others. She could tell I was trying my best and I guess that's why her face was one of only semi-criticism.

"You've seen most things, you just don't know you've seen them, that's all," she said when I'd exhausted everything. "Because there are lines, Nick. Very definite and very distinctive lines." She shrugged. "If you know where to look. Most paintings have lines, but these are very carefully constructed. Right, first let's build that 'almost' square I mentioned..."

She moved the cursor to the toolbox and selected one with which she could draw straight lines. In those days I was not as in-tune with computer technology as Deacon might have liked, but I at least recognised that much. "First the staffs," she said. "Very carefully placed. Why? Well, let's find out, shall we...?"

She pulled a black line along the length of each of the wooden staffs, but continued them to the scanned frame of the painting both above and below. "On the left, this crack in the bowl is our clue," she added, running a further line, vertically, through the crack and stopping it once again at the frame edge. "And on the right... it's the roof of the church. Or, more precisely, the apex of the roof and its relation to the window in the smaller building below."

She drew another vertical line, this time running straight through the point of the roof and the window. "Now, I'm doing this quick and rough," she said, "but trust me. This stuff is bang on, no matter how accurate you want to get. So now, we simply complete the square and then join the corners to find its centre." She connected the place where the staff lines met the verticals to form an approximate square. One of the 'staff lines' already formed a corner-to-corner diagonal, so she quickly drew in the one that was missing.

"Now a near-perfect square, at least one that's at ninety degrees to the vertical, is way too obvious for any codal system," she continued. "And besides, there's nothing of note in the centre which, if you know the rules, is odd to say the least. So I've drawn my square on a separate layer, because I just know it needs to be moved. So now we look at how Teniers wants us to move it."

"*Wants* us to move it...?"

"Oh, yes." As she looked at me her eyes became those of a naughty child trying to escape punishment with puppy-dog charm. "Okay, perhaps not us, but somebody." She turned back to the screen. "Look at those birds... very carefully placed and birds are always very symbolic in a Teniers. Usually in relation to the visible scene rather than to some embedded code, but they always have a purpose. So, we tilt the square, using the upper-left axis, until it passes through both birds. Or, more specifically, through their eyes. Because eyes are also very important. Eyes see things. And what's happened now....?"

She rotated a copy of the square she had drawn, leaving the original to fade into grey on the screen. And, as carefully pointed out without a single word, this new version followed the line of a stone to the bottom left of the image, as well as the slanting rocks which ran from the church toward the desert floor; perfectly.

"So where's our centrepoint now?" she asked.

"The skull." I said. And even I could see a strange kind of logic starting to unfold.

"The *skull*," she agreed. "Even better, it passes through the all-important eyes of the skull. All you need to do now is work out what the 'almost square' means and you're there."

"And where is *there*, exactly?"

"Well, if you happen to be the first to arrive then it's somewhere the U.S. government would really, really rather you weren't." She raised her eyebrows, devil-may-care. "Now, if you'd be kind enough to hand me the text...?"

THIRTEEN

Monday, April 2, 2040.
5th & Alameda, Los Angeles, California.

For all her 'glorious pedigree' as Josef Klein had once referred to it, Alison Bond could so very nearly have become one of The NorthStar Foundation's earliest and most spectacular failures. Throughout her life she demonstrated absolutely no telekinetic abilities, no extra sensory perception and only a very slight degree of telepathy; the ability to read the mind of another. Nothing, intrinsically, that couldn't be done by a million astute kids the world over.

Like the Siberium, it was nothing that KRT would ever be able to put to serious use.

But what she did demonstrate, and this was to be her saving grace, was prodigious learning ability and, with it, an almost photographic memory. If she saw it, heard it, or read it then it went in - and it stayed in. Coupled with this was a superbly logical mind, able to work through almost any problem placed in front of her by carefully calculating the odds in advance and setting herself on a clear route to an answer. At only sixteen years old she had, under NorthStar's supervision, achieved high-grade diplomas in gravitational physics, pure mathematics and biochemistry.

Alison Bond was, in a very real sense of the word, a child genius. It was little wonder then that after her seventeenth birthday, when her time under the wing of The NorthStar Foundation was coming to an end, KleinWork Research Technology should offer her a position within the group. Starting as laboratory assistant in the Microelectronics Division, she worked her way rapidly through Artificial Intelligence and eventually, at the age of twenty-eight, she headed the team known only as 'Computational Analysis'.

It was this division, whose work was not well publicised by KRT, which was directly responsible for the follow-up and ongoing investigation into both Dave Sherman's outlandish theories and NorthStar as a whole. The reason that Alison had chosen to head 'Computational Studies'; indeed the reason she had fought so hard for the position, was because by that time she had become fully aware of the aims of The NorthStar Foundation and why she had been chosen as one of its first acceptees. The fact that she herself had actually been one of those who had failed to demonstrate any abilities in no way detracted from her fascination with the subject.

What 'Computational Analysis' allowed Alison to do was to combine her fascination with pure scientific study; the study of time, gravity, light, biology, molecular and particle physics, with the study of things which were frequently demonstrated, even more frequently vilified and almost always never proved.

Her job, and that of her team, was to search for links between 'true' science and the paranormal: the fake stuff.

It was Alison's image that Klein was studying now, projected into the glass of his desk. It was her 'enrolment' photo, if you will. Five years old with shoulder length sandy-brown hair and an innocent smile; perhaps even a happy one which, given her circumstances, had been the biggest surprise of all.

A tiny red square, projected into the glass of the desk, flashed intermittently to the left of his file images and Klein reached across with one bony finger and touched it.

"Yes?"

The voice, that of an older woman, was curt and officious. "Miss Bond to see you, sir."

Klein smiled. "Send her in."

Alison, now a little over twenty-eight years old, entered. Klein clicked the image away from his screen as she walked the full length of the room, her head held high. She stopped immediately in front of the desk.

"You asked to see me, sir."

Klein smiled warmly and gestured for her to take a seat. "Indeed I did. I've been looking over some of the Micro-electronics data. Quite impressive. In fact, I've heard that some within the department have been referring to you as... how do I put this... a genius...?"

Alison smiled stoically. She was used to flattery, but rarely flattered. "Inspiration and perspiration, Sir."

Klein shook his head. "'Josef', please. And I think you undersell yourself."

"I do my best."

Klein leaned subtly backward in his chair and took a moment to think. It seemed that something was puzzling him. "Yet you choose, for the most part, to remain within NorthStar. Do you not feel you are wasted in such a speculative area?"

"It never crosses my mind," she replied honestly. "I was there myself once, I feel I have an empathy with the kids. And, as empathy is only one step away from..."

Klein gave one short nod of this thin head. "Understanding? Quite." He wheeled himself from behind the desk and toward the window, looking out for a moment over the extremely modern Los Angeles that had grown like shining mould over the old. Every week it seemed another glass tower was competing to get impossibly closer to heaven. "Tell me," he continued, "what do you know of Siberium?

Alison shrugged. "A little before my time, I'm afraid, but I've read the papers. As I understand it, the material was - and is - unlike any previously found on earth but is also... intrinsically... useless."

"Indeed," Klein agreed, nodding with a strained sense of reluctance. "The thing is, when we got around to cutting it up and distributing samples, we retained two spheres for ourselves, each approximately two feet in diameter. We've done nothing with them for a long time...."

Alison ducked her head slightly and looked at her employer inquisitively. Knowingly. "But...?"

"But then a few weeks ago, one of the aerodynamics guys, Strauss - who I believe you already know - made a request to borrow one of the spheres. He wanted to see what might happen if electricity was applied... in huge quantities I might add... in a perfect vacuum. In its native environment."

"And what happened?"

Klein thought for a moment, looking out of the window as though it were the answer itself that troubled him. "The results were... strange, to say the least. If I'm honest we cannot really make head nor tail of them."

"So you'd like me to take a look?"

"In a manner of speaking, yes. You see, Strauss is scheduled to run the tests again - with much higher numbers - this afternoon. We've increased the monitoring equipment made available to him... camera systems, temperature, pressure, gravity, magnetism, humidity. All the usual." He turned to look at his guest with already failing eyes narrowed further. "Tell me, Alison, are you still working with the mice?

"Yes, Sir." Almost as soon as she had uttered the words, she realised where this had been leading; what it was that Klein was wanting from her. "And... you'd like me to perhaps loan him one for the test? Perhaps even use that as an excuse to stick around and see what happens for myself?"

Klein smiled as a proud father might when a good report card came his way. "As I say, Alison, you undersell yourself. I believe he's booked the lab from three o'clock onward."

Alison smiled back, though hers was a dutiful one; the kind perfected by flight attendants the world over. "I'll see if I can't stop by."

"It would be appreciated."

* * * * *

The laboratory, housed in a bright white single-storey warehouse structure behind the main KleinWork Tower, was exactly fifteen metres in diameter, had coated titanium walls and was both air and water tight, allowing it

137

to be converted from a water tank one week to a perfect vacuum the next. And it was to be a vacuum today. Having pretty much shelved extensive research into the Siberium back in 2016, Strauss was here today because, as explained by Klein, he had wondered how the material might react when placed in a perfect vacuum and electrically charged to an immensely high degree. One so high that the heat generated would cause a thin layer of the surface - approximately 0.02mm - to melt.

It had already been demonstrated that Siberium's melting point in air was 2687° Fahrenheit, at which point it also reacted with the oxygen content of the air and 'sparked'. Strauss wondered if this melting point could be lifted substantially in the absence of air. If it could, then this - along with its low heat conductivity generally - would make Siberium an ideal candidate for ultra-thin protective sheathing on the upcoming Shuttle-X, on which his team had been handed fifteen research assignments by the GSA, the successor to NASA.

What Strauss also needed to do, as was the case in most budget-wrenching tests, was to get as many results as possible from just one run. So, positioned within the vacuum, would also be extremely sensitive devices for recording changes in heat, light, inherent magnetism, electrical fields and gravitational pull. A high resolution digital camera running at 136fps would be placed facing the Siberium ball and now, with Alison's attendance secured, Charlie would also be present.

Charlie, or DBX2105, was one of fifteen white mice that Alison used in her studies of ESP. He was also one of the smartest. Three electromagnetically-sealed carbon-fibre containers and Charlie wouldn't walk away from the one with the cheese. Every time. Take out the cheese and replace it with odour-free polystyrene. Same result. It was like Charlie could actually see inside.

When she entered the control room at a little after three she could see that Strauss was already suited up and inside the lab, making last minute adjustments to the camera system. She spoke to him through a microphone which, in the interests of a completely controlled environment uncontaminated by conventional audio speakers, gently vibrated the walls to produce sound. It distorted her voice so much that she sounded like a big butch guy, which made Strauss smile through his orange-tinted visor.

"Brought someone to see you," she boomed, holding up the case.

Strauss looked up, his face distorted by the plasti-glass and gave a thumbs up. "Great, bang him in the hole."

Alison moved over to 'the hole', a vacuum-controlled airlock system and placed Charlie down, tapping gently against the clear outer so that he could pretend to nibble at her finger in that adorable way that he did. The case was completely airtight, but possessed an air-feed system built into its base which would ensure that Charlie would continue to breathe comfortably despite the lab being devoid of any gases, breathable or otherwise. "Take care, baby," she said.

Strauss moved awkwardly across the lab, dodged around one of the two retained spheres of Siberium which was now supported on a titanium pedestal, and collected the case at the other side. "You will take care of him for me, won't you?" Alison asked, her voice bouncing like a huge rubber ball from the walls.

Charlie ran around in his tiny case, sniffing. Of course, he was completely unaware that he was about to become part of an experiment. Just as he was unaware that he would soon have no case left to run around in.

"'Course I will," Strauss replied with mock sincerity. "Who knows, ten minutes with the 'space rock' and he might even be more intelligent than before." He placed the case on another titanium pedestal then stood back and admired his work. Siberium, camera, mouse and digital recorders. Time to rock and roll.

Alison grimaced. Charlie was already fantastic. He couldn't be any more intelligent if he tried. Which, unlike the other mice, he did.

Five minutes passed before Strauss was out of the lab and back in ubiquitous jeans, sneakers and T-shirt. Unlike Alison, he never bothered with the white coat; figured it gave the wrong impression. Besides, there would be no need to suit up again once the experiment was over either; all the required results would already be in. He looked at Alison as she checked the backlit screens and recorded data, her long brown hair pulled impossibly tight and those black half-rims she always wore making her look more severe than ever.

Strauss, however, was a man used to finding hidden data within seemingly obvious results and he looked further than the glasses, his eyes running slowly along the length of her body. Underneath that clinical shell, he sensed, this was probably a very beautiful young woman. In fact, he might even be twisted to bet money on it. The problem was, everybody seemed to judge Alison's book by its highly officious cover. Nobody ever tried to turn the page.

"What do you say after this is over I buy you dinner?" he said, casually leaning against the console.

"I heard you were seeing Rachael?" She left it deliberately open-ended, but her eyes spoke volumes.

"Is that what they're saying?"

"That's what they're saying. They say you gave her a present. A cute little necklace, no less."

Strauss smiled a wry smile; part happiness and part kudos. He hadn't mentioned to anyone that he was seeing Rachael and the one date they'd already shared had been across town. Which, by logical deduction, meant that if anyone was saying that they were an item; it was Rachael.

"It was a good luck thing, that was all. A crucifix I made from 'Old Red'. She's visiting relatives in Europe for a couple of weeks."

She threw him a mock-stern look. "So... while the cat's away, you thought you'd play with my mice, is that it?"

"You know me, I'm only joshing." It was a lie, but becoming less of one the more he thought of Rachael. He smiled again; warmer this time. Maybe, once she got back, he actually had a chance with her after all. If so, it might take surgeons a good few days to get the smile off his face.

"So what is it with you?" he said, his tone firmly back in the realm of social banter. "You never go out, you never date. I mean, we all love our work

140

but we all gotta take a break sometime. Kick back and have some fun."

"I have fun," Alison scowled. "I just do it on my own, that's all."

Strauss laughed. "Well, if you mean what I think you mean then I know a guy in electronics whose working on a battery that recharges itself. I'll give him a call if you like?"

She gave him a slap on the shoulder. Gentle enough to tell him that she didn't mean it to hurt and hard enough to let him know that she did. "Are we ready to do this or not?"

Strauss looked her up and down. "Alison... darling... this is all so sudden. But I'm game if you are?" One look told him to quit it, and now. He sighed one more time, took a seat in a red-backed operator's chair and turned to the controls with an overtly hurt expression, the best he could manage. "Yes, Miss Bond, we are ready to go."

He pressed a green button and a long metal tube descended from the ceiling within the lab, five metal prongs arcing like a hand from its base. He kept the button pressed until this hand was almost touching the sphere and then let go. Another button press kicked in the auto sensor which positioned each of the fingers precisely 0.5mm from the surface of the sphere. It was imperative that they were close enough to deliver the actual charge, whilst never actually touching. Then he pushed himself backward, the wheels gliding across the smooth white floor, and keyed a required charge level of 389 into the computer terminal on the back wall. Then he turned, slid forward and, at arm's length, nonchalantly flicked a large orange switch on the console. There was a sound of humming, building slowly in volume as the system powered up. Then he smiled, flicked a second orange switch and...

All hell broke loose.

First there was a deafening scream which caused both Strauss and Alison to throw their hands over their ears. It lasted about two seconds, still tearing at the eardrums despite clasped hands. Strauss flew backward in his chair, causing it to tip and throw him onto the cold hard floor. Then, for the merest instant, there was a flash of light. The brightest and most

141

powerful blue/green light that either could remember seeing.

Alison, still on her feet, felt her ankles shudder, as though she was standing on a rug that had been tugged very swiftly. She reached over to the orange switch, faltering on her feet, and flicked it back upward, shutting the system down. Then there was nothing but the blissful release of silence. It had been over so soon, but even so Alison had never really appreciated until that moment just how alluring a concept pure silence could actually be.

Strauss, still laid on the floor, stared blankly at the ceiling. "What the hell just happened?" he said.

"I really don't know," Alison said, very quietly. "But I think we might be needing one of your good luck charms."

"It was one of a kind." Like its recipient, he thought.

Alison was staring into the lab, her eyes fixated on something. It was not what she saw now that bothered her, but what she was almost certain she had seen. Just before the flash.

"You're not going to help me get up are you?" Strauss said.

No reply.

"Did we break it? Please God tell me we didn't break the sphere? Because if we did then we were never here. Well perhaps you were, but not me. I was somewhere else. Eating chicken."

"No, it's fine," Alison replied, but it was obvious that her mind had moved to other things.

He rolled his eyes, climbed to his feet and joined her in staring through the glass, his hands pressed against the console edge. Everything, it seemed, was just as it had been before. The case, the camera, the instruments and the Siberium were all exactly where they had been only moments ago, and all were unharmed.

He breathed heavily for a few seconds, just watching. Then he inhaled one long gulp of dry, sterile air, flicked a switch and released the vacuum.

"I guess I'd better go check the results while I still have a job," he said.

They passed through the main airlock and into the lab. Alison stretched out her long fingers and ran them along the wall, the pure-white coating smooth under her skin. "What are these walls made from?" she said.

"Why do you ask?" Strauss said, already dismantling the camera.

"Curious."

Strauss looked up and saw her caressing the walls. Gently, like one might run fingers along the neck of a loved one. Or a work colleague, perhaps, once she returned from the other side of the Atlantic. "Ninety mil. titanium coated in heat-resistant porcelain enamel."

Alison's eyes narrowed. Then she couldn't really have seen what she had just seen, could she? She wanted to say something, but realised in an instant that it would have made her look foolish. Strauss had been on the floor, flat on his back and would have seen little, if anything. It was like he said; this was ninety-millimetre titanium coated in porcelain enamel. It was rock solid. She was mistaken and that was all there was to it.

She gave a last tap on the wall, unvarnished nails giving a high-pitched click-click against the cold white, then moved over to the case. Obviously Charlie should have been her first concern on entering the room, but he had been temporarily outweighed by other events. Other thoughts.

She looked into a case with a broad smile but then, as quickly as the smile had come, it disappeared once more. Strauss, now scrolling through a series of numeric readings on the display panel of the temperature reader, didn't even know that anything was wrong. Not yet anyway. The first he knew was when Alison 'kind of' spoke to him. She was distant, though, more distant that usual, if such a thing were possible. She didn't bother to look at him. She couldn't take her eyes off the case.

"Pete," she said, almost under her breath. "Can I ask you something?"

Strauss was too engrossed in his figures now to be flippant. "Of course."

Alison looked up; her face a blank canvas awaiting the first coat of understanding.

"Where the *fuck* is my mouse?"

143

FOURTEEN

Sarah scoured the Latin text again, translating aloud as she read. *"I bear a great secret, one that troubles me greatly. The Fate of the Knights seeks me and my time draws closer. So I take my secret from their reach and leave it in your hands. The Lord be with you and guide you."*

"You read Latin?" I asked.

She laughed. "Yeah, but not very well. I can do the basics but I find fricatives a bitch. Tina's so much better."

"So what does he mean by the *Fate of the Knights*?"

"If it *is* a he," she said chastisingly, "then I presume he means The Knights Templar. And their fate was death, in an exceptionally long and drawn-out way that you don't want to even think about. Now, for the Templars to be mentioned would make sense because The Knights Templar were the last people known to have held the tables."

And now I was back to not understanding again. "Okay, so what are the tables?"

"The Tables of Testimony. *The Divine Laws of God and Man...?*" Another glance upward and another instant where

I needed help again. Lots of it. "*Exodus 31:18: And he gave unto Moses, when he had made an end of communing with him upon Mount Sinai, two tables of testimony, tables of stone, written with the finger of God.*"

"So the divine laws are The Ten Commandments?"

"Hell no," she laughed. "Jeez, somebody here never went to bible class. The Ten Commandments were *dictated* by God, but *written* by Moses. '*And the LORD said unto Moses, Come up to me into the mount, and be there: and I will give thee tables of stone, and a law, and commandments which I have written; that thou mayest teach them.*' That, my friend, is Exodus 24:12."

"But you said that *Moses* wrote the Ten Commandments?"

"He did. You see, Moses came down from the Mountain and broke the originals, so God called him back, à la Exodus 34:27: And the LORD said unto Moses, '*write thou these words: for after the tenor of these words I have made a covenant with thee and with Israel. And he was there with the LORD forty days and forty nights; he did neither eat bread, nor drink water. And he wrote upon the tables the words of the covenant, the ten commandments.*'"

"You sure know your bible," I offered with a smile.

"I know a lot of things," she said a wry glint. "But what I didn't know, until now... was *this*."

She ran her finger along lines of Latin and read aloud as she did:

I TEGO ARCANA DEI
[ITINERIS HAUD TEMPTATIO] INVENIO INDICIUM
INEO CRUX DIABOLIS ADEO PINETUM
EXINDE CANCER ADEO CERVUS BALINEUM
OCCASIS ADEO ESPERAZA REVENIO CRUX
PERACTO QUADRUM TENIERS

"Which, when literally translated, means: *Go where I conceal the secrets of God, journey without temptation to discover proof; start at the Devil's Cross as far as pine wood; then south as far as the bathing deer; west as far as Esperaza, then return to the Cross; Complete the square of Teniers.* And that," she concluded, "is our map."

A couple of mouse clicks and Sarah's screen showed a highly detailed map of southern France, into which she zoomed tight. "Here's Esperaza," she said, "which is one of the towns mentioned. And here is the Devil's Cross." She gestured toward a feature marked only as 'Crx'. "So, with a bit of translation we now also have Lespinas, the pines and Rennes-les-Bains, the deer who bathe. The four points of our so-called square."

She selected the relevant area, copied it into the computer's memory, then switched back to the image of the painting complete with geometric lines and pasted it over. Moving the cursor to the bottom-right she adjusted a digital slider to reduce the opacity so that both images could be seen simultaneously.

She looked me straight in the eye and started laughing. Loudly. And, as she did, she shook her head in what I can only describe as despair. "Stupid, stupid, stupid," she said, as though watching a pair of delinquents playing chicken with an oncoming train.

"Who?" I asked.

"The U.S. team," she said. She hid the image for a moment, selected a folder on her hard disk called 'Cardou' and opened one of the files. She was still laughing when it came on screen.

"This picture here..." She pointed to the screen. The image was an aerial black and white; primarily hills but with dark rectangles located fairly centrally in the shot, "is where the U.S. Government currently have an archaeological dig underway.

They bought the land from the French in ninety-eight, or traded it for technology or something, I don't know. Either way, it's now five hundred hectares of U.S. soil and the world stays well away, that's the deal. Including the French. But the thing is, they've been digging for almost three years now and they've found... well... nothing. And boy, are they pissed."

She swapped the image to another, full colour this time, showing two stern-looking guys standing within what I presumed was the same encampment as the aerial.

The guy on the left looked early fifties and had a definitive military look whilst the other was younger but balding. He was pointing to a map on a foldaway table. In the background two much younger men, again with that military look I can spot so well, were wearing dark glasses. One was apparently mid-sentence whilst the other dragged on a cigarette. They and the foreground guys, the guys looking intently at the map, did not looked pleased. Not at all.

"This picture is from the U.S. dig itself," Sarah said. "I have a friend there, a photo-journalist called Kelly. She's got exclusive rights but can't publish any pictures until they find something. But, for a small fee, she's been known to send me one or two pictures when she can, just to show me what they're up to."

She pointed to the two men in the foreground. "These two are the dipshits in charge. General Peter Grier on the left and Professor Josef Klein is the one with the glasses on the right. Grier looks after security issues, internal as well as external, whilst Klein supervises the dig itself."

"So he's the resident archaeologist?"

"If only," she said disparagingly. "He's a scientist. Does research for MIT, freelances for the government and runs at least three high-tech companies that I know of. Very rich, very powerful and very, very stupid. I mean sure, he's got some good archaeologists on his team, some of the best, but he wouldn't know true archaeology if it ran into his tent and bit him on the ass." She looked at the image and shook her head, the smile still broad across her face.

"So... what's so funny?" I asked.

"Well, as I say, this is now completely U.S. soil, they were very careful about striking that deal. Presumably because they were so sure that they were going to find something. Which so far... they haven't. And this camp, in case you hadn't guessed Nick, is situated at the southerly edge of Mont Cardou."

I hadn't guessed. I hadn't even started to guess. "Mont...?" Sarah nodded toward the screen. And then I guessed. I just couldn't see why it was so funny, that was all. "The skull?"

"They've gone and bought the damn skull," she said, nodding with delighted satisfaction. "My God, I can't honestly believe they think it's that easy."

And now I really was confused. Not for the first time, and certainly not for the last. "It isn't, then?"

Sarah leaned back in her chair, looked at the screen and looked straight back at me. It was a look that said one thing, and one thing only: *duh*. "You're really not getting this, are you?"

"I'm trying," I said, and honestly I was. "It's just that I'm not very religious, that's all."

"You don't have to be religious," Sarah said. "You just.... Well, trust me, you just don't have to be religious."

"Look," she said, changing the screen back to the image of the overlaid map. "If you know the towns, then you have the Latin.

Because the names of the towns only appear on the Latin.Yes?" I nodded. "And in relation to the towns, the skull is where?"

I looked at the screen. I knew the answer, at least I thought I did, but given the fact that I was making an idiot of myself already I really did feel it better to check. "In the... centre?"

"In the centre. Get it now....?"

And still I didn't.

Sarah sighed. I've seen pre-school teachers do the same. "And if it's in the centre of your four towns... why the hell would you need the painting? If all the towns are known and all you have to do is criss-cross them to find the centrepoint, then why the painting?"

Now, finally, I could see her point. The painting would have no purpose to serve unless its content was designed to lead you to another location.

"Wherever it is," she continued, "you can *guarantee* it's not the skull.The skull's only there to show us that our angle of rotation is correct, that's all. Which is why the U.S. Government now owns five hundred hectares, which is almost exactly the size of this skull when laid over the map by the way, of totally useless French real estate."

I conceded. "So the tables are....?" And then, in the brief and slightly embarrassing silence that followed I - fortunately - answered my own question. "...under something else."

Sarah smiled. I'm sure she breathed a subtle sigh of relief as well.

"Yes," she said. "But now we have to find out under *what*."

I watched as she scoured the screen; her expression fixed but those piercing eyes she shared with her sister darting like comets from left to right. Her brow furrowed each time she came up empty and her breaths became more determined, like a swimmer preparing to dive. After maybe three or four long minutes, she breathed in. Long and hard. The brow lifted; the eyes widened and the mouth fell slowly open in dawning realisation. Whatever it was; *wherever* it was, I got the distinct impression that Sarah had just found it.

"*Journey without temptation,*" she said, slowly quoting the Latin directions I was now holding. She turned to look at me and repeated the words, stressing just one of them. "Journey *without* temptation."

"Go on..?"

"What do you do when you're not tempted, Nick?" she asked.

I thought for a moment and then said, "Just say NO!"

It was the best Reagan impression I could manage.

Sarah's face, singularly unimpressed, scrunched into a ball. "What else?" she asked.

"I don't know," I said. I tried to picture myself refusing some kind of temptation. Bearing in mind I now smoked (again), drank like a fish and yes, had I been given the chance I'd have done some serious womanising as well, it was not an easy image for me to create. "I'd just, well... I dunno..." I shrugged, "turn and walk away?"

Sarah nodded very slowly, eyebrows suddenly flicking upward as the eyes... those eyes... turned on me like lasers.

"So tell me, Nick..." she said gently, "...*who's not tempted?*"

FIFTEEN
FRIDAY, APRIL 20, 2040.
5TH & ALAMEDA, LOS ANGELES, CALIFORNIA.

It was one of the most hastily assembled teams in KRT's history; eighteen days flat, all other projects re-assigned. It comprised five men and one woman, all of whom were now seated at the head of a boardroom table designed to accommodate over three times that figure.

At the head of that table, as ever, was Josef Klein, the son of German immigrants who had studied at MIT and then gone on to work for the United States Government, funding from whom had led to the formation of KRT itself - a company which could not only perform government work, but also handle those projects from which that same government might at certain times need to disassociate itself.

At the age of sixty-seven, though still very active for a man of his age and looking not much older than fifty, Klein was now the seventh richest man in the United States, thirteenth in the world and very, very powerful. In his own eyes, however, never powerful enough.

Next was David A. Sherman, another MIT graduate and, prior to his recruitment by KRT, a one-time Alicium Professor of Particle Physics at the California Institute of Technology. Here was the man who had, whilst watching a coffee-table documentary, formulated a theory that on the face of it had sounded wholly ridiculous. A theory that suggested that the world in which we all lived was actually little more than an immense numeric grid, one that comprised billions upon billions of miniscule co-ordinates along which all particles went about their business. And this system was, for want of a better expression, 'computer-controlled'; supervised by a computational system not unlike (but infinitely more powerful than) a human brain. This computer laid down the laws and, on occasion, intervened to uphold them. With every thought that was generated by a living thing or every action that was taken, however, the computer was 'hacked'.

Some living things, however, primarily those who possessed the ability to utilise more than the 'regulation' 10% of their own brain, could hack a little deeper. Some could move objects without touch, others read thoughts without words and some could see events that had yet to happen. It was a ridiculous theory indeed, and one which (had it ever been openly publicised) would instantly have been the subject of great scorn from 'legitimate' scientists the world over.

Until, it would seem, eighteen days ago.

Third at the table was Peter Strauss, the man who's experiment into increasing the melting point of Siberium had led to 'the discovery'. He had seen little on the day, having spent the most important fragments of that time flat on his back, but what he had seen was the mouse or, conversely, the complete lack of one. And then he had seen the results; the changes in temperature, humidity, electricity, magnetic fields, and gravitation. And he had seen the tape. That, in addition to his expertise in particle physics, was why he was on the team.

Of all the men here today, however, it was the two others who were the most qualified engineers, both of whom having been seconded from other KRT divisions; one in Japan and one in the United Kingdom.

Nagariki Haga had extensive knowledge of the design and build of electrically operated systems and regulated charge dispensation, whilst Andrew Kerr had been one of the team responsible for KRT's patented waveless technology and was an expert in the field of transmittance and receival. At this point it was perceived that, on this basis alone, his inclusion in the team was a necessity. Even if it were not, he still had more than enough experience in a great many fields of electronics, including chip-assembly, integrated circuit design and data processing, to prove his inclusion more than useful.

And then there was Alison Bond. Young, beautiful and not nearly as 'sequence-aware' as her acceptance into the NorthStar Project might have suggested. Brilliant nevertheless, and able to theorise, deduce and apply something that Strauss, seated to her right, had always referred to as 'mindfuck logic' to almost any problem. The kind of permutative 'thinking ahead' that chess players could only dream of. That, plus the fact that she had possessed first hand experience of the 'sequentially aware' for over twenty-eight years, and the additional fact that she (like Strauss) had seen the results, made her inclusion a given.

Kerr, whose flight from London had been delayed, had been the last to arrive but now, with five sets of notes compiled by Sherman resting in front of them and coffee distributed, the team was now assembled. Klein stood at the head of the table, a fifty-eight inch flat matrix screen glowing behind him as he started to tell them all the things they needed to know.

"Welcome to you all," he said, the slight croak in his voice the only thing to belie his true age. "You are the complete contingent of what is to be known from here on as The Sequence Project. I don't need to remind any of you I'm sure that this, like all projects we undertake, is extremely classified. Not one word spoken in this room today leaves it." He smiled, but it had no warmth, just the same threatening cruelty that Klein always seemed to be able to turn on so well. "So what, you may ask, is The Sequence Project? Firstly, let me tell you that in many ways it has been one hundred and thirty two years in the making."

He pressed a button on a hand-held remote and the screen behind him changed to an image of dense forest, a huge swathe of barren desolation torn through it. "This is Tunguska, in Western Siberia," he explained. "The scene of the meteorite impact of 1908. As some of you may be aware, no fragments of the meteorite were ever found, indicating that the explosion itself had been many miles above ground level."

The image changed to that of a twenty foot diameter hole in the ground, presided over by a large rig containing five winches. "And this is the result of that explosion. Over four hundred kilometres from Tunguska we found, in 2011, the core of the meteor buried at a depth of eighteen hundred metres."

The image now changed to the ball in situ in Siberia, molten black rock still burned into its side. "On excavating the core, we discovered it to be an element unknown anywhere on earth and quite probably the result of chemical interactions created when a star somewhere in our universe reached the end of its natural life - thousands if not millions of years ago. The material is extremely dense, very heavy, conducts heat to poor effect but does, however, possess inherent magnetic properties to the point of exerting measurable gravitational properties, equivalent to half those discernible on our own moon. In fact, we believe that if this super-condensed material had the same atomic properties of, say, granite then it would need to expand to a size about a third that of the moon. You will understand then, just how condensed this matter actually is and we'll be coming back to that later."

He turned back to the screen, now showing one of the two spheres which KRT had retained. "Eighteen days ago, Peter Strauss here, formerly of our Solar Division, decided to perform an experiment on one of our Siberium spheres. And, much as I would love to give you the great news here and now, I feel that I must turn you over to him to give you some hard-data results. I think you will find them quite exciting."

Alison was already worried about the direction this was heading. In fact, she had been increasingly worried since she had seen the things she had tried to convince herself that she hadn't seen. The digital footage, however, unbelievable as it had been, had proved to her that she must have seen it, and her desperately logical mind had been kept awake far longer than it should - with good reason - every night since.

There was only one possible explanation for what she had witnessed in the sealed lab, she decided, and it wasn't good. Worse still, it was probably going to be unveiled here today and she figured that the only reason that Klein had so carefully chosen his attendees was that he somehow wanted to use what had been found. How, even her mind could not yet deduce, but that was immaterial. The fact that he did, and the knowledge she already had of Klein's quest for all-powerful supremacy, never more evident than in the way he conducted his business, literally gave her a chill.

In Alison's eyes, Klein wasn't that far removed from the Adolf Hitlers and Saddam Husseins of the world; he wanted it all and he didn't really care how he got it or, indeed, who might get hurt along the way.

She sighed at the thought because, given her conclusions, it was actually no longer 'the who' any more. It was more likely the 'what'. Klein might now actually be in imminent danger of screwing up the very planet on which we were all trying to live. Even now she could see that his eyes were saying 'Can I do this?" rather than '*Should* I?"

Strauss, as young, eager and unshaven as ever, almost bounced up to the front. He removed a metallic red three-inch disc from his pocket and dropped it into the vertical slot at the right hand side of the screen then turned to face the others. Klein had already retaken his seat and was now, out of sight to all but Strauss, smiling like the cat who had just perfected a cream-making machine.

"Right," Strauss said, nervously running his hand through spiky black hair, "Well...? First of all I must explain that the purpose of our initial experiment here was purely to analyse just how the introduction of a vacuum environment would affect the melting point of the Siberium during the application of strong electrical currents. In the interests of data collection, however, various measuring devices were placed on site including a camera, sensors, various data recorders and a mouse... by the name of Charlie," he smiled at Alison. "These are the results we extrapolated from the various pieces of equipment."

The screen showed a number of computer-generated graphs, each showing the usual 'x/y' co-ordinates and a series of undulating and interconnecting lines of varying colours.

"As you can see," Strauss continued, "electrical current was at 389, fairly high, and during that time there is a definite increase in magnetic and gravitational activity within the room, culminating at these peaks here and here..." he pointed to the relevant pinnacles visible on two of the graphs. "...as well as a very slight temperature increase. At the peak of activity, the temperature was raised almost instantaneously by eight degrees and gravitational pull became seventy-eight times that of earth's own."

"Jesus Christ," Kerr said, leaning forward in his chair. "78G?"

Strauss nodded. "That's right. Although it was omni-directional. Now obviously that was pretty much a cool result in itself, but it was the result of that gravitational increase which was to become the most amazing and, dare I say worrying, aspect of the experiment. As you will see from the video footage, as Alison and myself re-enter the laboratory, we discovered..." He paused, purely for dramatic effect, "...that Charlie was... no longer there."

"How you mean... *no longer there*?" Haga this time. Here was a big man with wide cheeks and heavy eyebrows. His voice was deep and pounding, his Japanese accent thick.

Strauss shrugged. "We don't actually know, although I believe that Dave's got a theory for you in a mo'. Anyway, Charlie's gone but we do have the digital footage. And this, my friends, is what it shows...."

He pressed a button and the screen changed to an image of the sealed lab. The sphere was perfectly centred, the lights reflecting in wide ovals across its now perfect laser-cut surface. Some of the instruments were just visible to the right of the image with Charlie scurrying obliviously inside his case to the left.

In the background of the image Alison had her eyes down whilst Strauss himself was leaning side-on and talking. Even from this distance it was obvious from his expression that he was basically chatting her up. Kerr sniggered but it didn't bother Strauss. He possessed many things, but a sense of shame had never been one of them.

On screen Strauss took his seat, leaned back almost disinterestedly and flicked a switch just below camera. A gentle hum built up on the audio. Then a loud noise, very loud, like a hundred shrieking women, followed by a flash of bluish light that obliterated the entire image. As the picture came back Strauss was covering his ears and arcing backward, eventually disappearing out of view. Kerr sniggered again. Then Alison, seemingly struggling to find her feet, reached over and appeared to flick the switch.

It was true. Charlie, formerly resident in the glass case to the left, had quite clearly disappeared.

But that wasn't all. Because Kerr had noticed something else, just as Alison had. Unlike Alison, however, he hadn't actually seen it in the flesh, only through a camera lens. Subsequently he went on to make an incorrect assumption. "It warped the lens," he said.

Strauss was shaking his head. "Not the lens, no. Here, I'll show you." He played the video footage back, pausing just after the first strains of the screaming noise could be heard, then frame-advanced it. "This footage is at one hundred and thirty six frames per second," he said. "And, whilst I can see why you might *think* it warped the lens, I can assure you that was not the case."

The frames continued to advance and, with each minor step, the walls of the laboratory seemed to bow inward, as if sucked close by the sphere. But, despite being coated in a smooth and very tough layer of enamel, they did not crack or flake. They bent like rubber and, true to Strauss' promise, this could not be an effect of the lens because, as they warped, they caught a glint of the lights embedded into the ceiling and reflected it back. Had it been the lens, the image might have warped, but not the lighting. Strauss paused the image at a point where one strip of light ran in a long arc across the glossy enamel, spreading as it curved toward the camera.

"It bent the walls," Kerr said. "How the fuck did it bend the walls? They're..."

"Titanium and ceramic," Strauss said with a smile. "And yes, it bent them."

"So what about Charlie?" Haga asked. "He's still there now, so where he go?"

Strauss continued the frame advancement, talking over the image. "Well, given the research that Dave has done subsequently, and adding to the information gleaned from frames 8568 and 8569, just over a minute after the camera was first activated, we're guessing at around...." he stopped the tape as Kerr's and Haga's eyes opened wide. Klein, Alison, Strauss and Sherman had seen this footage already; their eyes had already been opened. None more so than Klein's. "...1776."

The image on screen was no longer the sealed lab. It was no longer even a building. It was a desert scene. One long, endless stretch of ochre desert broken up by no more than a few cactus plants and a bright blue horizon.

Kerr could not believe his eyes. "You mean this is...?" He didn't even know how to finish his own question.

"Los Angeles," Sherman said, not even turning around. His eyes, too, were fixed on the screen. "Long before Los Angeles, as we know it, even existed."

Strauss allowed the image to remain in a permanent loop, toggling back and forth between frames 8568 and 8569, the only two to record the desert scene in full. Frame 8567, apparently, showed a mixed image of the lab and desert combined, but only the following two showed the true scene in full clarity. As the screen continued to alternate between the two he pointed to Charlie on-screen, his case temporarily removed from the image. Though only just discernible, it was clear to all gathered that the mouse was moving downward between the two frames. It was perhaps only one pixel's worth of movement on the screen, but there was no mistake.

Charlie was falling to the floor.

Kerr was looking at each of those gathered in turn. "But that's... I mean, what you're saying is... but that's..."

Klein turned to Sherman, his smile big and the lines along his cheeks creasing into something akin to deep wounds. "Dave, why don't you change with Peter here and... explain?"

Strauss took his seat again and smiled at the look on Kerr's face. That would teach him to laugh at his chat-up lines or his inability to stay on his chair, he thought. Don't look so clever now, do you wise guy?

Sherman rose to his feet and left Strauss' images flickering on the screen. He smiled a wide smile and held the air of a defending politician. His mousy blond hair, mid-length, was curled backward to allow just the right amount of lift above his scalp. He smoothed it over with his hand. Both his suit and tie were expensive and immaculately tailored. In true politician style he had even gone to the trouble of wearing a pin-stripe shirt.

Alison looked right at Sherman's face and frowned. For the most part scientists, like computer-jocks, were pasty. Not only did they rarely venture into the sun, but even more rarely did they care. Only those who saw discovery as a stepping stone into something far more corporate cared about their appearance; only they went as all out as Sherman to get themselves a tan that deep.

However many bottles it took.

"Given the gravitational pull already exerted by the Siberium in a state of rest," he began, "and the increased levels registered during electrical input, we believe that this sphere has, in effect, exerted a force so great as to pull time toward it, releasing it once the current is broken."

"How that possible?" Haga asked.

"Well," Sherman continued, strolling left and right and rubbing his chin as he fought for the words. Sometimes it was hard to explain gravitational science even to other scientists - lesser scientists. Especially those whose work was centred very much on the limitations of this world. "Mr. Haga, could you explain to me what a black hole is?"

Christ, Alison thought, now he's even acting like a Goddamned politician. All measured strolls and deep thought as he addresses the common man. What next? False promises and unfeasibly optimistic manifestos?

"Is a dense star, imploded." Haga explained. "The density exerts an immense gravitational force, very strong, and this can even pull light to it. To a point light itself cannot escape, so only a black sphere is seen to the eye. This sphere, it is believed, is a thousand times the size of the star itself so very heavy pull."

159

"And in addition," Sherman continued, "could you explain to me what, from a 'time' perspective, would happen if one could travel at the speed of light?"

"Time stand still," Haga said bluntly. "Einstein and relativity."

"And if you could travel *faster* than light?"

"Time seem to go backward, yes?" Even Haga knew that this was standard stuff.

"So what we are intrinsically saying," Sherman mused, still pacing the room in measured steps, "is that something with an immense gravitational force can bend light and, if we appear to be travelling faster than light, then we appear to be going backwards in time?"

Haga was already working it through. His thick brow was furrowed and his head nodding very slowly.

"You think this sphere pull light past us... and time come with it?"

Sherman raised his eyebrows and grinned those perfect white teeth of his; all veneered.

"That's exactly what I think, Mr. Haga; I think it bends light... and time comes with it. The more charge you apply, the more time you pull. Now obviously, time is already running forward and it would be impossible to speed that action up. But, what is theoretically possible, and I think Charlie would back me up on this, is that we can appear to be travelling faster than light. And therefore faster than time. It can be pulled beyond us so fast that it actually appears to be travelling backward."

He pondered for a moment. "Imagine throwing a milk carton out of a car at fifty miles per hour. To us, the carton appears to be travelling backward, when in reality it is still moving forward at, perhaps, thirty miles per hour. It's the same with Charlie. From our vantage point, our little mouse friend appears to be travelling backward."

"So how come Charlie went back, yet the other items in the lab remain unchanged?" Kerr asked. He looked flustered, his usual smooth-guy image rumpled, like this had really shocked him. It would probably take a long time to come to terms with this theory, Alison thought. She wasn't even entirely sure that she had. Not yet.

"Because he's a living thing," Sherman explained. "When you look through the briefing notes you will see a section entitled 'Computational God' which details my theories on the way objects interact with the world around them. From that, you will see the important role that living, breathing, world-altering entities play. In a nutshell, I believe it's this..."

He pointed to the tiny image of the white mouse on the screen. "Charlie is affected by a time sequence because Charlie *understands* a time sequence. Unlike rocks and metal and wood and water, he knows what time means and can therefore discern changes within it. One cannot be affected by an alteration in the pattern of time if one cannot see or understand that it has happened. So he went, everything else stayed."

He changed the screen to a graph. Along the base was time, the present day at the left hand edge and up the left hand side was the amount of charge applied to the sphere in a vacuum environment. The red line that began in the bottom left hand corner ascended gently at first, but became steeper the further back in time it went. By 600AD, the last point on the graph, this line was nearly vertical.

"This is all theory," he explained, "but it is based on the results we obtained from the measuring devices, the image we saw on screen and some independent submissions from external specialists in this field, none of whom were aware of the true nature of our request."

He pointed to the near-vertical area. "The problem... is that the more charge you apply, the less specific you can be. To send somebody back to say, the turn of the century would allow you to almost pick the day, perhaps even the hour, that they arrived. By the time you get to the previous millennium," he pointed to the line as it crossed the vertical for 1000AD, it is very difficult to even pick the year. Beyond 600AD one would really just be keeping their fingers crossed as to whether one was placing someone into a scene from Jesus of Nazareth or Jurassic Park..."

"Wait a minute," Alison interrupted. She had just heard a word. It was a word she did not like one little bit. In fact, it was the one word that would make all her sleepless nights and nightmares thereafter come true. "Did you just say 'placing *someone*'? As in a human being?"

"That's exactly what I said."

"No," Alison said. "You can't do that."

Klein turned to face her, a mischievous glint in his eye.

He had known Alison for the major portion of her life and had been just as impressed by her inherent genius as the others she had come into contact with. As such, he also respected her opinion. Hearing it would not change his mind, not for one second of that time which was now proving itself to be so very controllable, but he was interested in hearing her thoughts anyway.

"And why can't we, Alison? Why can't we send somebody back?"

Alison's eyes narrowed, one step away from scorn. There was a healthy smattering of disgust within them as well and for once she didn't mind showing it, Klein or no Klein.

She looked at the image of Charlie, still flickering high above a desert landscape, then back to her boss.

"Because it would be the worst idea in a long history of really bad ideas."

With her long brown hair, as ever, pulled tight against her scalp and small horn-rimmed spectacles accentuating her eyes, Alison had never looked more serious in her life. No mean feat.

"And quite probably the single most pointless thing that mankind has ever - *ever* - achieved."

SIXTEEN
Thursday, June 9, 2011.
Downtown Los Angeles, California.

She made it look so easy.

There he was all along; our lowly little Shepherd at the right hand side of the painting, disappearing off into the distance. Turning and walking away. And yes, when laid over the map, those tiny feet of his stood directly over a small town; Serres. And a town, Sarah explained, would be a far better place if you wanted to hide something than open countryside. As long as you still hid it well; i.e. you didn't choose somewhere within the town where people might accidentally stumble across it.

Open spaces are too vague, she explained. Because she needed to. *Fifteen steps north from the big tree just didn't cut it in accurate crypto-cartography.* And, lacking the benefits of Global Positioning Systems such as those available today, anybody drawing a verbal map in the 1600s would need to be very precise indeed unless they wanted to risk all their careful work being in vain. *In such a building, in such a town* was by far a more accurate system.

Unfortunately, as Sarah further explained, getting Serres was only getting 'the town'.

Now we needed to find 'the building'.

Over the past couple of years Sarah, it seemed, had acquired as much research as she could - research she felt she might one day need - on every single town located in the Béziers and Perpignan areas of France, and some way beyond; Esperaza, Couiza, Rennes-les-Bains, Rennes-le-Chateau, Alet-les-Bains, Veraza, Terrolles, Casseignes... and, of course, Serres.

Most of the information had been downloaded from the vast expanse of knowledge that various computer geeks had chosen to store on the internet. Everything from official French documentation to the wordy ramblings of travellers who had merely passed through the area. Some people, it seemed, had an almost pitiful desire to share holiday experiences with anyone who could be bothered to call up *www.doreenstravels.com* and bore themselves rigid. Stories of broken down camper vans and shitting in holes in the ground were rife.

Sarah, it seemed, cast nothing aside. She had it all; street plans, descriptions, photos (old and new, official and happy snaps) and she had history. And it was within the soils of history, as she informed me in that know-it-all tone she slipped into on occasion, that every seed of knowledge had chosen to first extend its roots.

It all came back to the Knights Templar.

As she printed out every file she had acquired on Serres, she made coffee – real coffee - and explained how the town had been one of many on her list of prime suspects. It was, like a good few others, more than ideal, standing as it did about half a kilometre from the main road between Narbonne and Quillan. This road, now Route D613, had in medieval times been one of many used frequently by the Templars on their passages through this region of France. Not in a broken down camper van, I'm sure, but probably still shitting in holes.

The Templars had, for the most part, chosen that time-honoured career path known to you and I as 'stealing' with which to furnish their lifestyle. And what they stole were religious artefacts. They claimed, as indeed they would, that their thefts were 'in a good cause' and that they 'stole in the name of God'. In their eyes they were merely returning his treasures to the faithful. And it made them rich. Very, very rich. All of which made their original title of 'The Poor Knights' something of (and these were Sarah's words, not mine) a crock of shit.

And for Sarah, the Templars were very much a part of the search because, as she explained, it was in the furthest depths of Templar lore - 1128 to be precise - that the last sighting of the Tables in history had been noted.

The coffees complete, she placed the cups on the desk and looked over to the bookshelf, the bottom shelf of which heaved under the weight of five or six of the larger volumes. When she saw what she needed, bound in faded blue leather and thicker than my wrist, she bounced over to retrieve it. "This is a reproduction of a journal called *Liber de acquisitione terrae sanctae*, written in 1309," she explained. "The original is currently stored within the French National Archives." She flipped through the many pages, eventually locating the one she sought and reading aloud:

> *Visum: inter Templariis sunt forte secreta thesaurus*
> *mensii de quibus poterit orribilis revelatio*
> *deus itineris inter Templariis evenir*

"Meaning?" I asked. *All I got was blah, blah, templaris, blah.*

"*Understand:*" she said, "*there was among the Templars a treasured secret; tables from which one particular secret may cause incredible revelation, God did journey with the Templars.*" She looked up from

165

the page. "And the Tables of Testimony were never mentioned in history again. Now if the Templars really did have the tables, probably having stolen them from their previous owner," she explained, "then they could very well have taken them to France. This area specifically is where they lived, where they kept many of their possessions and where, in October 1307, the die-hards who remained were arrested, tortured and burnt. And if they knew that they ran a high risk of being arrested, one of the first things they would do is stash the loot."

"But that was the thirteen hundreds," I said. "And your painting is dated 1645."

She nodded. "And 1645 is slap in the middle of the thirty years war;" she said, "a time when France is siding with Protestant Sweden and the Netherlands against the Catholics. Including the *Spanish*, whose border is only 60km south of the area in which we're now looking. My guess is that either somebody *found* them or inherited them through descendency. Then things started happening that maybe, just maybe, he blamed on some sort of vile curse. Perhaps the Spanish were stealing over the border and burning villages or raping the womenfolk. Perhaps he lost his son in battle or maybe his dog got a chesty cough, I really don't know. People would put almost anything down to a curse in the sixteen hundreds."

"But when he hid them again he left clues?"

"Of course he left clues. *Just in case.* And he was undoubtedly a wealthy man, because whoever he was he commissioned none other than David Teniers the Younger to paint his map, one of the few artists respected during his own lifetime, and that won't have come cheap. During his life Teniers was Court Painter to Archduke Leopold William and had the patronage of several crowned heads including William II of Orange, Christine of Sweden and Don Juan of Austria. Not only that, but he was also married to Isabelle de Fren, daughter of André de Fren who was a direct descendant of Godfroi de Bouillon, no less than the man who led the first crusade and captured Jerusalem."

"So, he would have known that an artist like Teniers could be trusted with a Templar secret?"

"Exactly."

She leaned backward, wrapped her fingers around the now lukewarm coffee and thought for a moment. "Although in truth I doubt that Teniers ever really knew the complete answer to the riddle, even though he unwittingly helped to create it. The absence of complex symbolism in most of his other paintings tends to suggest that he might have simply followed a plan drawn up by someone else. That 'someone' would have known exactly where the Tables were hidden, but lacked the artistic ability to ensure that the painting was accurate. Or the name to ensure that it survived."

She looked at me knowingly. "I doubt that Teniers would have known anything at all about the Latin text being tagged on to the back of his painting once it was complete."

"But the U.S. Government must have a copy of the text if they're digging the skull?"

"I think they might even have the original and, if they do, I think they got *that* in nineteen-ninety-two," she said. "There was unconfirmed speculation around that time during renovations to the vaults of the *Abbaye Fontfroide*, which is.... here..."

She scrolled the digital map to the right and pointed to an area just below, and just inland from, Narbonne. This was the nearest major city to Serres, but still around 80km to the north-east.

"Some of the locals said that during excavations a 'parchment' had been found and that the American architect who was doing the 'sympathetic renovation' suddenly went from boasting about 'an important discovery' to denying vehemently that anything at all had been found. Then more Americans began to arrive, the official story being that structural problems had been uncovered and that the new arrivals were simply specialist engineers."

"But you don't believe that?" I asked.

Sarah shook her head. "Engineers don't carry etched 9mm Smith and Wesson semiautomatic pistols under their jackets. But U.S. agents do," she said. "They thought the locals were stupid. It never occurred to them that one was President of the Narbonne Rifle and Pistol Association. But what gets me is that until now - until you showed up I mean - no-one has ever seen another copy of that parchment. Which begs the question *where did you get it...?*"

I finished my coffee. As the cup came down I couldn't help but smile.

"Well, to be completely honest with you, it was stuffed up a dead guy's ass."

Sarah's eyes narrowed slightly, but it was not in the way I'd expected. Not in the way I'd almost banked on.

"This guy?" she said, questioning, "Five-eleven, dark hair, goatee beard?"

"How the hell do you know that?"

She didn't answer. She just said, "And was he naked?" After which there was a long pause. Long enough for her to register what she saw in my eyes when I didn't answer. "Hey, I didn't kill him, Nick, honest," she said quietly, raising her open palm.

"But was he naked?"

And now I paused. Because with that one question she'd caught me full in the balls. It meant only one thing. Tina Fiddes might have known my dead stiff - or she might not - it was hard to tell, but *Sarah* Fiddes *definitely* knew him; there was no 'might' about it. And, whether she killed him or not, she also knew that he'd been wearing nothing but a shocked expression when he bought it.

"Totally," I said. I could feel my eyes tearing into her.

She smiled again as she began to gather the printed pages and slide them into a blue plastic wallet. "Somewhere in here is our answer," she said, "but to get it I think we need to visit Tina."

The smile was thinner and more cryptic now, like a concave and very secure zip across her mouth. It told me I was only going to find out the things she wanted me to know.

For now at least.

Sarah stood, picked up both cups and checked her watch. "That can all come tomorrow. Right now I think it's time I found out a little something about my new partner in grime."

She smiled mischievously and moved to the sofa, sitting with her legs drawn like her sister had been. She looked like a monochrome photograph, one of a very beautiful, and very excited, young woman. She patted a space to her side, indicating that I should join her, and I did.

We talked for over an hour. Me offering a few snippets of my life and she a few about hers. Although, it has to be said, she was a lot more sparing with the details than I was. As time rolled on her eyes started failing and the big black lashes started trying to close, but still she squeezed in one more question:

"Do you have any regrets, Nick? I mean, if you could travel back in time, is there anything you would change."

"I can't," I said. "So the question is irrelevant."

"But if you could," she said. Her smile begged me to answer.

I thought for a moment, Sarah's heavy breathing to my right. I had plenty of regrets, truth be told, but only one seemed to come to the forefront of my mind. Same one as always. "Maybe my relationship with my daughter," I said. "You...?"

She laughed quietly. "Too many to mention. Thing is, you have to accept that you can't change the things that have happened, don't you? No matter how much you want to. It's the future that really matters."

The silence returned.

"Your daughter...?" she said eventually.

"Vicki?"

"Vicki. Tell me about her. What's she like?"

And I told her. The good and the bad and the I don't knows. How much Sarah heard I don't know because ultimately those eyes lost the fight and she fell asleep on my shoulder. I learned many things about Sarah as time rolled on, but one remained firmly implanted in my mind.

Though I did not know it yet, her childhood had not been a happy one. Indeed, for much of it she had been almost totally alone. And one thing she had always dreamed of, it transpired, was the day that she would fall asleep just like the 'normal' children did; to the sound of somebody telling her a story.

I'm glad that it was me who gave her that.

I carried her upstairs to her bed and laid her down, covering her fully-clothed body with the duvet. Then I watched her - just for a moment - a smile of admiration creeping across my face. Dressed head-to-pointed-boots in black, the area around her eyes and lips painted into strange shapes of a colour picked to match the ragged jet-black hairstyle and yet this girl seemed to know more things about more things than many of the scholars I had met.

As I moved to leave she opened her eyes, sleepy, and smiled.

"Don't go worrying about naked guy too much, Nick," she said.

"No?"

"No," she said, her eyes already sealing the black shape again. "I don't think he's dead yet. Not really."

Then, with the seductive air of some weird B-movie vampiress returning to the land of the dead, she slept.

SEVENTEEN

FRIDAY, APRIL 20, 2040.
5TH & ALAMEDA, LOS ANGELES, CALIFORNIA.

"Pointless?" Klein said. "And what on earth would make you say something like that?" He seemed really put out, as though Alison's off-the-cuff analysis had somehow been some kind of attack on him personally, rather than merely an idea he had formulated or approved.

"Because history cannot be changed," she said. "So... what's the point in even trying?"

Klein, rather than looking as though somebody had stolen his balloon, now sported a smile which seemed wider even than before; as if he had known this was coming. Worse, it seemed as if the too-clever Alison had just played straight into his hands.

"I'm sure we'd all be very keen to hear your thoughts on the matter," he continued. "If you'd be so kind...?"

She had indeed played into his hands; she could just feel it. Something about what she was about to say was now going to be picked up, reconfigured and thrown right back. Somehow. She just didn't know what. The only way to find out would be to go ahead and say it. She cursed herself for her stupidity.

"Okay," she began, "let's say you send, for example, a man back in time, there is nothing about history you could change. Not one single action."

"Why not?" Kerr asked. He wanted to go back and not make an almighty mess of his one date with Akira Okinawa, the American student he'd met

172

and fallen for in London six years ago. The self-same date who later became the *movie star* Akira Lake.

"Because it's already happened," she said, but she could see that it was not just Kerr whose face was blank; there were others. "Okay, imagine I send you back with a nuclear bomb to blow up Berlin in 1939, kill Hitler..."

"You can't take a nuclear bomb," Kerr said, "It's not a living thing."

"Ram it up your ass," Alison said in mock annoyance. Although she had, unwittingly just openly voiced what had once been one of Klein's biggest problems with the whole project. "OK, so I send you back to *steal* a very powerful explosive device," Kerr nodded his approval of the revised scenario, "and detonate it in Berlin 1939. You failed. End of story, goodnight."

"How do you know I failed?" Kerr said.

"Because no very powerful explosive device was ever detonated in Berlin in 1939," Alison explained. "It simply never happened. And if it never happened, you can't just go back and make it happen."

She looked around the table, looking at each face in turn.

"I mean, if you *had* succeeded how would that affect me, still sitting here in the future? Would the text in my history books suddenly change? I hope not because our Mr. Klein here is the son of German immigrants who came to the United States just after World War Two. If you succeeded, which you didn't, then Mr. Klein might never have studied at MIT, never done research for the U.S. government and so, ultimately, KleinWork Research Technology might not exist. Therefore I'm out of a job. And that's just two German people. What about all the other consequences?"

She pointed to Strauss. "Maybe Pete here was never even conceived as a result of the knock-on effect of your little bombing spree. And whilst I'm sure we can all understand that this might be no bad thing in itself, what would happen to him after you've gone back? Would he suddenly just... disappear?"

Klein smiled his approval for Alison's mini-thesis. Strauss just looked hurt.

173

"So what you're saying is that if it never happened, then it can never happen?" Klein asked.

"Exactly," Alison said, "So what's the point?"

Klein thought for a moment, his thick eyebrows causing the creases across an ageing forehead to join forces. "But what if you were the man who went back in time to 1939 and, I don't know, suggested to our Mr. Hitler that it would be a great idea for him to wake up on September 1st and invade Poland, thereby starting the Second World War?"

Alison looked astounded. People were nodding for Christ's sake. Had everybody else in this room taken some kind of stupid pill this morning? "Again... what's the point? It's already happened, so what would anyone have to gain by being the reason it happened?"

Klein smiled an old man's smile. Satisfied, but with what, exactly? "Ah," he said gently, "and therein lies the crucial word, young lady, the *reason*." He thought quietly to himself for a moment, his hands together and his fingers pressed against the base of his nose. "Tell me, Miss Bond. Where are the bones of Christ?"

"Nobody knows," Alison conceded with a gentle shrug.

"Exactly," Klein replied and now the passion, the desire for something she could not yet see, was intensified. "So what if we were the reason that nobody knows?"

Her eyes narrowed as Kerr and Haga leaned forward in their chairs with anticipation. "To what end?"

"To hide them where they would never be found," Klein said. "At least... not until we decided to dig them up."

"You've got to be kidding," Alison said. "Sending people back to hide things. Digging them up? That's too many levels of crazy for me to even get my head around."

And, strangely, that's what was now scaring Alison the most. She knew that it *wasn't* crazy. Not at all. It was actually very, *very* clever. And it should never be allowed to happen. Which is why she was fighting so damned hard. "Besides, what about the people you send back?"

"What about them?" Klein asked, and here's where the hint of evil really started to come to the fore.

"They couldn't come back," Alison said, there was an anger in her voice now. "*Ever.* Whatever period in time you sent them to they would lack the resources or the technology to return. They'd be stuck there. Forever."

"And that's a bad thing?" Klein said.

Alison's eyes widened and her neck dropped into her shoulders. "Duh...?"

Ordinarily, of course, nobody would have been allowed to get away with speaking to Klein that way; not even the boldest and brightest. Today was different. Today, Alison Bond was saying all the things that Klein wanted her to say, which was always the thing with people whose train of thought was so very logical; they were also so very *predictable*.

"If you would all like to turn to page fifteen of your notes," Klein said, oblivious, "you will see a section headed 'REPRIEVE'. I think you will find it most illuminating."

Alison opened the document and flipped to the relevant page. She studied the text for over a minute, digesting every word and, worse still, every implication. It was a list of statistics, along with names, numbers and backgrounds. In amongst, and asterisked, were also some dates. All of which could be described, at best, as imminent.

She realised now that Klein had turned a corner. That he had, in a very clinical sense of the word, gone mad. She had known this man most of her life and, if she was honest, watched every episode of his descent like a weekly sitcom. It had started as simple ambition then progressed through craving and desperation until it had become his only narcotic; the quest to be supreme. She had seen more of it in his eyes over the past few years than she had cared to mention. And now age of body and constant failure to achieve his one true quest, it would seem, had brought with it the kind of anger that throws reasonable thought to one side.

The senile old bastard really had finally lost it. This was too much; too far.

"Please God, Josef," she said, shaking her head. "Tell me you're joking."

EIGHTEEN

Friday, June 10, 2011.
Downtown Los Angeles, California.

I didn't sleep well that night. All I truly remember, however, was lying on Sarah's sofa, listening to the world beyond the blinds and staring at the tiniest sliver of moonlight as it gently made its way across the ceiling. When I first noticed it, it was to the left of the light fitting in the centre of the room. The last time I saw it, it was creeping over one of the abstract pictures I mentioned earlier. I've no idea how many hours passed in between. Maybe three, maybe four. Either way, I just lay there. Thinking.

As I started to run events through my head, and I knew I was following a spiralling path here, the first thing that became clear was why the F.B.I. had whipped in and stolen the case. Of course, the government would have been made aware of 'a parchment' being found in the Abbey at Fontfroide and they'll have done what they always do; they'd have swooped in, stolen it and kept it for themselves.

Then they would have bought or traded the 'skull' land with the French, without the French knowing why of course, and set about digging it up. But, stupid as they were, they'd missed the plot, quite literally, and failed to understand the crucial relevance of the 'without temptation' line.

So, year after year, they would have been getting increasingly more pissed off. Then, who should turn up in an alley in downtown Los Angeles, six thousand miles from their dig, than a naked dead guy. All unrelated until stories start flying around that nestled in this guy's ass is a copy of a Latin text. So, they come and they check it out and, oh shit, it's the one thing they don't want *anyone* to have a copy of. Hell, they don't even want to admit that the original even exists; probably because that way they run the risk of somebody cleverer than they are, and trust me people like that aren't difficult to find, working out exactly where they went wrong. Worse still, keeping it secret from *them*. And they can't have that now, can they? No, sir. So they take the case away. Problem solved.

Except that it's not. Because the one thing you can guarantee is that if *I* had been made aware of Tina Fiddes, then so had they. After all, her name and room number had been scrawled across the top of the note. But this is where a difference in investigative styles came into play, or so it seemed. We, by which I mean the LAPD, wanted to know why the guy was dead.

They didn't.

They were just rather pleased that he was.

So whilst we would look into the why, and actually visit 'Tina Fiddes - 113', they would simply sit and wait and hope that their problem went away. They probably wouldn't even visit her themselves; *they would just make sure that nobody else did.* Which is why Sarah, when I'd told her that 'nobody knew I'd come to see her' had somehow managed to squeeze the word 'naive' into her answer. I was being followed. And as yet, if you can recall the timeline, I had no idea that the love-sick puppy that was Billy Roberts in Apartment One, so desperate to please the FBI, was helping out.

There would be no point trying *not* to be followed because they'd be pretty careful about it, I figured, so I'd just have to run with it. Later that day I'd be back in Deacon's office, supposedly to give him an update, but it wouldn't pan out like that. Instead I would find out exactly to what degree I'd been followed and yes, it was good. Until then, I just had to run with the knowledge that being tailed everywhere I went was a distinct possibility. One that I did not like one little bit.

Probably because I'd lain awake for so long, I was still fast asleep when Sarah woke. That was, of course, until she shouted, "Nick! Ass off my couch. Breakfast on the table. Things to do."

"What time is it?" I asked.

"Time only affects living things, Nick," she said wryly. "When... and if... you resemble one, I'll be sure and let you know."

The Jack she had plied me with had been the green label – the good stuff. So good, in fact, that it had somehow enticed a small creature into my mouth overnight. A furry creature, no less (and a smelly one, probably a raccoon or something) which had subsequently died from alcohol poisoning and disintegrated, leaving only a still-warm pelt which was now determinedly clinging to the back of my throat.

By the time I'd pulled myself up and made a futile effort not to look like shit, Sarah was already dressed, this time in khaki combat pants, a white tee and olive sneakers. Her hair was tied back into a straggly pony tail, her Gothic sense of make-up fifteen times more restrained than had it been the night before and she was reading the Latin in one hand whilst holding buttered toast with the other.

"Sleep okay?" she asked, her mouth still full and her eyes still fixed on the text.

"Like a log," I lied. It was that bit easier than explaining why I hadn't.

"Eggs over-easy, hope that's okay?"

It was fine. Truth was, I felt so hungry I'd have eaten them raw. So we sat at the kitchen breakfast bar and ate, Sarah poring over the text and one or two questions being passed back and forth. Nothing major; small talk really. After half an hour or so, we prepared to leave.

"We'll have to go in yours on the grounds that... well... I don't have one," she said, picking up a khaki rucksack and slinging it over her arm.

Thirty-eight minutes after I had managed to peel my eyelids apart we were climbing into the car. It was gonna be a hot one again and I immediately wound the windows; by which I mean I wound Sarah's full down and mine the few inches it chose to allow me. Except this time the fact that it was sticking really got the better of me so I turned, curled my fingers over the glass and pulled down on it. Hard. Enough for something else to break and the glass to shoot straight down into the frame. I smiled, embarrassed, and tried unsuccessfully to gloss over it for fear of looking as stupid as I felt.

"You want dropping back here when we're done?"

"Not here, no," she said. "because if Tina does her thing, or even if she doesn't really, I'm gonna be on the next flight to France. I'll go to Serres for myself and see what I can uncover, so to speak." She reached into the rucksack and retrieved an A4 envelope which she handed over. "Will you do me a favour, Nick. Will you hang on to this for me?"

"What is it?" I asked, turning it over. It was sealed and fairly full, the brown manila expanded to about half an inch thick. I'd seen it once already, laid on a glass shelf under the coffee table.

"Some files we might need later," she said, without emotion. "Will you keep it safe?"

"Sure." I leaned over and carefully placed the envelope in the glove box, alongside all manner of other shit I kept in there and turned the lock.

As we drove out of the city the local station was playing jazz. Sarah turned to me and scowled. "Is this the best you can do?"

"Pick something," I said.

So she did. reaching into her bag she pulled out a CD and slotted it into the deck, cranking the volume slightly.

Hard rock. The hardest to get into.

"What the hell is this?"

"Cool music," she said.

"If you say so."

"You should like this track," she said. "*Flawed to perfection;* it's about a girl who isn't really a rock chick, she just plays at it. So the tights are very carefully laddered and so on. Remind you of anyone?"

I laughed and she rocked her head up and down to a beat I couldn't even begin to pick out from the noise. We didn't speak again for a while; partly because I didn't know what to ask and partly because Sarah didn't yet know what I wanted to know. And yes, I suppose, it was partly because she'd cranked the music too damn loud, but to admit that out loud will only make me sound as old as I'm rapidly starting to feel.

So I just drove and she just leaned against the open window, her fingers tapping against her hair and one of those Mona Lisa smiles etched across her face. The kind that reached six thousand miles to Mont Cardou in France and said to the team over there, Grier and Klein included, I haven't won yet, but I'm a good few steps ahead of you. I couldn't see her eyes, not through the shades, but I guessed they were smiling just as enigmatically.

"So... what exactly are these tables?" I asked. "What are *The Divine Laws of God and Man?*"

She turned toward me, creased her face and wiped perspiration from her nose and cheeks. With a gentle curl of her mouth, she thought for a moment. I'd become increasingly more used to that curl. It was the one that said *how best do I explain this?* To a scientifically challenged moron like me, I presume.

Eventually she said, "Tell me, Nick, what's the difference between 'God' and 'Mother Nature'?"

"You mean, apart from gender?"

And I'll bet you five dollars those big brown eyes rolled behind the shades. "Yes, Nick, assuming that something as clever as God stood even the slightest chance of being a man... apart from gender."

And I thought. For quite a while. Twice I nearly came out with an answer and twice I realised just how stupid that answer would have sounded. Which is good for me, because usually the sequence happens the other way around.

"I don't really know," I said eventually. "I suppose they pretty much share the same duties."

"Indeed they do," she said. "And so, if one has the Divine Laws of God and how they might relate to mankind, then surely what one actually has is..?"

"The laws of mother nature?"

The brow furrowed again, thin lines of sweat glistening. "I think we can lose the maternal bit now, Nick, but yes... we have *the laws of nature*. The laws of creation, the laws of the universe, the laws of physics. You know, Einstein worked for years before he published his Theory of Relativity., but he still called it a 'Theory' because it couldn't yet be proven. If it could, it would become a Law. But what Einstein was actually looking to prove, what he spent the last 30 years of his life trying to develop in fact, was the Unified Field Theory."

"Which was?"

"It *is*," she corrected, "a theory that proposes to unify the four known interactions or forces; the strong, the weak, the electromagnetic and the gravitational. These forces are known to control all of the observed interactions in matter. Einstein believed that one day all physical phenomena would ultimately be explainable by one underlying unity."

"Something that explains the laws of nature?" I asked.

"That's the *theory*," Sarah said with a wry smile. "Obviously things have moved on since Einstein, but if the Unified Field Theory *could* ever be proven then it would offer a knowledge and an understanding over the world around us that would be unsurpassable in every sense. One might even manage to *control* nature. Imagine what the world would be like if mankind could quite literally *move mountains*."

"You're shitting me, right?" I fully expected to see Sarah laughing. But she wasn't. Not at all.

"There's a gas station just outside Victorville," she said. "We need to get a couple of Snickers bars for Tina."

Her face held no indication of the implications of what she had just said previously. It was as though, to her, the very thought of controlling nature was... well... normal.

Then she turned and smiled. "You know, you really do have so very much to learn about the way this world actually operates. And personally..." she turned back to the window, "...I think a couple of Snickers bars might just help."

NINETEEN

FRIDAY, APRIL 20, 2040.
POLUNSKY SECURE UNIT, HUNTSVILLE, TEXAS.

Marshall looked every inch the lawyer. Slicked back mousy-blond hair, small round spectacles, sharp features and even sharper suit. In his right hand he carried a tan leather briefcase, the clasps only a few inches below the rattle of a gold Rolex. The shoes were 'crafted' as opposed to 'made' and very high-priced, Italian soles clicking metronomic pace along the tiles as he was escorted by Joe Drinkard, no less than the governor himself, toward the man he was so eager to see.

"Bit late in the day for a change of attorney," Drinkard said, almost disinterestedly.

"Never too late," Marshall replied without feeling.

They turned at the end of the corridor, a guard dutifully opening the gates to the most secure section at Polunsky; The Row.

"Take an act of God or the devil himself to get this guy off the hook," Drinkard explained as though his guest might be interested. "He's already on watch and I got him pencilled for The Walls day after tomorrow. After that he's heading straight for the Byrd this kid... bet your ass on that. Never yet had a stay from The Walls."

'The Walls' was the name given to the unit at the very heart of Huntsville, a devout Baptist town 70 miles north of Houston. This was the 'prison city' of Texas, where every fourth inhabitant was an inmate and the Texas Department of Criminal Justice (TDCJ) was by far the biggest employer.

The Walls, approximately twelve miles from Polunsky, was where all State executions took place. Until the middle of the twentieth century inmates also lived at The Walls, until an excessive increase in the number of offenders of that nature meant that they were systematically moved to the larger facility at Ellis.

After the failed escape attempt of three inmates in 1998, the facility was then moved to a more secure unit nearby; the Terrell Unit, which was, at the same time, renamed 'Polunsky'.

'The Byrd', meanwhile, referred to the Joe Byrd cemetery. Whilst some prisoners could, if they wished, donate their bodies to the medical facility up at Galveston, many could not see the point of helping the system that had just so disinterestedly taken away their lives. Some handed their bodies to next of kin but there were others, Mason included, who had no known kin to accept such a privileged gift. In these circumstances, such inmates went 'straight to the Byrd', their graves marked only with a simple white cross. No epitaph; just name and number.

"Mind you," Drinkard continued, "I reckon he's got God or the devil on his side anyway for them to allow you to come onto the scene so far down the line. Stuff like that don't normally happen either."

He looked to Marshall as he spoke, his pace still swift. "So which is it...?"

"Sorry?" Marshall said. He wasn't really interested in making small talk.

"God or the devil?"

Marshall smiled to himself. "A little bit of both."

"Death row inmates...?" Alison said. "Tell me you're not serious, Josef. You can't do it."

Klein's eyes told her he was. Deathly. "And why not, exactly?"

"Because it's wrong," she said angrily. "It's inhumane."

"More inhumane than... ooh, I don't know... *killing* them?" Klein said, with deliberate emphasis. "Taking away their lives? I'm their saviour, Miss Bond, not their enemy. I'm putting the length of their miserable lives back

185

into their hands, giving them the chance to live to a hundred if they can."

"But where? When?"

"Do they care? And should we? Anything has to be better than death, wouldn't you say? And all these men would have to do in return is locate the items we need, art treasures, religious artefacts, valuable assets seemingly lost to the world forever and become the reason that they are lost to the world. Not such a difficult task for men who are in most cases experienced killers and thieves, wouldn't you say? And then, when they've done as we've asked, they can live their life as free men in whatever period of time suited our needs."

"And if they fail?" Alison asked. "What then?"

Sherman leaned forward, his arms folded on the table. "How do you mean?"

Alison turned to face him. "Well, suppose you are aware that, I don't know, the bones of Christ - to use your example - were still in circulation in, say Persia, in 1200AD. You send a guy back, one of your little guinea pigs here..."

"I think of them more as *mice*," Klein interrupted. "In honour of young Charlie."

Alison shook her head in despair. "So you send one back to steal whatever it is you need and they... bury it. Presumably somewhere in Europe, because he'd have a hell of a job if they landed in an undiscovered continent. Then what? What if he decides 'fuck you, Klein' and doesn't bother to do what you sent him to do? He can just go off and live his life a free man if he wants. Why bother risking his ass to do it? And what about language? How the hell would he speak when he got there?"

"Language can be taught," Klein said. "As for his task, he will perform it. Because, if he doesn't... if he *fails*... then the next man to go back will, quite simply, become the *reason he failed*. And he will dispose of the man who failed so miserably in the process."

"And so on and so on...?" Alison asked. "Until what? You run out of people to send back."

SEQUENCE

"There are plenty more fish in the tank," Klein said calmly.

Kerr closed his folder and pushed it across the deep-shine mahogany. "That's right," he said. Alison, to her dismay, could already see he was thinking things through in his mind. He almost looked excited. "I mean, we could become the reason that the first man failed just as much as the reason that the bones of Christ are missing at all. Guy 'A' might not even know he'd failed, not until he meets Guy 'B'. But we'll know he did, because we've just dug up plot 'A' and there's no bones. So we allocate Plot 'B' and send Guy 'B' back. His task is then to steal the bones from, and of course kill, guy 'A'. Or just kill him if he never bothered stealing them in the first place. Then he can get the bones and put everything right again so we don't have to send Guy 'C' to deal with him. It does make sense,"

Alison turned to him, venom in her eyes. "Sense? Christ, none of this makes sense. You're not putting things right. You're making things very, very wrong - and screwing with the entire flow of history in the process. How the hell can that concept make any sense?"

Klein smiled. "As you've already explained quite clearly, Miss Bond, we cannot, as you put it, 'screw' with history. These men will be a part of existing history. In fact, who knows...? Perhaps they already are."

"That's right," Sherman said. It was obvious that he was in on this little plan. Christ, it might even have been his suggestion. "Who's to say that in every history book we have on our shelves, any reference to Nostradamus is not a reference to..." he scoured the page of names and dates, "... Michael Davies? Especially given that 'Nostradamus' was nothing more than the Latin name assumed by Michel de Nostradame. Or that the man we know as Isaac Newton wasn't really, I don't know... Jeffrey Mason. I mean, these are obviously extreme examples of men with knowledge clearly ahead of their time, but the principle is the same. We could be reading history books now with references to men we have yet to even send back."

"And how do you fund them?"

187

"Pieces of gold, diamonds, precious stones," Sherman said. "I believe that such items can pretty much be used as currency in whatever century we choose."

"But they can't take anything that isn't 'living' with them," Alison said, "in fact I doubt they can even take clothing. So they end up naked and penniless in a century they don't understand. Hardly a recipe for success, now is it?"

"And that's precisely where Charlie proved to be so useful," Sherman said with a knowing smile. "Especially the fact that, like all of your beloved little vermin, he was data-tagged."

And Alison suddenly realised something that had completely escaped her. Charlie was indeed data-tagged; a small capsule placed into his neck which kept his complete records and could be scanned and read at any time. It could also have been used to track Charlie through the building should he ever have escaped his cage. And yet, after Charlie's departure, the case was empty. No mouse. No data-tag capsule.

Which could only mean that, because it had been completely surrounded by living tissue, the capsule went with him.

"Ram it up your ass," Kerr said, quoting Alison's earlier comment and smiling a small but decidedly sanctimonious victory.

"Ram it up your ass," Klein agreed, a glint in his eyes showing that even he saw the humour.

"Christ, you make it sound like it's actually going to happen," Alison said. "Like it's not even a discussion."

"It's already happening," Klein said matter-of-factly. "I've already spoken with the Attorney General - who is very excited by our research I have to tell you - and we're negotiating conditional releases as we speak."

Alison shook her head and voiced one word under her breath.

It sounded something like 'shit'.

Mason was already waiting, his face showing no emotion. In the flesh he looked even bigger and more aggressive than in the many photos that Marshall carried with him today, and never was Marshall more thankful for the invention that was 'toughened glass'.

He wore the regulation orange overalls, his sleeves rolled to show the many tattoos along the length of his huge arms. Many demonstrated his previous gang affiliations and one said 'Kitty', Mason's only tangible memory of the girl killed in the shoot-out that had ultimately led to his arrest and conviction.

Of the 'big ten', the capital offences currently listed in the United States, Mason was guilty of eight, and many more than once. Having murdered both before and after he entered prison life (murder of a correctional employee; murder by a state prison inmate who is serving a life sentence for any of five offences - murder, capital murder, aggravated kidnapping, aggravated sexual assault, or aggravated robbery), only 'murder during a prison escape' and 'murder of an individual under six years of age' had eluded him.

The others: murder of a public safety officer or firefighter; murder during the commission of kidnapping, burglary, robbery, aggravated sexual assault, arson, obstruction or retaliation; murder for remuneration and multiple murder had all been committed in one long spree between 2024 and 2026, during which Mason had believed himself not just to be above the law, but probably above even God himself.

He was, as Drinkard had told Marshall in no shortage of excruciating detail on the phone only the previous day, 'not a man you wanna go fucking with'.

And yet Marshall was just about to go fuck with him. If Mason was up for it.

He picked up the handset. Mason didn't. He just sat and stared, his eyes cold and without feeling. Marshall indicated and still Mason remained perfectly still; staring. Only after about two minutes, and when he was good and ready, did he choose to pick up and speak.

"You ain't my lawyer." His voice was coarse, his drawl undeniably Texan.

"No, I'm not," Marshall said. "I made a deal with your appointed attorney

189

and now I'm here to help you."

Mason laughed scornfully. "Help me? Ain't no fucker but Mason gonna help Mason. Mason gonna live on."

"Maybe you will," Marshall replied, unaffected. "But where?"

Mason leaned toward the glass and rubbed his patchy beard with his free right hand, like he was thinking real deep. Like he was even capable of deep thought. "Well, see, I been readin' up on that. Had plenty time, see? Seems I go to The Walls in a real nice van. Then, next day, they gonna put me in a gurney, like I was a patient or sumptin', and they gonna inject me. But dey ain't gonna cure me, no sir, 'cos only Mason can cure Mason. So dey gonna try get rid o' me."

He leaned back with a huge wide smile, the phone still pressed to his ear. "But Mason gonna live on. In de hearts and de minds of every guy who ever tried to fuck with Mason. And der family and der friends and even der fuckin dog. Nobody gonna forget Mason. Not never. He still be living long after the chloride done its thing and dey wasted der hundred."

The smile grew even wider and more pronounced.

And Mason was right. Unless Marshall could strike a deal, he would indeed spend his last day at The Walls. Then, twenty four hours later and indeed strapped to a gurney, he would receive an injection comprising a lethal dose of sodium thiopental which would sedate him; pancuronium bromide, a muscle relaxant which would collapse his diaphragm and lungs; and potassium chloride which would, regardless of the other chemicals, bring his heart to a complete standstill. Seven minutes later he would be dead and the cost to the TDCJ would indeed work out at just under one hundred dollars.

Mason's face was one of simply not caring. He'd seen enough lawyers in his time to know they weren't worth a fuck. Like that other fella, the court-appointed. Couldn't even remember his name, except that he was a dirty spic. Had his face on TV more times than he had it the other side of that glass. Lawyers, he thought. Fuck 'em all. They cared about the dollars, not the client. Maybe this one, with his expensive suit and his nice tan, wanted to get those big pearly whites of his on TV too, pleading Mason's case when he knew it was too damn late.

Not a fucking chance. Not if Mason had his way. He could just go back to whatever la-di-da office he had somewhere and pick another patsy for his career ascent. Mason didn't give a shit.

He smiled broadly and blew Marshall a kiss. "So what say you take your pretty lawyer ass back to the big city and let Mason handle this little sid-u-ation Mason's way?"

"I never said I was anyone's fucking lawyer," Marshall said with quiet contempt, his eyes curled in a similarly 'don't fuck with me' glare. "And, unlike any lawyer you care to name, I can have you out of here by morning. If, that is, you can shut that big ugly mouth of yours for a few minutes and listen to what I have to say."

Mason's eyes narrowed and he leaned back. This was not what he expected. "If you ain't a lawyer," he said eventually, "den who da fuck are you?"

"My name is Marshall," he said, calmly removing a business card from his breast pocket and holding it firm against the cold glass. "And I work for some very important people. And now it seems..." he smiled a strange smile, one that Mason did not know how to take, "...so do you."

Mason leaned toward the glass and read the card. By his own admission 'Mason don't read so good', but he read enough. He could not avoid mouthing the words as he read them to himself.

Robert L. Marshall.
Senior Acquisitions Executive
KleinWork Research Technologies.

TWENTY
Friday, June 10, 2011.
Lenwood, California.

Because Maggie had taken the night shift it was a different face on the Oakdene reception desk by the time we arrived. Not one I recognised, but he - a young guy about twenty-two - clearly recognised Sarah because he smiled broadly when he looked up and offered a genuine 'Hi.' Then he turned, selected the relevant key, and handed it over without question.

"Thanks, Carey," Sarah said, and we walked. "Carey," she explained to me. "He's a young kid, but he's cool. Heart in the right place." As she looked ahead her face changed. "Unlike somebody I could mention...."

I looked along the corridor and saw in an instant what she meant. Creed, squeaking toward us along the vinyl with that self-effacing smile he managed to put on every morning when he dressed himself for work.

"Detective... ? And *Miss Fiddes...*?" he said, surprised. "What an unexpected honour to see you both again so soon. Visiting the lovely Tina, no doubt. Nothing *wrong* I hope." He stopped in front of us, ready to pass the time of day. I didn't like the way he stressed the word 'wrong'.

"Just business," I said. I didn't offer out my hand and he didn't bother to offer his.

"Ah, I see," he said. "Something I can assist you with, perhaps?"

It was Sarah who answered. "No thanks, Mister Creed, we're fine. It's like you said; we're just visiting."

"Actually it's *Doctor* Creed," he said, somewhat indignant. However, a raise of my eyebrows told him that both he and I (and Sarah as well, most likely) knew that a Doctorate in Philosophy didn't really count in the case of remedial or rehabilitative care. Unless, of course, it was your desire to simply ensure that your patients were 'philosophical' about the fact that most of them wouldn't be leaving the depressing confines of these walls until they were carried out with their faces covered. "But you are here en masse today, Detective," he continued, his smile forced. "So this must be *important* business."

"Yes, it is, Mr. Creed," Sarah said, brushing past him. "Thank you very much for asking." She gave me a sideways glance, laden with victory as I followed. I could only picture the expression which chose to etch itself onto Creed's face.

"I so *hate* that man," she said, making double sure we were out of earshot.

"That'll make two of us then," I replied. "I'm sure he's dirty."

"In more ways than you know," Sarah replied.

As we started up the stairs, the handrails flaking and the insteps thick with grime where the mop had struggled to reach, Sarah asked for my take. I almost didn't tell her. After all, her sister had to live here.

"Doesn't matter," I said. "It was a long time ago."

Sarah smiled knowingly. "Don't spare me because of Tina," she said. "She's here for the time being whether I like it or not and it's like they always say... knowledge is power."

And so I sighed and I told her. By which I mean I told her *everything*. About Jennifer Sanchez, how she had once been a beautiful Costa Rican girl, placed at Oakdene when her Tourette's got too much for her elderly folks to cope with. I told her how, according to the information I'd been given, one minute you were having a conversation with a girl who looked and sounded like an angel and the next she was kicking, spitting, screaming and calling you the kind of names you pray to God your kids never learn.

Of course, most Oakdene staff are trained to deal with such outbursts, whereas Creed wasn't even trained to tie his own shoelaces. Which is why, I long since figured, he always wears those moleskin slip-ons. He claimed she'd freaked out, *like she did*, and run at him hard. When he'd moved she'd caught the door full on, fracturing her skull. It was a Friday and Tony, Maggie's nocturnal Latino equivalent back in those days, had been taking the day's sheets to the laundry.

He was downstairs for maybe half an hour.

Long enough for Creed to get fed up of Jennifer's screams, walk from her deliberately spartan room back to his office and grab his brass football trophy from the shelf, then come back and crack her over the head with it. The trophy he claimed to have suffered a nosebleed over when I noticed spatters of blood on it the following day.

He'd seen damn well where my eyes had been. He was wiping it clean before I even posed the question.

"She kicked off when he went in to administer her pills," I explained. "Something he claimed he was doing because they were short staffed. My guess is when he went into her room

194

she started calling him some of those names I hinted at earlier. And, who knows, maybe one of them struck too heavy a chord with him. Given the circumstances I wouldn't have spared him the crime of losing it, not for a second, but I'd at least have *understood* it. I mean, she must have been damned hard work. But to lock her in, which I think he did, go back to his office and then come back. Carrying something big and heavy…"

I took a deep breath. "Of course, I couldn't prove anything…" I walked without talking for maybe twenty seconds and, after a brief glance at my expression, Sarah extended me the same courtesy. Eventually I decided to close off the conversation. I felt it needed closure before I lost it myself, went right back downstairs and kicked the living shit out of the slimy little bastard. "What is it about guys with clean hands," I said angrily. "Always so careful not to get them dirty."

Sarah shivered. "I hate this place so much," she said with deliberate emphasis. "Not as much as I hate Creed, I gotta tell you, but I even hate the walls." There was a pause. "Tina deserves so much better."

"So why keep her here?" I asked. We reached the top of the stairs and turned along the corridor, gentle moans permeating the battered door of 106. "There's plenty of other places."

"There are reasons," she replied in that cryptic way that she had. "I mean, one of these days I'll find the things I need to find and then see about moving her to one of the government facilities. I mean, sure, they're all varying levels of crap, but the standards of hygiene and care are usually that bit higher. And, whilst there's a Creed at just about every place you visit, the State-owned usually keep them on a much tighter leash."

She thought quietly to herself. "One of these days. But, for the time being at least, Sarah being at Oakdene is the only reason I can be here for her."

I knew what she meant about the higher standard at equivalent government facilities. The only one that I was familiar with; Thousand Oaks, was a damn sight cleaner and better run than Oakdene. It was a fairly modern building a little way up the coast from L.A., just off I-101; lots of glass and bright white pathways which overlooked the sea three miles from the town of the same name. And yes, the Pacific Missile Test Centre was right next door, which wasn't ideal, but then again what better security could one ask for? I also knew that Oak's popularity amongst the rich folk of L.A. whose nearest and dearest had lost the plot had meant a healthy waiting list, but surely that again went in its favour.

We reached 113 and Sarah peered in and smiled.

Tina was seated at the table, reading in the sunlight which, unlike during my previous visit, now extended far into the room. Again the bed was perfectly-made, something I would later learn that Tina did for herself, regimentally, every morning. She was reading a book which, even from a distance, I could see was by Émile Zola. Remembering what Maggie had said about her being able to read five languages, I guessed the book was in its original form; French.

We entered the room. Tina looked up idly at the sound to see her sister walking through the door and her face lit up like fireworks were exploding behind her face. I remember once (a long, long time ago) asking Vicki if she wanted to go to Disneyworld and her face lit up just the same. It's the kind of childish excitement that gets lost as the years are added and it seemed strange to see it now on someone of Tina's age.

They hugged like long-lost relatives, the kind who have been separated at birth and reunited on a TV show after some global search.

"Hey, pumpkin, how are you today?" Sarah asked.

Just the expression, still spreading like a warm blanket over Tina's face, gave Sarah the answer she needed; better now. As they pulled back, Tina merely threw the lightest glance at me, then back to her sister. I wasn't important. Then she began to fondle Sarah's pockets, searching like a dog for treats when they just know they've been good. The longing in her eyes placed her only a few steps away from panting and barking excitedly.

"In a minute, pumpkin," Sarah said gently. "I've brought some work."

And Tina stopped. Just like that.

I leaned against the wall, facing the window as Sarah and Tina took seats at either side of the basic table. Sarah pulled a file from her rucksack and loosely explained to her sister how the painting and the Latin had pointed in the direction of a town in France called Serres. Then she showed her all the pictures and notes she had printed out on the town.

"I think there's more," she said gently. "I think the Latin will tell me where else I need to look." And Tina listened intently to every word. She looked as hungry to help as she had when she'd been searching for the Snickers. "Do you think you could take a look, pumpkin?"

Tina's bright, piercing eyes were impossibly wide and they said 'yes'. But, wide as they were, they somehow managed to grow even wider when Sarah pulled the two Snickers bars from her rucksack. "I figured you might like one now and another once you've seen the file. What do you think?"

Tina's smile widened and she reached across, but Sarah pulled the bar back, gently. "I'd like you to take it from me *your* way," she added. "Do you think you can you do that for me?"

Tina looked straight at me and the excitement in her eyes was lost in an instant. I had no idea what Sarah meant by 'her way' but I could see that, whatever it was, it was not something her sister liked to do in front of strangers. "It's alright, pumpkin," Sarah added. "He's a friend of ours. Honest."

A friend of *ours*. I liked that.

Tina smiled. She still looked a little unsure, but her face was saying that if her sister said it was fine then maybe, just maybe, it was. Sarah made a gesture aimed behind me and I turned to see a small canvas blind mounted over the glass of the door. As I looked back she nodded so I pulled the blind down and tried hooking it into place.

Creed. Now that's someone Sarah does not want peering in on whatever it was she wanted to show me.

Unfortunately, there was no catch to hold the blind. All I had was a string on the blind itself and a circular hole in the door, maybe twenty-five millimetres across, where a clasp had once been inserted.

"Don't suppose you've got the world's biggest lipstick in that bag of yours, have you?" I asked Sarah.

"This place," she said damningly, bending to rummage in her rucksack. Eventually she produced a wide black marker pen, roughly the correct diameter. "Here, try this," she said, and flung it across.

"You always carry a pen this big?"

"Writes on anything," she said. "It's an archaeology thing."

The pen was only slightly too large but, because it was tapered toward the end, it went in after a bit of wedging. Once it was holding firm I pulled the blind down again and wrapped the string around enough times for it to hold.

Sarah carefully placed the Snickers in front of Tina on the table, maybe three feet away. Her fingers were only just hooked over the table side, her thumbs touching and she just stared at the bar. *Hard.* She didn't strain, or even seem to focus, she just kept her eyes firmly on the object of her desire. It was the kind of look that seemed born of longing. *I want it. I want it sooo bad.*

And the Snickers moved. Only slightly, but I swear to God it moved. I was damn sure of it.

I started to speak, but Sarah made a subtle gesture under the desk designed to silence me. So I watched, my jaw still hanging in whatever form my first syllable had been going to take. For the next few seconds I wondered if I'd simply imagined the movement or whether it had actually moved. Or indeed, if it had, whether one of them had accidentally nudged the table. Perhaps it was nothing more amazing than gravity.

I didn't wonder for long. Because then she did it. Tina took the Snickers from her sister *in her own special way*.

One more slight judder and the Snickers rushed along the table like an arrow shot from a bow; as if it had been made of steel and Tina's fingers had been concealing some powerful electromagnet. Somewhere in her head she had flicked a switch, then simply raised her fingers and accepted it; a receiver accepting the pass. She knew it would come straight to her and she knew precisely when. Her fingers barely moved and her expression never changed.

Sarah smiled lovingly. "Well done, pumpkin." She looked at me.

God only knows what she saw written across my face but she, like her sister, was filled with childish glee. And, I dare say, a hint of pride. Tina already had the wrapper open and, as she ate, was moving the pieces of paper Sarah had brought, placing them into some form of order that might make her task that bit easier. She looked like someone about to take an exam; pen there, eraser there, drink there, calculator there. Ready to go.

"Detective Lambert and I are going to go for a coffee," Sarah said, "because I get the feeling he could do with one now."

Tina barely even looked up. It was as though she had tried but she couldn't because her eyes were held to the papers by taut elastic that had pulled her head straight back down. And that's the point at which I realised that this was a passion they shared. Tina Fiddes had not seen her sister for perhaps two or three days, yet here she was now and she was going to be left alone again almost immediately. Not for long, I'll grant you, but alone all the same.

Still she was far more concerned with the 'work' that her sister had brought.

"We'll take a walk when we come back, eh, pumpkin?" Sarah suggested. "Does that sound good?"

Tina didn't look up.

"Told you a Snickers would help," she added as she walked toward me and grabbed my arm. "Come on, Detective. Wipe the 'startled bunny' look off your face for a few minutes and I might just let you in on how this world actually works."

TWENTY-ONE
FRIDAY, JUNE 10, 2011.
LENWOOD, CALIFORNIA.

"So tell me," I asked, with just a hint of the probing we detectives seem to rely on so much. "What was it like having a little sister who'd steal chocolate from you without actually touching it?"

Sarah blew fast ripples across the top of the hot tar that was reputedly 'coffee with milk'. By which, I guess they meant 'dark sludge, further accentuated by non-dissolving lumps of white powdery sludge'.

"We lived separately as kids," she said, and I heard a sadness that she seemed eager to suppress. "I didn't even know that Tina existed for a long time and didn't manage to track her down until about two years ago. By that time she'd pretty much been institutionalised all her life."

I fell silent. There was no doubt that she and Tina were cut from the same cloth, one look was enough to tell me that, and it was apparent without looking just how much Sarah adored her sister - and vice versa. I could not even begin to imagine what it must have been like for either of them to learn, after years of blissful ignorance, of a sibling's existence.

"So when, and how, did you find out that she can... you know... do what she does?"

It was a side-step, sure, but somehow I felt that I should be changing the subject to one which might bend the sense of sorrow she was feeling right now back towards something akin to pride.

And yes, with a flick of the right switch, the pride came hunting. It even brought a slight smile along for the ride.

"Change the sequence?" she said. "That's what I like to call it, because that's what she does, I think. She lets the time sequence run normally, but makes all the other numbers within it move in a new direction. Change the sequence," she repeated the words as though describing some unattainable prize for us all.

"It wasn't until I got angry one time..." She looked into her memory and smiled. "I was here... maybe my third or fourth visit... and I didn't really understand how to cope with her back then. Patience never was one of my better virtues. I was trying to brush her hair and she was scrabbling for a Snickers I had in my bag. It was mine, by the way, not hers. I didn't even know she liked them yet."

She took another drink of coffee. "So I'm combing and she's pulling away and I guess I just got a bit frustrated and shouted at her. And she freaked." She shook her head. "God, you'd have thought I was killing her, the way she lashed out. Maybe a minute into this fit my bag moved about half the distance between us, three or four feet. I figured I'd just imagined it."

"But you hadn't?"

"Definitely not," she replied. "A few weeks later it happened again. This time I knew she liked Snickers and I'd brought one especially for her, but I said she couldn't have it until her hair was done. Anyway, I guess I must have taken that little bit too long over the combing because she got annoyed with me again, started scrabbling like she does and it just... slid along and fell off the table. I mean, it had been at least a foot from the edge."

Sarah took a deep breath. "Right there and then I knew it was no accident."

"So what did you do?" I asked. What *do* you do?

"I started talking to her about it, trying to understand, and that led to me asking her if she could develop it. It took months, but even she was pleased when she finally got it under some kind of control. She doesn't focus or anything, she just looks at something and wants. If she wants badly enough then it happens."

"Isn't it dangerous?" I asked. I'd seen far more Stephen King films than I'd care to admit.

"I suppose it could be if she got *too* angry but, to be honest, Tina doesn't have a nasty bone in her body. She's probably the least likely person in the world to misuse the gift she has." She glanced up. "Unlike somebody I could mention."

"Who?" I asked. "Creed?"

"Nah," she laughed. "Creed wouldn't know his ass from a hole in the ground. But you remember when I told you that the guy at the U.S. dig, Klein, was a scientist?" I nodded. "Well, in addition to his own companies, he also handles certain projects for the government and has even been known to advise on matters such as paranormal studies."

I took a large mouthful of sludge and then regretted it. "Paranormal studies? And he works for the government?"

"Oh yeah," Sarah said, real matter-of-fact. "ESP, telepathy, telekinesis, future projection, apport, you name it. Plus some of the darker stuff like 'remote viewing', you know? The ability to lie in a bed in Washington and see what's happening in some remote terrorist hideout. The ability, perhaps, to even pinpoint that hideout. That's something the CIA have been messing around with since the late fifties."

She looked at me as though she expected me to laugh, but would kill me on the spot if I did. Had I not just seen what I had seen – and I was still fairly certain that I had seen it – I would still be thinking that this all sounded worse than ridiculous. But Tina's Snicker's trick, and the look in her sister's eyes told me she was deadly serious.

"Hence an interest in the laws of nature?"

Sarah shrugged. "Yeah. I mean, there's no guarantee that the tables offer any understandable answers, but I'd guess that finding them in the first place is a pretty healthy start. In truth, particle physicists have already come pretty close to realising how the world actually works without them. They've already figured that it's numeric, and that there are rules. Being scientists, they just refuse to believe that these rules are not accidental, that's all. As such, they've just been stuck in a pretty deep rut for the past few years."

"So tell me," I said, recalling her words, "how *does* the world work exactly?"

Save for Sarah and myself, huddled over steaming paper cups, the room was empty, cold and dirty. Still, it was the closest Oakdene had to a canteen.

In the days of the school, this had been the far more romantically titled 'refectory': fifteen or so staff cooking great smelling food for wave after wave of hungry kids. Now all Oakdene's food was delivered in a van, pre-cooked and wrapped in polythene, and this room was nothing more than thirty cracked laminate tables, chairs that refused to stay level and a desperately ineffectual coffee machine.

She thought for a moment, her usual 'how best do I....?' look creeping across her face and then went over to the vending machine and stole eight of the paper cups.

"Well, see, there's a problem that's baffled scientists for years," she explained, taking her seat again.

She lined up three of the cups, leaving a very narrow gap between each and then, a short distance along the table, carefully placed the other five. With the five, however, she spaced them a full width apart with distance enough to have inserted another cup in between if necessary.

"And it's this... When you have a sheet of card with two slits cut into it, symbolised here by the two narrow gaps between these three cups, and you shine a light through the slits, what you get on the wall or screen behind is a series of light and dark vertical patches of equal space and width. And that is my five cups and the spaces between them. Light-dark-light-dark and so on." I nodded. "And that's fine, because light it seems, travels in waves. So all that's happening is that the waves, when they emerge from the slits, are interfering with each other like ripples on a pond, and at the point they hit the wall they are either accentuating each other or cancelling each other out."

"Like waves in a pond?"

"Exactly. In fact, if you do this same experiment in a wave tank, sloshing water through the slits instead of light, you get the same result. And that's cool because that's what all waves... water, sound, radio and every kind of wave function you can name... do when they bump into each other. They interfere. Make sense?"

205

"I think so."

"But there's a bit of a problem here, Nick," Sarah continued.

I pushed my chair back and crossed my legs. Like I was getting really into this, you know? "There is?"

"Yes, indeedy," she offered, nodding with her eyes wide. "Because in 1985 some scientists in Germany conducted the exact same experiment I've just described. But... instead of a wall or a screen, they used very sensitive photo-detectors and instead of a light they used a light particle emitter, capable of firing just one photon of light at a time. All this was housed inside a perfect vacuum, with no interferences. So now, there was no way for 'waves' of light to be formed, not from a single particle, and therefore there was no way for those waves to clash with each other." Her eyes widened further. "But guess what...?"

"They did?" I was coming dangerously close to not even noticing the taste of the coffee any more.

"Indeed they did. Even though it was scientifically impossible for it to happen the photons, rather than find their own way and land at random intervals on the photo detector, still formed patterns. It was like they were being told to land there. Pretty much whether they liked it or not."

"By who?" I asked. Sceptically. "God?"

Sarah shrugged and smiled. "If you like, sure. Certainly they were adhering to some set of rules, and if that was the case then something was not only *creating* those rules, but also *ensuring that they were followed* even when environmental circumstances dictated that they no longer had to be. Whatever it was, it sure as hell wouldn't have expected mankind to get to the stage where we could fire one particle of light at a time and tear the whole rule book up."

"And this means.... what, exactly?"

"It means that everything in this world, every particle of matter from which all things are composed, must only go where they are allowed to go. Light can travel through glass but not brick, even though they're made from the same base material; silica. When the material is changed, new set of rules. And the only way for anything to be enforcing those rules is with an enormous set of co-ordinates and pre-sets."

"So the world is nothing more than one big set of numbers?"

"That's precisely what it is; with every single thing being told where it can and can't be within an immense grid. And we're not just talking at object level, or even at molecular level here. This is at *particle* level, the things from which molecules are composed. Billions and billions and billions of them, all adhering rigidly to their place on the grid at a given point in time."

"And this is all controlled by some kind of God? That's one hell of a lot of particles to keep track of."

Sarah was drinking her coffee now, without wincing, and shaking her head.

"No, that's the thing. You can't control it all, so you have to set the rules for key particles which the others have to follow. For example, when you move your finger, you're not adjusting the movement of every single particle within the muscle system which controls it. There's a key element. You don't know it exists and you don't even think about it, but it's there. You simply move that key element and the others follow."

She pondered. "As for the 'rule-maker', if you will, I don't see it as a god but rather as a kind of Divine Computer. And I don't mean some bland IBM or even anything with circuit boards and software, I mean the greatest number-crunching force imaginable."

"So God is a computer?"

She nodded confidently. "Any brain is a computer so, for want of a better word, yeah - it is. And, on a very small level, I think that we - indeed *all* living things - are hacking that computer on a daily basis simply by interacting with it. We decide where we go and what we do, using our brains to make things move. But we also have to adhere to the rules. Open-minded people like Tina, however, and many others around the world it seems, can simply hack on an even deeper level. It's possible that they can see the numbers, perhaps without even realising it, can detect changes and, in the case of true telekinesis, can even be the ones to change them remotely. It's more sensory than mechanical."

I was starting to see why Sarah had chosen to show me the Snickers trick immediately before launching into this conversation. Firstly, I would have assumed that she should have been sharing a room with Tina without it and secondly, I guess she had felt the need to show me what a person on a 'higher plane' could achieve before trying to explain how such a plane might even be able to exist.

"So you think Tina can what...? Hack the Laws of Nature?"

"Why not?" she said. "It's no more unbelievable than what you've already seen for yourself. In fact, I think it makes it all the *more* believable if there's some explanation as to how it might actually be achieved. You see, Tina often looks blank, as though she can't actually relate to people or what they're saying. But I think that, because of her condition, all she really is... is tuned out. She can focus just as well as you or I, she just can't do it *on our level,* that's all. Her mind is much more open; expanded. As I believe I mentioned before, she sees things that you and I will never ever dare to see."

I looked around the drab room, a brown walled box with insipid yellow-cream arches. And yes, crazy as it all sounded, it did have a logic attached. And logic was something that I, as a detective, knew you had to trust. Not all the way, perhaps, but you had to be open to the chain of events it was suggesting.

Not only that, but I had seen things in my life. Things I simply couldn't explain.

Once I'd strained to open the lock to the police stores for five minutes, having been assured by the duty sergeant that the combination for the day was five-eight-three-seven-one. Eventually Phillips, my partner at that point said, 'try one-five-eight-three-two'. So I did, just to humour him really, and click; it opened, simple as that. Phillips never knew how or why he knew that number. He said it just came to him. It changed daily. There was no way for him to have known.

Another time, I was chasing a purse snatcher down 3rd, past the Centre for Performing Arts, and I just knew I was going to lose him. The guy was just too fast for my twenty-a-day lungs. Plus it was raining like a bastard so my clothes were wet, heavy and clinging like Bacofilm. Then this guy turns and disappears down an alley and by the time I make the corner he's gone. Poof! And there's, like, *twenty* doors down there. Some are unlocked, I suspect, some not. And I'm tired and wet and ready to give up, but I just know he's gotta be at the other side of one of them.

Then, almost without thinking, I walked up to door number eight on the right, pulled my gun and opened it up. I ran up the stairs to find a one-way fire door at the top; one that can't be opened from the outside. And there he is.

Trapped.

Don't ask me why I chose that door because I really don't have a clue. All I know is that I did. I called it intuition at the time, and got really proud of myself.

But then, what the hell is intuition?

Sure, these two events might not be on a par with human levitation, or locating a crime scene from nothing more than a piece of the victim's clothing, or even making a Snickers bar slide three feet into my hand, but they had carried their own restrained sense of weird at the time. So, I figured, why not? Give me a better explanation and I'll run with that instead.

Until you do...

The coffee was nearly gone. And with each mouthful the surprises it offered up became markedly less wonderful.

"So these tables?" I asked. "They're the key to unlocking this computer?"

"That's the theory," Sarah said, finishing her own coffee first and basket-pitching the cup a full eight feet into a brown wire-mesh bin. "They are an explanation of the rule; something that could be reverse-engineered and ultimately understood. Understanding is always the first rung on the ladder of control. What worries me most, however, is that the kind of hacking Tina can do, whilst it beats you and I hands down, is still extremely mild. Think what would happen if you could hack completely. I mean *really* control the numbers for yourself?"

"You'd be playing God, surely?"

"Exactly. And *nobody* should be allowed to do that."

I could agree with that. "So the actual tables," I asked, "What are they? What do they even look like?"

"Nobody really knows," Sarah said. "According to the Exodus they were written on both sides, by God, and they offered complete power over the elements; earth, sky, fire and water. In fact, I think that God showed Moses just what kind of power was attainable with them before he handed them over."

"Showed him how?" I asked.

Sarah smiled. "*Lift thou up thy rod, and stretch out thine hand over the sea,*" Her tone changed to one more akin to a TV evangelist delivering a prophecy. Slow, clear and deliberately well-enunciated. "*and divide it: and the children of Israel shall go on dry ground through the midst of the sea.*"

I tipped my head backward, toward the cold high ceiling with its dusty cobweb strands and laughed. "The parting of the Red Sea? You actually think these tables would offer the power to part the sea?"

Sarah shook her head; looked serious again. What she said next was just one more of the things that stayed with me the rest of my life.

"No, Nick. I honestly think these tables would offer the power to make the Red Sea look like some cheap little party trick."

Silence. Long, drawn and awkward. Then the door flew open with a bang and I damn near went for my gun. I looked over to see Carey standing in the doorway, still catching his breath.

"Right," he said, tone loud and angry but eyes suggesting that he wasn't entirely serious. "Which one of you wants me to go through the reasons – yet again – why we don't allow any of our patients to have access to big, black marker pens?"

TWENTY-TWO

Sunday, August 2, 2043.
5th & Alameda, Los Angeles, California.

It hadn't been quite as easy as Klein had hoped.

How, in the name of God, could he ever have thought it would?

First there were the 'mice'. Running for him and running from justice, he'd said with a smile. Big nasty bastards, every last one of them, and there were five in total, though he suspected that it was a number which would increase following a high degree of success, or an even higher degree of failure. For a start, these men had to remain completely segregated from the world at large; there was no way Klein could risk one of them opening his big fat mouth to a guard, an inmate or to the very few relatives they had who now believed their kin to be dead.

It had meant the construction of a special facility which, to aid logistics, had been housed beneath the single-storey 'sealed lab' behind KleinWork Tower. The lab which, for the time being, had been given over completely to The Sequence Project. Maps and charts showed that this position, two miles from the area in which Los Angeles had first begun to sprout like a concrete flower, had remained unpopulated until around 1892 and Klein could not think of any reason, for the sake of testing at any rate, why he would ever need to send somebody back to arrive after that date.

So a complete facility, housed in a purpose-built basement, became the new 'Polunsky' for five angry men. They ate there, slept there, took every damn shit they ever took there and never again saw daylight. Still, they

212

were still alive, weren't they? And there'd be time enough to see the sun once Klein had dropped them into the cheese maze and watched them run. Hell, it might even give them something to look forward to.

But with hardened men came even harder guards and with hands that can kill came guns that do the same, just that little bit quicker. Klein hated guns, always had; especially on his facilities. Like every other corporate overlord, he understood that they were a necessary evil and every member of his door staff possessed them, but then they weren't spending their days and nights with hardened killers, were they? One human error and the effects could blow his whole project, quite literally, out of the ground.

In the 'old days' Klein had been able to hand excessive security issues to Grier and his team and never be directly involved. Now, however, he was playing in a much bigger league with men who, whilst they were initially supposed to endure these conditions for four to five months at most, had now been cooped up for almost two and a half years. What was euphemistically termed a 'disturbance' was becoming an almost weekly occurrence and Klein, now seventy years of age, had become prison governor to the most explosive tinderbox imaginable; men without families or responsibilities; men who didn't care.

Then there were the tattoos. Whilst the application of tattooed images had been recorded since the Egyptians in 2000BC and had long been prevalent in Japanese society, three runners had needed to be rejected on the grounds that their tattoos depicted definitive twenty-first century scenes. Those men only ever had one more needle pierce their skin and that had been back at 'The Walls'. Some had needed laser removal on certain aspects of their decoration, but even those without any tattoos at all prior to conviction still had the 'prison mark' shared by all convicted men since 2023; the unique tattooed pattern on their left ankle indicating that they were, or had been, a state convict. In the end Klein chose to use this final mark to his own ends, to prove that his project would indeed be successful.

The first run, the sequence test, had initially been scheduled for late

May, and was a send-back to 1865. Unfortunately for Klein, and due to a fight in the canteen resulting in the chosen (and fully briefed) man, Jake Edison, having his throat sliced with a broken plate, the test had subsequently needed to be postponed. Whilst Edison survived, it was Klein's suggestion that the man who had sliced him, Leroy Stubbs, take his place. It was only when Sherman pointed out that Stubbs was black and 'they'd lynch that nigger within an hour of him arriving' that a suitable replacement was found.

Greg Castle took Edison and Stubbs' place and was none too pleased to be 'the little ginny piggy'. He was certain that this would all go wrong, that he'd die in pain and he hadn't been further impressed when Klein, through toughened glass, had told him that if he was right he could merely balance the pain against the extra eight months he'd been allowed to suck air.

In reality, however, Castle should have been pleased. After all, his was by far the easiest run because he didn't actually have to steal anything or risk his neck in a distant world. All he had to do was acquire something, something definitely mid nineteenth-century and bury it where he was told, along with a sketch of his prison tattoo so that there could be no mistake. He could add as complete and accurate a record of the time and date he arrived as he could be bothered to compose, along with anything else he saw fit to leave or tell them.

On the morning of Sunday August 5th, Castle was prepped in his cell, given a final meal of his choosing, a full medical and handed a yellow rubber bullet containing a small quantity of gold grains, three uncut diamonds and five matches. Like all the runners he had already undergone a surgical laser procedure to remove his fingerprints. After all, fingerprints could survive for hundreds of years under the right conditions and nobody wanted to see a historic artefact being dusted by a TV archaeologist only for it to reveal the prints of a man who until very recently had been sitting fair and square on Death Row.

On arrival, if indeed he survived, Castle was to use the gold and diamonds to buy clothes and supplies and use at least one of the matches to burn the rubber, thereby destroying the one remaining piece of incriminating evidence. He crammed the bullet up his own ass, under strict supervision, and was led in shackles and hand restraints by four members of KRT's security staff to the lift which would take him upstairs.

On the way up, so they said, he sweated, he cursed and he prayed.

At ten-forty-seven in the morning Castle, shackles and red jump-suit still in place, was led into the sealed lab and a mask was lowered from the ceiling to enable him to breathe once the vacuum took over. The only other alteration to the lab itself had been a raising of the floor by two feet, as further investigation had placed the desert floor of Pre-L.A. at anything up to one foot above current level.

Within reason, Castle was now allowed to move freely through the room. Which he did, pacing awkwardly and never once looking toward the window. All five members of the project team were there to watch, all wearing corporate-red ear protectors and wraparound red-lens goggles. All looked expectant. Hopeful.

All save for Alison Bond. Having swallowed her pride deep enough to remain on the team, it's bitter taste was making her feel physically sick.

Klein, a mild stroke three months prior having temporarily confined him to a wheelchair, looked through the glass and smiled. "This is it, gentlemen." He turned to Alison and raised his eyes, "And, of course, lady. This is where the past really does become the future."

Strauss, as he had once before, held down the green button on the console to lower the arm, then flicked the auto-sensor to position the fingers. Castle, sweat dripping down his face and running into his thick biker moustache, looked desperate and uneasy, his eyes darting. Alison doubted he would looked half as worried if he'd been laid on the gurney at "The Walls', because at least then he'd have known what was coming. Here he had no idea and neither, if they were honest, did any of the men now standing to her right.

Strauss idly keyed 371 into the computer terminal on the back wall; the number which, it was theorised, would send Castle somewhere pretty close to 1865. As if anyone knew for sure. Then he slid forward again, his finger poised above the first of the orange switches. He looked to Klein who - after a pause and an expectant smile to himself - nodded and, with a flick, the buzzing began to build around them.

Castle, more agitated than ever, began to swagger around the room, looking anywhere and everywhere; his face full of uncertain panic. He didn't like this one little bit. He didn't like the noise, the feeling, didn't want to be here and maybe, for the first time in his thirty-seven years, he had wished to God his mother was leaning over him and stroking his brow.

When the digital read-out ascended toward, and then stabilised at, 371, Strauss looked again to Klein. He didn't turn, his eyes never leaving Castle and his mouth curled into a gentle and unfeeling arc, but he nodded again and the second switch was flicked.

The screaming came like a burst and, though it could not be picked out individually, it was obvious that Castle was now contributing some high pitched audio of his own. It looked almost comical, as though he were miming to a pre-recorded soundtrack. He moved quickly but clumsily, his manacles dragging on the floor as he shuffled his feet. Then he froze, staring directly at Alison. What she felt and what she saw in his eyes, she would never, *could* never, forget.

Here was a man who had whipped his wife to death with a motorcycle chain, the grease mixing with her blood, and then taken his pistol and slaughtered three more innocents who worked at a gas station on his getaway route. He killed in the coldest blood possible; innocent and point blank. A man who had faced almost certain death at the hands of fifteen police marksmen and lived to tell the tale, only to face death again at the squeeze of a needle. Here was a man who probably did not even truly understand what fear was, until today. All she could see in his eyes now was the kind of horror normally associated with five year olds and monsters in closets. He thought he was going to die in the worst way imaginable, his expression told her that much. His jaw was hanging so far open that even at this distance she could see the bad teeth nestled like long-forgotten heirlooms at the back of his mouth.

And then the flash; the blinding incandescence filling the room and turning everything a pale vibrant blue, one step removed from white. And somewhere in amongst that light, in an instant, Castle was gone. At this stage it was still little more than numbers-on-paper theory as to exactly where that might be. Strauss leaned forward, flicked the switch again and the screaming stopped.

Everywhere, save for Alison's head.

The lab was calm and ghostly, the fingers still the required distance from the sphere and the mask swinging gently from the ceiling. To the right of the sphere, crumpled, was the red jump-suit; lying as if discarded by a lover in some passionate leap into bed prior to the earth quite literally moving in the most unimaginable way. Creeping from underneath, just visible, was one ring of the manacles that only a few seconds ago had been clasped securely around Castle's feet.

"Excellent," Klein said calmly, as if in his world this kind of occurrence was an everyday one. He wheeled himself behind the camera and pressed 'stop', then a second button and the DVX disk slid upwards into his hand like toast. "Now then," he said, "shall we take a little trip?"

The sun, a rich blood red, was low above the horizon by the time they reached the site. Strauss, designated driver, pulled the SUV to a standstill on his superior's swift instruction, then he and Sherman climbed out and lowered the ramp for Klein's chair. On the way he had watched the DVX disk on the vehicle's on-board system, carefully pausing it for the two frames where Castle could clearly be seen against a desert environment. His clothes, having not fallen from gravity in such a short space of time, could still be seen against his body, although they were now semi-transparent, his nakedness visible underneath. His mouth was frozen in horror. There was no way yet to tell if this was a look that had actually been accentuated by an instantaneous and extremely painful death.

The ground outside was hardened by the sun and the wheels on Klein's chair moved quite freely. Without even acknowledging the assistance he

217

had received, he began to wheel himself away from the track toward the bright red of the rock-face beyond.

"Why here?" Kerr asked, always the one for questions.

"Why not?" Klein said, his hands still pushing hard against the wheels. "I couldn't think of a safer place on earth."

They were now 80 miles from Los Angeles at the base of Eagle Crags Mountain and only a mile from Cuddeback Dry Lake. Klein had been here just over a month ago, along with Sherman, Castle and two guards to select the site. It had needed to be easily identifiable, both then and now, and had taken over an hour to find the ideal place.

Klein stopped at the base of a pillar comprising multiple colours of rock maybe thirty feet high, which was around three feet from a cliff face of similar height. A lizard which had been seeking shade in its base watched him approach and then hurriedly scurried under a rock. Sherman, spade in hand, stayed by his side, leaving the others to follow close behind.

"If you'd do the honours, Dave," Klein said.

Sherman smiled. You could take your mice and you could screw them up the ass 'till they spat teeth. If they found today what he prayed they would find today then his theory was correct; the world was nothing but numbers. Better still, those numbers could be controlled. Sending people back was merely the start. He didn't give a shit about the past, or indeed the future. What he cared about was today, and how it could be manipulated via the truth that he, and he alone, had delivered to Klein.

Indian kids bending steel would look like clowns at a circus compared to the possibilities that would start opening up. Klein wouldn't be around for long, his chair today and slightly lop-sided features from the stroke were proof enough that his health was failing rapidly, and he had no children.

Whether or not KleinWork Research Technology passed to Sherman, and there was nothing to suggest such a thing, the technology undoubtedly would. He understood it and he could manipulate it. Even the vast wealth that Klein had amassed during his lifetime would start looking like little more than chump change once Sherman held the purse strings.

He thrust the spade into the ground and scooped a hardened chunk of pale red earth to one side.

"I really don't like this," Alison said. She had meant only to think it but, unfortunately, she hadn't. She'd actually voiced it out loud.

"You opinion, as ever, is respected, Alison," Klein said, his back still to her, "but you're not paid the sums you are to like what we do, only to make sure that we do it."

Kerr and Haga looked at her. She could feel the combined weights of their stares and she didn't say another word.

Sherman was sweating now, the hole almost two feet deep. It had been expected that the hole would need to be deep, especially given the build-up of erosion from both the rock face and the pillar at ground level, but with each thrust of the spade he became increasingly frustrated. There was nothing here. Nothing at all. If Castle had ever made it back in time then he had, quite clearly, failed miserably in his set task.

He stopped digging and leaned on the spade. The anger etched across his face spoke volumes. "Nothing," he said.

Klein sighed. His expression showed that he too was annoyed, but this was by no means the end of the road. Indeed, what was the dark road of discovery without a little failure to light the way? "Then we try again," he said, calmer than his face suggested. "And we keep trying until we get it right."

Sherman sighed and looked into the hole. He could not believe he'd driven all this way, in this heat, and busted a gut over a spade for what... nothing? Donkey work. "Never should have trusted the hillbilly," he said, referring to Castle. "Guy couldn't even tie his own Goddamned shoelaces." He bit into his lips, anger burning his eyes, then he raised the spade high in the air and thrust it into the hole. "Goddamned son of a bitc...."

And the spade stopped dead, as expected. The sound it made, however, was completely the opposite. This sound was not metal cutting through hardened sand but metal hitting something tough. Tough and hollow. Something that sounded not too dissimilar, perhaps, to a wooden box.

Slowly, all bar Alison moved toward the hole, then looked to each other. For a moment Sherman did not start to dig again. It was almost as if he daren't. Just a few moments ago he was worried that he might not find anything, now he worried about exactly what it was he had found. There was something in the hole, right where it was supposed to be, and that could only mean one thing....

"Is a box, yes?" Haga said, moving forward.

And even Alison, worried as she was for the implications of such a find, and praying as she was that the experiment would fail, could not help but be caught in the moment. "I guess there's only one way to find out," she offered slowly.

Sherman carefully scraped away the earth to reveal a sliver of wood. Then he reached in with his hands and brought out one fistful after another of rich red sand. After a few minutes he could just get his fingers at either side of the box and he lifted it carefully out. The wood was dark and ornately carved, the hinges and clasp brass and still shining in the warm light of sunset.

He laid it on the ground ahead of Klein who just looked at it for a moment, his smiling eyes seeing so many things he was not about to share.

"It's beautiful," Alison said.

Klein nodded. It was. In ways he could never have imagined.

"Open it up," he said.

Sherman undid the clasp and eased up the lid, the sounds of creaking and silence of expectation filling the air. He opened it a little, as a bomb disposal expert might, then pulled it full back to reveal the contents. Six anxious pairs of eyes peered inside at contents hidden for one hundred and seventy-seven years by a man who had been screaming into their faces not four hours earlier.

"Gentlemen," Klein said eventually, his voice straining. "I believe we have a winner."

TWENTY-THREE

FRIDAY, JUNE 10, 2011.
LENWOOD, CALIFORNIA.

Tina had done it. Whatever *it* was.

The blind on the door was up and she was standing in half shadow to the left of the room, her back against the wall as she stared in admiration. She had a gentle smile, a light in her eyes and her head was tilted like someone who'd just decorated their apartment and was now admiring a rather excellent choice of colour.

Which was not a bad analogy, really, because in terms of the room that had become her life, Tina had indeed done a bit of decorating. It just happened to be of the kind that a three year old might do if you left him or her alone with a ten foot high pale cream canvas and a big black marker pen, that was all.

On the right hand wall, almost framed in a broken arch of that sunlight tinted yellow by grime I described earlier, she had written her answer. It was creative. Expressive. The kind of thing you might expect from someone who has not been allowed such freedom for way too long. She had broken out and gone wild with the brush. Or, in this case, the pen. In thirty centimetre high, inch thick letters, surrounded by workings:

ET IN ARCADIA EGO

Sarah turned to Carey. "You got some paint in your stores?" Carey, still looking more than a little shocked and inquisitive, nodded. "Good. If you'd be a darling and grab a tin I'm sure Nick here will take care of this whilst I take Tina for a walk." I nodded, because I could see exactly what Sarah was doing; *Getting rid of Carey*.

Once he was gone, Sarah closed the door and looked to Tina. She could see in an instant that she was fine, happy, so she moved to the table and scrabbled though the pieces of paper, eventually locating the Latin text. She moved to stand in front of Tina's handiwork and I could see that she too was pleased. Her face was being pulled upward by invisible threads. "It's an anagram," she said, a lilt in her voice indicating that even she could see the obviousness of it now. "And an address."

"How do you mean?" I asked.

"Like when you write a letter," she said, her eyes still fixed firmly on the wall. "You write the house number first, then the street and so on. But the Postal Service work from the base up. First they need the state, then the town, then the street and then the house number. Reverse order. It's the same with the Latin."

She sounded as though, whilst she had accepted that it was obvious, she still could not quite believe it. "From the base up it tells us to complete the square of *Teniers*. So first you've got the painting; then the towns, then *journey without temptation* and then, at the top, I TEGO ARCANA DEI; *go where I conceal the secrets of God*. But that's not it, is it pumpkin?"

She turned to Tina, but her sister didn't respond. She just kept admiring her handiwork with a proud and gentle smile lighting her face. "It's an anagram isn't it sweetheart?"

"And would you be so kind as to translate it for me?" I asked.

"And in Arcadia I am," Sarah said. "Or rather; *And I am in Arcadia.*"

I walked over to her side and studied the words. "Arcadia's is a suburb of Los Angeles, isn't it?"

"Yeah, and it was a suburb of Los Angeles in 1645 as well, dumb-ass," Sarah said sarcastically. "No, the reason there's a suburb of L.A. called Arcadia is because it's home to the Los Angeles Arboretum and so, in 1888 when they built the place, they named it after a region of ancient Greece known for its pastoral character."

"Jesus, woman, is there anything you don't know?" I said.

She smiled at the compliment. "Not much. Although I have to admit that I don't know - yet - where *our* Arcadia is. Because of the Greek pastoral connotation, Arcadia can now mean a kind of Heaven; or a... *Utopia*, if you like. Any place of ideal rustic simplicity or contentment. Now I'll bet you that somewhere within Serres I'll find a building, probably one of rustic simplicity, that has some reference to Arcadia in its name, its walls or its history."

Sarah, given her strange look and immense knowledge had started to remind me of another young kid I once met; Kenny Wilding. He was another who's overall look and dress sense indicated a leaning toward the satanic. His leaning, however, was just that little bit more fully fledged given, as he was, to blowing up buildings. He was a pyromaniac in the simplest sense, but also an explosive one who got a sheer thrill from watching immense detonations. It was about seven years ago and it had taken us nearly a year and six explosions to finally catch up with him and give him fifteen years.

Credit to the kid, he always worked on empty buildings, at

night, and hadn't taken even one life during his brief and somewhat downbeat career. When we tracked him down he was, like, *nineteen* and living with his ma, yet to have seen his devices you'd have him pinned as some war-hardened I.E.D. expert. Every component he used he had either constructed himself or, more worryingly, bought over the internet and he'd ultimately fashioned some extremely elaborate devices. Very clever kid.

The kid was, in reality, a genius in ever sense. It just so happened that the thing that most gave him a kick couldn't be done in his bedroom at home without sending that self same bedroom into the heart of the nearest city.

So very like Sarah. Young, weird looking and yet extremely gifted. To look at either of them you'd never have thought it, but underneath... I could only hope that Sarah was in the process of using her genius for good. With an intellect such as hers I figured the world could be well and truly screwed if it ever chose to piss her off.

Carey came bouncing back through the door with the can and brush. Sarah took them with a smile and placed the brush in my hand with a slap. "Thanks, Nick. You're a star."

And so, whilst Sarah and Tina took a walk around the grounds, I slowly started painting over the solution.

TWENTY-FOUR

TUESDAY, AUGUST 11, 2043.
5TH & ALAMEDA, LOS ANGELES, CALIFORNIA.

'Our Lamb has conquered, let us follow him.'

Alison's impromptu and potted history of Josef Klein when she had scoffed at the ideas laid before her had not been entirely accurate. Klein's parents had indeed emigrated to the United States and he had further studied at MIT, but not 'just after World War Two'. Initially his family had relocated, with official assistance, to the United Kingdom. The government there, like those of the Americans and the Russians, had been keen to employ the services of scientists, engineers and, more alarmingly perhaps, geneticists from the fallen Reich. With respect to the advancement of propulsion systems, they were especially keen to relocate those who had been so senior in the V2 rocket programme. The United Kingdom might have missed out on securing the services of Werner Von Braun himself (he would initially help the V-rocket programme to graduate from a U.S. High School and ultimately be instrumental within NASA itself), but in the form of Johann Krass, the fifty-three year old Dietrich Klein and Erik Valk they got the second, third and fourth best things respectively.

Krass, Klein and Valk were clearly card carrying, brownshirt-wearing and Führer-idolising Nazis, but like Von Braun they were also useful Nazis and, in the cold light of peace, perseverance with their plans suddenly seemed a much better proposition than persecution of their ideals. In the cold war that followed the novel '1984' was retitled '1948' (because the former year had been and gone) and, in the style of another Orwellian work, everyone who had been equal now wanted to be that little bit more equal than the others. Above all, everyone wanted to win the space race.

The Klein family name temporarily became 'Cain' (and for a time it made Dietrich feel as important as Lord Mountbatten himself), papers were issued and, in order to give some sense of stability to the already thrice-uprooted (twice by no less than the Führer himself) 'Joe Cain' was ushered off to boarding school. A Moravian boarding school in the North of England called 'Fellbeck'.

The Moravian Church Movement was founded in the fifteenth century in what is now the Czech Republic. As a weak group with strong ideals they suffered persecution during the counter-Reformation and subsequently survived for little more than a hundred years. The Renewed Church did not surface until 1727 when refugees from Moravia were granted permission by Count Nicholas to settle in Saxony near the border with Poland. It was this area in which Dietrich Klein, his father, his father and all their fathers before him, had been born and raised. The settlement was known as 'Hermhut' - 'under the watch of the Lord'.

It was from here, and under that auspice, that the church began to spread their simple message. Rather effectively, it seemed, for such a seemingly small institution.

The aim of Count Nicholas and his disparate group was not that the Moravians should become a separate church at all, but that they should form societies within the more established churches and build from within. Even now that was a trait which Josef admired. Indeed, he had used that same technique to good effect throughout his corporate life. Never try to compete directly, rather; step inside, listen, learn, bond and ultimately surpass. Having formed early alliances with, and drawn from, some of the most powerful corporations and governments in the world, KleinWork Research Technology had itself been built on the Moravian philosophy.

Every Sunday afternoon during term time, Klein and over three hundred other pupils were forced to attend a small chapel within the school grounds. For many of the boarders it was one of only three instances during the week when they could mix (albeit from afar) with their counterparts from the neighbouring girls' school; the other two being mixed sports on Saturdays and Tuesday evenings when use of the playing fields overlapped. Klein never bothered with girls, then or now. As a shy, gangly child he was friendly with all the other pupils, but never their friend, and was far more often to be found poking his nose into a book rather than into any trouble. So, each and every week for three years, he simply did as he was told; sat in almost the same seat and was faced with exactly the same inscription; the one which, at over eight feet high, surrounded the stained glass image of a small lamb carrying a righteous red cross standard. Over and over he read the words until it every one of them was inexorably burned into his pre-teen mind.

> *'VICIT AGNUS NOSTER, EUM SEQUAMUR.'*
> *'Our Lamb has conquered, let us follow Him.'*

Even as a young child, Josef Klein...

(Joe Cain)

...whose father had been a fervent supporter of the most powerful leader in German history, a man selected by God himself to lead and reform the known world, only to have done the impossible and failed, had felt an affinity with those words. They said so much. They spoke right at him, and told him that not only was it a good thing 'to conquer' - that it was something to be respected - but also that meekest of animals, like the feeble, studious young Klein himself, were capable of such victories. Moreover, they told him that when he did, people should follow. That they should be called to follow.

During his final summer at Fellbeck, it was in that same chapel, squeezed like a barricade of righteous thoughts between the girls' school and the boys', that Josef also decided for the first time that God probably did not exist. Or, conversely, that if he did then he wielded little or no power, having unwisely handed it over to his free-thinking creations. It was late June, the world was the same as it always was and the last of a solstice sun, already tinged with red, was stretching its arms through the high windows, light swirls of dust broken into a rainbow of colours by the stained panels.

He was a good boy, always well behaved; both so that he did not bring shame upon his family name and also because, at his father's request, he had agreed not to call attention to himself lest his Germanic descent be uncovered. It was not yet 1970 and so nobody really called each other 'bastard' or 'fucker'. Indeed, why should they when 'Kraut' was as powerfully dirty a word to a Briton as any yet to be invented.

Klein dutifully attended the chapel that Sunday with all the other boarding pupils. He had fulfilled the three main criteria; attendance, punctuality and pressed appearance. He had shuffled his way to the centre of the third row, along with the other twelve year olds and his sandy coloured basin of hair had taken its rightful place in the colourful tapestry.

It was not long before that flash of light ochre was gone from view, and with those who were charged with overseeing the pupils, its sudden and inexplicable absence did not go unnoticed.

In the space of five minutes Klein had suffered the onset of the first of the many crippling stomach cramps he would suffer throughout his life, the opening scene to the Crohn's Disease for which he took immunomodulators to this day. He was almost paralysed with pain as though a nest of razor-backed snakes were writhing in his gut. Whilst the other children listened attentively to the minister he placed his head between his legs, his face curled in torment and his teeth gritted. When the others stood to sing the chosen hymns, shoulders straight and chins angled to the Lord, his head remained down, tears slowly dulling the shine on his freshly polished shoes.

God's vengeance never came. Only that of man. And how.

Following the service Klein decided to forego the evening meal, despite his attendance (like the service) being obligatory, and opted instead to retire to his bunk in the dormitory. There he gently laid down his head, his legs drawn high as he hoped to any god that would listen that the pain would subside. He was there for no more than fifteen minutes before Martins, one of the seniors resident at the school, appeared at the foot of the bed with a knowing smile. Klein had been summoned by Chamberlain; the headmaster. An ominous calling, if ever there was one.

Chamberlain was a busy man, one with five hundred pupils, including non-boarders, and a million diverse things to do. A man too busy to waste time on congratulations for his wards, which meant only one thing: a call to 'Chamber's Chambers' as it had been titled, was rarely a good sign. More often than not it was a bad one.

A *very* bad one.

Klein tried and failed to rise from his bunk, pain ripping through his gut like a saw and so Martins, still smiling, had grabbed him by that same head of hair - the one whose absence along the line of row three had been his downfall - and wrenched him from the bed to the floor. Then, as though hoisting an sack of potatoes, he lifted the now screaming child to his feet.

The young boy was kicked down the first flight of stairs, dragged down the second and he cried all the way down the third.

Chamberlain was a tall, thin man with tiny wire-rimmed spectacles and a backward sweep of greying hair. He lived by two things; the bible and the stick; with an unhealthy bias toward the stick. More 'old school' perhaps than even the hallowed history over which he so vehemently presided. Where church was concerned there were the three pre-requisites, all of which Klein had fulfilled that afternoon, but where God and Chamberlain were concerned there was a fourth to be adhered to rigidly ; respect. 'Woe betide those who don't show it'. If respect was not available then fear, it seemed, would make a suitable replacement. To that end he kept a deep brown Malacca cane resting on brass pins behind his desk. A cane that was smooth and glossy in the central area of one edge, indicative that it was wielded often, and that when it was, he had a time-favoured grasp.

Over the next few minutes, in the near-perfect soundproofing of deep mahogany panelling and numerous unread classics, the normally flinty-eyed Chamberlain struck that cane with jackal-like vigour across Klein's palms until the ten year old boy felt that the soft skin which had graced them would never return. For days after he genuinely believed he would never close his fingers toward a fist again.

Chamberlain recited an array of stirring passages from the New Testament

229

each time he struck but where, Klein wondered, was God himself whilst this torture was inflicted? God the merciful, God the great. God who was so omnipresent in this world and the next that he could see a person's every transgression. If that was so, then surely this great all-seeing eye could also see when a child was sick and forgive him his trespasses. Fighting the pain, Klein closed his eyes and thought back to the one passage that he had caught during the seemingly endless service. Mark Chapter 2 Verse 10:

The Son of Man hath power on earth to forgive sins.

The Lamb. The Lamb had power to forgive.

As did man. He simply chose not to use it.

Rather than beat the goodness and the word of the Lord into his soul, every stroke, every new crease of pain that carved into his tiny palm pushed God further from the young Klein's body. It was not religion that was at fault, he realised. Not the belief in a higher power. It was simply the rules that were set by man in His name. 'Thou shalt not do whatever I damn well decide'. Rules that came from nowhere and would ultimately return there when and if the End of Time fell like mist and settled like low plague across the surface of the world.

Men of God always advocated (though whose advocate were they really?) that they held the answers to everything. They never handed those answers over to the minions, of course, because what were the needy once their need was assuaged? In fact, Klein mused, perhaps the priests and the ministers and the bishops held absolutely no answers whatsoever. What if all they held, in reality, was unattainable promise of them? Have belief, my child. Have faith, but never, *ever* have proof.

If redemption had a colour then it was orange. It was a carrot, dangled on a very long stick.

As he lay in his bed that night, his palms open and bleeding into the sheets, Klein understood with finality that God was not the power in this world. God could never *be* the power because God was invisible. Even electricity, whose ability to give light was utilised more widely by mankind than that of God and the sun combined, could be rendered visible in its pure form under the right circumstances. God, on the other hand, could not. He could be thanked when it suited as easily as he could be blamed when it all fell apart. Whether or not anything had been a result of his bidding could never be proven either way. Therefore, if a man was a man of God then he expected his word to be believed without question. If a man was a priest then he held a congregation in the palm of his hands.

Suddenly in Klein's eyes, along with the tears, was the clear realisation that the 'ordained' ministers - the bishops and the priests - were no better than the pay-per-view TV Evangelists; the men who were clever enough to find and hold those same answers - apparently - but never clever enough to remember that when they told their square-eyed congregation to 'get on their knees and start praying', the word 'praying' was damn-well supposed to have an 'r' in it.

People were sheep who would blindly, and gladly, follow men who held answers. They might take some persuading but sometimes, given the right answers, sheep could even be persuaded to follow Lambs.

At ten years of age a young boy with Aryan-blue eyes, a mop of sandy hair and a desire to succeed on at least some of the levels where the Führer and his father had failed decided that if God would not supply the world with the answers it so desperately craved, then perhaps the scientists could.

> *'Our Lamb has conquered, let us follow Him.'*

Klein would be a scientist. He would bring answers, and the world would love him for it. They would follow him. Blindly.

Confined to a wheelchair, the sandy hair (initially replaced by thinning streaks of grey) was long gone. Klein had chosen to shave the last of it away completely at the beginning of the year, leaving him completely bald and adding to the severity of his already sharpened features.

He was seated in his office, triangular and comprising one wall entirely formed from smoked blue/grey glass, situated on the uppermost floor of

231

KleinWork Tower. He was poring through a digital file projected into the curved area of glass that formed the rear of his desk. He smiled gently, deep ridges forming in his gaunt and deeply-tanned cheeks. The answers were close. He had barely been able to appreciate the taste of food on his tongue these past few years but he could taste *them*. They tasted exactly as the future should taste. Metallic and sweet.

Looking markedly out of place on that glass desk and mounted on a three inch high titanium pedestal was a roughened bar of soap made from rendered animal fats. Despite the fact that animal fat manufacture had been superseded by sodium carbonate as far back as the late 1800's, the bar was pristine. It could well have been made and sold that very morning. A note on rough, pulp-rich and heavy paper: *Hands Clean Now? - September 10 1852 (morning)* and a crude sketch of Castle's prison-mark tattoo now hung in a frameless frame behind the desk, the only icon hanging on the two dark-panelled walls that was not a backlit digital projection and that did not blend softly into a new image on a half-hourly rotation.

Both the soap and the note had been discovered inside Castle's wooden box, along with five authentic nineteenth century bullets - a chamber full for the 1836 Paterson Revolving Pistol to which they belonged - and a blurry sepiatone photograph produced from a wet collodian negative, another process long-since superseded and lost to the world.

The picture, taken facing a crude farmstead surrounded by stunted mesquite grasses, showed Castle, fully bearded, along with what was assumed to be his wife and young child. A detailed check of land and historical records showed that Greg Castle had almost certainly become Gerald Castell, a frontier timber worker who had resided with his wife and daughter some two hundred miles north-east of the retrieval site. His new surname was presumed to be a simple bastardisation stemming from mis-pronunciation, given the spoken language of the time, and that his amended forename may have been a vain attempt at social climbing within a society he did not fully understand. Castell purchased the farmstead land in 1867 and remained there until his death in 1898 from a condition described only as 'a fearful distemper'. He was, the records claimed, seventy-two years old.

Klein closed the file and looked up as Alison entered the room, walking purposefully across the polished floor.

"You asked to see me." she said. It was a statement, not a question.

Right on time and right to the point, he thought with a smile; forever Alison. "Take a seat."

She sat across the desk from him, her legs crossed so that the skirt beneath her white lab coat rose a little above her knees. "I need you to do some research for me," he said.

"You're taking me off Sequence?" Alison replied. She looked surprised, but deep down she wasn't; not really. She might have lacked extra-sensory abilities but, given her attitude to the project from the outset, an enhanced sense of perception was hardly required to see something as predetermined as this turns of events ambling slowly down the road.

"Not at all," Klein replied, his hands clasped pensively in front of his face. "Quite the opposite, in fact. This is very much part of the project and that's why I have to utilise someone from within the team."

"Why me?" Alison asked. She seemed upset by the implication that in such a team the woman might just have become the glorified research assistant. "I'm not a researcher. You'd be better utilising someone like Haga who's...."

Klein was already shaking his head. He turned and moved his chair away from the desk and toward the window, looking out over the spread of New Los Angeles. Three new golden-glass skyscrapers had been erected since KRT's Head Office had been built on these five acres of reclaimed ground and their combined presence, annoyingly, now obstructed his view of the hills which lay beyond.

"I genuinely feel that you're the only one that can do it," he said.

Alison was puzzled. Research was research, wasn't it? She had no special access privileges to information. At least, none that she was aware of. "I don't follow...?"

Klein thought for a moment, then looked up. "Because this is more than just research," he said, though it was clear that he was speaking from another place. "I need someone who can make sense of the things they find; perhaps even draw conclusions from them. I need *answers*, Alison, and I need those answers very quickly, I'm afraid."

Alison narrowed her eyes. "How quickly?"

"Before Friday."

Her eyes narrowed. "What happens Friday?" she asked.

Klein smiled. "I leave for France," he said.

"France? Why the hell are you going to France?"

Klein looked back out of the window, across the city. This was it, he thought, this was where he needed to be completely assured of Alison's discretion. He wondered if he was. He wondered if he was assured of anyone's discretion but his own, but then he surely would not have invited her to his office today if he were not?

"I'll be working in Cardou for a few weeks."

Alison was really puzzled now and that happened so infrequently as to shock her with its appearance. She knew about Cardou. At least, she knew as much as anyone else within KRT. Didn't she? It was the land purchased by the United States government at the turn of the century. Klein himself had worked there once, apparently using his scientific expertise to offer guidance on an archaeological dig. Nothing had been found and the site, ultimately had been traded over to KRT, who now utilised it for much less exciting purposes.

"But there's nothing there. Well, except for our ELRC." She was referring to the Cardou site's new position as KRT's European Livestock Research Centre. It was a small centre set in acres of open land; populated by just three men, fifteen cows with a higher than average milk yield and some sheep whose fleece, with a little more work, would perhaps grow that little bit faster.

Klein's eyes were serious. He looked around the room, out of the window and back to Alison, still patiently awaiting an answer. They looked everywhere, but she did not know for certain what it was that they saw. Not yet. He nodded to a file, sitting on his desk and bound in translucent red plastic. "It's all in the file," he said.

Alison did not pick it up. She sensed that there was something he wasn't telling her, even now, and her senses might be no more powerful than Klein's own, but they were rarely wrong. She knew that it would be merely facts - and not answers - that she would find within the pages.

"What's going on, Josef?" she asked softly.

"Six months ago we transferred the ELRC to England," he said quietly, as though confessing a sin, "and restructured the building at Cardou. We created a sealed room with coated walls, increased the power supplies and added a vacuum pump. On Friday that room will be functional and I would very much like to be there when it is."

And she could see it now. Very clearly. Another site; a *European* site. A place from which mice could be sent further back without fear of being stranded in a desolate environment populated only by Native Americans.

Her own words from the meeting came swiftly back to haunt her; suddenly and painfully. *Presumably somewhere in Europe...* So that's what Klein had done. In amongst KRT's numerous and global assets he had found the ideal location to further his ridiculous aims.

"And you've sent the second sphere," she said, her eyes still thinking through the consequences. "That was why you cut two before distributing the rest. You knew this was going to happen."

Klein shook his head. "Not then I didn't, no," he said. "But God does work in mysterious ways, doesn't he? I just felt it prudent to keep something in reserve, that was all. Had I not, then I could still have taken the one from downstairs. Still, fortune smiles on the cautious and now it seems I don't have to."

Alison rose to her feet and walked to the window, no doubt seeing a completely different vista laid out before her than her employer had seen.

She saw the world as it was today. Her desperately mad employer saw it in another place; a place he wanted to herd it.

She turned suddenly, her wide eyes probing and demanding an answer to her next question.

"What are you really looking for here, Josef?" she asked. Because there was something very specific now about all this. That was why he needed her to do some 'research'. He needed her to find something for him. Not just anything. *Something*.

He looked at her almost apologetically. "You always were very perceptive," he said. "One of the traits you did demonstrate in your NorthStar days, as I recall." He smiled lamely and took a deep, long, rasping breath.

"In truth I have searched for something all my life," he continued, "and now that life is drawing to a close. Then suddenly, like a gift from God himself, I am handed the opportunity not just to find it now, but also be the reason I never found it before. It's almost as if He *wants* me to find it, as though I'm am in some way blessed." He looked over to the file, and squinted as though achieving the impossible and reading the words within. "Who knows? Perhaps I am the very last of the Templars."

Alison fought hard to control her thoughts and the words that might spin from them like dealt cards. What did Klein know of God? What did he believe of Him? Little or nothing she suspected, and yet here he was now, his body weakened from the stroke and his mind similarly challenged, talking of being 'blessed'. Of being a 'Templar', as though his enduring quest for power and profit had become some kind of twisted Crusade.

"What is it you're looking for?" she asked, deliberately calm. "What do you want me to find answers to?"

"Our Lamb has conquered," Klein said, almost to himself. Then he looked up and Alison saw the light burning in, around and behind his normally dark eyes. She saw his final burst of life. "Everything," he said cryptically, his passion adding a short spike of energy to his tired voice.

"Don't you see? I want you to find the answers to *everything*."

TWENTY-FIVE
Friday, June 10, 2011.
Los Angeles, California.

It had taken a while longer than I expected to bring Tina even close to being settled. Giddy as she was, like a child at Christmas; a child on a birthday or even a child as the ice-cream van came calling; an ice-cream van she had never seen. She was excited in so many ways but they all belonged to a person not yet a third her age. It made me wish that I could be a child again; to see the world and the people who inhabited it with the same degree of innocence and unknowing acceptance that she did. The world was a shit place. Whenever I looked at a child I wanted to tell them - to scream at them if need be - that it was a shit place, just so that they might gain a head start on their contemporaries.

When I looked into Tina's eyes, bright and innocent, I never once felt that desire. I only prayed that she would never ever get to see just what a truly shit place it really was.

I never got my wish.

Whilst Sarah did her best to bury her sister's head into the escapism that was Dumas' *La San Felice*, in its original form, I retreated outside for a cigarette.

If eighteen square concrete blocks - each around two feet in diameter, surrounded by a low brick wall and accessible only via a rusting fire escape constitutes a roof-top garden, then that is what I have back at the apartment. It is to that place that I go when I need to think, reflect, deduce and, on numerous occasions, feel way too damned sorry for myself.

Once, perhaps three weeks after Katherine left, I even went out there and placed the barrel of the .357 in my mouth. It tasted of warm oil, silky yet sour - like bad fruit. The gun was not loaded, of course - I'm not stupid - but for the few seconds it was pressed against my tongue it made me a little feel better about myself. I realised that there were, in fact, worse things in life. Like death. I've never done it before and I've never done it since, but sometimes I figure that has more to do with the fact I did not actually believe that I would even be missed.

And that hurt almost a much as a bullet.

My apartment block was a six-storey building with no favouritism shown when it came to which was most neglected and consequently the 'garden' had a clear and occasionally relaxing view over a moderately large area of Southern Los Angeles. It was undoubtedly an area more likely to make an appearance in a Spike Lee movie than in any of the tourist guides, but I loved it for what it was. For what I will always be. It was my place and to some degree I thrived like bacteria on the crap that surrounded me.

Today, as I got the strange feeling that I might not be back in the garden for quite a while, the overgrown expanse that surrounded Oakdene became a green and strangely less pleasant substitute in which to gather my thoughts and try and make some sense of where this might be going in the few minutes it took for Sarah to bid farewell to her sister.

My mind was as chock-full of potentials as New York is of bad drivers, little yellow cabs of indecision violently cutting up any rational suggestions that tried to make their way across town.

As I understood the situation at this point, which almost implies that I understood it at all, I had a very dead and extremely naked stiff. Why he was naked was unclear but why he was dead was starting to make itself known. He'd latched onto something, either for himself or on behalf of a third party. That something was a coded map which, if it could be deciphered, would possibly lead him – or them – to treasures lost for centuries. I doubted very much that these treasures held the answers to life itself or would herald any new dawn of mankind, but I did not doubt – even based on their age alone – that they would be extremely valuable. They might even be worth enough of the green stuff to kill for, especially given that it seems to take less and less of the green stuff to make murder a viable option with every year that passes.

So this guy, whoever he was, had found himself a map. Now all he needed was somebody who could translate it for him, bearing in mind that a computer system would be neither use nor ornament. Okay, it might make a nice ornament, but not a particularly useful one, so he brought his map to L.A. because somehow he had come into possession of Tina's name as the kind of walking, talking (sorry, *not* talking) miracle he might have been searching for. What worried me at this point in the story was that he was not only killed, but also killed with a high degree of professionalism, hence the fact that Deacon had placed three teams on the case. He had no fingertips, no identification and he had been found sunny side up. Which told me that he had not been invited to the alleyway, but rather that he had been prepped and stripped before they had taken him there to finish the job. Why his killers had not killed him and then taken him to the alley was still one of the answers I would be filing under 'elusive'. Unless, course, he had been stripped in the alley. In which case.... why take his clothes? What was it his threads would have told us?

My fear, which I was loathed to voice out loud, was that this man had been killed by 'our side'. The good guys, if you will. I realise that such an accusation sounds crazy; it did then and it does now, but according to Sarah *they* were the ones with the site in France; the one which even the French were not allowed to penetrate and *they* were the ones who had on the face of things invested most money into this project. What I did admire, at this point, was the fact that it was clear that my dead guy had balls long before he showed them to the world at large. If Sarah was right then the map was the key and, regardless of who it was that had ultimately punctured him, my guess is that they had spent a very long time asking him for that map in as forceful a manner as they could muster. He never gave it up. It was hidden up his rear end the whole time and he never gave it up. They sure as hell did not put it there, because they wanted it.

Unless, of course, we were being set up...

Perhaps the text had always been a false lead; a white elephant herded in so that the dumb shits at the precinct, myself included, would find it and waste a good few hours following it up whilst they got on with the serious business of cleaning the whole mess up. I hoped not, because if it was then I would hate to spend my later years explaining to the next generation of bar-flies at Cody's how I'd once found a naked guy dead in an alley with a white elephant stuffed up his ass.

But if our only lead on the case was false, why did the Feds take that same case away?

Something about this whole sorry charade was not right. Something smelled and it smelled bad; a clear indication if ever I needed one that it was all going to get a lot worse before it even spared a thought for getting better.

The door clanked shut behind me and I turned, Sarah walking down the steps with a reluctant smile.

"She's okay now."

I could tell that however much she and her sister might relish the times that Sarah came to visit, both of them hated the times that she had to leave again a whole lot more.

"So where now?"

Sarah sighed and looked beyond the line of bristlecone pines and the deserted strips of I-15's dusty tarmac to the cactus and sagebrush desert which stretched to the horizon and beyond. It had been a hot one the world over this year. It seemed to get hotter with each summer that passed. The TV told us that it was global warming; man's slow cancer on the world to those who cared. Personally I came from the school of thought that if the world was still inhabitable when the time came for me to shuffle my way off it, then that was more than long enough.

She drew breath raggedly and straightened her back toward the possibilities. "Airport," she said, pulling a loose strand of hair behind her ears and replacing her sunglasses.

She smiled again. Perhaps a little wider this time.

★ ★ ★ ★ ★

When she stepped from the car at LAX, Sarah offered me three distinct promises. She would call me the instant she returned, she would tell me exactly what she had found, and she would be very, *very* careful. In that instant I knew that the entire matter was now firmly out of my hands. For all her sincerity, her promises sounded little more than awkward compromise. One that came with no guarantees. All I could do was let her go. I'd sure as hell got nothing to hold her on. What I had was the sum total of nothing multiplied by very little else and however long it might take Deacon to follow that information up, it would be time wasted because Sarah would almost certainly get to Serres, and 'Arcadia', long before anyone else he might think to call.

I doubted very much that, given the circumstances, Deacon would be calling the U.S. Archaeological Team in France to share his new-found knowledge. Instead he'd have to go through his own channels to find out what, if anything, was hidden in the village. Channels which, at best, were mere trickles compared to the flood of excitement which was now guiding this girl.

Back at the precinct, and back on two, I sensed that all was not well in paradise. The room had an air, and not a very pleasant one at that. Most of the precinct were there, which in itself wasn't unusual, but they were not scurrying like the busy little swarm of worker bees they normally were. Today they ambled, as if honey futures had halved in value and their worlds had somehow decided to run at half speed for a while by way of compensation.

Ellis, whose desk was immediately and immaculately located behind my own sat rigid, his elbows resting on a pile of un-filed paperwork. For Ellis, 'un-filed' was the kind of sacrilege that would usually result in him pre-booking an extended stay in a confessional booth followed by a week of Cistercian underwear and Hail Mary's. His glasses were removed, his fingertips pressed firmly around his nose and his eyes stared at something only he was privileged enough to see.

"How you doing with naked guy?" I asked, deliberately oblivious. Knowing that I had uncovered so much more than he and Dean, it was all I could do to stop myself smiling as widely on the outside as I was within.

He didn't answer. For a moment I don't think he even registered my existence. Or indeed his own. After a few protracted moments he looked up, still expressionless, and said in a voice that would have made a Speak and Spell machine sound as though it had won the Minnesota State Lottery; "Deacon wants to see you."

I turned to see the obligatory Post-It plastered over Vicki's face. Why did he never stick them over the face of somebody I didn't actually want to see, like Katherine? As ever, I peeled it away, ready to throw it in the trash along with the archetypal 'fuck you', but Deacon hadn't stopped there.

Not this time.

Underneath the Post-It was another sticker - one of those white ones that needs a bucket of warm soapy water before it will even consider coming off. All it said was *NOW!!!* Whistling every breath that followed through gritted teeth I turned and made my up to the third.

Ellis went back to staring into nothing.

Deacon was peeling open the blinds and staring out of the window, watching the traffic making its way along Fifth. Red braces today; nice touch Deac'. In his hand I saw a glass with coke and ice, but on his desk I saw something that told me this wasn't just coke: A half-drunk bottle of single malt and another glass, empty save for melting cubes. Whatever the reason; single malt only ever meant one thing; today was not a good day.

"Wells and Rodriguez are dead," he said bluntly. He didn't bother to turn around. I had my own way of entering his office that had told him he didn't need to check it was me. "And you're off the naked stiff. In that order."

"Dead?" I said. Then a little too much silence. "How?"

"Unrelated," he said, like it mattered. "They were leaving City Archives when a mugger took a case from a guy in front of them. They chased, the mugger chose his route well and when he found an empty street he stopped and turned. Got them both as they came round the corner. Head shots."

"Did we get the guy?"

I saw his head shaking. "Nah... and I doubt we will either."

And of all the words on the list of those I had expected to hear, Deacon had chosen some fresh. These were not the words a chief said when two of his men had been taken out in an alley. These words worried me.

"So why I am off the case? I mean, I've just been..."

Deacon turned around and I didn't like what I saw in his eyes. It was rare that I did, in truth, but this was different. This was nasty.

"I know exactly where you've been," he barked. "So, I might add, do the Feds. Christ, could you not have been a bit more *discreet*? You might just as well have been waving a God-damned flag on your way to Oakdene. You pissed off Creed... *again*, and then you scoot off to see the sister. Worse still, you ask the neighbour for directions, for God's sake."

He sat down in the high back, the leather creaking against the damp that seeped through his cheap tailored shirt. "So the Feds come in here and bust my ass. And we lose; just like that. Thanks a lot Lambert. As of now it stops. Go get some of that other shit off your desk instead."

Silence. Save for the gentle flicker of the cheap bulk-purchase blinds and the low rush of traffic. So when I chose words with which to break that silence, I chose them carefully. And I leaned across his desk and spaced them evenly so that the clarity of not one single syllable was lost.

"You... must... be... joking...? This is big. No... correction... this is fucking *huge*."

I was still trying to retain the case. I *wanted* the case. I felt bad for Wells and Rodriguez, sure, but that was the business we were in. One day it might be my turn to chase the wrong guy into a quiet alley and take a bullet. But in the meantime I could still get one over on Ellis and Dean. "You invited me to the party, you're not sending me home now."

"Big?" Deacon laughed, but he didn't find it funny. Not one bit. "Of course it's big. That's why I've spent the biggest part of the morning getting one hell of a big kicking from the big Assistant Director at the big white building down on Wilshire." His voice was raised. Not much, but enough for those at the other side of the blinds to take a quick look up from their work.

Charlie Petersen. Assistant Director at the F.B.I.'s L.A. Field Office down on... well, Wilshire. So now I knew who'd been drinking from the other glass.

"And they're shutting us down?"

"We shouldn't have been open," he said. "We stole it, remember? They just took it back again, that's all.' He looked at me with narrowed eyes, the kind that come along when you're thinking what you ought to say now; or how you ought to say it. With the slightest sideways glance of recognition he smelled the air. It was as though something in Deacon's walnut-faced mini-fridge had suddenly gone really bad.

"Aw shit, Nick, have you been drinking?" Now it was like he was trying to find things to pin on me.

I leaned forward again, my fingers firm on Deacon's desk and looked him right in the eyes. "Look," I said, near spitting the words, "You *asked* me to steal it and I've made good progress. And no, I haven't been drinking," I lied. "Smell my breath."

He looked up, placed his glass back on the desk with a distinct clink of resignation and stood to face me; eye-level. His words were as deliberate as mine had been, but his arm was outstretched, pointing toward the fishtank.

"The goldfish can smell your breath, Nick. But no... you haven't been drinking and you've made good progress? Well, you'll forgive my scepticism, but those are two things we just don't hear from you very often, aren't they?"

He was picking a fight.

"Fuck you, Deacon," I said. Stock response, hardly creative.

"And I didn't *ask* you to steal anything," he continued. "I asked you to play as part of a team, that was all. Which you didn't. You were sent to Oakdene and nothing more, I don't remember sanctioning you to go visiting any Goddamned sister. So now the team is calling it off and I expect you to do the same."

I laughed through my nose, sardonically, and pulled back from the desk, shaking my head like I'd given up on his very existence. "Team? And which team would that be exactly?

Ours... or *theirs*?"

He sat back down and took another long drink, drawing the last through the ice. "Either? Both? It's the same goddamned thing, isn't it." His expression and his words were far from reaching an agreement. "You don't follow this case any further. You don't go back to Oakdene unless someone pulls a gun and you don't go visiting the sister again. Understand? You let it die."

"What about Wells and Rodriguez? You letting them die?"

"In case you hadn't worked it out already, Lambert, this is not a discussion. It's a 'you come to my office, I tell you how and when to piss and you go away again' scenario. Tail between your legs would be greatly appreciated." He swirled his glass until the ice gained centrifuge, his face creasing deeper the more he thought. "To whit, you are off the case. End of story. Why? Because you're a liability."

"Double fuck you."

"That's the second, and either one's enough for me to place you on suspension." He looked me right in the eye and I saw something that I suspected he'd been holding back. There was something that reeked of 'clever' creasing them now. Some kind of punchline. What was it they said about trump cards? Only play them when they're funny. "Although you do have holiday owing, and that would look a damn sight better on a piss-poor record such as yours. So... personally... I'd like to suggest, very forcefully, that you take it now."

"I don't want to take it now."

"Then I'll log that comment on your file and, given the inescapable truth that charges are currently being prepared against you and that you seem incapable of following even the simplest instruction, *and* the fact that I suspect you're giving my goldfish a hangover, *and* the fact that you cost me twenty dollars by lasting four days without a cigarette, I'll suspend you." He smiled at his own joke. "You will let me know if I run out of things to pin on you... Nick... won't you?"

In that one closing line he lost the last of his edge. The clever plan, whatever it might be, came right to the fore, pushing his anger to one side. Temporarily, I was guessing. His voice had become gentle, calm and almost persuasive.

Nick? But we already know that Deacon only calls me 'Nick' when....

There they were. The answers to all the words I didn't like, delivered on a plate with a sprig of something green adding unnecessary garnish. Rodriguez and Wells were dead, yet Deacon *doubted we'd ever catch the guy*. This was a cop killer and we always put full weight behind catching cop killers, don't we? That's the way it had been since the dawn of time. So where was Deacon's weight now?

He knew full well that this was big. He'd had Petersen drinking in his office, for Christ's sakes, how much bigger did you want it to be? So big, in fact, that he couldn't risk any of his officers. Maybe there was some link that I wasn't seeing and he wasn't going to point out to me; one that said 'any more of his officers'. But, if that was the case, he'd sure as hell risk me. Because in Deacon's eyes Nick Lambert was worse than useless. Yet he wasn't *telling* me, his change of tone had indicated that much.

He was *asking* me.

It was the coward's way, sure, but even I could see it was perhaps the only door that Petersen had left open for him. I've said it before – I'll say it again. Perhaps Deacon was not quite as stupid as he looked.

Perhaps no-one is quite as stupid as Deacon looks.

"How much leave do I have exactly?" I asked, very carefully.

He must have done some calculations in his head, because we both knew I had less than a week.

"Two weeks," he said, firm like fact. "And I suggest you use it wisely. *Soberly*."

I narrowed my eyes and smiled. It told him I knew. That I kind of understood and that I'd fill in any blanks at a later date. I pulled out my gun, unclipped my badge from my belt and laid them both gently on his desk. "Fuck you, Deacon." That was three of a kind.

And he actually smiled back, albeit lamely.

Sometimes I picture him after I'd left his office. Sitting deep, low and creaky in his high-back cattle ranch, still twirling the glass in his hand and wondering what he'd started by ever trying to take on that case. He wouldn't have had any idea that Wells and Rodriguez had been government hits, of course. At least I would hope not - and it would be months before I myself was in the unfortunate position of learning that little home truth, but he would have known that their deaths were excruciatingly connected.

Perhaps Petersen himself had hinted at it, used it as leverage. Not that he would have needed leverage over Deacon, but in situations like these I would assume at some gentle attempt at diplomacy if nothing else. That's the thing with games of policy and politics; you never stab someone hard in the back who might be able to come along and scratch yours a damn sight harder a few years down the line.

So perhaps the big old Assistant Director looked right into Deacon's ambitious eyes, all serious, and said words that rhymed with… "*These are seriously bad guys we're chasing here, Paul. Maybe they were watching your officers at the galleries, or checking out the Latin. Maybe it's safer if you let us handle it. You know? Like you said you would.*"

Unlike Deacon, though, Petersen would not have been asking. No way. Diplomacy would only be there to act as a plane, smoothing the edges of the door so that it was a real tight fit when he closed it tightly behind him.

So now, when I picture Deacon, I picture him sitting in that carefully stitched expanse of cow, ashen faced. I picture him sitting there for quite a while in fact, all the while wishing that he'd passed the F.B.I. medical the previous year. Because if he had, if he'd actually got the eighteen-plus average instead of the sixteen-five, then maybe - just maybe - his little stab at petty revenge might not have been a contributing factor in his precinct losing two of two of its best officers. And husbands. And, in Eric Wells' case, a father.

★ ★ ★ ★ ★

Back on two I gathered the few things I needed. In actual fact, there wasn't anything I needed, but it just seemed like the right thing to do. It fitted the mood, and I guessed that if they ever made a movie of my life then it would allow the actor who played me a small scene in which to deliver a plot-shifting line. To Ellis, in fact, when he wandered over with the smirk he seems to reserve solely for my benefit.

Ellis never misses a trick. He's a good guy, if you have a penchant for people whose only aim in life is to wear their boss as a hat. Unfortunately, that means that the day they make sycophancy an Olympic event will probably be the same day they bring a platinum medal into play just to grace the buttock-tightened neck of little shits like him.

"Enforced leave," I said. There was no point leaving out the 'enforced' bit. The words 'I suggested he...' would be snaking their way out from Deacon's lips the next time Ellis sat across the desk from him anyway.

"Anywhere nice?"

It was a joke, and a bad one at that. He'd already got me pegged for a few weeks sitting at home, drapes closed, a few bottles of Jack, take-out cuisine-du-jour and hour after interminable hour of re-runs of Jerry Springer carefully stage-managing another ratings-winning fight on trailer-trash-TV.

I had better plans than that, as it happened. Much better. In fact, I had some plans that I was actually quite proud of, and that's something that deigns to make an appearance less often than my 'not been drinking/have made progress' speech.

I slammed the drawer closed and turned around, straightening the collar on my jacket in some pathetic attempt to look as cool and unaffected as he would have hated me to be. Truth is, I pulled it off as well, primarily because I really was *that* cool. *That* unaffected. I looked for the briefest moment as though I was actually sifting through the international directory of endless possibilities.

"Dunno," I said. "Somewhere warm. South of France, maybe...?"

And with that piss-you-off smile I do so well, I was gone.

Now stick *that* little exit in your movie.

★ ★ ★ ★ ★

Of course, I realise that I'm a heavily biased individual, but in

251

my opinion there were few jobs in this world less gratifying than mine. Actually, shitty is the word that does it most justice. Not that officers of the law are supposed to seek gratitude for what we do. Hell no, we're supposed to do it for the sense of community it etches indelibly into our soul or some such crap, but the odd pat on the back, genuine or otherwise, wouldn't go amiss.

Conversely, there were few things more gratifying, again in my opinion, than not having to do that job for a given length of time. Officially at any rate. And here I was, with clearance to do whatever the hell I wanted for two weeks. And I could do it *wherever* I wanted. Which, whether Deacon knew it yet or not, was going to be in a tiny village in France, searching for some long lost religious artefact with a beautiful young woman by my side.

Assuming, of course, I could make that flight.

I mean come on, when your nine-to-whenever is a shitty as mine, this just had to beat working for a living. Didn't it?

So, as I walked through the underground lot to my car, I have to admit to smiling like I hadn't smiled in a long while and throwing my keys into the air like a star quarterback heading off to football practice. You would have thought, however, given that Wells and Rodriguez had recently head-butted a bullet apiece a great speed, plus the fact that I no longer had a gun and Deacon's hint about me using my time 'soberly', that I'd have actually bothered to keep my eyes open. But I didn't. All I heard was the dripping of a fire hose that had been leaking for as long as I could remember and the dull drone of midday traffic on the street above, the sound permeating down through the vents.

I walked - no, scrub that - I *sauntered* - through the lot as quickly as I could. If I was to catch the same flight as Sarah, then there would be no time to go home and pack a bag. I'd have to travel in the clothes I was wearing now - which were not only the ones I'd been wearing yesterday as well, but also the only clean clothes I currently owned. So, in the great scheme of things, not making it home actually mattered little.

Caught in this little world I'd created for myself, I didn't hear the footsteps coming up behind me. They had seen me exit from the stairwell and followed me the full length of the lot; never too far behind. In fact, they were advancing with every step I took, slowly drawing closer. I didn't hear a thing. Not until it was too late. By this time my uninvited guest was right behind me and all I heard was the voice...

"Hello, Detective."

I turned around like a shot, nearly reaching for a gun I didn't have. Then blew all the breath I had with relief.

"Jesus wept, don't do that."

Sarah was leaning on one hip, a huge cheerful grin on her face, her shades tucked into her straggly hair and the rucksack thrown over her shoulder. "Mind if I share this cab?" she said.

"Aren't you supposed to have checked in already?"

"Later flight. Couldn't go without you, could I?" she said.

We reached the Taurus and I opened the door like the gentleman my mother tried and failed to mould me into. "And now that you've got two weeks suspension disguised as leave, I figured I'd better come and give you your ticket."

She flashed her eyes and waved a white envelope.

"Besides which, you need a change of clothes."

TWENTY-SIX
Thursday, August 13, 2043.
Los Angeles, California.

The reflections were fuzzy. They always were.

It felt as though she were in a corridor and it smelled like a bad one. No clear light, just one long undulating shadow. Always the same. Certainly the overriding smell she sensed was one of bleach; antiseptic perhaps, but it did not bring with it an air of cleanliness, rather the suspicion of what it might be covering up. She swept along this place as though she were floating. Across the Styx? If there had been a light at the end - if there had been any light at all - then she might have wondered if she were dying.

Then a dark shape; a door. Black. Slowly - silently - it opened and what might be a room beyond was nothing more than a three-dimensional sheet of haze. Milky white. Sour. The sky on a cold February morning.

It's not a dream. It can't be a dream.

(Because I'm not asleep.)

It should have been cold. All the laws of colour and sense told her that a chill should have flowed within her. Yet all she felt was warmth. She was supposed to be here. She needed to be here. It was her place.

(To be here.)

Dull light cut through the thick air from the near distance. Square light, perhaps, in a clear room but now it was hard to tell. A small shape outside. Lighter than the light. Reflecting.

The shape moved back and forth, awkward. Nothing was smooth, yet in this world perhaps it should have been. But the head. The head of this small shape did not flow. It bobbed like flotsam in the harbour.

Something about that shape. Something important.

(White.)

The first time she had visited this place she had noticed instantly that she was not the only visitor; that there was another already there. A thin shape, sitting on a bed of rough blankets. She sensed that the head was lowered, though in her dream state it was hard to tell. Initially she had focused all her efforts on that other. Something told her that it would be fruitless to try to talk, sound did not exist in this place, but she had tried as hard as she might to see the person's face, perhaps in the hope that it might explain where this was. Why this was.

She had never found out. The face had never been clear enough and the eyes were mirrors.

It were as though she were watching this place through a veil. A living ghost. What she could sense of the room told her that it was a prison cell, spartan and bare. It was so hard to know for sure and so hard to glean answers from what little she could make out. Everything in her view was nothing more than a blank canvas because everything was a shape without form. Without history.

Still, she had known. She had not found out, but she had known.

Who she was. Where she was.

It made her smile. Made her warm and happy. Truly happy, perhaps for the first time in her life.

The second time was the first. Everything the same. The third time she saw another shape. The one in the light.

She did not know what it meant or why it should be there, only that it meant something and, like everything in this place, it was there for a reason. A reason that eluded her then as stringently as it eluded her now.

It was there now. Head bobbing. Flotsam.

Many years after she had first visited this place - or rather, after some intangible friend had entered her mind, gently taken her hand and led her here - she was allowed to stay a little longer; environment permitting. Real world permitting. If there was such a thing, because this place was not only hazy, but it had also cast a dizzying spell across the line which had once separated the two.

She never knew when she might be brought here, or how long her world might allow her to stay...

(allow her to see)

...but her visits expanded in length. Longer every time. There was no point trying to come here, because she had. Tried, that is. No, she was brought here at the request of another. One whose stay here was a little more permanent; whose visits could not be handed back like screaming children to their parents. She came here to see the world as it truly was. Twenty-four-seven.

Head bobbing. Flotsam. In a harbour.

The door behind her opened again. Though she did not remember closing it. Had she? Did it matter? Another shape stood within. A dark soft-edged silhouette in the haze. Not black, rather a dull grey like a reflection in a pond. That was all this was. It was all he was, and she knew it was a he because she could sense something on his breath as it swirled the mist. Reflections.

This was the third time she had seen him, or rather his form. The first time, perhaps three weeks ago as she sat at home reading Catch-22 by Joseph Heller, the lighting toned to 'nocturne', she was suddenly back in this place, only this time she had felt as she should have felt all along. Cold. Inside, outside and all around, as though the mist was freezing around her and clamping itself to her skin. This shape - this man - brought this feeling with him. The worst cold she had ever known. Colder even than death she wondered? Perhaps it was just as cold as because that's what it was. Death.

Yet she felt something else, even then, and it was stronger now. It was not just death that travelled with this man, there was life as well. Not warm life, loving and giving, but life all the same. This man carried with him a blanket for the streets, not for the nursery. Then as now he stood in the doorway, prouder than she felt he should be allowed, as the dim light seeped around him like an optical illusion. Faces and vases, what do you see? What do you want to see?

(I want to see what happens. I want to know why he is in my place.)

A voice in her head. A voice she recognises as surely as she knows she has never heard it before. Soft, consoling. Saddened. "You will know. You need to know. But don't hurry. Because once you know, you can never return."

Once you know you can never return.

Catch-22.

The man in the doorway took a step forward. Just one. Always one. It was not a long stride but it carried with it a sense of purpose. Things to do. Things that have already been done. Things that cannot be changed.

History, she thought. History cannot be changed.

As he came toward her she sensed this man's eyes, seedy and dark. Like his stride they held a purpose; a dark goal of which she was unaware and was afraid to even attempt a guess. She wanted to shout. Not for herself because she could sense that this man had not come for her. He had come for the other, the one who had called her to see, but would not allow her to see everything. Not yet.

Once you know you can never return.

A shape in the window. Stark white. Like an angel. Moving. Bobbing. Watching. Could it see her? Could it see the other? Or the man? The man who is entering. Could it see anything?

Or was it all just reflections? Of the real world.

If there was such a place then she had to go back there. A voice she could not hear was telling her that it was important not just to her world, but to both worlds, that she go home. Now. She had things she needed to do. (He is inside now.) She did not know what they were, only that they were

257

waiting for her. Like a supermarket. What did she come in for? She might not know, but she knew that she had come in for something.

He's inside the room.

Something to do.

He's in my place.

Important things that told her they might take that line and erase it forever. My place is full of fear, but it's not mine. They might take away the haze and bring some clarity not just to this other place, but to her life in both. Fear. She could taste it in this place.

Reflections. Clarity. Like new spectacles.

The small half-rims resting on Alison's nose now, back home, were reflecting three computer screens, each showing a different image. She stared intently, then tapped the pressure mat with her long fingers to alter the information presented before her and sipped coffee that had reached the wrong side of lukewarm at least half an hour ago. As was always the case when she returned from this place she could hear her heart, tumbling like an empty barrel down a hill. She had no idea how long she had been gone. Time was not important in the real world, only in the other place. The place where she could sense that it was running out.

She needed to do something. To find something.

But what?

It had been like this for three hours now, five the previous night and six the night before that. The dark shade of her eyes was showing the strain. She blinked away sleep and did her best to carry on. She did not fully understand why, but she needed to get all the answers before Klein left for France.

The answers to everything, to quote him directly.

Not his answers, though. Not any more; *hers*.

In reality, Alison already had everything Klein needed printed and filed, and that file had been sitting on his desk well before he arrived at 7:30

that very morning. And, whilst she had not spoken with him since, she knew that he would undoubtedly have been very pleased. What he was looking for, indeed what he had been 'searching for all his life', she had discovered, were something called 'The Tables of Testimony'. Ancient stone tablets. They were described with holy Aramaic writings, described as both the 'Cosmic Equation' and 'The Divine Laws of Number, Measure and Weight'.

The mystical art of reading the inscriptions was said to be achieved by utilising the cryptic system of the 'Kabbala'. Which, if myth, tradition, speculation and God only knew what else was to be believed, were indeed Klein's 'answers to everything'. Two tablets of stone, supposedly carved by the same hands that moulded the earth itself, and placed in the Ark of the Covenant or the Ark of Zion which, for a period of time, travelled with Moses, ultimately delivering he and his followers into the Promised Land.

But where, Klein had wanted to know, had these tables ended what was, quite literally, an epic journey of biblical proportions? Through extensive research, the cross-referencing of innumerate digital archives and biblioteque centres worldwide, Alison had managed to demonstrate that the Ark itself had very probably followed the 'known path'; the accepted path. There was certainly no information to the contrary. This huge container, carefully constructed from ancient shittim wood, had been carried by Joshua seven times around the walls of Jericho, carried against the Philistines by the sons of Eli, taken by David into his new capital, Jerusalem and it was there that David's son, Solomon, had constructed a magnificent temple in which to house it.

After centuries in which the Ark was mentioned very little, it subsequently vanished completely in circumstances about which even the Hebrew Bible had very little to say. The Temple itself was destroyed by the Babylonians and then rebuilt. No Ark, however, was ever replaced in the Inner Sanctum. Ultimately, if even more rumour, speculation and myth were to be believed then this, the holiest of all vessels, was stolen and ultimately ended its life somewhere in Ethiopia.

The 'Tables of Testimony', however, would appear to have taken a different route. According to documents uncovered by Alison, along with the writings of Philo and Josephus, it would appear that the Tables themselves stayed in Jerusalem. There, according to the Talmud, the tables were hidden by Josiah when he realised that the Temple was to be destroyed. In AD36 Josephus reported that a false prophet had told the Samaritans to accompany him to Mount Gerizim where he would show them the 'Holy Tables' that were buried there. The Samaritans were known to have believed that a holy prophet, like Moses, would restore the hidden tables to the Temple so they agreed to the journey. The Memar Marqah, an Aramaic text written in the fourth century AD, referred to Mount Gerizim at a time where 'what is hidden will be revealed'.

The Tables were not, however, to be found at Gerizim. Instead they had remained hidden deep beneath the Temple, in the great stable of King Solomon. During the First Crusade in 1091 the enormous underground shelter had been described by one Crusader as 'a stable of such capacity that it would hold more than 2000 horses'. It also, apparently, held 'great treasures, including the Tables of Testimony'.

If Templar lore held any degree of accuracy, and the speculations of such a self-effacing group was always to be taken with a least a tiny pinch of salt, then it was the finding and opening of this immense store that had been the ultimate aim of the Knights anyway. A confession after the event.

By 1127 the Templars had all they needed. They had uncovered and seized not only the Tables of Testimony, but also an inordinate quantity of gold bullion and treasures, all of which had been safely stowed beneath the ground long before the Roman demolition and plunder of the Temple way back in AD70.

After the raid Hugues de Payens, leader of the Templar Knights, was summoned to a Council at Troyes, to be chaired by the Cardinal Legate of France, and he left Jerusalem, writing: *The work has been fulfilled, and the Knights will journey through France and Burgundy, under the protection of the Count of Champagne, where all precautions will be taken.* The Court at Troyes was to perform extensive translation work on the Tables, having long sponsored a school in esoteric and Cabalistic studies in readiness.

They never got the chance. Somewhere en-route the Tables were stolen, and Alison was well aware that if Klein had this information in his hands, as he now did, then his next move would undoubtedly be to ensure not only that the tables *were* stolen, but that he and his messed-up sense of perpetuity were to be the reason why.

And there was no way to stop him. If she lied or changed the facts then Klein would simply uncover the fraud and set a new researcher onto the task. Then, over a period of time, he would ultimately 'put things right', having the ways and the means already at his disposal.

If Alison was to be the one to stop him, then on the face of it she was pretty much screwed. Klein would ultimately retrieve the one thing that no man should be allowed to possess; The Divine Laws of Number, Measure and Weight and there was nothing she could do to stop him. Nothing she could think of, at any rate.

Indeed Alison stayed screwed for quite a while; all through Tuesday night and all through Wednesday as she printed and bound Klein's new file. All until tonight, when she had decided that the direction her research had been taking needed to pull off the main highway and take a turn into previously uncharted territory. Territory for which Alison would now need to become both explorer and cartographer royal.

She had a logical mind, one of the best, and two things had stayed trapped within that mind of hers since she had become aware of them. Firstly, that Klein had searched 'all his life' for the Tables; his own words. Yet she herself, knowing Klein for a great many of those years, had never seen any evidence to that effect. Secondly, and more damningly, she had become aware from dated files that Klein had 'advised' on an archaeological dig in the Cardou area as far back as 2011.

Why? She thought. Why had Klein been advising on an archaeological dig in France? Had the Tables not been taken to France by Hugues de Payens in 1127? Had they not been stolen in France? What had Klein not been telling her? Could it be that, even as far back as 2011, Klein had somehow believed that he had found them?

If so, what went wrong? What, when and how?

Using government issue codes, she accessed every file she could relating to the 2011 dig. Klein, she discovered, had been heavily involved in the Cardou excavations from the discovery of a parchment in 1992 at the Abbaye Fontfroide in France. He had remained involved right through to June 2011 when he was called to Siberia to investigate an unrelated site of scientific importance there. The site had heralded the discovery of Siberium, hence the name. During his five days in Russia, however, an e-mail had been sent to Klein by his chief of Security at the Cardou site, General Peter Grier.

The e-mail read: 'Site empty but have located and intercepted what you seek. Stolen by LAPD detective and girl, now deceased. Tables in Los Angeles; to be transferred to Washington for decoding. Grier."

The site was closed. Klein never returned to Cardou.

Two years later, ownership of the Cardou site transferred to KleinWork Research Technologies, to be used for livestock research.

So, if Grier had 'intercepted' what Klein was looking for, and she could only assume (dangerous as assumption was) that it was a reference to the tables themselves, then why did Klein not have them now? Why was he still searching? There was no reference to where the items had been intercepted or how on earth an 'LAPD Detective and girl' had come about them in the first place, but Alison was hooked.

Suddenly, what happened in 1127 became irrelevant - that was solely Klein's problem - and what had happened in 2011 became very important indeed. Something about the events of those few days was the key to why Klein was still searching for his prize after all these years.

All she had to do was find out what.

Then, to quote Klein himself again, to put things right.

* * * * *

Beneath the main laboratory, in a subterranean level that many within KleinWork Research Technology were not even aware existed and would not have the genetic fingerprint to access even if they did, eight guards, four apiece, arrived to escort the men from their cells.

Two remained at the door, name-labelled buttons in their hands, a press of which would activate the red light on the steel bands the men wore around their wrists and ankles. Were such a situation to arise, guard-safe explosive devices detonating inwards would blow the hands and feet clean off the unlucky wearer. Technology, it seemed, had delivered instant coffee, instant micro-pizza and, more worryingly, instant incapacitation for those who did not play by the rules, no matter how messed up those rules might be.

The other six guards split into two sets of three, visored helmets and protective clothing disguising both their bodies and their identities. Calmly and in perfect synchronisation, they moved to their respective positions.

Two of the incarcerated men were told to rise from the bunks in their five-by-nines and turn so that their backs faced the bars; their hands held through. The armbands were clipped together with steel rods, keeping the men's arm and leg movements to a minimum should there be any failure on the part of the explosive devices.

When the shackles were in place the guards stepped backward and signalled to their colleagues at the door who input the codes which activated cell doors three and nine, the bars sliding down into the floor to release the men.

Michael Davies and Pierrot D'Almas, as personally selected by Josef Klein, were on their way.

"Where?" Davies asked. "Where we going?"

"Shut the fuck up, Davies," one of the guards said.

"Hey, fucker," D'Almas complained, his accent thick with Mardi Gras as he was pushed along faster than the shackles would allow. As a result the guard pushed him yet harder, causing him to stumble over his own feet.

Davies was made to wait three feet from the door until D'Almas, further along the corridor, caught up. Then both men stood together, surrounded, as one of the doormen explained the rules.

"You will not speak to anyone except a guard, which will only be in direct response to a question. Do everything you are instructed to do and you will be no trouble to us whatsoever. Disobey a direct instruction, regardless of the reason..." he held up the button, "...and you will become an instant quadriplegic. Do I make myself clear?"

Neither man nodded, but both understood. They looked to each other with puzzled expressions; two atheistic Christians pushed to the gates of the Coliseum. They knew why they were here, of course they did. Or, at least, they knew *some* of the reasons why they were here. But why did they need two of them? And why had they been led to the main door? Why not to the other end of the pale corridor where the lift would take them directly upstairs. That was where Castle had gone and, from what they had heard on the greasevine, he'd survived the trip as well.

One of the other guards had told them that, just to keep them quiet.

To their right as they were escorted from the room, a pair of dark eyes. Cold and leaden. Jeffrey Mason stood against the bars and scowled. Like Davies and D'Almas he wore the regulation red jump-suit; in his hand he held a steel cup from which he had long-since finished his coffee. It had been thick and black, like Stubbs in cell eleven he liked to think. It had also tasted of urine. Guard-piss.

This was the cleanest and most modern block Mason had ever served time in. High-tech. Pure white walls; clean, mirrored glass doors and almost disgustingly modern lighting. Yet the human element, that inescapable constant that seemed to follow him wherever his crimes took him, made this white place darker than hell itself. He hated the prospect of spending another day here more than he hated the certain knowledge that he had once served nine months of hard time in his bitch of a mother's womb.

He wanted out, and he really didn't care where that took him any more. Anywhere they told him to go. A man who had never cried in his life was almost bored to tears. So how come Davies, D'Almas and Castle had gotten out before him? Wasn't Mason good enough for them?

"What 'bout Mason, fuckers?" he shouted as though the whole sentence was one thick word poured from molasses. "Don't Mason get out of this fucking hell-hole as well? Why they get to go and not little old Mason?"

Nobody answered. In a few moments, all ten men were gone and the main door, a full length one-way mirror through which the corridor could be monitored twenty-four-seven, slid back into place with barely a whisper. The lights along the corridor, as was always the case, dimmed back to one-third strength. Mason threw the cup through the bars. It hit the mirror, not even causing a crack on the toughened surface, and clattered loudly around the corridor, disappearing into a darkened corner of three.

"Hey," he shouted again. "Don't go leavin' me 'lone with the fucking nigger."

"Keep it down, shithead," Stubbs shouted from eleven, out of sight. His voice echoed along the bleak walls behind the bars and made one angry man sound like three.

"Yeah...? Fuck you, nigger. Mason talking here." He looked back to the door and the image of the men who had gone, still fixed in his retina. When was he going to get the hell out of here? Quietly, almost under his breath, he said, "Fuckers."

And now, one of those images reflecting in Alison Bond's glasses, was the image of a man. An ageing, world weary man who had clearly not wanted his photograph taken. A man by the name of Detective Nick Lambert. A man who had, at the age of twenty-three joined the Los Angeles Police Department, becoming detective at twenty-eight. He had been married, divorcing in 2002 whereupon his ex-wife took their eight year old daughter to live with her and her new lover in Seattle. Since that point, the man's career had been on a steady slide. He had one or two notable successes over the following years, but his career ultimately reached a nadir from which it would never rise. In 2011 he was handed the task of investigating a Latin text discovered on the body of a dead man and travelled to see an inmate at an institution referred to as 'Oakdene'. Alison smiled to herself when she read this. Latin text. This was how Klein had been led to believe that this beloved tables had been found and intercepted.

Having done a complete search of V-2102 police records for the period June 2011, Alison eventually uncovered file BX9906808 detailing the death and subsequent investigation of the individual who had initially been in possession of the Latin. It was from this file that she had been made aware of Detective Nick Lambert.

And then she had seen the pictures; fifty-four in total. Some were of the crime scene itself, the man covered by a sheet as huge pools of blood seeped out onto the ground from beneath, others of the ensuing investigation. And some had been taken during the actual autopsy of the dead man.

For almost an hour she sat in front of the three screens and she thought hard; her superbly logical mind trying to piece together what had already happened. How it could have happened. Even for her it wasn't easy; this was an equation more complex than any she had ever faced in her life. The pieces were there, every last one of them, but understanding how and why they interacted was something different altogether.

She got up and made coffee, but it didn't help. Her eyes were still staring into nothing, knowing that somewhere out there was an answer which was eluding her. She knew the man in this picture, she had seen him herself, so why could she not work out what had actually happened to him?

And then it came; a flash far brighter than any she had seen in the sealed lab, and her mouth fell wide. "Oh sweet Jesus," she said, louder than intended, and she ran back to the screen, calling up yet another image. Now Alison Bond was smiling so wide and so broad that it actually hurt the jowls of her slender cheeks. She looked back at one of the screens and knew only one thing: that she had just realised *exactly* what was going to happen.

The man sneered back at her from this new image and, although caught and convicted only very recently, his features showed no remorse for the crimes listed beneath his name. His eyes, staring now from the screen, held no feeling other than some kind of unspoken knowledge. Not for anyone or anything. Only for himself.

That was the kind of man he must have been, she mused. Cold. He probably believed that he would live forever, spiritually at least, and his selection as part of the Sequence Project had only served to accentuate that belief.

Alison stared right back at him, her own smile also never falling. Because she had seen the autopsy pictures. All of them. She knew that this man's face belonged to each of them as much as it did this rap sheet. As such, she knew full well what would ultimately become of him, even if he was telling the guards just how great he was across town even now.

"Somebody's gonna find you dead very soon, aren't they?" she asked the picture, leaning right toward the screen with narrowed, knowing eyes of her own. She smiled at the word 'soon'. Because this had already happened. A very long time ago.

Oh, they would find him dead alright, the autopsy pictures told her that much. Dead as his eyes. She smiled and sipped at her coffee, voicing his name gently to herself. The words were formed around a smile and kept apart by small silences of self congratulation.

"Jeffrey. Fucking. Mason."

TWENTY-SEVEN

SATURDAY, JUNE 11, 2011.
EN-ROUTE TO FRANCE.

I hate flying. I cannot emphasise that enough. Always have. And it's not the take-off and landing either which, statistically, is the portion of the flight most likely to end in death - a period of time representing only 4% of the total flight. The closer the plane got to the ground and the faster it did so - within reason - the happier I would be.

What I couldn't stomach was the knowledge that, as I looked down at my feet, there were only a few half-inch thick metal plates between the soles of my shoes, 35,000 feet and eight and a half lingering minutes of certain death, during which - in any conscious moments offered me - I would undoubtedly embarrass what would soon be my corpse in far more ways than simply screaming my head off.

The seat belt lights went off, the seatbelt stayed on and I ordered a drink. Sarah idly added half-and-half to her coffee and said, "So... why aren't you a good detective, detective?"

I narrowed my eyes without looking directly at her.

"In the car last night. You said you weren't a good detective. You said that you got the shitty jobs because it wouldn't matter if you messed things up. So...? Why do you mess things up?"

I looked at my drink. The reason was swirling around the glass. "I just do."

She leaned closer. "There has to be a reason. I mean, you said you'd been a detective since you were twenty-eight. I'm guessing you can't always have been crap at it."

"I wasn't."

"So what changed?"

"Things."

"What kind of things?"

"I don't know," I said. Though in reality I knew exactly what had changed. "Everything I guess."

She dipped her head. "Define *everything*."

I shook my head. "The job changed. It got too quick... too, I dunno, *technical*... and I have absolutely no idea how a modern police department works; no knowledge of... computers... or systems" I turned to face her. "You know, we have a system called ViCAP. It's fantastic, apparently. It gathers nationwide information and kind of, I don't know, puts it together into one big file. Me? I have no idea how to access this thing."

"You mean a database?" Sarah said.

"There," I said. "See what I mean? What the hell is a database anyway? How on earth does it work?" I sighed again. "I'm not what they want any more and its starting to work both ways. I get my results through instinct and hard work. I don't get a computer to sift through files for me. It might miss something. And, do you know what...? I don't *want* to change. If I'm a cliché, then so be it. Leave me be until I can claim my pension."

"Sounds to me like you stopped trying."

I sighed. "Maybe so."

She turned to face me with a 'spill it' expression. "So what was it that made you stop trying?"

"You ask way too many questions."

"I know,' she replied, 'throwing a knowing'. "And you give way too few answers."

I sighed. "It's a long story."

She mimicked the sigh. "It's a long flight."

There are times in any human existence when people simply do not want to talk.

There are other times where they have no option but to talk. It's a kind of 'now or never' thing. Those are the awkward scenes in life's play, quite often played out in front of a parent or loved one whereby an individual simply swallows what little pride life has allowed them to retain and starts blabbing it out as coherently as possible. Such conversations can involve phrases such as 'I'm gay', 'I like to dress up in women's clothing' or even 'I have a thing about squirrels, but it isn't pretty'. Often salient points are left out in order to soften the blow. Such as telling your mother (or loved one) that her underwear is more comfortable than any available in the shops.

Such times in life, I guess, make you feel better because they convince you that ultimately you were left with little or no choice in the matter. You just have to take the baton and run with it.

"My wife left me." I finished my drink and beckoned for the stewardess.

"Why?"

And now I really did have to be honest with her; not least because the stewardess, trolley wobbling ahead of her, was already three quarters of the way up the aisle. "Because I started drinking."

"And why did you start drinking?"

Christ, did she ever give up?

I looked straight at her and could see that she knew damn well that she was probing me. I could also see that no, she wasn't going to give up. Not until I spilled every last sorry detail.

"Why do you care?" I said with a sigh. Why would anyone care?

She smiled. "Because of who you are."

"And who am I exactly?"

She smiled an odd smile, as if she genuinely knew something that I didn't. "Oh, that's for you to find out." Then she stared right at me. Right into me. "Come on, Nick, tell me why you started drinking...?"

She was right, it was a long flight. And by the time we landed it had seemed even longer. Because there were things in my life I had never discussed. Not with anyone. Not whilst I was sober at any rate.

Yet on that flight, to Sarah, I did discuss them. I don't know why, or what it was about her that allowed her to pull them from me like bad teeth, but she did. All she forgot to do was tell me to relax and gargle, and that it wouldn't hurt a bit. But it did hurt. It always did. So much so that generally I needed an anaesthetic. Or two, or three. Straight up, with ice.

"I was on a case. Long time ago. A girl died."

"And it was your fault?"

I smiled at that, though I'm not sure why. I guess it was just the fact that somebody was finally voicing something that I had kept to myself for many years. Too many perhaps. "Yes it was,"

I said eventually. "Very much so."

Three days after my twenty-ninth birthday, less than a year into my new role as detective, I had a drugs case. No surprises there. In those days, and in the Wholesale District generally, I guess most of them were. We'd studied the guy, a smart-assed young Puerto Rican by the name of Freddy Casparo, for over five weeks. We knew his territory better than he did and, more to the point, we knew when and how he travelled through it. On the morning of 15th March we knew he'd be carrying; not his biggest load, but enough to send him away for seven to ten.

Things didn't go to plan, though I guess that such trivialities had stopped hitting me by surprise a long time ago. Casparo, unbeknown to us, was flying to Mexico that evening. Why he was going was of little importance at the time, but what was important was that he had, for the first time in those five weeks, moved his schedule forward to the tune of three hours. Each of his subs knew, and each were prepared, but our line of informants didn't run as deep as we would have liked.

Fifteen officers, myself included, were sitting in unmarked cars at carefully spaced intervals waiting for a man who had already been and gone; would-be passengers waiting at a long-dead rail-line. Almost an hour after he was supposed to walk right into our hands, we gave up and went home.

Myself; I went and parked my butt under the shade of the red, white and green canopy of Gray's, the Italian-American Deli on the corner of Alameda and 4th. In order to feel a little better about the whole damn thing I subsequently ordered a cappucino and a pastrami on rye. I was due in court at midday so there was no point, I'd convinced myself, in fighting the traffic back to the precinct only to set off again maybe fifteen minutes later. So I sat, and I ate, and I cursed Casparo.

This was the kind of fiasco that wouldn't be sitting well at the lunch meeting of Deputy Chief David who headed Operations. He would have to explain to Perkins, our short-sighted wood-for-the-trees Chief of Police, why so many officers had been removed from normal duty for a total of four hours and why they'd come back from the market without so much as a handful of magic beans.

Which meant, if you pulled it right back to the nuts and twisted, that David would probably be told to shove a hot spike up his ass and sing 'Hello Dolly' the next time he even considered requesting extra personnel. Short of stumbling upon Casparo carrying four of five keys of Colombian in the lining of his trademark Armani, he was off the hook. For now.

Which is almost exactly what happened. Except it wasn't in the lining of his jacket. It was laid very neatly in a smart brown Berrick briefcase. And it wasn't Colombian, it was American. I just didn't know that yet.

So there I was drinking coffee, and I just glanced up. Like people do. Bang. The slimy bastard just walks straight past me, less than three feet away, with not a care in the world. In one hand he's got a cellphone pressed to his ear, in the other he's got the case. I only heard a fraction of his conversation but it was enough to get a smart-assed hothead like me onto my feet. *Relax, Carlo, I god-dit. Wit' me now; m'on my way.* I finished the last mouthful of coffee, just to place a few pedestrians between the two of us, then I too was on my way.

He walked, or rather strutted in the way that arrogant young shits like him do, along Alameda toward Produce. My choice was simple: follow him and bust him with the case or sit in a draughty courtroom and watch another half-hour bail hearing presided over by yet another Judge Judy wannabe. If you've ever attended a bail hearing, further weighted into the creamy depths of boredom with the kind of caring family man bullshit that they think will buy them more time on the streets, you'll realise just how easy a decision this was to make. So I kept my pace and I kept it even; no more than six and no less than four behind the jumped-up coke-shifting little bastard.

Until I saw the Porsche up ahead, hood down and driver's-side mirror glinting from behind a dark blue box-van. Silver late-model 911, black hood. Just like they'd told us at the briefing.

It hit me like a bullet. If he gets in the car he goes and if he goes then, just like that morning, I get nothing. Zip. Zilch. So as he got closer to the car, I decided to make a move, call a bluff. I moved out, walked roadside along the length of the van and took my position by the passenger window. Casparo slid in, placed the case on the passenger seat and stared right into the dark tunnel of my snub-nosed .357.

"Morning, shithead."

His pock-marked face curled and looked at me like I was scum. "Hey! Who da fucka you?". Anger. Defiance. But within it, hidden from all but his voice was something else; something our Casparo did *not* want to feel: *fear*. Goddamned piece of shit thought i was here to deliver a bullet on behalf of one of the many he'd no doubt screwed over in his time.

I pulled my badge with my free left hand and held it over the sill. "Keys on the seat, hands on the wheel."

And the son of a bitch *relaxed*. I mean, do you believe that? Like... *hey... it's okay... it's only the cops or something.*

"Open the case," I said. Slowly.

"You said hands on da..."

"Open the God-damned case, you little shit. Now!"

He moved slowly, just like instinct told him he should. "Hey, *little shit*," he mimicked, then turned to me looking all serious. "Now dat hurtin me bad, 'tective. Dat gettin' me right dere, y'know." He banged his fist on his chest, then moved to open the case. The latches slid with a loud thwap and he eased up the lid. Let it be Columbian, I thought. Please God, let it be coke.

But it wasn't Colombian. It was American. All of it. Washington, Lincoln and Jackson all counted out and laid in neat little bundles. Must've been fifty-k at least. I tried not to let it show but inside I was shouting 'fuck' over and over like it was the only word left in the dictionary. *Fuck, fuck, fuck. I am so... very... fucked.*

Casparo voiced what I already knew. "Cash, 'tective. Cold, hard cash. Hey, whaddayou expect? Drugs or sumptin? Nah, just some little money. I sell my car today so I have all... dis... money."

"You're sitting in your car, shithead."

He shook his head in mock dismay. "Ooh, now *shithead*. Dat *definitely* not nice. You see, I sell my odder car, 'tective. My 'cedes. Now you can 'rest me if you want, but I get da sale papers sent down by my law-ya. You see, I on a flight at three and you know...? I be out in time to catch it. So whadda we do, hey?"

He reached into the case, careful that I could still see both his hands, and picked up one of the wads which he then wedged into my breast pocket. You get that? He wedged it in my pocket. And I didn't stop him.

"You a good 'tective, I can see dat. And you know you ain't got nottin'. So what you say I just start my car; drive away now, 'cos we is bot' wastin' time, yeah?"

Two solid gold teeth glinted in the light. "You get your girl sumtin' nice, 'tective, 'cos we both know this..." he gestured around, "this never even happen."

The wad was a thousand, bang on. I know that because I took it. Hear that? I took it. And Casparo drove away.

I tried to convince myself that he was right, that I had nothing on him but the money and that it simply wasn't enough. Sure, any forensic scan would have shown traces of coke on the money but only because, as defence would so clearly point out - though I doubted it would even get that far - ninety-five percent of U.S. currency has traces of coke on it. The car sale documents would have been put together within the hour and I'd have been the laughing stock when Casparo walked.

So why the did I keep the money? Sure, I got my girl *sumtin' nice*, but it wasn't Katherine. Hell, no. Instead I got a game console for Vicki.

Over the next few months I pretty much drank the rest.

Am I proud? Hell, no. *Would I do it again?* Never. But I did... once... and whether that actually makes me dirty or not, it sure as hell makes me feel that way.

Feeling dirty was bad enough, but that was nothing when you stood it beside the things that followed. Because it seems Casparo got home in a real foul mood that night. Maybe I was to blame for that or maybe he was just the kind of guy who blew off regular, I don't want to know. Either way he launched into one steamer of a row with 'his girl', a twenty-three year old called Monica. She was young, very young and a real looker from the pictures. *A good looking kid.*

So they rowed and they fought and they screamed at each other in that way that 'Ricans do sometimes, fiery Latino and all that. Then, in the midst of this very audible fight, Casparo was seen walking angrily out to his car, where he retrieved what neighbours described as something that looked like a gun. Then he went back inside and dropped her with three shots. Bang, bang, bang, dead. Quick as that. Bad enough for ya?

Well, young Monica was eight months pregnant as well. They'd bought the crib and everything. I tried to convince myself that maybe that was why they'd rowed. That it had nothing to do with me putting a rocket up his ass and giving him the kind of fear that had made him feel as embarrassed as if his Ma had caught him with his dick in his hands. I mean, given Casparo's reputation as *one for the ladies* he won't have liked the idea of being tied permanently to one girl, not a bit. But his Latino honour would have demanded it. Credit to Casparo, though, he felt bad for what he'd done afterward. Bad enough to let himself take one of the three remaining bullets anyway. Upward; through the chin.

Now either you choose to see me as fatally flawed or simply human, that's up to you. But I don't honestly think there's anything I haven't screwed up at some point. My career, my marriage, too many cases to mention (though I had the odd success) and yes, even Vicki. That beautiful twenty-five year old daughter of mine? Therapy. Shrink reckons she has a deep seated crisis of self-worth and an inherent distrust of men, probably stemming from early childhood or some such crap. Stemming from when I was her dad. Or rather from when I was the man who was supposed to be her dad but simply never managed to be home long enough, even before Jack's intervention. I just know that who she is - *everything* she is - is my fault somewhere along the way, that's all.

I should have checked the car, found the gun and taken Casparo and his smart-ass comments somewhere where they might have had an appreciative audience. Like a cell. I should have spat on his dirty money, thrown it back in his face and thrown him over good and proper. But I didn't. I let him go and the girl died.

There was no need for her, or her child, to die.

I knew nothing of what happened until I read the paper the next morning. Pictures of Casparo (little inset of Monica). And details. Lots and lots of details.

I didn't want details, not the kind that explain that she fell backward and police found her lying across the baby's crib, blood from her stomach, from her unborn child, dripping on to the cold white sheets.

Like I say, the paper printed a picture of her. Just so that I would never forget it. Has a day passed since that I've woken up without seeing that face? Not one.

"And that's when the drinking started?" Sarah asked. Gentle, sure, but with the same unbridled hint of probing.

I nodded. "Pretty much. It makes it easier."

"Makes what easier?"

I laughed quietly to myself. "Being me? Convincing myself that it wasn't my fault? Both? I'm no alcoholic, I still function. I just find that I function that bit better with a little help, that's all."

"Your wife couldn't hack the new you?"

"No," I said. "And I don't blame her. First I started coming home late, then I started coming home drunk. Eventually it got so that I'd got the two cuffed together and it was the only state she and Vicki ever saw me in."

I thought for a moment, then tried to laugh it all away. I failed.

"Talking of which I need another," I said. "After all, I need something to liven up this pitiful existence, don't I?"

I smiled, just to let her know I was joking on at least one level, then signalled once again for the stewardess.

Sarah didn't say anything. Not a word. The stewardess arrived once more and handed me a chastising look, another glass of ice, one more of those little square soaky-up things and my third whisky miniature.

I grabbed another two from her trolley. Save her a trip.

When she had gone, Sarah leaned back in her chair and relaxed. Without turning to me, almost as if talking to herself, she said; "You know something, Nick? The real beauty of your existence is that – as yet – you have absolutely no idea just how unbelievably important it actually is."

TWENTY-EIGHT

SATURDAY, JUNE 11, 2011.
SERRES, PERPIGNAN, FRANCE.

They knew damn well that we'd flown to France.

I know that *now*, I just didn't know it *then*, that was all.

Save for more detailed forays into the pre- and post-Casparo world I inhabited and more detailed, weird, fascinating and somewhat far-fetched explanations of Tina's gift, I pretty much slept most of the way.

With time differences and connections we landed in Salvaza, Carcassonne's tiny airport, around eleven o'clock the following morning where I rented a car from the Europcar desk. It was a small, brown, ugly Fiat thing and an absolute pig to drive, but it had both a sunroof and windows that worked. After a bite to eat overlooking the sixteenth century ruins of Notre-Dame-de-la-Santé, we headed south along the D-118.

Away from the city and without the blood-flow of electric lighting to feed its course, the dual freeway eventually withered into a tiny road. We made the turn east at Couiza and, for the final ten kilometres to Serres, drove through tight valleys of rich green hills and vineyards, rich with the kind of beauty I'd only ever seen once before. In a book.

Throughout the drive, Sarah leaned quietly and thoughtfully

against the frame, as she had on the way to Oakdene, and watched the world go by with her eyes hidden by the same enigmatic sunglasses, loose strands of hair blowing in the wind and that ever-present all-knowing smile. By one-thirty we were covering the last straight and approaching the half kilometre side road that led into Serres itself.

I flipped the indicator, but Sarah leaned across and flipped it back up. "Not yet," she said. "Keep driving."

Seconds later the turn appeared and, just as swiftly, it was gone again. "We're not going to Serres?" I asked.

"Soon," she said. She turned to me with a knowing smile. "There's someone I'd like you to meet first."

We continued along the main road, not stopping until we reached the town of 'Arques', announced by a small black and white sign desperately losing a fight against vegetation some six kilometres further on. The keep of a large Gothic chateau looked down from the hills to the left as we entered, Sarah directing me to pull up on a main street bordered by tatty craft shops, all seemingly selling pretty much the same very poorly hand-crafted souvenir.

We climbed out of the Fiat and with a nod of her head she walked purposefully towards a tiny stone frontage, a large black sign hanging from a pole which read 'Bar Roché'. Next door was a similar stone building which, in both French and English, announced itself as the birthplace of Déodat Roché, a 'prominent Cathar historian'.

A few metres down the hill a group of student tourists, perhaps eight or nine in total, clustered in a doorway with coloured backpacks firmly in place as one tried in vain to decipher a map. They appeared to be the only people in town as both the streets and the air felt unnervingly still.

Sarah headed through the open door of the bar without slowing her pace and, with a swift glance at the students, I followed, ducking to clear a beam. Inside was the kind of gloom that normally suggests deserted, with only the weakest of orange wall lights, two of which seemed not to be working to full strength. The ceiling was low and the walls bare stone, just a few framed etchings of the old town arranged at carefully spaced intervals to add any life.

There was only one other patron; a blonde girl in her late twenties. She looked like yet another student, albeit a mature one, but she didn't bother to look up. Instead she continued reading a copy of *Le Monde* spread wide and drinking bottled beer whilst an obese barman with convex red cheeks and a large white apron looked bored and cleaned glasses that were probably spotless at least an hour ago.

He stepped forward with a half-smile and Sarah, in French, ordered two beers. After paying in Euros, she led me to one of the enclosed booths which hugged the right hand wall, away from the window but still close enough for her to look out across the street; which she did. Endlessly. Silently she watched and waited, hushing me each time I made an attempt to speak and sipping beer as though it were not even there.

The group of students came back into view and she looked each one up and down. They, having presumably deciphered their map, or at least figured out which way up it should go, were now heading along steep cobbles to our right. In a few moments they were gone again, the view through the tiny panes as empty as it had been before. Whoever it was Sarah had wanted me to meet, they sure as hell weren't here yet.

After three or four more interminable minutes, Sarah coughed, the way one might to catch someone's attention, and the student girl at the bar turned, but not to us. She too glanced anxiously toward the street, then carefully folded the paper and came over to the booth. She sat down without a word and laid the paper on the table in front of her.

"This is Kelly Brown," Sarah said, introducing the girl with a lowered voice. "She's a photographer."

"From the U.S. Dig?"

The girl ignored my question and looked suspiciously at Sarah. "Who's this?" she said bluntly, nodding in my direction without ever actually looking at me.

"He's good." Sarah said, then turned to me, her voice still lowered. "Kelly is a friend of mine. She's freelancing for *National Geographic*, but her pictures can only be published when and if they find something. She gets a little... *twitchy*."

Kelly scowled and took a swig of her beer. She was perhaps twenty-seven or twenty eight years old with a heavy tan and she wore no make up. Her hair was pulled into a short pony tail, sunglasses resting on top and her expression cold and hard. It was deliberate, I sensed, designed to give the impression that she really wasn't the kind of person to be fucked with. Something about her overall look told me she probably was - if taken a little more literally.

From between the pages of the now-folded *Le Monde* she slid a small brown envelope in Sarah's direction. I presumed these were the pictures she fed Sarah, similar to the ones I'd already seen on her computer.

"Kid yourself I'm a friend all you like, sweetheart," she said, "but anything on that disk get out and I ain't never seen you before in my life. Bet your ass on that."

Sarah smiled and pulled a much smaller envelope from her rucksack and slid it back. In an instant it took the now empty space between the pages of the newspaper.

"So what's new up there?" she asked.

Kelly's face stayed cold. "Not much," she said, placing the bottle down hard on the wooden surface. "They still haven't found anything and trust me, they're getting *real* pissed off about that. Skull's nearly up. Meantime, Klein disappeared in a chopper a couple of days ago, some big find in Russia or something. Don't know when or if he'll be back. Grier still comes and goes as he pleases, like he does, and I'm damn sure tweedle-dum and tweedle-dee are up to something."

She shook her head knowingly.

Sarah leaned forward, interested. "Such as?"

Kelly shrugged. "Dunno, but Grier's been getting real edgy over security of late and the tweedles have been clocking some serious mileage. They've been over in the states last few days, landed back this morning and now it's all real hush-hush and shit. I don't like it, whatever it is. I think I might even need to pull back a little. Just 'til the heat's off"

Sarah nodded. "Probably best," she said.

"How's Tina?" Kelly asked, though there was no real concern in her voice. Or maybe there was but she'd gone to great lengths to ensure that she didn't show it. I wondered how and why she knew of Sarah's sister.

Sarah smiled. "She's great, thanks."

Kelly nodded. "Give her my love, yeah?"

"Always do," Sarah said.

"Anyway," Kelly said, finishing her beer. "I'm outta here. Anything big crops up and I'll try to get word, but don't expect to hear from me otherwise. I'm gonna be a real good girl 'til I know what the hell's goin' on up there."

She stood to leave.

"Kelly," Sarah called after her. She turned. "You be careful, eh?"

"Always do," Kelly replied, deliberately emulating Sarah. With a quick flick of the eyes she pulled her sunglasses down and disappeared out into the brightly sunlit street.

Sarah ran her finger up and down her bottle, small pools of condensation collecting along her finger. "Kelly's one of the best photo-j's going. I know she can be a bit abrasive but she's cool with it," she said.

"So she gets you pictures and you pay her?" I asked. I took s quick drink of my beer.

Sarah shook her head vehemently. "I don't *pay* her. She does it as a favour."

"The envelope," I said. "I presumed that was..."

"Ah," she said, her finger waving chastisingly in the air. "You *presumed*. What the hell kind of detective are you anyway?"

"So what was in the envelope?" I asked.

"A letter."

"From?"

"From the reason I know Kelly," she explained. "And the reason she knows Tina. We met about a year ago when she was still at the *Tribune*. Her mother's at Oakdene; been there for about eight years. Altzeimers. Some days good, some not so good."

I noticed that, like many who have sick relatives, she avoided using the word 'bad'.

Nothing was ever bad, just 'not so good'.

"Thing is, that's also one of the reasons I'm not too enamoured with our Mister Creed. See, Kelly once told me to be very careful when writing to Tina and vice versa, because if a letter enters or leaves that place and he doesn't like what's in it..."

"He... *opens* them?"

She nodded. "Oh, yeah. And if it mentions him, or any of his dirty little scams, then it somehow manages to gets lost in the mail. Kelly reckons she'll do a feature one of these days; open the box and expose the slimy little shit for what he is."

She opened the envelope she had been given and pulled out a memory card for a digital camera, protected in a clear plastic case, and placed it in one of the smaller pockets of her rucksack. Then she removed a smaller cream envelope; bond quality. On the face, in a neat script of deep blue ink, it said simply 'Ma'.

"So, if I'm ever over this way, I act as a kind of unofficial two-way courier."

"And is that often?" I asked, probing.

"Every couple of months," she said. She knew I was probing.

"She feels she owes you?"

"Perhaps, but if so then it's more to do with something else. When we met and got to talking, she told me that she was thinking about branching out from the *Tribune* and going freelance. She said that she knew the picture editor at *National Geographic* and that he'd promised her a break if she came up with anything good. So I kind of...."

"Let slip about an important archaeological dig in France?" I was nodding in admiration.

She smiled at my intuition, limited as it was.

"Well, I might have suggested that there was one, yeah. And that it had government funding. I might even have suggested she get in touch. Just to see if she might secure an exclusive."

"And they agreed?"

"Klein did," she said, nodding. "He loves publicity; positively thrives on it. Obviously, he told her she'd have to keep everything under wraps until 'the discovery', but once they found something, and he was damned sure they would, then she would have kept a complete photo-record for them. Shit like that can make for good P.R. after the event."

She stared forward for a few minutes, her mind on a pilgrimage. She looked worried.

"Grier, on the other hand, positively *hates* the fact that Kelly's there, always has. If it was up to him that site would be tighter than a virgin's knickers. He's been waiting a long, long time to catch her out."

"You think he will?"

"Already has," she said. She sighed deeply. "Kelly just doesn't know it yet, that's all."

I didn't need to be a detective, not even a piss-poor one, to see that whatever Sarah had meant by that, she was already blaming herself for it. She looked straight at me, her face unnaturally devoid of emotion.

"Sometimes, whether you like it or not, Nick, you have to face up to the things you've done," she said.

"Before it's too late."

TWENTY-NINE

Standing in just under five hundred hectares of open fields, hills and outcrops of blackened rock, what remained of KleinWork's European Livestock Research Centre looked exactly as it was supposed to; abandoned. For fifteen miles in every direction the fields, owned entirely by KRT's European subsidiary, were empty save for a low mist which clung to the rich green, covering the entire site like an off-white sheet thrown over a dead man's body.

There were things in His world that not even God took pleasure in seeing.

Outside the single-story roughened stone building, rain glistening from the dark tiles which lined the roof, was a solitary vehicle; the four-wheel drive which belonged to Klein and his team. There was no sound, but there had been, and recently. Minutes earlier a scream had flowed from the building and chased across the fields as though escaping some unknown fate. It was the kind of scream the world at large had never heard, had prayed they never would.

★ ★ ★ ★ ★

Another vehicle, one that had been parked outside the ELRC building for most of the morning, was now gone.

It was now parked three and a half kilometres away; in Serres. And now, following radio clearance, Kerr was standing in a light rain, knee deep in

288

wet grass in a graveyard at the uppermost edge of the town. A red laptop case was slung over his shoulder as he watched the guard dig into the hard ground. The guard who had, that same morning, been one of three to escort D'Almas into the chamber.

The mound of heavy soil, saturated near black, was growing larger by the minute to his left and his laboured breaths were becoming more and more audible in the isolation which surrounded them.

Back at the centre as Rachael, the Sequence operator flown in from Los Angeles to run the newly constructed lab, continued to check the readings, Sherman continued to pace the adjoining room. Surrounded by empty white desking, he was growing increasingly impatient.

"How long can it take to dig up a grave?" he said, to nobody in particular. He turned defiantly to Klein. "This had better work."

Klein, still seated in his chair, stared through the tiny window and smiled to himself. "Your problem, Dave, is you have no faith."

Sherman sneered. "Yeah? Sometimes, Josef, you have a little too much."

Klein was in no mood for discarnate semantics. In the end he simply said; "It'll work."

Because it would.

The guard's spade hit something hard.

"I think we're there, sir," he said.

Kerr smiled, pulled the radio from his belt clip and reported in. The guard, standing knee-deep in the hole he had dug, turned the spade upright and thrust hard down into the remaining centimetre of soil, the aged wood of the coffin cracking like an eggshell with the force.

"Jee...sus Christ," Kerr said, turning away with head down. "That reeks."

The guard turned puce, as though ready to retch. With one arm now held decisively across his nose, he reached down with the other and, one by one, broke a few more slivers of wood. Then he reached inside with a gloved hand and felt around. Nothing.

"Keep looking," Kerr said, now standing well back from the smell.

The guard kept fumbling, periodically trying to catch his breath whilst inhaling as little as possible, and pulling even more of the wood away, throwing it up so that it landed on the mound of soil. Inside felt soft, mushy and strangely warm. The kind of warmth that walks hand in hand with the biology of decay.

Eventually he said, "I got something."

"Get it out," Kerr said, walking to a long-felled tree stump, opening the case and laying the computer down.

A little under a minute later the guard climbed from the hole, retching, filthy and carrying a metal case. Kerr fought for a moment to open it with his fingers then suggested angrily that the guard might like to bring the spade. With a few hits at the seam the case split open, corroded metal flaking like dark confetti to the floor. Kerr reached inside.

Carefully he lifted a rolled-up parchment, dirty and held by a deep red ribbon. As he pulled at the bow the ribbon all-but disintegrated in his hand, the parchment falling open. And he smiled when he read the base and saw the sketch of the tattoo. This was from D'Almas alright, no doubt about it.

Klein, the bastard, had actually pulled it off.

He laid the parchment flat, unclipped his touch-phone and, with a swift on-screen selection, passed it over the parchment's aged surface, scanning in the handwritten text. Then he hit send and waited.

The secure, heavily encrypted connection went straight to Sherman's own phone, a small 'ping' alerting him to the fact that the message he was waiting for had finally arrived. He looked to Klein, who smiled.

"I think that's for us," the old man said.

Klein wheeled himself over as Sherman called the image on screen. Every detail, every nuance, had been caught by the scanner, including the mark of a fingertip, no visible ridges, just in case there should be any doubt. Klein, his voice showing the stresses of his condition and his journey, read the text aloud.

Despite the fact that D'Almas had performed his task well and included a great deal of detail, the main facts Klein needed were actually embedded in only the first and last paragraphs;

1307 not 1311! Three Templer (sic) friends. Tables taken from Jerusalem to Troyes in 1132. Stolen on the way, possibly during stopover Narbonne late year, October or November, but no-one knows for sure. Stayed at 'main inn in town' for one night and tables will have been heavily guarded. Best estimate ten men on waking duty through night. Will have been in wooden box with Templer cross - here D'Almas had included a crude sketch of the cross in question - Tables not reached Troyes and no-one in Templers heard of them since. Friends suspect that I ask so many questions but was nearly two hundred years ago so I guess should be ok.

The following two paragraphs detailed various Templar traditions and other items he had been made aware of that had been in their possession after the Jerusalem raid.

The final paragraph related to the burial sites:

This grave second only in graveyard (hence 1311 on stone). No graves here until 1309. Had to wait four years for any suitible (sic) funeral (two people). Buried this following day. Have done what required but no-where to bury here until 1309 earliest. Am told that first church built 850AD. Church different to yours, though structure same so probably renewvated (sic) and altar now is same as yours so may be original?

I am free man, yes? Have a shit life.

Klein ran his finger over the screen, tracing the crude sketch of D'Almas' prison tattoo.

"We did it," he said quietly. "We actually did it."

Sherman was already nodding. "So what now? Do we brief Davies?"

Klein nodded. "Indeed we do."

THIRTY
SATURDAY, JUNE 11, 2011.
SERRES, PERPIGNAN, FRANCE.

I think about Sarah all the time.

These past few years I've really missed her.

I find it embarrassingly difficult – even today – to put into words the kind of man I had become in the years before we met. I was hollow, empty. Clichéd words I know, but I'm nothing if not a clichéd man. Even then I recognised my shortcomings, but I had no real desire to accept any business cards or to give them a call with a view to sorting things out. I just let my life flow over me, took everything one day at a time. Then, as often as not, I either headed for the 'rooftop garden' or to Cody's, drank enough to blot the day from my short-term memory and repeated the process the following morning with an open – for which read dampened – mind.

What I despised most about myself back then, if I'm honest, was not the whole Casparo thing, or the drinking that made me a shit or even losing Katherine and Vicki as a result. What really hurt – what cut me deepest inside – was the fact that I was alone through failure and, worse still, that I not only felt it but also knew that it would be a state of affairs that would probably continue the rest of my natural life. I knew that I'd messed up. If I had trusted myself not to mess up again (which I didn't) then I might have made some effort to right the wrongs of the past, instead of which I pushed people as far away from me as I could, especially those I truly cared about. My fear was that they might somehow get their feet caught in my belt loops at whatever point it was that I lost my grip on who I was and then - inevitably - get dragged down with me.

I had given up, quite simply, because whilst I knew that tomorrow was indeed another day, I also knew that I would still be the same person trapped within it and I figured I lacked the strength - physical or otherwise - to fight against my own shortcomings. When every result is the same, every conclusion forgone, and you feel age creeping into your limbs, you really do get so that you stop attending the training sessions that full participation in the human race requires. You start looking forward to the day when you stop being asked to turn up for the race at all.

Which is why what I remember most about Sarah, aside from her infectious knowledge and wide-eyed passion, was the very subtle way in which she somehow brought me back from the dead. I guess she understood, as I do now, that a crash-bang-wallop start invariably ends the same way. She didn't want to start a fire inside me. Well, not just any old fire. She wanted to start a campfire; something that would burn slower and longer. Something not only to keep me warm, but alive. So she let the tinder take before she threw the bigger sticks on.

She had some logs waiting - big gnarly ones – but she was saving those until she could leave me to tend the fire on my own. By which time, let me tell you, the fire in my bloated and clichéd belly had really gotten going.

Which is my long-winded and rather less than eloquent way of explaining to you that Sarah Fiddes did everything in her power to piss me off.

At the time.

In less than two days she had managed to extricate feelings of guilt from me not only for my daughter, which were known but never discussed, but also those for Monica, Casparo's girl. Nobody – and I do mean nobody – has ever managed to do that, before or since. In fact, nobody but Sarah even knew that I'd even seen Casparo that day, let alone taken the cash. Worse still, with those few words, sometimes, whether you like it or not, you just have to face up to the things you've done, she'd managed to make me feel like shit about both.

I hated her for that.

Sarah spotted, and very considerately chose to point out, that the one thing I was not doing, or had ever done, was facing up to the way the world had changed around me.

It wasn't that I'd given up on something, more that I'd never bothered starting it in the first place.

The fact that it had taken a girl almost eighteen years my junior to point out my failures, one who hadn't known me long enough to even begin to understand, made me angry.

Not angry with Sarah. I tried that, but it didn't seem to sit right.

Just angry with myself then.

Which didn't, incidentally, mean that I was suddenly and miraculously going to change overnight; take responsibility for the way my life had gone and go running off on some desperate quest to put things right. As far as I was concerned way too much water had passed under the bridges I'd been burning and

I honestly didn't think I had the strength anyway, but she did set me thinking. And that, 'whether I liked it or not', is what I did all the way from Arques to Serres.

I just thought.

There really is a first time for everything.

I didn't give too many neurons over to young Monica, to be honest, save to accept that her death had ultimately been where it had all started, but I did think very long and hard about my daughter; Vicki. The last time I had spoken with her was almost a year ago when I called to wish her a happy eighteenth.

Almost a year ago. Three hundred and sixty something days. And if that wasn't bad enough, it had been closer to three years since I had actually seen her face. Three hundred and sixty something multiplied by three.

I'd tried kidding myself that Seattle was a long way away. Which it was. But I think we both know, you and I, that it was me who was too far away, not Seattle.

During that last call, on the phone, and right after I had wished her happy birthday and offered more false promises about seeing her soon, she had told me that she had to go; that she'd put her mother on instead.

I didn't want her to do that. I almost begged her not to do that.

She put her mother on.

Katherine and I rowed. Again. For a great number of reasons, but primarily because Vicki was not only seeing a therapist now, something of which I was already painfully aware, but she had also seen fit to drop herself out of college as well.

Katherine said that, little by little, Vicki was spiralling out of control. You know the sort of thing; hanging with the wrong crowd and bringing home another messed up priority every night of the week. And though Katherine never once said it, at least not in so many words or to my face, she fairly well insinuated that all this, despite a ten year period of me not actually being there, was all my fault. Which in many ways was typical of Katherine; always one to pass the buck, but in many ways was also true. Vicki had been steadily going off the rails since a young age. She'd been disruptive at school, abusive to her mother and the good dentist and had recently started dressing 'kinda weird' and having things pierced that God, if he existed in her world, did not intend his beloved children to puncture.

I knew the truth just as well as Katherine did. The reason we fought was that I just didn't like being reminded that it was my fault, that was all. Vicki hadn't been going off the rails 'since a young age', it was far more specific than that. She'd been going off the rails since the day her father messed his existence up and set her on the road to throwing what was left of hers away.

One day, whether I liked it or not, I might just have to face up to that.

As we arrived at Serres, I managed to wrench hard at my thoughts and turn them toward something more positive – like just how unbelievably easy this task would prove to be.

Serres, this historic town we'd travelled half way across the world to visit… was *tiny*. Imagine the smallest town you have ever visited, small one horse stuff, and then divide it in three smaller ones and bin two of them. What you have is what we had. A one third of a very small horse town. One perhaps capable of supporting, at most, a single laxate donkey.

"This is it?" I said, somewhat critically, "*This…* is your town."

"I know," she smiled. "Fantastic, isn't it?"

One main road and only five sideaways which were really little more than painfully thin alleys cut between high rendered walls. The entrance to the town was guarded, if you are so romantically inclined, by the 'Château de Serres'; a thirteenth century building constructed of stone with a turret hanging from its western face. When a place is as small as Serres I guess it's easier to make the history stick.

The chateau was, I figured, one possible hiding place for the things Sarah sought, but there were others...

A statue to the virgin Mary stood to one side of the road and, at the top of the hill, a small church with a tiny graveyard nestled in the overgrown grass behind. Ideal locations, Sarah explained, because they stand the test of time. Year after year nobody messes with the holy shit. All we had to do was find one that had some reference to 'Arcadia' marked upon it. We parked under the shade of some trees just below the town itself and climbed out of the car into the afternoon heat.

We walked up the steep, cobbled street, the sun cutting through the gaps to form bright bands across the road and Sarah carefully scrutinising every building, statue, sign or stone.

It took less than ten minutes to cover every avenue, finishing with the church and gravestones located at the uppermost end. All the buildings were nondescript; all faced directly onto the road and, short of the different brightly coloured paints their occupants had chosen for the wooden doors and shutters and the varying styles of plants and flowers tended carefully in each of the window boxes, they were pretty much identical. All were very Mediterranean, very picture-postcard, and of very little use. There were no carved words or wooden signs, no inscriptions and no dates.

Around half way down the cobbles a local came into view, ambling laboriously up the hill toward us.; a real old guy, wobbling on his feet. His face was full of chasm-like wrinkles, he had more teeth missing than remaining and wore an ill-fitting suit he'd probably owned for fifty years.

In Greece he'd probably have been dragging that donkey I mentioned earlier, stopping only when it needed to go.

Sarah sauntered over with a broad smile whilst I took a seat and watched.

Her attempt at French wasn't bad, ten times better than I would have achieved, but even she had to admit afterward that she lacked Tina's grasp of languages and, with a wry smile, that even Tina herself lacked the ability to actually *speak* them. After a few 'Est-ce que un sign d'Arcadie's', a few 'pardon's' and a few 'non's' she gave up and let him on his way to the top of town.

In the toilets on the plane, immediately prior to landing, Sarah had managed to change her clothes; khaki combat pants being replaced by olive shorts and her tanned legs now glistened in the afternoon sunlight.

I'd always pictured the women of archaeology to be big and burly with harsh faces and wide biceps, and religious women to be plain and conservative, very prim and proper. Sarah was neither; like her sister she was an incredibly beautiful young woman with a body to die for and a personality that simply shone from her eyes and smile.

I wondered if she had any idea just how beautiful she actually was, or indeed if she cared. I felt it was the latter. In her mind, there were far more important things for her to attend to than personal vanity and it made me realise something very important; Tina wasn't, in fact, one of a kind, as Sarah had described her.

What the world had delivered us was, quite clearly, a very valuable matching pair.

She stood to my right, hands on hips. "Well, that's five minutes of my life I'll never get back again," she said sarcastically. "I don't think he had the first idea what I was talking about."

"I need a coffee." I said. In fact, I needed something a little stronger, but figured I'd be safer keeping that little gem to myself.

Sarah looked around and scowled. "Yeah? Like... where from?"

I shouted up the road after the old man, who was by now opening the narrow wooden door to what was quite obviously his humble abode. Maybe he knew if there was a café nearby. "Monsieur...?" He turned and looked back with deep-set eyes. "Un café, s'il vous plaît?"

It was pretty much all the French I knew and a crying shame that I wasted it all in one go.

"Oui," he called back with a broad, toothless smile. "Oui, naturellement. Entrez!" Then he disappeared into the shade of his home.

I looked at Sarah. Blank.

"O-kay... am I going mad or did he just say his house was a café?"

She gave me an indignant look. "I really worry about you," she said. "Café...? *Coffee...?* He's offering you... Oh, never mind, come on." She picked up her rucksack and headed off up the hill.

Toothless guy made the coffee. Thick and black but damned good and pulled some chairs onto the street where we all sat in a thin sliver of sunlight opposite the church. I say church, though it was actually little more than a chapel; a small square building with a tiny crumbling bell tower that probably once contained an even tinier crumbling bell.

There was no point talking to the old guy, but we talked at him for a while and he nodded and smiled and did all the things that polite hosts are supposed to do. In time I even stopped seeing him as some kind of elderly simpleton because he had life in his eyes. Passion, and I was really starting to admire that in people. It was something I couldn't remember having had myself for a very long time. His was a passion for nothing more exciting than the game of life.

Which was probably how he had managed to keep playing that game for so goddamned long.

Suddenly, Sarah placed her cup down on the floor, stared open-mouthed at the church and said; "The *Ark of God*."

I didn't understand, but the old guy did. Now he was laughing and chuntering something, over and over.

Sarah repeated it slowly, as though she wasn't so much saying it as thinking it out loud. What he'd been saying, as he laughed and swayed on his chair the way old people sometimes do when they're excited, was "Oui, Arca Dei, Arca Dei."

It was the Church of The Ark of God.

In Latin, the church of the *Arca Dei*.

And that sounded very much like....

I looked across the road. The sign above the door was in a fairly impressive state of disrepair, but even to me there was no mistaking what it said, and what it *might* say, once translated.

We thanked our host for the free coffee, taking time to shake his hand and extend true gratitude, then I left him sitting where he was and walked across the cobbled road to the chapel. Sarah didn't follow, not immediately, and I turned to see her still thanking the man, her smile wide and genuine.

"You coming?" I said.

"Even the most adventurous travellers can't be in two places at the same time, Nick..." she said, almost as though she was quoting. Then she cast me a knowing smile. She shook the man's hand one more time and hurried over.

The doors were wide, arched and made of wood barely held together by flaking crimson paint. They were more like barn doors than those of a church. In fact, the whole building looked more akin to a barn than a church. In the centre of each of the doors was a blackened brass ring which acted both as knocker and handle.

We tried both. One turned, the other didn't, but nothing happened either way. The church was locked solid.

A very loud and heavy jingling sound came creeping from behind and we turned in unison. There was the old man, still sitting where we'd left him, huge wide toothless smile and a big set of black keys dancing like marionettes on an impossibly large loop. He wasn't a priest, so I'm guessing he must have been someone's low rent version of a caretaker.

Which would offer a fairly adequate explanation as to why he lived directly across the street.

"Vous voulez entrer?" he asked. We nodded, almost violently, and he climbed slowly to his feet, mumbling just loud enough for us to hear, "Mais oui, mais oui. C'est la maison de Dieu, après tous. Il est pour tout le monde."

THIRTY-ONE
Friday, August 14, 2043.
Kleinwork European Livestock Research Centre, Mont Cardou, France.

The plan was a simple one, if such things could ever be simple. D'Almas had done what he was supposed to do – find out where and when Klein's prize had been stolen - and was now a free man. Or, at least, he *had* been. Unlike Castle he was certainly never heard of again. Now Davies, his every move being watched by the five remaining guards, and armed with the information Klein and Sherman had only just received, was to be sent back.

Even earlier.

The timing would be approximate, but it would be imperative that he arrived at least two years before 1132. Whatever else he did for those two years he would ultimately ensure that he made his way to Narbonne, found a place to stay and waited. He would remain in the port for every waking second of the year 1132 if he had to.

One day, a group of soldiers would arrive in town, returning from victorious conquests in the Holy Lands. They would disembark from a crude boat which had made the painful journey from Palestine, would have broad smiles etched across their faces and bright red crosses emblazoned on their tunics. Believing themselves to be invincible, or perhaps protected by God, they would probably start boasting about the treasures they carried and Davies, having had a crash course in Medieval French, would just about be able to understand the things they were saying.

They would be tired from the journey choosing, for one night only, to find the first comfortable lodgings they had been granted in months before continuing on their journey across southern France.

Davies would watch them drink and cheer and generally make asses of themselves all evening. He might even attempt to befriend them if he felt he could pull off such a feat, and then he would watch them retire for the night. Wherever it was that they chose to keep their treasures, some of which Davies would take for himself, he would then place a half-finished tankard of ale with something resembling a dead worm resting at the base of the liquid.

Four centimetres long and less than one in diameter, this additional bung, made from a material which would allow it to be immersed in the liquid for almost ten minutes before it deteriorated completely, would contain enough VX228 nerve agent to knock out everything that breathed within a half-mile radius. Having been protected whilst within Davies himself by the outer bung comprised of hardened rubber, the capsule would now start to dissolve, leaving the agent to bubble up and spread into the atmosphere without colour, odour or, more importantly, warning.

A few people, certainly those closest to the tankard when the gas entered the atmosphere, would be killed. Not that such trivialities bothered Klein or even Davies. The majority of the group, however, would simply be rendered unconscious for anything up to eight hours and severely ill for the weeks that followed. After half an hour's patient wait, the air would be safe enough to breathe again and Davies could go back inside.

He would need to avoid those unconnected and unaffected at the periphery and enter the inn under cover of night.

Then he would find the tables and steal them back again. Along with anything else he could carry. And sell.

When those who had not suffered a rather painful death awoke they would have no idea what the hell had just happened, how it had happened or even who was to blame. The tables would be long gone. By this time they would be secreted within the altar of the Cathar church at Serres and remain very carefully hidden for hundreds of years. During that time various renovations to the building's structure would take place but the altar itself, as confirmed by D'Almas, would remain untouched. Only Klein, Sherman and Kerr would ever see those tables again.

And they would see them approximately twenty-eight minutes after Davies had gone

Due to hasty construction, there was no way to see into the sealed Cardou lab, but it mattered little. Davies would be there when the doors were closed and gone by the time they re-opened. There was no way he could find a way out of this, even if he had wanted to. Which, given the options, he probably didn't anyway. All he had to do was perform one simple theft and one simple hiding job and he would be free to live the rest of his life in an environment where he was certain he would excel, given that his knowledge of the world would be so much greater than those who surrounded him. He would be a king amongst men.

Sure, there would be none of the luxuries to which he had become accustomed, but there would be the two primary things this man had lived without for almost four years now; alcohol and women. Who knew, perhaps Davies could even finish off the things he had started. The Texas police had caught him after only twelve of his rapes and murders, nine of which had been committed during his time in Tennessee, but he had always hoped to steer that figure closer to fifty.

A new world beckoned for him now and it was just bursting with delicious opportunities.

The loud screaming filled the small building and spread through the empty fields which surrounded like a wide-shot in a horror flick. There was nobody close enough to hear, and nobody who would know what it might be if they did. The digital read-out, tweaked by Sherman himself, was reading 527, almost the maximum the system could handle, and the ground moved slightly but violently as though feeling the effect of some distant earthquake. There was probably a bright flash from somewhere within the room, but it was invisible through the titanium walls, all of which appeared to stay perfectly flat from the outside. Only their inner faces, it seemed, were affected and distorted by the temporary fluctuation in time.

Sherman waited until the dust had settled, metaphorically, then entered the room. He returned a few moments later holding Davies' crumpled red jump suit at arm's length. The tough guy, the one who had raped all those women and declared during his arrest that he was afraid of nothing and no-one had, it seemed, pissed all the way down the front of it in the few seconds before he had gone. Perhaps he was still pissing when he arrived. Cold, naked and in a world he would never understand he would, quite literally, have been pissing into the wind.

Klein, seated in his wheelchair, smiled broadly. "He's gone then?"

Sherman nodded. "Literally."

Klein was already turning his chair around. "Then let's bring them home."

"Perhaps you should wait here?" Sherman offered, hoping that Klein read only concern for his deteriorating condition in his tone. "I'll meet Kerr at the church and we'll bring them back here for you."

He was praying inside that Klein would agree, but the old man was already shaking his head defiantly.

"Not a chance," he said. "We'll take the guards. I've searched for these all my life, Sherman, and I want to make damn sure I'm there when they're found."

On the face of it, everything *had* gone to plan.

Davies' only mistakes, it seemed, were to mouth off when he had drunk one too many, telling the kind of wild stories that for hundreds of years would become the subject of folklore, and spending a night in Montpellier with an African whore named Emerie. Three months after he had hidden the tables he had spent over an hour brutally abusing her body sexually before turning over with a cruel smile etched into his features. She, in turn, brutally beat him to death with a stone slab whilst he slept. Then she took the other treasures he had stolen from the Templars and boarded a boat bound for Egypt.

Folklore led to suspicion and suspicion led to a sense of inquisition. Early in 1631 Pierre De Montfort, a devout catholic and owner of much of the lands in Perpignan, heard stories of a great treasure - stolen from the Templars themselves - buried somewhere on his land. Convinced that this horde would include gold and jewels he searched his entire territory for over eight years. He found nothing.

Then, in 1640, De Montfort and 'any man of his lands capable to raise a sword' was called to the Principality of Aragon so that they might aid the Catalans in their civil war with Spain at large. He immediately visited his private chapel at Serres where he prayed to the altar that God would ride with he and his men. That he would deliver them home, safe and victorious, to their families.

The cold stone was smooth and well-preserved, despite its age and the golden bars, symbolic of the shittim-wood originals which had been overlaid with gold at God's command, were still in place in the gleaming brass rings, just as they had been designed to be. But, as he knelt and prayed that his life would be spared in the conflicts to come, De Montfort's eye level fell on the underside of the representation this altar embodied.

De Montfort then noticed that one of the many stones comprising the altar was not quite a perfect fit...

★ ★ ★ ★ ★

Twenty five minutes after Davies' departure was confirmed, the four wheel drive pulled up sharply outside the church, Kerr and the guard already waiting.

Kerr had been smoking a cigarette which he flicked hard against the wall, tiny sparks splaying across the stones like a miniature firework. Sherman climbed from the driver's door and around to the sliding panel on the side, lowering the ramp for Klein to disembark. He threw Kerr a set of keys and watched as he opened the lock on the chain; strung across the doors and held by the two blackened loops. The chain that Klein and Sherman had placed there the previous day when they had chosen the church as their site and discussed the location with the heavily guarded Davies.

The church had been empty for twenty years now; the few local residents who remained in Serres having long-since lifted their faith and taken it the few miles to the services in Arques. In the early part of the century it had been decided to close the doors to the church for the final time and allow what was left of the mortar within to crumble at its own pace.

Klein knew nothing of this, of course, and had no desire to learn. All he cared to know was that the altar had been intact in 1132 and that it was, for the most part, still intact when he arrived.

The door creaked as though suffering pain, thick piles of dust falling from above and clouding the air. At the furthest end of the aisle the thin light which fought its way through the cracked and dirty windows added a deep hint of yellow/brown and gave the room the appearance of a sepiatone photograph; a relic of the past. When it had cleared, Kerr stood back to allow Sherman to push Klein's chair inside. The guard waited on the door.

"Look at this place," Kerr said, piercing the dusty air with the tight beam of a powerful torch.

The sun was across the furthest side of the church now and the inside, devoid of lighting, was even gloomier than their last visit. There were no pews, all having been taken by the final caretaker and used as firewood during his similarly final winter. The mortar from within the walls was all but gone and just one pane of stained glass survived: that of the baby Jesus staring down at the visitors as they made their way inside.

"What happened here?" Kerr said, his eye drawn to a deep red stain, seemingly a very old one, which due to an ongoing lack of caretaking facilities was still visible across the stones just inside the entrance.

Klein looked, then just as quickly looked away again. He pursed his lips. "Who knows?"

"Who cares?" Sherman added. He didn't even bother to look.

His eyes, like Klein's, were now locked firmly on the prize which lay ahead of them.

THIRTY-TWO
SATURDAY, JUNE 11, 2011.
SERRES, PERPIGNAN, FRANCE.

If the church looked like a barn from the outside then its interior didn't disappoint.

Or rather it did, if you see my point.

It was cold, dark and empty. The kind of empty that suggests always empty, as though the place hadn't been used for a hundred years. Two rows of dark wooden pews ran forward, some of which were chipped or had accoutrements broken off long enough ago for the lighter, exposed wood to have turned grey with wave after wave of dust; now permanently ingrained. The only light reached like coloured arms through the large stained glass window, its backlit appearance glowing with a typical Virgin Mary and Child scene in far duller hues than they had been originally.

The walls were bare, crumbling almost as much as those outside and small piles of mixed rubble had gathered at their bases having fallen from visible gaps between the stones. In the corner to our right were two dirty bell-ropes, tatty and frayed and a narrow iron ladder, covered in deep orange rust. Once, it had no doubt acted as access for repairing or replacing the long-gone bell.

At the base of the ladder were various tools and cast iron bars, no doubt left over from the last repair job. A wooden collection tray lay beside them with hardened grey sludge covering its base, having been put to more profitable use as something on which the last set of workmen could mix cement.

The place needed a caretaker, there was no doubt about that, but what it needed was one who could walk faster than he aged; one who could not only hold a broom but also find the strength to push it and one who took pride in the building, rather than letting in strangers and muttering "Là vous êtes," as he ambled back across the road to take his place in the sun, as ours just had.

Sarah's gaze was fixed directly forward; straight to the focal point of the broken seating; the altar. A place where once – and I myself had no idea just how long ago that might have been – a man might have stood in white glory and order those gathered to confess their sins to the Lord or face eternal damnation. I was guessing, given that particular analogy, that the building itself had never made such a confession in its life.

She walked slowly forward, placed her rucksack on the floor and ran her fingers along the altar's roughened surface. "Oh yes," she said, her voice laced with a breathy sense of wonder. "This is it."

"How do you know?" I asked, moving closer as she covered a full three-sixty around the base, eyes scouring.

"Because this is the Ark of the Covenant," she said, as though this were somehow as obvious as my lack of education was proving to be.

I had very limited knowledge of the Ark of the Covenant, and most of that had come from the final scene of a Harrison Ford film. Unfortunately, that was the bit where you were supposed to look away.

"The Arca Dei," Sarah continued. "It's a heavily damaged representation of it, I'll admit, but that's definitely what it was designed to represent. See?" She pointed to two corroded brass rings embedded into the stone. "These were the loops where handles would have gone."

She worked her way around and did her level best to enlighten me. The original Ark - the biblical ark - had been a box seated on four brass feet which, for the purposes of the altar, were carved from stone. It had been carried by means of two poles inserted through the four rings already pointed out. Above those rings a large bevelled area represented the lid.

Seated on top of the original lid had been two angels of gold; their wings reaching toward each other. As Sarah quoted, gently caressing the one remaining stone angel and the broken stump of the other; "And the cherubims shall spread out their wings on high, and covered with their wings over the mercy seat, with their faces one to another;"

She rubbed gently at a last piece of gold leaf clinging desperately to the stone and it fell, gliding slowly downward to join a few others beside the heavy base.

"I'll bet this was one hell of a beautiful piece."

Then she blew dust from the surface, a cloud rising up before her face, and coughed. "So how do we get in," she said slowly, clearly thinking as she spoke.

"Lift the lid?"

"This is one piece," she mused. "Unlike the original it doesn't actually have a lid."

"So how do we get inside?"

"I could have sworn I just asked you that," she said. It was an idle comment. She never looked up.

She pushed stone, pulled brass and tweaked a cherubim until the head came off.

"Oops," she said with a naughty smile.

I doubt it mattered, given the already crumbling state of its long-beheaded partner.

Sarah looked closer at the base; the area where the feet were carved. They were formed in the shape of upturned acorns which ran upward to the flat stone above. As the original would have been seated on these feet, however, leaving a gap underneath, the stone behind was heavily recessed to create a darker area when lit from above.

Sarah's mouth started to curl upward again, the foundations of a smile.

"Hello? What have we here...?" She sounded like a customs officer who had just uncovered a rich seam of cocaine under a far less rich (metaphorically speaking) seam of used underwear.

She moved around to the back of the altar and started to push, gently at first, at the thin slab of stone housed under the main block. The stone which, by being deliberately recessed, had created a sense of shadow between the feet. Nothing. She pushed harder. Nothing multiplied by nothing. Before long she had stretched her legs out to the back wall and placed them in such a way that she could put all her weight behind the task, limited as that weight might be.

The stone moved. The tiniest fraction. Enough.

"Yeah, I'd love some help, Nick. Thanks," she said.

Moving around the altar I placed my fingers into the gap, barely three inches high, and pushed as hard as I could. I could feel the stone sliding little by little. My fingers breaking at roughly the same speed.

"You pass, I'll receive," Sarah said, moving to the other side.

As the stone edged slowly in short bursts, Sarah took possession at the other side, gently guiding it through. I could see nothing of what she was witnessing as the surface came into view, but I could see her expression; wonder, awe and God only knows what else, spreading like flames across her features.

Whatever the hell 'they' were, they were there. The - what did she call them? - the 'tables', were there.

At which point the stone stopped dead. Jammed solid. With my hands deep within the void, I had lost any or all leverage. I stopped pushing, or trying to push, and caught my breath. Rubbing strained fingers I looked around the church for anything that might help finish the job.

"Support the stone," I said eventually. "I've got an idea."

I walked to the base of the bell-ropes, pushed them aside with my feet like dead snakes, and selected one of the steel rods. With a broad smile I slapped it hard against my palm, the way one might when threatening some obnoxious little punk with a baseball bat.

Suddenly - loudly - the door to the church flew open and Sarah turned, her mouth and eyes fixed wide.

On seeing who it was, she relaxed. "Jesus, Christ," she said, "you scared the crap out of me."

From the depth of the angle in which I was standing, I couldn't see who she was speaking to, but I heard his voice. Old, slurring,

French. It wasn't the same though. Either it had acquired an edge, or it had just lost one. I couldn't be sure, but something was suddenly very wrong, which was pretty much what the old guy was now trying to tell us anyway.

"Il y a un problème."

Then a shot, muffled from a damn good silencer, but a shot all the same. I'd heard enough of those in my time and the use of a silencer meant only one thing; professional or close enough. Someone, it seemed, wanted to come and go unnoticed and my guess was that they'd prefer to take the tables with them.

A spurt of blood flew across my line of vision like discarded coffee. The old guy's body appeared next, falling forward in complete silence and with a disconcertingly real sense of slow motion. His body hit the floor not three feet in front of me, the bones in his face cracking like a dropped egg on the cold stone floor.

"Where's your friend?"

And here was a new voice; one I did not recognise. Nor, for obvious reasons, did I particularly like the sound of. It was deep, coarse and unmistakably American. Midwest I guessed from the way he had made the word 'where' become two painfully elongated syllables.

I reacted, as you might expect. Initially by watching a very short and boring documentary of my life flash before my eyes and secondly by raising the bar to shoulder level and edging forward. Very carefully; my eyes fixed both on the doorway and the chance of adding some more interesting scenes should I ever be forced to watch that documentary again. For only a split second as I stepped into view I saw the front end of the silencer and the harsh look beyond it. Then I slammed the bar into this new face with every ounce of strength I had. His nose exploded and the gun fell only a moment before he did, his body slumping to the floor as heavily the old guy's.

Except that the American was still very much alive and still very conscious, his face covered in blood. I back-heeled the gun away from his hand and stepped two paces back to pick it up, the bar raised again.

By the time he realised what had hit him, quite literally, Sarah had the bar and his own gun was pointing directly at his less-than-smug face.

"Use the bar," I said to Sarah, insistent, "Get the stone out."

"Don't shout at me," she said.

"Please, Sarah. Just... do it."

Given the urgency of the situation she did as she was told.

As I heard the first low strains of grating stone behind me I stepped over the old guy's lifeless body and crouched to look the American full in the face. It was one of the two faces I had seen behind Klein and Grier in Sarah's pictures; mid-sentence guy. He had flattened features, no pun intended, spiky black hair and deep set eyes sheltering under thick eyebrows.

The kind of face that makes one realise just how on the money Darwin had been.

"Give me one good reason why I shouldn't make your ugly face a doughnut." I held the gun close enough to be threatening, but far enough away for him not to knock it clean across the church if he decided, albeit stupidly, to take a swing.

He touched his nose with the back of his hand and winced. "Go for it," he said, his voice nasal and bubbling yet still remarkably and annoyingly calm. "Go on. Knock yourself out."

He smiled at the irony of his comment.

"Nick you really should see this," Sarah's voice from behind.

"Kind of busy at the moment," I offered sarcastically. "Think you can manage without me?"

"It's. Just. So. Beautiful," she said, as though delivering four complete and unconnected sentences.

I knew she was no longer talking to me. She was talking to it, or them. Whatever it was that she'd just found.

"On your feet," I said.

Reluctantly, he climbed to his feet, the gun still inches from his face, and I edged back toward the altar, signalling for him to follow. At the end of the aisle my back reached Sarah's and I glanced quickly over my shoulder. I knew that whatever I wanted to see, I would have to see quick. This guy was no fool; he wouldn't allow me to take my eyes off him for a second.

What I saw, at least what stays in my mind of what I saw, was that the extracted slab of stone had two perfectly symmetrical holes cut into it, like some kind of medieval DVD tray. Within those recesses were what I assumed to be the tables; a combination of disk, industrial gear and jigsaw carved from dark stone.

Like the holes in which they had been seated they were circular but with numerous hook-like curves carved smoothly around their circumference. Deliberately, it seemed, as the markings on the face of the disks followed the shape of those indentations perfectly.

But what I *really* remember, and I know why now, was that in the fifteen centimetres or so of stone between the disk holders was another marking; deep and sharp and carved with the skill of a monumental mason.

It was a symbol, a weird symbol and not one I recognised. But I'd seen one very like it. Not the same, even a glance told me that, but very similar indeed.

It had been tattooed onto my dead stiff's left leg.

As I flicked back to the American's sneering expression, I could hear Sarah carefully extracting the tables from the recesses and placing them in a container she had taken from her rucksack. I expected then to hear the zip, but I didn't. Instead I heard a strange 'popping' sound. Like a bubble bursting or a fuse blowing in the distance.

Or, like somebody excitedly removing the lid from a large black marker pen.

Like department store animatronics, Sarah and I turned and looked over our shoulders at each other. My eyes were questioning whilst the emotion within hers had ascended far higher than her usual sense of mischief and was now planting a black flag on the summit of naughty child. She looked to all intents as though she was just about to cover her teacher's chair with quick-drying glue.

"Nearly done," she said.

THIRTY-THREE

FRIDAY, AUGUST 14, 2043.
5TH & ALAMEDA, LOS ANGELES, CALIFORNIA.

Time was running out and Alison could have done without spending almost ten minutes of it sweet-talking the guards on the door. They'd been suspicious as to why she would want to enter the cell area but she had easily pulled rank on that one. But why did she want to do it alone, they asked? Surely it would be so much safer for her to have the guards enter with her, then they could hold the detonator buttons and make Mason or Stubbs, the only inmates left, swiftly lose a limb or four if anything started kicking off.

Alison had needed to stress the extremely confidential nature of the visit, numerous times, and that it had been on Klein's express instructions. When that had failed she had resorted ultimately to an uneasy mix of threat and fluttered eyelids. In the end they backed down, handing over both Mason and Stubbs' respective detonators and agreeing to remain outside whilst keeping a watchful eye through the mirror door.

She smiled a thankyou, picked up one of the guard's chairs and carried it inside.

In the time it took to walk the short distance along the corridor to Mason's cell Mason himself, no doubt alerted by the lights reaching full strength, was already at the bars. He was drooling like a St. Bernard puppy.

"Pret-ty lay-dy. You been getting bored up there? Been hankering after some of Mason's loving?"

"Shut the fuck up, Mason," she said, placing the chair directly in front of his cell and never once catching the lascivious line his oily black eyes were now following.

He pretended to be hurt. "Ooh, I can just see you begging for it there, lady. You talkin' dirty to Mason now."

Alison laughed and shook her head in dismay. This was probably going to be much harder than she thought, she figured, but undoubtedly a lot more fun in the long term. Perhaps not as hard as Mason was at that moment, but pretty tough just the same.

"You know who I am?" she asked.

"Pretty science lady," he said, his head jerking upward from her skirt. "Pretty good fuck and pretty desperate for it I'm a-guessing."

"Maybe she wants some nigger cock in her?" Stubbs gravelly tones from further along the corridor.

Alison turned but Stubbs wasn't at the bars, so she rose and walked slowly - purposefully - along the corridor, stopping directly in front of his cell with a deliberate click of her heels.

Of all the men shortlisted for this crazy scheme, Stubbs was the one she hated the most. He was pure evil; no middle ground. Every crime he had ever committed had been for the sheer hell of it, and that had been up to and including slicing Edison's throat with the plate back in May. He was laid on his bunk, big black arms behind his head and the sweat on his thick biceps glistening in the light from the corridor. She stared straight at him, expressionless.

"What about it, lady?" he said, his eyes on the featureless white expanse of the ceiling. "You want some big black nigger cock in you?"

Alison smiled. "Mason's an opportunist," she said, her voice deliberately lowered and lacking any trace of affectation. "A thief. He only ever killed people to get away. He isn't exactly sweetness and light, but you...? You, as I recall, are a much nastier little piece of work altogether..."

"Bet your ass, sweet thing," he said, not moving but distinctively flattered

318

at what he took to be a mighty fine compliment.

"I think the last thing that you put your big black nigger cock into - before you killed her of course - was an eight year old girl. And that makes you one seriously fucked up individual. And now, especially after your little stunt with the plate, the people who run this project, myself included, have absolutely no plans for you to go anywhere."

She held up the detonator, bright red and little bigger than a key fob, with 'Stubbs' etched in white across the top.

"So I doubt anyone's going to lose any sleep if I accidentally drop this now, are they? I mean, just to see if it can withstand the shock without ending the close relationship you seem to have enjoyed with your hands." She stared right at Stubbs, her delay well calculated. "Because really... I'm interested."

She slowly opened her long fingers, releasing her grip on the fob. Stubbs' eyes widened as it descended to the floor almost in slow motion. A second later, though it seemed so much longer, it hit the hard tiles with a click, bounced twice and came to a halt at the side of Alison's feet. She watched it the full way, then looked up and saw the expression now etched across Stubbs' face.

Abject fear, just as she had hoped.

For a moment she wondered what the little girl had seen in that same face as he'd thrust himself into her. Desire, probably; the worst kind. The kind that, with damned good reason, she hated more than anything else in this world.

"What's the matter, big boy?" She said, bending to pick up the detonator and flicking it in her hand, just to piss him off. "Scared of dying?"

Stubbs still looked stunned. When he said nothing, Alison smiled and started to walk back along the corridor to Mason. A few seconds later, having no doubt recomposed himself just enough, Stubbs called out behind her, "I ain't scared o' dying, little lady. Just scared you gonna leave me with no hands to jack off over you when you're gone, that's all."

Mason was grinning wide at the comment when she got back. She

319

ignored him, turned the chair so that the back was facing the door and sat down; close but out of reach. "Wipe that grin off your face," she said.

Mason made some disgusting noises and started flicking his tongue up and down. Alison, feigning ignorance, took both detonators, out of sight of the guards, and carefully started removing the backs from them.

"Hey...? What da fuck you doin'?" Mason said, edgy now. He looked at the bands on each of his wrists in turn; checking; making sure that the red lights did not come on. "If dem tings go off...?"

Alison placed both detonator backs on her knee and started to pull the workings from inside Mason's. "They're going to kill you," she said. As the words came out she looked at him as though the best thing he could do right now would be to keep extremely quiet.

"Who gonna kill me?" His voice was lowered. He was stupid but not so stupid that he didn't understand when talking should give way to listening.

"Klein and the rest of the team," Alison said, now removing the workings from Stubbs' detonator. "Don't ask me how I know, but I know. Think you're going on a journey of salvation? You ain't going nowhere, Mason."

"Why they gonna kill Mason?" he said. He believed her. "What Mason done?"

Alison swapped the detonators over, trying not to give too much thought to the things that Mason had actually done in his life to warrant administering a painful death at least three times over. Very carefully Mason's workings went into Stubbs' case and vice versa. She started replacing the backs, using her flattened palms to squeeze them into place with a loud snap and hoping to God that the guards hadn't picked up on what she was doing.

"Nothing," she said calmly. "Yet."

"So why you tellin' Mason if Mason not don' not'in?" He was looking nervous now, perhaps even sweating a little, she couldn't tell. "You come to gloat you pretty ass?"

"Nope," Alison said casually. She looked up and smiled. "I've come to save your sad, pathetic little life."

Mason's face turned to one of contempt. "You fuckin' wit' me," he said defiantly. "Dey ain't gonna kill Mason. You jus' trying to fuck with my ass." He nodded and smiled, swiftly like he got the joke. "Very funny dat. You almost got Mason dere."

"I'm not fucking with anyone," Alison replied, her voice still desperately calm. "Least of all..." she looked at him contemptuously, "...you. Before today's out, those two guards are going to be sent in here, they're going to shackle you and they're going to take you out through the main door. Then, I don't know when and I don't know where, they're going to kill you."

"How you know this?"

"Thought I told you not to ask that."

"And you gonna save me?"

"Not necessarily," Alison said. "But I'm gonna give you a chance."

She held up the detonators so that he could see them. He'd watched every move she'd made like a beggar staring through a restaurant window. He had no idea why she was doing this, maybe he didn't need to know, but it damn sure looked like she was helping him. What the fuck was she playing at?

"So what Mason gotta do?"

"Shut up, listen and learn. In that order," Alison said quietly. "If I'm wrong then you lose nothing by keeping your mouth shut for five minutes, but if I'm right then you might just get away with your life, shit as it is. Choice is yours. And then, once I've helped you out, you'll do me a little favour in return."

"Which is....?"

Alison deliberately didn't answer the question. Mason stared straight at her, thinking it through as best he could. He couldn't tell if she was for real or not but it was like she said; he had nothing to lose. Not by hearing her out at any rate.

"Okay," he said eventually. "Mason listening."

THIRTY-FOUR
SATURDAY, JUNE 11, 2011.
SERRES, PERPIGNAN, FRANCE.

Sarah scurried ahead of me on the way down the cobbled street. American guy's considerate silencer use had raised no alarms and the place was as dead as it had been when we had arrived and the caretaker was now. I have to admit, begrudgingly, that inside the church I had been frightened. The kind of frightened I could remember having been only two or three times in my entire career. Outside was a different story, written in a markedly different style of writing. Outside I was angry.

Two things were getting to me.

One would have been bad enough.

The first was that Sarah, whilst looking a little angry at what had occurred not ten minutes earlier, hadn't actually looked frightened. Like me. Not in the least. More worryingly, she hadn't even managed to look surprised.

This gnarled at me somewhat. As did the fact that she had just carried on about her business afterward. She had simply extracted the tables, done what she had needed to do with the marker and then calmly replaced the stone. I was not a little surprised that she hadn't chosen to discuss the benefits of a single global currency whilst she was about it.

Then, as we had left the church, I had taken the trouble to watch her as she passed the body of the dead Frenchman. Nothing. No compassion and still no fear. She simply stepped over his lifeless corpse like one might a log in the countryside. It was not what I'd expected and it made me ask questions like 'what kind of a archaeologist is she?' Not one to be around if you want to stay alive; that was my thinking.

You have to remember that I was still working blind at this point. I was still of a mind that if the deaths of Wells and Rodriguez were in any way related to the text, then they had been killed by 'the bad guys'.

Therein lay the second of my problems...

I grabbed Sarah's shoulder and spun her around, hard. "What just went on up there?" I asked. Although I was speaking as low as my anger would allow so as not to alert the locals, I couldn't hold the question any longer. I just had to know.

"Please, Nick, there's no time for this now." She turned to walk away again.

I span her around a second time, even harder than before.

"Like hell there isn't. An innocent man gets his face blown off not fifteen feet from you and you know what...? You don't even flinch. Like it's no great surprise."

Sarah sighed gently and looked at her feet. It wasn't shame she was feeling, though. It was despair. Despair that I was still, despite her protests, choosing to hold this conversation here and now.

"And the guy who kills him," I continued, "just happens to be one of the guys in your set of happy snaps? In the background of the Klein/Grier picture? Mid-sentence Guy? And that picture, in case you hadn't noticed, was taken at a government dig. Which means he works for the government. Which I doubt is much consolation to the guy whose face is currently seeping into the floor back at the Arca Dei."

Sarah looked up, oblique, but remained calm. "In the picture? You noticed that?"

"I'm a detective, Sarah. I get paid to notice shit like that."

Suddenly Sarah got angry. Venomous angry.

She leaned forward and placed her face against mine, almost spitting the words down my throat. Her eyes were telling me to think very carefully about interrupting and then, if I felt it might be a good idea, to think again.

"So now you know just how real this is, Nick. This isn't nuclear weaponry, internet domination or even the Presidency of the United States we're dealing with. This is something much bigger and infinitely more important. And you're somehow surprised that the good guys are killing as well? This is how it is. Wake up to what you're involved in here."

"What *you* involved me in," I corrected.

"You've seen the text, Nick. Which means that the only reason you're still alive is because I brought you here; because they figured that you and I were on to something and let us get on with it. If we'd looked like we were getting nowhere they'd have taken us both out yesterday. Just like your two friends back home."

I felt myself pull back. "Wells and Rodriguez?"

Her face relaxed and with it, so did her voice. The venom was gone. "Yes."

"How."

"You'll see. In time."

I was fed up with playing the 'you'll see, in time' game. It was bad enough before people were dying, but now?

"No way. I want to know and I want to know *now*. Who exactly are the bad guys here?"

She sighed again. "*Everyone*, Nick." She lifted the rucksack. "Everyone who wants to get their hands on these tables is a bad guy. Is that simple enough for ya?"

I leaned forward, my eyes now fixed straight into hers. She never blinked and all I saw was defiance. She wasn't scared of me any more than she was scared of Mid-Sentence Guy. "So what about you, Sarah? What does that make you? You a bad guy?"

"I think you already know the answer to that," she said. "If not... you soon will. *If* you choose to stick around. But I'll tell you something for nothing. As long as we have these we stay alive. Lose them... or walk away... we're as good as dead."

She looked down the hill. "And the guys in the picture? Sure, they work for the government, but guess what? They work as a team, Nick. They get paid to do one thing and one thing only. They *kill*. But they never, and I mean *never*, work alone. So if I were you I'd stop worrying about me, and start wondering where his little friend is."

She slung the bag over her shoulder and started walking. Or rather, ambling, like she still didn't have a care in the world. I took a moment then followed...

As we edged closer to the parking area at the base of the town, though still just out of sight, I reached my arm across and held Sarah back. Along the road ahead, through the treeline, I could see another vehicle parked adjacent to ours; an olive-green Land Rover. Not military but decidedly similar.

Worse still, through the more open base of the trees I could see a pair of heavy duty boots and on the breeze now channelled along the narrow street I could smell smoke. Cigarette smoke.

I was really starting to hate the fact that Sarah was always so Goddamned right.

Without a sound I indicated that she should stay put and walked within the line of shade cast by the Château, sticking to the grass and edge of the trees as best I could so as not to be seen or heard.

It was smoking-guy alright; so laid back and relaxed, as though he was just waiting for a bus. A guy was dead and he was leaning against his car smoking yet another cigarette and catching rays. Unlike his friend, he was wearing his sunglasses. The cigarette was in one hand whilst the other, worryingly, held a radio. He wore a navy T-shirt, his arms exposed and the further round I moved the more I could see of his tattoo, deep blue/black set on one of the widest upper arms I had ever seen.

The tattoo wasn't 'weird' or 'trendy' like the stiff's, but it was instantly recognisable. Navy SeAL insignia. Which explained why these two hadn't held any expectations of failure; why they'd taken the easy option of parking their vehicle next to ours rather than hiding it further along the road. They thought it was going to be easy and, granted, it very nearly was, but they were complacent and, when it came to opponents, I just loved those who were blessed with complacency. I looked at the Fiat and realised that it was a trap I had to avoid falling face first into.

I edged my way behind him, waited until he blew a plume of smoke into the air and cocked the gun I had taken from his colleague; the silencer three centimetres behind his right ear. Then, over his left shoulder, I dangled a set of keys; the Europcar logo emblazoned on the fob.

"Drop the radio, take these keys and start my car," I said.

He didn't turn around; he knew the drill. "Do *what...*?" His tone was scornful.

"I said... *start my fucking car*. It's a hire car and they'll charge me if I don't take it back. In one piece. So I'd like you to get inside, start the engine and make sure that that's exactly how it's going to stay when I get in it."

The radio fell to the ground with a dull thump. As he moved toward the car I beckoned for Sarah, picked up the radio and threw it hard into the trees. Then, my eyes never leaving him, I removed the Land Rover keys from the ignition. I didn't throw them, though. Not yet.

Smoking guy stubbed his latest under his boot, climbed into the Fiat and, keeping the door open as I stayed well back, slid the key in the ignition. I held my breath, as indeed did he, although I still don't know why because I was only making sure he hadn't rigged the Fiat, not anyone else. It sparked into life.

I threw his keys in roughly the same direction as the radio and signalled for him to step back from the car as Sarah climbed in the passenger side. Then I edged over to the driver's door, still wide open.

"You do know we'll get you?" he said, mouth and eyes sneering with equal intensity. "Real soon."

He had the face of a man who would cheerfully kill you with one hand whilst calmly eating ice-cream, or indeed smoking a cigarette, with the other. He also looked cocky, like he was seriously looking forward to getting that chance.

"Your friend probably isn't dead... *yet*," I said with the most callous grin I could manage, then slid into the seat and found a gear.

Sarah looked back through the window, then at me. Her face said it all. "All you did was strap him to the bell-ropes."

"I know that and you know that, but fortunately he's too damn stupid to know that."

There aren't many police tracking the speed of passing vehicles along the D-613, thank God, and Fiats may not be the fastest cars in the world but I got nearly one hundred out of ours on the road back to Couiza. All the time I watched the rear-view, waiting for the Landrover to sneak into view at any moment.

It didn't.

Some way after Couiza I threw the gun from the window into endless fields bordering the road. I still wanted it, obviously, because it made me feel safer, but there'd be nowhere to ditch it once we hit the highway and I sure as hell didn't want to walk into an airport with it tucked into my belt or leave it for the Europcar guys to find. I felt I had my fair share of problems already.

Every car that passed, turned in front or appeared as so much as a speck in the rear-view mirror was a potential threat. These guys were serious. Big time serious. They'd whacked the old guy, shot him in the back of the head and splayed his face over the stone without a second thought, and they'd done it just to prove to us that they meant business. So that hopefully we'd do exactly as we were told.

Life never quite goes the way you plan, does it?

As we passed the signs for Alet-les-Bains, I took a deep breath and turned to Sarah.

"So... what are my chances of getting you to enlighten me about the pen thing?"

She looked straight ahead and said nothing. For a good few seconds I thought it was going to stay that way, then she too took a deep breath. Except that hers was the 'I'm not going to tell you what I don't want you to know' kind.

"It's nothing really," she said.

"You wrote the words: *'Fuck you, Klein,'* and that's nothing?"

"He won't see it until it's too late, anyway," she said. "Anyway, it's not what I wrote that bothers you, is it? It's what I *drew*."

And she had me there again. I had only glanced, but I knew full well what I had seen.

"How do you know that symbol?"

"It's on the pictures you have. The autopsies of dead naked guy."

"You haven't seen those pictures," I said.

"Oh no, I haven't, have I?"

She smiled in a way that told me she had wanted me to catch her out. Like I'd just played right into her hands.

"So... are you going to tell me how the hell you know about that tattoo?"

"No," she said softly, turning and grinning at me like she held every ace in the pack and a spare up her sleeve.

"Well, not yet, anyway."

THIRTY-FIVE
FRIDAY, AUGUST 14, 2043.
SERRES, PERPIGNAN, FRANCE.

The irony that they were in a church was not lost on Klein. If indeed he found the answers for which he had spent a lifetime searching, then this would be rather an amusing place in which to do it.

It did not escape him the Moravian Chapel in which he had felt the first of his increasingly regular stomach cramps, more frequent as the Crohn's won its battle against an immune system that had slowly adapted and fought back against the modifiers - along with making his shit a constant blood red - had borne a similar layout to the chapel here. But then, were churches the world over not intrinsically the same? There was a central nave stretching away from the main entrance, two side aisles, the altar located centrally and raised respectfully at the front and a stained glass window behind, positioned in such a way as to spread maximum light across the gathered congregation. The chapel at Fellbeck had possessed two such windows, one located either side of the pulpit, but they both showed the same image: the lamb of God, its foreleg curled around the wooden pole of a flag which bore the red cross of the crusaders.

The lamb, as in all the school's publications, had been shown within the coloured panels as standing on a slight tor; symbolic that it was that little more elevated than those around it; symbolic that it had conquered; that it had been victorious in battle.

The winning of battles and the spoils that were bestowed as a result did not require swords and death, Klein realised. Not any more. Indeed most weapons development now concerned itself with the destruction of systems rather than cities. From the United States to China, everyone was starting to realise that the chronic and often plague-like spread of information was far more effective in deciding the course of warfare than the equally chronic - and equally plague-like - spread of fire, death or chemical and biological agents. In the modern world, the greatest prize to be seized was not land and property but the hearts, minds, ideals and trust of the population. It could be achieved in many ways. Indeed, given the advancements in media and technology, it could also be achieved far quicker than ever before.

Once Klein attained his answers and once he further advertised and spread them via the world's rapidly-expanding networks, then technological victory would be his. He might not govern the lands but he would control the people therein. He would have one of the most powerful weapons in history, the one that even the child looking down from his mother's arms on the stained glass window here in Serres had failed to fully attain: overwhelming public support.

Using one of his travel chairs, more traditional in design, he wheeled himself the full length of what had once been the main aisle, the thin, hard rubber clunking rhythmically on breaks in the cold stone. Though he did not see it as he approached the altar, he passed within inches of an age-old mark, deep and sharp, carved into the stone floor. It looked like the kind that might have been caused by a chisel.

The cherubim which had once adorned the altar were little more than stumps now and only one of the four stone rings remained. The main edifice, far from being the glorious homage to the vessel of God it had once been, was cracked from tip to base and peeling open like a ripened seed-pod. Large chunks of broken stone littered the base; ancient shrapnel from an desperately unarmed and ultimately fruitless battle against the hands of time.

Kerr wandered the room, casting the torch up and down the walls as if horrifically transfixed by the sheer darkness of the place. Periodically he kicked pieces of stone or shards of broken glass and they echoed back

331

from the reticent walls as they slid. Having been used to vulgar levels of luxury his entire life, he clearly considered this place the pits. He stared up to a corner of the ceiling where a spider had spun its web across a broken plaster cornice and was now motionless, staring back at them.

"What a dump," he said.

"Good," Klein offered. "Because that means that we are the first ones to come here for a very long time."

Sherman nodded across to Kerr who turned the beam, allowing Sherman to move around the back of the altar and place his weight against the slab. He shoved hard. Nothing. So he shoved again, his face growing steadily more reddened and grunting gently until he could push no more.

He offered one last desperate gasp and gave up.

At Klein's request Kerr moved around to help. He laid the torch facing the stone and, once Sherman's breath had returned, they leaned and pushed, sweating like breach-birth mothers. The broken slab above, the deep crack rendering it increasingly incapable of supporting its own weight, was now acting like a junkyard car-press on the inserted stone and making the job three times more difficult than it should have been.

Klein sighed impatiently and bit deep into his blackening lower lip in readiness.

Alison stared at the only screen currently alight with colour, the central of the three. Filling the frame was a picture of Mason, dead on the autopsy table, his twisted and tattooed ankle clearly visible. She leaned back, blew gently across coffee cupped in both hands, and prayed to whatever she took for God that she was doing the right thing.

This had been the most complex puzzle she had ever needed to solve and also the one which allowed her the least time for completion. In her head she had tried to take the facts and from them build a full and very intricate picture of the sequence of events.

Who could have been where, and when.

SEQUENCE

Why something would have happened, and when.

Who, why and when.

And how..?

In the end, she had given up on technology, relying instead on an archaic method of colour-coded index cards. On them, in neat blue script, she had written each event and where it had, might have or might one day take place. Then, by carefully reassessing the scenario at all levels, she had periodically amended and juggled those cards until they had seemed to make some kind of sense. All she could do now was sit back and hope, because it would be a very long time before she knew with any certainty whether or not her estimates were even close to being correct.

Among her many hopes was one that Klein did not find in Serres the one thing he so desperately craved.

What she did know at least, based on the pictures and the autopsy report, was that if her synopsis of events was correct then Mason had to escape, and she could no longer leave that to chance. Even though the consequences would be immense were her involvement to be discovered, she somehow had to make sure that he escaped. She had to help him. It was a huge gamble, the biggest of her life, but Klein needed to be stopped.

But was it really Klein she feared? Even she now was getting increasingly less worried about her employer; his failing health seemingly making him more impotent and unlikely a candidate with each day that passed, and more about the up-and-coming Sherman. She had started to see something in that man's eyes that Klein himself had once had; a burgeoning quest for wealth and power.

He wanted money, regardless of the cost. Even as a scientist, well-versed in Keplar's Laws of Planetary Motion, he still thought it was cold hard cash which made the world go round.

He was a young man, and not a very nice one. Ambition combined with youth and a complete lack of moral standards formed the kind of alliances that often lacked charitable subdivisions.

333

Either way, Alison reasoned, somebody had to be stopped. Even if that somebody transpired to be her. The tables could not be found, ever, no matter what form they took. If indeed they existed then any trace of that existence would need to be erased. No clues. And for now Jeffrey Mason, pretty much whether he liked it or not, had just become the key to the imminent failure of Klein, Sherman and whoever else chose to throw their hat into an increasingly lawless ring.

She closed the picture of Mason and brought up another which showed one of the detectives who had been assigned to Mason's case; Nick Lambert. She stared at his cold features, his hung, drawn and quartered dog expression and the weary shape of his eyes. In them she saw something else. It looked like compassion, as though this man - hidden deep below a hardened exterior - did indeed possess a heart.

She smiled. This was going to work out.

She just knew it was.

The stone started to slide. Slowly. With each push the crack in the upper structure fractured a little more and slowed the operation further. With the combined strength of Sherman and Kerr, however, its fight to remain in place was proving a vain one. As the slab eased into view, Klein stared expectantly, his failing eyes still showing that they were capable of hunger. With the rug across his legs to protect against the cold and in his weakened state he looked more akin to the inhabitant of an old people's home eagerly awaiting a plate of mashed food than the CEO of a multi-billion dollar empire waiting for proof of the ultimate technology.

Centimetres of movement became mere millimetres as the stone above pressed resiliently down, its crack increasingly becoming both visible and audible.

"After three," Sherman said, exhaling deeply and preparing for one last desperate shove.

He made the count and both men pushed hard, their combined weight pressed hard against the slab. It stayed put for the briefest moment, then broke free to an echo that bounced around the bare walls. The slab tilted toward the floor, remaining angled toward Klein as it hit. It faced him in all its glory as the stone above, the one that had formed the main body of the Ark, finally gave way and imploded into the void that was left. Segments broke and fell, shattering like glass across the cold stone floor.

Sherman and Kerr collapsed to their knees, breathless and red. Nobody wanted to see the tables more than Sherman, but they could wait.

They had been waiting for centuries, they'd sure as hell be waiting when he finally got his breath back.

The two men shook hands briefly as they climbed back to their feet and took opposing routes around the altar. Klein was still in his chair, his eyes fixed on the slab that faced him. Those eyes were wide, but not with awe and wonder. With shock. Despair. Both men could see in an instant that something was wrong and, almost in unison, took a step forward, looking down at the piece of rock that had nearly offered them a hernia apiece.

"I don't believe it," Klein said, slow and resigned. "I don't believe it." He looked to Sherman, the answer to all things sequential, the man who had uncovered the science and who knew precisely how it worked. His face was almost begging, pleading for an answer that he himself was unable to find. "How could this happen?"

No answer came. Klein turned back to the slab, stared again in disbelief at the empty receptacles and the highly skilled carving of Davies' tattoo. The man had done his job, as briefed, and the Tables of Testimony, lost to man for hundreds of years following their theft from Narbonne in 1132 had been placed exactly where Klein had ordered them to be placed. The marking alone was confirmation of this.

Yet they were not there now, and there was no point sending somebody back to deal with Davies, because the carving showed that Davies had not been the one who had failed. The blame lie at somebody else's door, somebody Klein knew all too well. He just didn't know how the hell it could possibly be, that was all.

Not yet.

Kerr looked at the writing; *'Fuck you, Klein'*, his expression demonstrating that he too was short of answers. He looked to the symbol; not the sharp edges of Davies' design, but the rough felt-pen scrawl of another.

"Who's tattoo is that?" he asked.

"Mason's," Sherman said. He couldn't believe what he was seeing any more than Klein. Any more than Kerr.

"It can't be," Kerr replied. "Mason hasn't gone anywhere. He's still in L.A., isn't he?"

Klein's face curled in anger; his top lip rising slowly to expose his teeth like a wolf protecting its young and he almost snarled the words...

"Terminate Mason."

"But sir," Sherman began. He was going to explain that terminating Mason would do no good; that history could not be changed and that if Mason had got here then, like it or not, there was absolutely nothing he or Klein could do about it. Even if Mason was still in Los Angeles now, this had already happened. It could not be changed.

Klein didn't want to hear it. When he spoke again it was more akin to a long desperate scream; the kind one makes when losing a loved one.

"I said terminate the little shit. *Noooow!!!!*"

THIRTY-SIX

SATURDAY, JUNE 11, 2011.

PERPIGNAN, FRANCE.

'The first man's wish had been for death, and he got it.'

After we passed Limoux the road split into two lanes and the volume of traffic built steadily to take full advantage. Suddenly Sarah did something that I was not a little surprised she hadn't done much earlier in the journey; she opened the rucksack to take a look at her treasure.

In the church she'd placed them in a small wooden box which she'd brought specifically for the purpose. It was light in colour, basic and traditional in design, the kind into which you might place memories before tucking it safely at the base of a wardrobe. Of course, I doubt that she had known exactly what size of box would be required, but it was big enough, the tables being little more than six inches in diameter. Inside she had placed cotton wadding and whilst the box was at least an inch and a half too large in either direction, and much more rectangular in shape, they appeared to have been kept as safe as she had intended.

They were carved from a satin-black stone; the darkest and truest black I can remember seeing, but the slight gloss of their surface gave them a rich purple hue at the highlights. Intrinsically round, they had strange shapes missing at various intervals around the circumference, perhaps fifty or so in total. It was these which gave the stones the appearance of some kind of ancient gear mechanism.

Rather than being simple indents, however, these were curved like a letter 'S' in some kind of yin/yang affair. I could see, on my glances away from the wheel, that the shapes were perfectly symmetrical and that the tables would probably interlock with each other at any point of choosing. The face was hewn very intricately; carved and embossed in a series of symbols the likes of which I had never seen before. They did not look dissimilar to the kind of hieroglyphic symbols one might see on ancient Egyptian tombs, yet they also had the appearance of crude lettering, similar in style to Aramaic.

Or, perhaps, a combination of the two.

What the hell did I know?

The symbols were arranged in a series of undulating rings which created interlocking waves, and were so tiny as to have been laser-etched. Presumably, to rotate the disks and lock the two together at different angles would offer differing combinations of symbols and, conversely, differing results. Perhaps all results stood on their own merits, or perhaps they simply led to a further, more deeply embedded result.

Then another and another.

Again, what the hell did I know?

"How do they work?" I asked, focusing instead on a deep blue people carrier that had just indicated to pull in ahead of us.

"I haven't the faintest idea," Sarah said, turning them both in her hands and carefully interlocking the grooves. she looked like a teenager trying to solve his first Rubik's cube. "I count forty-nine hooks, and four planar sides, so that gives combinations of forty-nine to the power of four. Which is..."

In less than a minute she did the kind of mental arithmetic that I could not even hope to do in a week, "...nearly six million combinations. And that's before you get to the internal rings."

"That would take one mother of a computer to decode."

"Maybe. Except I'm not about to let anyone's computer get the chance."

"Isn't that the point? To decipher them?"

"Nick... these are the answers to the way the world works. I have a very clear theory about what would happen if somebody gets those answers... and let's just say it isn't nice."

"Which is?"

She leaned back and held the disks toward the windshield, turning them over and around and watching the light as the symbols broke it into a host of tiny speckles.

"You once said to me that if somebody could control the numbers, then they'd be playing God, yeah?" I nodded. "Well, I don't think so," she continued. "I think that they would come close to actually *being* God, and that's a whole different thing altogether. If whatever it is that's keeping track of us at the moment isn't required any more and, worse still, is replaced by the thing it always endeavoured to control, then the world as we know it ceases to be. We dabble too much and understand too little. We really shouldn't be allowed to succeed in this."

"It's like being a politician," she continued. "Anyone who actually wants to be one should automatically be excluded from ever being one."

We took an underpass that fed us under France's equivalent of a freeway and I indicated left onto N-161.

"So you think that anyone who wants to unlock these things wants to be... *God*?"

Her attention was back on the tables, her expression one of intense appreciation at what they might be. She stared at them like someone looking at an old photo. "Well, perhaps not God *per se*, but they sure as hell want to be something they shouldn't, that's for damn sure."

She turned to look at me, her eyes formed into an inquisitive slant. "What we have here, Nick, is a monkey paw."

I turned, very briefly, and scowled. "What do you mean? What the hell's a monkey paw?"

"W.W. Jacobs," she said. "He was a horror writer although, like many horror writers of his day, he was much more of a philosopher really. He simply used horror to accentuate what he felt were frighteningly real problems."

"And he though a monkey paw was frightening?"

"Indeed he did. The story concerned the White family: Mother, Father and their beloved son, Herbert. One night an old friend of Mr. White's arrived at their home following travels in India and he brought with him a mummified monkey paw. He said that it had been cursed to offer three wishes to each of three men. He had used his own three, as had another man, though he did not seem happy about those he had made himself and never explained what they were. What he did say was that the first man's third wish had been for death, and he got it. He was persuaded to give the paw to Mr. White, though he admitted that he would rather see it burned."

"So did he take his three wishes?"

"He took *one* of them," she explained. "He wished for two hundred pounds. All night nothing came but in the morning Mr. and Mrs. White received a visitor from the factory where their son worked. Herbert had been caught in the machinery and the man had been sent to offer them financial compensation."

"Two hundred pounds?"

She nodded. "Two hundred pounds. So then Mrs. White told her husband to use the second wish; to make it so that their son was somehow still alive. And it worked, Herbert was raised from the dead and came-a-knocking."

"But...?"

"But before Mrs. White could open the door, her husband came to his senses and used the final wish to send whatever it was that their son had become back to his grave."

I laughed quietly to myself at that. "The moral being what...? Never trust a monkey paw...?"

"Not at all. The paw was never the bad guy in the piece and was never referred to as such. The paw was merely the conduit for somebody else's desires. *Human* desires. Just as money is not the root of all evil."

I nodded in understanding. "But the *love* of it is....?"

"That's the motto. It's not about what these tables can or cannot achieve; it's about what people can or cannot achieve once they have them. For every person out there wishing for world peace and for its occupants to feel as free as the birds, I'll find you at least two or three eager to kill some birds and rule the roost."

"So what are you going to do with them?" I asked. It seemed to be the most obvious question, given that I have always held an inherent distrust for people who hold on to things because they believe them to be too dangerous to hand over. "Presumably you've been commissioned by somebody and receiving your fee involves handing them over in some way? Or have we just busted our asses and nearly died for the sum total of sweet nothing?"

Sarah smiled. "I have been commissioned by somebody," she said. "But as I've already told you, the payment I receive isn't always the kind you'd expect. So he isn't going to get them. The only payment I want now is the knowledge that these will never be found. Ever."

"So what *are* you going to do with them?"

She started to place them back in the box, as if she suddenly felt that she was treading on ground too holy for her shoes just by holding them. She closed the lid and they were gone. "If there's one thing I know it's that this world is what it is because two very distinct sets of things have happened to it."

"Which are...?"

"Firstly," she replied, "there are the things we know about. And secondly there are the things we don't. And just because we don't *know* about something doesn't mean that it hasn't shaped things far more than we could ever know."

She took a breath and looked around. "Who knows, maybe somewhere out there the technology exists to build a device so powerful it could destroy the entire planet in the time it takes for a light to flash. Perhaps it's already been built and it's just sitting there, waiting. If someone's *aware* of that kind of technology, then I think the best thing they can do for us all is keep their mouth tight shut, wouldn't you agree?"

"And you think that what you have in that box is a flashing light?"

"I don't know what I have in this box, really. In all honesty I don't even want to know."

"But what if the thing you have there is not going to blink out the world? What if what you hold in your hand is every cure for every disease we've ever known?"

As we pulled the Fiat into Europcar's dedicated parking area she smiled a resigned smile and carefully placed the box back in the rucksack. Safe. "Even if these *are* the ultimate in disease prevention and cure then the world would be just as screwed, and you can quote me on that."

"I don't follow."

"Millions fewer people dying prematurely? Overpopulation reaching epidemic proportions? Don't you think our fantastic.." and she used the word sarcastically, "...advances in technology make enough of us redundant already, without adding to the problem? A loss of natural selection would lead to nothing less than a global economic meltdown. Not enough jobs, food, housing and an entire medical industry which, despite its blacker points, helps support that economy, now in tatters. And what about religion? Would people still need something to turn to in the absence of pain and suffering? What is God without begging and what is begging if there are fewer things left to beg for?"

She glanced out of the window and watched the world she was trying to protect as it carried on about its business. "Don't be fooled, Nick; even things that look like fluffy little sheep can be wolves in woolly jumpers."

"So why not just destroy the tables and be done with it? Surely no matter where you hide them, they'll be found eventually, even if it takes another three hundred years. Law of averages."

"What God hath joined together, let not man put asunder," Sarah said, her voice reverberating defiantly through the car.

Her reasoning was simple; save for the possible exception of his almost ceaseless attacks on the planet earth itself, how could man destroy what God had created?

I gave her an appreciative look. "Said it before, say it again. You know your bible."

She smiled. "Occupational hazard."

"So what do you do with them? Hide them?"

She thought for a moment, considering the options. When she spoke, it was as though she had still not found an answer; as though the one she chose to deliver was actually nothing more than a 'best so far' option.

"No, I don't think I'm going to hide them."

At which point I was elevated from the point of 'a little unsure' to 'seriously confused'. "You're not?"

"No," she said. She unclipped her belt, climbed out of the car and turned, ducking slightly to look at me through the open door; the way she had when we had first reached her apartment. "I think *you* are."

THIRTY-SEVEN
Friday, August 14, 2043.
5th & Alameda, Los Angeles, California.

The corridor lights glided back toward full power and a few seconds later the mirror door slid open with a whisper. Two guards entered, one remaining by the door and holding the remote whilst the other moved the twelve or so feet further down to stand directly in front of Mason's bars.

Mason hadn't bothered standing.

Not this time.

"On your feet, turn around, back against the bars."

And, for the first time in his life, Mason didn't know what to do. It looked like this was going down just the way the bitch had said, but he couldn't be sure. What could she have to gain from helping Mason anyway? She hated him, which pleased him no end. Maybe this was a set up. Maybe Miss Pretty-Britches just wanted him to try something so they'd blow the device. But then, she'd swapped the device, hadn't she? He sat on his bunk, motionless, and thought for a moment, trying to decide what the hell to do. He sat and thought a little too long.

"I said on your feet, you little shit. Turn around and put your back flat against the bars."

It was a set up. It just had to be. He should never have bothered sticking that damn thing she gave him up his ass anyhow. They'd find it now, even if he behaved himself, and then they'd do him for sure. Still, he doubted they'd kill him. Not for having a rubber bung where the sun had

345

no privilege to shine.

He rose slowly from the bunk, muttering like he did, and turned, leaning as instructed against the bars. And, just before he did, he looked to the guard at the door, who was probably smiling his little ass off under that visor as he held up the fob; Mason clearly visible, white on red. This was definitely the wrong device.

Or was it? Had the bitch swapped them back after she'd gone? Had she and the two pretty boys here got a bit of a thing going, a kind of cat's away type affair and they wanted to play with Mason's little mouse-ass? Lose him some limbs for a two dollar bet? Perhaps they were testing little old Mason, just to see if he really was as dumb as he looked?

Lacking immediate answers, or options, he rose slowly from the bunk and did as he was instructed, turning to place his back firmly against the bars. With a metallic clank the shackles were clipped into place and the guard stood back, nodding to his friend. He keyed in the relevant code for Mason's door and the rack of bars slid down into the ground.

He felt naked. Worse than that he felt scared. Jeffrey Mason actually felt the hairs standing on the back of his neck and his stomach churning like he needed to hurl. He turned to face the guard, shaking gently.

"Where ya takin' Mason?" he asked.

"Move forward," the guard said.

"Where ya takin' Mason?' he repeated, and he didn't move forward.

The guard looked over to his friend, making sure his finger was firmly on the button, then he stepped forward himself, his visor right in Mason's face. "You're in deep enough shit already, Mason," he said, his voice harsh. "I suggest you don't make it any worse for yourself. Now move along like a good little boy."

You're in deep enough shit already, Mason.

Just like the bitch had said. Deep shit, and Mason didn't even know what he was supposed to have done. According to the bitch he couldn't know because he hadn't even done it yet. But something big was going down,

346

something the bitch had warned him about, and Mason didn't like it. Didn't like it at all. No, sir.

He stepped forward and turned toward the main door, as ordered, the guard coming up on his left. Then, quick as a bad memory he swung, the shackles catching the guard full in the visor and sending him violently to the floor. Stubbs, who'd been sitting on his bunk not giving a shit about anyone or anything was now against the bars himself, his black knuckles paling as he gripped the steel and his head pressed tight against the gap so that he could see at least part way along the corridor.

The guard's helmet flew off, skidding a few feet further along the floor than he had, and for a second he was shaken. Then he looked up, saw the stance of his partner and could tell that his friend was wavering; unsure how to react. This was a real situation, just like they'd trained for, but was it actually a button pressing situation or just a petty scrap like Stubbs and Edison's little fracas in the canteen?

But then, hadn't Edison got his throat cut? Was his partner now gonna get cut? Shit, just how serious was this?

The guard who had barked the orders was laid on the floor with Mason already bearing down on him again, the heavy shackles raised above his head, and he made his colleague's decision for him. "Press the button. Press the fucking button."

"Yeah, fucker," Stubbs shouted from down the hall. "Press that fucking button. Blow that loudmouth motherfucker's ass off." And how he smiled. This was gonna be some serious fun.

It took another moment but then the guard did it - he pressed the button. Mason was striking down on the guy on the floor now, beating his head with the heavy steel bar that connected his wrists. Each time he jammed his eyes tight closed before it hit, but not before he had noticed one thing; the red lights on each of his wrists.

Neither of them had come on.

Suddenly Stubbs felt uneasy and he looked down. He'd seen something out of the corner of his eye, but he didn't know quite what it was. Not straight away. Even when he saw it for real it took an instant to register. The red lights on both his wrists were on. He turned his arms and stared in disbelief. Then he looked up and screamed,

"Hey, you got the wrong fuckin...." The four seconds had passed and they all went detonated with perfect synchronicity. Six small explosive devices on each limb, evenly spaced and designed to fire like miniature rockets direct into the flesh. There was a slight flash from beyond the metal and Stubbs' eyes widened. This couldn't be happening. This was one mother of a bad dream. But it was happening, because in the instant that followed he saw his hands, his own hands, falling to the floor; separated from his body like in some sick movie. And his balance? Where was his balance? Because it wasn't just them big black hands that were falling any more, it was also Stubbs himself. It was probably two or three seconds after he hit the floor, watching more blood run like spilled wine from his extremities than he had ever seen before, that he finally felt the pain; like nothing he could ever have imagined. It was as though someone had not only taken off his hands and feet but shoved red hot pokers deep into his wounds as well.

He screamed the place down.

Mason had finished beating on the guard and was shuffling his still manacled feet along the corridor; away from the door but toward the lift. The lift to the lab. The guard on his feet looked down the corridor, watched as he passed Stubbs' cell and saw one black stump hanging out through the bars, blood pumping onto the floor. He realised what had happened. Somehow he'd got the wrong detonator. But how...?

Quick as he could, the guard re-entered the door code and ran outside for the other. Mason glanced at Stubbs, lying on the floor almost foetal now, screaming and wailing and smiled; just couldn't help it.

He never slowed his pace, but still found time to say, "Bet that hurts real bad, don't it nigger?"

What was it the bitch had said, Mason thought. The code? She'd given him a way to remember it, made him feel stupid but she had said it would work. It was like some kind of memory trick of something. *It's a good position for the people you killed.* He reached the keypad, hoping to God she wasn't fucking with him now. If she was then ten seconds from now it wouldn't just be Stubbs lying there with no hands and feet, screaming like a baby that ain't been fed.

He reached the keypad and lifted both hands, the shackles still forcing them eight inches apart. *A good position*, he remembered it now, *sixty nine*. Like the sex position thing. *For the people you killed.* Well, every shithead and their dog knew that Mason had taken down *fifteen*. The fat judge had repeated it three times for the benefit of the dailies not five minutes before he'd swung down that big ol' gavel. So there it was, and don't you let Mason down now bitch, he thought. He keyed it in as quickly as his limited arm movements would allow. Six-nine-one-five, and...

The doors opened.

No time to rest 'cos resting was dying. What else had she said, about the lift? About the cells being sealed 'cos there was offices in the building next door. Sound proof, bomb proof, sodding water proof and everything. Yeah, everything. Like the key fobs. They didn't work, not through walls and doors this thick. But if there was a gap, so much as a millimetre of gap when the guy pressed the button, then it was all over.

He pressed the door close button, the guard he'd beaten the living shit out of now running down the corridor toward him, slipping on the bloodied floor whilst his own blood streamed down his forehead and into his eyes.

The doors started to close.

The guard got his fingers in the gap. Just the tips of his fingers, red with blood, that would be enough. In fact, if that button got pressed it was more than enough. Mason banged the guy's fingers with his hands, the rattling of the steel echoing through the walls of the metal lift. Then he heard the other voice; the other guard.

"Get out of the way, Karl."

Karl, the guy who's fingers were taking a pounding. His pal didn't want him to get caught in the mini-explosions, maybe lose a finger of his own.

So the fingers pulled back and the door nearly closed. Not quick enough, Mason thought. Plenty time to press that button and Mason's limping home. Close for fuck's sake.

But then another sound. Like plastic on something solid. Like what? Like the sound you make when you drop something. Yeah, that was it. Fucker had been panicking so much that he'd dropped the Goddamned fob.

Mason couldn't see, but the guard himself dropped straight to his knees, giving chase and caught the fob on the first bounce. He pressed the button in one seamlessly fluid movement. He looked up, his friend sitting with his back against the lift door, exhausted. The door that was closed. He pressed the button again. Nothing. He threw the fob down the corridor. It hit the wall to the side of the lift and bounced into cell nineteen.

"The stairs," the seated guy, Karl, said, climbing to his feet. "Get the guns."

They ran out of the corridor. Karl grabbed two submachine guns from a rack at the base of a stairwell and threw one to his partner. Both ran upstairs, heavy boots resonating from the metal treadplates.

Mason, meanwhile, was already in the lab. So much to remember, but he was not really being presented with a choice. They'd be coming and they'd be coming, like, real soon.

Okay, he thought, big room. Console first. The big one by the windows. Very bottom left, button called ARM. Flick lever up to AUTO-POSITION and press red button. Then over to computer, hold... shit what was it?... ESC and RETURN, that's it, until the box comes up. Then key in one-eight-seven and hit RETURN again. Then, back over to the big console. Red switch for DOOR, left hand side, hit it.

Door is open, that's good. Arm is coming down onto ball, that's good as well. Now orange button one, top left. Flick it. Where the hell is orange button one?

He looked the entire console up and down, no memory of where it was supposed to be. Then he saw it, or them, middle right. Two orange buttons side by side. And the one on the left is number one. Flick it - good - digital display is rising. Then get ready, because the bitch said that the second you hit orange button two you've got less than three full seconds to throw yourself to the left and through that big door. That was the maximum delay allowed by the system. Three seconds is hard enough with freedom of movement, let alone when you've got an eight inch hinged steel bar joining your Goddamned legs together.

Mason took a deep breath, held his shackled arms over the switch and prepared. He looked at the digital display, it had completed its climb and stopped; one-eight-seven. All he could hear now was a buzzing sound. He wasn't sure if it was just in his head.

Then he heard them, the dumbasses, coming up the stairwell; coming fast. Shit, shit and more shit. He couldn't think any more, there was no time to think. He hit orange button two, the one on the right and dived to the left, spinning on his feet and falling backwards into the airlock. He hit the button and the semi-circle that enclosed him rotated so that he faced into the lab.

He tried to breathe but nothing would come; it was as though all the air had been stolen from around him but still he stumbled blindly in. He saw the other door to the lab thrown wide open and through the glass was Karl, the guy with the fingers. But one of those fingers was now pressed against the trigger of a gun. Still he couldn't breathe; the air felt as though it was pulling at his skin.

There was a loud screaming sound, louder than he had ever heard before and even Mason wondered if it was coming from Mason. Then a bright light, brighter than heaven itself, and some smaller flashes of light in between. These, however, were coming from the direction of Karl. Karl and his big-ass gun.

Sounds. Loud sounds. Like the smashing of glass. Not in front or behind but everywhere; all around him, the fragments clattering like steel plates to the floor. But not just glass. No, some of this was thicker, heavier. Ceramic tiles being broken with a hammer maybe, shards flying everywhere and a sudden rush of cold air circling around his body.

Followed by the most warm and soothing sensation Mason had ever felt in his life; like being in a warm bath after spending a week in the cold.

And that light. So very, very bright. Almost blinding, yet safe enough to stare right into the very heart of. He turned his head and looked around. Everything was white, though he could sense that things were hiding within. Objects that he recognised, but all... white. Huge white trash cans with white wheels next to white cardboard boxes. And there were white doors, too, and what looked like a fire escape. He looked back to the boxes. All of them had writing on them, but it was all shapes. Like symbols. Oriental symbols perhaps. Japanese? Chinese?

Where the fuck was Mason anyway? Was he dead or alive? He'd never felt more alive in his life but if he was dead then he must have ended up in Gouk heaven by mistake. And he could feel warmth from his chest and his arm. Not a still warmth, though, but a runny warmth. Like warm treacle running all the way down his body.

There was something he needed to do. He remembered that now. Something for the bitch. Some kind of 'favour' and it involved the thing she'd had him ram up his ass; a piece of paper or something. A name written at the top and a number. A girl. He had to find that girl for the bitch. *(He felt weak.)* She was at some asylum or something. Some kind of tree. Oak something. Think. But he couldn't, his mind was a mess. Oakdern? No, that wasn't it, it sounded wrong. *(Oh, God, Jesus he felt weak.)* What did it matter anyhow? He was going and shit there'd be no fucking panic then. Hard to grasp but he'd be safe. Be free. All the time in the fucking world. He could worry about it then. *(Why can't I breathe?)* He might deliver this thing after all. I mean, the bitch had saved his ass, hadn't she? Even if she hadn't, she'd still found him a way out of the cells; set him free. *(Oh God and sweet Jesus, what's happening to me?)*

And still everything so white. Gloriously white and getting whiter with every second of his life that ticked slowly away; the finer details of the objects which surrounded him getting steadily lost. Whiter and whiter until there was nothing but the pure white of whiteness itself.

Mason, curled foetal on the cold stone of the alley behind Mr. Yang's Chinese Supermarket, was dead.

THIRTY-EIGHT

SATURDAY, JUNE 11, 2011.
CAUCASSONNE, FRANCE.

Salvaza airport at Caucassonne is hardly LAX. In fact, it's doesn't do a very good impression of an airport at all. It's situated right out in the sticks, in a huge area of desperately sparse countryside, two kilometres from the city centre and has one terminal and one runway. Which means there aren't a great many places to hide. Despite the fact that we would almost certainly be needing them.

Pretty darned soon I was guessing.

After handing back the Fiat and being stung on the mileage we entered the terminal itself and headed straight to the all-yellow Air Liberté desk to buy tickets for the next flight to Paris. As the woman checked our documents I tapped my feet impatiently, periodically looking around to the main doors. They'd know exactly where we would be heading and they'd be here real soon, I was sure of it.

Eventually the tickets were handed over and the woman informed us, speaking like a ventriloquist through that painted-on smile that airline staff seem to have perfected, that we had half an hour to the flight. I hoped to God it was enough.

I moved to head straight for the gate, but Sarah asked me to wait and disappeared into the tiny gift shop. What the hell she was doing I had no idea. I divided my time watching nervously through the glass and even more nervously looking up and down the terminal; waiting for the two faces I did not want to see to come busting in.

They'd shot the old guy full in the face, so I doubted they would be debating whether or not to save our puny asses. I was also betting the two of them did not actually exist; at least, not officially. Like the parchment they had been so keen to decipher. They probably held no driving licenses and no medical insurance numbers. They would come straight in, see the two of us and turn us into tea-bags on the spot, even if there were fifty people nearby. Then they'd just walk over like they were picking up mail, take what they needed and go.

By the time anyone might have started to register what had happened in front of them, they'd have been and gone. Disappeared. Nobody would see or hear from them again. I looked around and through the other passengers.

Safety in numbers, it seemed, had banded together and taken a well-earned vacation.

Sarah emerged a couple of long minutes later with some brown wrapping paper and clear tape. Despite my face stressing the urgency of getting the hell out of France she then went and made it even worse, if that were possible. She excused herself to the Ladies' room and I cursed her for it. I got to thinking that maybe she actually wanted to die that day; that she had made some secretive arrangements to meet her maker that I was completely unaware of.

When she returned, five of the angriest minutes of my life later, she carried what appeared to be the box.

Wrapped in brown paper. Like a gift.

"What the hell are you doing?" I asked, following her as she swiftly walked the full length of the terminal. She weaved without a care in and out of those who had no idea where they were, let alone where they needed to be.

"I'm sending a package to myself," she said bluntly, stopping in front of a DHL desk and exchanging pleasantries.

In the time it took for her to hand over the package, I started to realise why she was making me so angry with everything that she did. It was the same reason she'd set me thinking on the way into Serres and shouting at her on the way out. It was because of the feeling she gave me.

I had thought it was guilt, but it wasn't. Guilt I could have lived with, given that it had been a fairly regular drinking buddy for as many years as I could recall. No, what I was feeling now, in her presence, was inadequacy. I had been unable to cope with the aftermath of the Casparo deal and it had been that which had led to my inability to even let it pass through my mind without being numbed by the kind of complacency that only alcohol could offer. It was that which had led to Katherine leaving, taking Vicki along with her, and I hadn't coped with that any better. I was not a bad man, just a thoroughly... inadequate one.

Which was why I was so angry now. It was starting to dawn on me, even though I was here on this merry little jaunt, that I was playing absolutely no part in it whatsoever. I was an understudy to the healthiest actress in town.

It was Sarah who knew what the Latin meant, it was she who had traced it to France and it was her sister who had given us the clue that had led to the church. The clue that Sarah, yet again, had spotted as we sat drinking coffee. It was also

Sarah who had decided that we would side-track to meet with Kelly and Sarah who had decided to waste valuable time buying packaging materials in order to send the parcel to herself.

Why was I even here? All the detective work was being done by some young kid who was now signing forms on the desk in front of me. Was I really that useless, I wondered?

Was that why I was so angry?

Having signed everything requested of her, Sarah paid in cash and the package was added to an outgoing pile. She had requested that it be collected in person by the recipient, which they were unaware was herself, from the DHL office at LAX. Then she turned to me and with a fired-up smile.

Job done, let's go.

"They do international cargo direct from here on a pre-ten," she explained as we finally headed toward the gate, now with less than five minutes to spare. "With us transferring in Paris, we don't land in Los Angeles until 11.30 tomorrow. The package will beat us there and we can collect it when we land."

"And is that safe?" I asked. I mean, wasn't she now trusting the 'Divine Laws of God and Man' or whatever they were to a courier service. I'm casting no aspersions on DHL whatsoever, I'm sure they're very careful, but personally I wouldn't have been letting those damn things out my sight.

"I took out the extra insurance," she said with an oblique smile. The call had already been put out for our flight and a small queue of Paris travellers were already having their boarding cards torn. "Besides, it's a damn sight safer than hand luggage," she said. "Especially if those two decide to follow us on to the plane..."

Her eyes moved backward very slightly.

I knew immediately who she meant. I only glanced, and my face registered no recognition whatsoever, but they were there alright. Watching.

Mid-sentence guy was standing with his face half obscured by a square beige pillar some thirty feet behind her, his nose looking like he'd done fifteen rounds. Smoking guy had his back to us, the radio to his ear. I don't know if he'd retrieved it with the keys or whether his friend had carried a spare. I guess in all the excitement I forgot to check, though it didn't really matter now either way. They knew we were here, they knew the flight we were boarding and now, given the use of the radio, so did somebody else. I was guessing at... what had she called him?... Grier.

I had no idea when they had arrived, what course they were being told to follow or what they had managed to see so far. I could only hope that their arrival at the airport had been a little too late to see what Sarah had been doing at the DHL desk.

"Relax," she said, handing over her card. "We'll be fine. And so will they."

Much later, perhaps two years after all this happened, I was sitting alone in my new quiet place - the cliffs at Montalvo - just listening to the cymbal-crash of the waves below and thinking strange thoughts to myself and something very important occurred to me. Smoking guy, whatever he had told Grier - now or down the line - had not actually told him where in France they had followed Sarah and I to when we had found the tables.

Or, if he had, Grier had never bothered to tell Klein.

After all, Klein was little more than a scientist, wasn't he? He was only employed to help find the tables and then do whatever was needed to unlock the information contained within them. But they'd been found now. Suddenly the where and why had become little more than a extraneous information.

Which was a big mistake on their part, I have to say; so very typical of those differing investigative styles I mentioned earlier. We wanted to know why the guy was dead; they didn't. They were just glad he was. And now they didn't care where the tables had been; or how we had found them. They just wanted them back.

Now maybe, if they'd failed to retrieve the tables at all, they would have looked deeper into our investigation and deeper, conversely, into the sleepy village of Serres. Except that they didn't fail. They got exactly what they wanted and they set the best mind – the most powerful brain – they had available to work on them.

With Tina helping, I'm told it took Klein's team less than seven months to decode them.

THIRTY-NINE
SUNDAY, AUGUST 16, 2043.
5TH & ALAMEDA, LOS ANGELES, CALIFORNIA.

Klein, already an old man, looked fifteen years older as he sat and stared out across the modern skyline of Los Angeles.

All the scientific advances in the world were no use to him now. He wasn't going to recover from this latest descent in health and he knew it. He could *feel* it, and still the world went about its business, desperately oblivious to the truth about how it even functioned as the minions used what little hacking ability they had to dream up what they should have for supper that night or where to spend the statutory two weeks that their employers would pay them for not coming in to work.

His eyes were glazed and his breathing deep as he contemplated just how close he had been to finally achieving a lifelong ambition. He had worked all his life, quite literally, for a day that was already at an end and he was no better off than before. He had never married and rarely even dabbled in his younger days, preferring only to immerse himself in his work. Such things had never been an issue until now.

Until today.

What others might have felt Klein had been missing he knew would more than compensated for when his day came; when he was recognised the world over as the greatest scientist ever to have set foot on its surface. And it would happen during his lifetime, he had always assumed, not via some kind of posthumous shit of which he would never be aware.

Newton, Einstein, Hawkins, Crick and Watson would all pale into the shadows once Klein attained his prize; their spirits would bow down to him and applaud him for finally putting all scientific dilemmas to rest once and for all. For all time.

No longer. Now it was all gone and, unlike his failures in the early part of the century, Klein knew that if this was a hiccup then it was the ultimate hiccup and not even the shock he felt now was going to cure it. There would not be another chance. Klein's day had come and then it had gone again with nothing but the weight of his thoughts to show for its existence. He wondered if things would have been different had the decision not been made to terminate Mason immediately. Would he not then have broken free? Could the tables have been saved?

Even the answer to that seemed to be a resounding 'No'. As Sherman had gone to great pains to explain on the return flight from France, the tables were lost long before he, Klein and Kerr had even entered the chapel in Serres. They had been lost some time around the middle of 2011, given the number that Mason had somehow known how to key into the Sequence.

That, more than anything, was what was burning at Klein right now.

Somewhere, somehow there had been a betrayal, and to start with he had no idea who or why. Initially speculation had fallen on the guards but if they'd had anything to tell, then the techniques that had been implemented would undoubtedly have brought it out of them. Nothing.

With further investigation, speculation fell onto just one other person; the person who in a few minutes would be entering Klein's office where he and Sherman were already waiting.

She had never liked the idea, not from the start. What was it she had said? *'The worst idea in a long history of really bad ideas'*. So, because she had no control over whether or not the plan would actually go ahead, she had bitten her tongue and bided her time. She was, after all, a very clever girl. When the time was right and the others were in France she had simply chosen to sabotage it all. She had visited Mason without authorisation that very morning and had taken both his and Stubbs' detonator fobs into the cells with her.

Somehow, as she spoke to Mason, she had swapped those fobs over, giving Mason the chance to escape and blowing the extremities off the foul-mouthed Stubbs. As Mason had made his escape, the guards had fired their weapons and were sure they had hit him. Mason, however, had not been killed. He could not have been, not when the crude sketch of his tattoo was still burning its image into Klein's mind in super-heated black felt pen.

How could Alison, of all people, have betrayed him? If Klein could not trust *her* then who the hell was there he could trust? He had known her almost all her life, for Christ's sake.

Despite having been dealt one of the worst cards possible in terms of her childhood, Alison Bond had spent almost her entire life wanting for nothing. And this was how she chose to repay the debt? Bitch.

"What are you going to do?" Sherman asked, seated in front of Klein's desk and drinking thick black coffee.

Klein snarled quietly to himself, still in a world of his own, and then said. "Kill her."

He took a small red case, half the size of a spectacle case, from his pocket and opened it wide. Inside were an array of tablets of varying colours. Blue, red, green yellow and pink. To one side, held in its own clasp, was a black capsule, twice the size of the others. It was this tablet that most who knew him were trained to force down his throat if he ever blacked out completely. It was the one chance he might have to prolong his life. He extracted a yellow pill, an aspirin-like mesalamine that might just assuage the burning sensation he was now feeling inside, and closed the case.

"And the tables?" Like Klein, they were all Sherman truly cared about.

Klein rolled the tablet around his tongue for a few moments and then swallowed. In the early days he had hated the taste of almost all his medication and had done what he could to swallow without ever feeling

361

them go. Now, it seemed, due in no small part to the fact that he was up to eight a day, including three of these little beauties, they were little more than the taste of stale air.

He took a deep breath, his throat rasping. "They're gone," he said, though it pained him to hear his own words.

Sherman sighed and bit his lip as the light flashed on Klein's desk. Klein nodded and he pressed the red square, not even waiting for the voice on the other end.

"Send her in."

The door opened and Alison entered. She knew exactly what this was about, of course she did. Christ, she'd left enough clues for them to follow. No sniffer dogs needed here, just a keen eye and a healthy dose of common reasoning. Now, however, she was stepping into the next realm and its success depended on her taking great care over every damn word she said. She would either be leaving this room dead or very, very much alive. Like Klein opening the altar, this was her moment of truth. The one she had waited for all her life.

"Miss Bond," Klein said, still staring through the glass. "Glad you could join us."

They'd caught her alright. Klein was back to calling her 'Miss Bond'. She tried to convince herself that this was good, that this was phase one complete, but she struggled to allow it to make her feel any better. She was a wreck inside.

She walked halfway across the laminate floor of the office, high heels clicking her pace and stopped in the centre of an ornate Japanese rug, its shape almost framing her stance. Her hair was tied back, as ever, her white coat draped over her more casual clothing and Klein turned just in time to see something behind those tiny half-rims of hers; fear. She had every right to be scared, he thought. Every right to fear for the well-furnished life he had laid out for her. The one that he, and only he, could take away again in an instant.

"What can you tell me about Friday's little disaster?" he asked, trying as hard as he might to remain calm.

Alison's expression never changed. She stared right at him, though she had to force herself to do so, and said; "Mason escaped."

"And *why* did he escape?" Sherman asked.

Without any hint of remorse in her voice, as though she was stating the most natural turn of events possible, Alison said; "Because I helped him."

Klein looked up. He was hurt, she could see that. "You helped him?" His voice was croaking with disbelief, the kind that comes when a wayward son realises for the first time that it was his mother who turned him in to the cops. Betrayal.

"Yes."

"Christ Almighty, Alison, why the hell did you do that?"

"I had my reasons."

Sherman glared at her. He tried to remain expressionless, uncaring, but even she could see that he held a sense of superiority that was hammering at him from inside.

"Then, given the whole heap of shit you're in right now, I suggest you share those reasons with us."

Klein also looked at her, waiting desperately for an answer that would make him feel less shafted by one of his own than he did right now. "Go on," he said.

Alison looked to them both, very calmly. "Because I continued the research after you'd gone," she said. "And I found out why you were in Cardou all those years ago."

Klein looked puzzled at the change of tack. "I was advising on a dig," he said. "That's no real secret."

"You were digging for the tables," Alison continued. "In fact, that whole site was nothing more than a search for the tables, wasn't it, Josef?"

Klein looked to Sherman, then back to Alison. "Yes," he said. "again, that's no secret. What does this have to do with Mason?"

"When were you there?" Alison asked.

Klein shrugged. His memory wasn't quite as good as it should have been. "I'm not sure. 2010 maybe? 2011?"

"2011," Alison said bluntly. "And why did you abandon the dig?"

Klein thought back to the events of the time. This had all happened whilst he had been in Siberia, attending the discovery of the Siberium. He had received an e-mail from Grier who handled security at the Cardou dig site.

"Because we believed that the tables had been found." he said. "So I came back from Russia and we started the process of decoding them."

"But they weren't the tables, Josef. Were they?"

He shook his head. "No, they weren't"

"Wait a minute," Sherman said. "You're digging in France for tables in 2011. You think you find them in 2011 and we've just found out not only that Mason stole them but he also stole them in 2011? Am I the only one who can't see a problem with this?"

Alison smiled, allowing her own superiority to break through. Now it was she who had them by the balls.

"What are you saying Alison?" Klein asked.

"That we can make this all work out, if we're very, very clever about it."

Sherman sneered. "You're suggesting you can succeed where we failed, is that it?"

"Try to remember, Sherman, that genius is not about concocting hair-brained schemes." She turned and glared at him. "Genius is about making them work."

Sherman started to speak. "I don't see how you of all people..."

"Go ahead, Alison," Klein interrupted, causing Sherman to grit his ridiculously expensive teeth.

"I discovered, after you'd gone, that Mason got to the tables first," Alison explained, "hence the drawing of the tattoo, and realised that even if we wanted to, we couldn't change that. How he managed to find them is irrelevant now, but he did. What happened to them *afterwards* is very important. So what we can do is the one thing you suggested at the very first Sequence meeting. We can be the *reason* that Mason ultimately failed."

Sherman narrowed his eyes. "But Mason didn't fail. He got the tables."

Alison smiled. "In which case, where are they now?"

Klein and Sherman looked to each other.

Neither man knew.

Klein leaned back in the wheelchair and thought quietly to himself. Sherman just looked back and forth like an animal trapped in a rising flood; ready to drown. He had uncovered this science, for Christ's sake, he knew better than anyone how it worked. How was it then that Alison had answers that he didn't? How was it that he still couldn't work them out now?

Klein looked up and smiled gently. "So you're suggesting that we send somebody to steal them from Mason?"

Alison nodded. "Exactly. From or, more preferably, before. We know he stole them and we know where from. All we need to do is steal them back, something he probably isn't intelligent enough to be expecting. Then we choose a new site and, wherever that may be, that is where they are right now."

"And the drawing? The message?"

"My guess is that he wrote that when he discovered they weren't there."

Klein looked worried. "So what do we do about the fakes? They happened. Presumably that also cannot be changed."

"No, it can't," Alison agreed, "But we can take care of them. We know that Grier is the one who found them. As I understand it the fakes were too big for us to send back now. So, what we have to do is have the person we send back create the fakes for Grier to find. That way you get some fake tables in 2011, spend seven months trying to decode them and realise that they aren't the real thing. Nothing's changed."

365

Sherman's mouth was open wide.

"Let me get this right," he said. "You're suggesting that Josef has some fake tables created so that he himself spends more than half a year trying to decode them, only to discover that they are fakes he learns many years later that he created. And he does this without ever realising he's doing it?"

Alison smiled confidently. "You're the one who decided all this could be done. You just didn't realise it at the time, that was all."

Klein was still thinking it through but he didn't look too enthused. In truth he still looked worried. Alison did have a point, he thought. Mason had indeed stolen the tables and, for all he himself knew, had replaced them with the fakes that had once been the bane of Klein's life. If somebody could be sent back to steal the tables from Mason and either allow him to create fakes or create some of their own, then the originals could indeed be hidden in a new location. As Alison had pointed out, they could be there now, just waiting to be uncovered.

Still there was a problem; and it was a big one. One that came down to the one word that had been lacking in Klein's vocabulary since before Alison had entered his office less than ten minutes ago. Trust.

"I don't know," he said eventually. "This is complicated. More complicated than any of the others. Stubbs is dead and that only leaves Edison, who'll be in hospital for at least a few weeks yet. Even when he's released I doubt very much that he has the qualities we need for this kind of job. It's very clever, Alison, but if I'm honest I just don't think there's anyone who can be trusted to pull this off."

Klein was right. Stubbs had bled to death in his cell, the guards being far more concerned with Mason's fate than his and Edison was only a few steps short of a retard even when his throat was intact. Which meant, in Klein's eyes, that - for now - all options had been expunged. Perhaps he could get somebody else from Polunsky and train them up, but that would take time and she doubted very much he wanted to sit around and wait for it all to happen whether it made any difference or not.

He did not have much time left. Not in this life.

"How long will it take to repair the tile damage?" she asked.

"It could be complete by tomorrow if necessary," Klein replied, "but there's no point if there's no-one ready to go."

"There is," Alison said, raising her eyebrows well above the level of her half-rims.

"Who?"

"Me."

Sherman was nearly choking on his coffee. "You are joking?"

"I have a funnier repertoire than that, David," Alison said.

"You're the reason we're in this mess. You let Mason go and you think you can be trusted? Not a chance."

"No," Alison said deliberately. "Mason *had* to go. And, by the laws of how this whole shitty thing works, he had to be gone before you opened the altar. Which left me with no choice but to help him on his way. He had the tables years ago and nothing was ever going to change that. It went wrong because it had to go wrong, and I did what I needed to do, for us all, by making sure that it did."

Klein was nodding. "She has a point, Dave. Without Alison's help we'd be in a far bigger mess than we are now."

Although addressing Sherman, he was looking at Alison as he spoke. "At least this way we had some hard evidence of Mason's departure and could see where it was that he went back. If he'd done it in the middle of the night with someone else's help the computers could have been cleared and he could have gone to 1850 for all we knew. Besides, let us not forget that it was Alison's hard work on the research that stitched the sequence of events in 2011 to Mason leaving in the first place. All of which she managed before the altar was opened."

He looked at her now and smiled gently. Gone was the sense of betrayal and in its place was a sense of pride; almost paternal. She really was one intelligent young girl. He had been right to approve her acceptance into the NorthStar Foundation.

And yet there was still one thing that Sherman could not, for the life in him, work out.

"Why you, Alison?" Everybody in this room knew the harsh severity that such a task would entail for her. She would never, ever be able to come back.

"I'd like to speak to Josef," she said, looking back at Sherman. "Alone, if I may."

"Not a ch...." Sherman began.

Once again he was cut mid-sentence by Klein. "David, why don't you fetch us all some more coffee?"

"But...?" he began, but Klein's hand was up in the air, stopping him. There would be no negotiation.

Reluctantly, Sherman rose to his feet and walked from the room, casting a harsh glance at Alison as he passed. The heavy oak door slammed hard behind him.

"It's because..." Alison began, but Klein's hand was in the air once more.

"Don't worry," he said, a sense of pride now smoothing some of the many wrinkles on his aged face. "I think I already know."

FORTY

We were forced to queue for over ten minutes at the DHL desk. Some spoilt old trout whose face had been surgically stretched so far back that I'm surprised she could close her eyes at night was sending something to her cousin in New York.

"And you make sure you treat that with care, young man, that's a five hundred dollar bottle of scent in there, and it's fragile. Do you understand me?" She repeated the word like the kid on the desk had never been to school, *"fra... gile."*

It made me laugh. She was concerned that they might somehow damage some overpriced water designed to make her elderly cousin stop smelling of urine and Sarah had just sent some age-old old tablets of stone which, if authentic, had a value probably exceeding the combined worth of the NASDAQ. She had done it without any fuss on sending or impatience on collection. Without even the slightest hint of 'now you listen here, young man'. She had just waited calmly.

As if she had known they would be safe.

Yes, it bugged me a little that sending and retrieving the tables had been so easy. Well, for all of about ten minutes it did. You see, good fortune isn't like Columbo's wife; you do actually

369

get to see it from time to time, and if it comes knocking on my door I'll open it up and invite it in for a beer any day of the week.

The package back in Sarah's olive rucksack we headed out into the morning sun and collected the Taurus from long-stay. It had been parked there all that time and nothing, least of all the car itself, had actually been stolen. I ask you, how big a heap of shit did you need to drive to be able to leave it parked up with no driver's-side window whatsoever and for it to stay put? As we pulled through the barriers and headed out through the traffic toward I-405, I put my sunglasses on and asked what I figured at that point would be the most important question of the day. Of course, it wasn't.

"So... where now?"

Sarah, as ever, was watching the world float by. "Hardware store," she said bluntly.

★ ★ ★ ★ ★

We stopped at the All-Mart on Dewberry; Everything you need under one roof – and so much more!! Sarah asked me to wait in the car and I obliged. She was gone for no more than fifteen minutes, during which time I climbed out and leaned casually against the car smoking a cigarette and getting myself a sweat. When she returned she had managed to prove All-Mart's adage remarkably well, carrying as she was two shovels, a box with Magellan written on it on deep red letters, a map of California, a bag of sandwiches, assorted snacks and a twelve pack of Bud. "King of Beers," she said with a wry smile.

She placed the shovels in the trunk, her sunglasses back on and our temporary respite from the thick heat of the Taurus came to an abrupt end.

"OK, now where?"

"You keep driving," she said, "and I'll keep directing."

She directed me along I-405 until we joined I-5 to travel north. As we started to leave the sprawl of Los Angeles, the surrounding area became more and more like open desert and the sun seemed to get infinitely hotter through the glass. Sarah reached into the back and retrieved two bottles of Bud, cranking the tops with her keyring and handing one over.

After an hour or so we entered 'Grapevine Canyon' and passed the signs for Fort Tejon State Historic Park, now seventy miles from Los Angeles.

"I brought my wife here once," I said. "Before she was my wife. Back when I was still trying to impress her. She had a real interest in history so we took a drive out."

Sarah smiled. "You old romantic." The sarcasm was evident.

"Hardly. I hated it. Spent the full stretch of the return journey telling her so. Somehow I had managed to spend an entire day, one that I'll never get back I hasten to add, listening to hammy actors in 1850's costumes grumbling about fatigue details, shoeing horses or doing crap carpentry. We even got to watch a re-enactment of a Chemeheui Indian raid on the barracks by a horde of even worse actors. I had no interest in the past then, I have none now. I was just trying to get my rocks off."

"Did it work?"

"It sure did." I smiled to myself.

"No interest in the past then?"

"Nope."

"So you don't believe in time travel?"

I laughed. "Hardly."

"I do," she said, and left it at that, turning away from me.

"You do what?"

"I believe in time travel," she said, her voice lowered. "I believe in it very much."

"You mean, the real H.G. Wells type stuff?"

She nodded. "You don't think it's possible..?"

I laughed. "Not for a second, no." Considering myself a moderately sane man, there was no particular reason I should believe in such a thing either. "Why do you ask?"

"But do you believe in what Tina can do?"

"You mean with the Snickers?"

"I mean with *anything*. You've only ever seen it with a Snickers, that's all."

I thought for a moment. "I don't know," I said, and it was the truth. "I don't think you faked it, if that's what you mean, but it's still kind of hard to get to get my head around."

"But will you accept that it *might* just be possible that she moved that bar of chocolate just by thinking about it; by merely wanting it to move?"

"Okay. If it helps, then it *might* be possible."

"So time travel *might* be possible as well?"

"I didn't say that," I corrected. "And nor did I say that aliens exist or that Kennedy was part of some government conspiracy either. They're hardly the same."

"Aliens, no; Kennedy, no, but Tina's trick and time travel, oh yes. They're *exactly* the same thing."

I scowled. "Not from where I'm sitting."

"But they are," Sarah protested. "They have to be. Because if

Tina moves anything... anything at all... then she has to change a sequence of numbers, those which dictate where the Snickers bar is. Three dimensions; width, depth, height. Agreed?"

"Agreed."

"And what's the fourth dimension?"

"I have absolutely no idea, Sarah. What is it?"

"Time, stupid," she said, as if it was so very obvious. "It's a scientific fact that time is the fourth dimension because an object is only at point 'x comma y comma z' at a given point in time; 't'. Before and after that point in time it could be somewhere else altogether. So Tina can only change points 'x', 'y' and 'z' if she also knows point 't'; the point in time at which the object is there in the first place. Then, as time; 't' carries on at it's normal pace, she changes the other co-ordinates and the Snickers moves towards her... *over time*. Doesn't matter if it's a minute, a second or a blink of the eye, there's got to be a time element attached."

"So what are you saying? That if Tina could adjust point 't' in her mind as well, then she could actually make the Snickers disappear, only to reappear maybe an hour later?"

"Something like that, yeah. Or earlier."

I was shaking my head defiantly. "I don't buy it."

She wiped a dribble of Bud from her chin with the back of her hand. "But it *might* be possible?"

"If it will keep you any happier then yes; I'll concede that it *might* be possible."

Sarah smiled, happy with her days work. "But I still don't believe it actually *is* possible," I added. Deliberately.

"And I'm very certain that it is," she said quietly.

"Ah," I said, having suddenly remembered Sarah's initial question. "Wait a minute, we're talking here about time *travel*?"

"Yeah," she said.

"As in *human* travel? Like I said; the real H.G.Well's stuff?"

"That's right."

"So how would Tina do that? How would she change the sequence for a human being? Answer me that."

"She wouldn't," Sarah said nonchalantly.

"So who would then?"

"Not who, Nick.... what."

"Okay," I said. "What would do that?"

"Something powerful enough to bend time."

"Such as?"

She thought for a few seconds. "Do you know what a black hole is?"

I shrugged. "A very poor Disney film with Maximilian Schell and a very scary robot?" She glared at me chastisingly. "No,' I said, "I have no idea what a black hole is. Not really."

"Good," she said, fanning herself with the map. "Allow me to explain...."

A few miles further along from the highway from Fort Tejon toward Mettler, Sarah directed me to make a turn off I-5 and we reached the kind of territory where roads totally cease to have any meaning and become one long stretch, like a Marlboro ad. At the end of each straight was the horizon and over the horizon was another long straight leading right the way to the next horizon.

And so on.

At least I knew that we weren't being followed by the killer twins or any of their colleagues.

Unless, of course, they were tracking us by satellite.

Which was just one more of those things which proved to me that irony also tuned into Columbo, perhaps when the schedules were slim, and realised that playing his wife was a very poorly paid job indeed.

FORTY-ONE

Tuesday, August 18, 2043.
5th & Alameda, Los Angeles, California.

The room again. The dark place, and the only square of light - the window - was diminished as though time had perhaps moved on; though not by much. The room was a lot colder now, though she felt that this had little to do with the world outside. It had to do with the emotion inside; sharp icicles of fear behind her face.

The man with the dark eyes, the eyes that could not conceal their even darker intent, had been and gone. She did not know how she knew, or even if she knew, but the sense she felt was too powerful within her to ignore. It was like blood in her veins. She could smell nothing but she knew that if she could, if she had been allowed, then his fetor would be clinging in the air. The figure on the bed was now curled tight, as though in pain.

She tried to reach out to this figure, as one might a victim in a public place. In the street.

(in an alley)

...but it was as though the air had thickened impenetrably between them. She pushed her fingers into the gloom but she could not pierce the barrier.

(Reaching out)

She felt emotion rising within her. Fear, yes, but also anger and sorrow. The kind a social worker might feel. I need to help if only the...

(victim)

...would allow her to come close. She wanted to hug this person, to make them feel warm and safe but now was not the time. She felt that too. There were barriers. They were there for a reason and they needed to be broken down. Slowly. This person, this...

(victim)

...was as afraid of her as she was afraid of everybody. Trust had been broken so there was none left to give. Perhaps she had felt safe before. Perhaps she had felt no reason to feel otherwise. Until today. Until this man. The man with the dark eyes; the dark intent.

(reaching out).

(victim).

(in an alley).

When she came back from that room she did not travel alone. She brought with her the fear, the anger and the sorrow - the sorrow that would stay with her until she died - but she also brought answers. In an instant she knew what she had to do and how she could make this work. Because nothing had been more firmly ensconced in her mind these last few days than the certain knowledge that she *had* to make this work. It was too important to her, certainly, but perhaps it might prove to be too important to the world as well. It would take years to achieve and she would miss out on witnessing its conclusion, but she must not fail in the things she needed to do. In her dark and fertile mind, like the richest soils, she might be carrying the one and only chance for growth.

(Once you know, you can never return).

No-one would ignore a victim, not if they were wretched and they begged... pleaded like sinners at the feet of God. Some might choose to hide it, but everyone had a beating heart lurking inside. It was the living affliction of the human condition.

No-one would refuse her pleas and, until barriers were broken down and trust restored, no-one would ask too many awkward questions either.

She knew what she had to do.

377

* * * * *

Alison couldn't even sit down, her ass was hurting that much. Christ knows how she'd gotten in all in. Fortunately, they'd allowed her to do what she had needed to do in complete privacy. Hell, they were all crazy as loons but they weren't perverts. In addition to currency - and this time it was diamonds and notes - her ten minutes of seclusion had allowed her to add a few little gems of her own, so to speak.

Christ, how crazy was this anyway? It sure wasn't the kind of thing one dreamed of doing when one graduated high school. That said, Alison had had more than enough dreams when she was a kid and some of those were about to be fulfilled, if everything went according to this crazy plan she'd somehow concocted in that over-active imagination of hers.

Would it be worth it?

She wondered. She pondered.

But not for too long.

So she paced up and down the control room wearing the red jump suit with arms folded. She was so Goddamned nervous, even though she knew it worked. They all did. Castle, D'Almas, Davies and even Mason had proved that it worked, but none of that seemed to make it any easier to bear. Five hundred people could have gone and she'd still have been just as apprehensive. It was like space travel; been done many times before but still a highly stupid thing to do to any right thinking individual.

She was thinking right, wasn't she?

What about the pain? She had no idea whether or not this was going to hurt. There might have been nothing to suggest it from any of the mice, but then each had been leaving notes a long time after they had made the journey. It might have been the worst pain they had ever suffered and they'd just neglected to mention it. She took a deep breath then exhaled it in one long, highly audible sigh. Why the hell was she here?

Then she remembered. And yes, she thought, even if it was the most excruciating pain she ever felt, it would *still* be worth it. She would walk over hot coals with her bare feet doused in gasoline if it would get her where she needed to be.

"Nervous?" Strauss asked, deliberately stating the obvious with his feet resting on the console.

"Shitting bricks," she said.

"Not surprised." He also took a deep breath as he looked through the new glass to the sphere; the broken tiles from the gunfire on the far wall now fixed. "I can't actually believe you're actually doing this."

"Me either."

"So I suppose any chance of a date's out of the window then?"

"It was anyway." She threw him a look. "How is Rachael, by the way?"

"She's good. Running the Cardou lab for a while. Back next week, though!" He rubbed his hands together in only semi-forced excitement. He smiled. "And... I *might* just have bought her another little gift!"

Alison narrowed her eyes as Strauss reached into his pocket and produced a red velvet ring box, flicking it open to reveal the platinum-set diamond inside.

"The good luck charm didn't work then? At least, not for her." She thought for a moment and smiled. "Ah well, I guess we all have our cross to bear."

Strauss leaned forward. "You know what gets me, though?"

Alison faked intrigue. "What's that?"

"Well, I'm thirty-nine, and you're going back maybe thirty-two or thirty-three years, yeah?"

"Yeah."

"And yet *never* as a six or seven year old kid do I recall a stunningly beautiful woman calling round my aunt's house and taking me out for milkshakes."

"Your point being?"

Strauss looked hurt. "Well, you're not only blowing me out now, you blew me out then as well. That's two chances you've missed."

Alison thought for a moment and smiled gently. "Do you remember you once told me that when you were around seven you found a little dog abandoned outside the front door and you fell in love with it and kept it?"

"Joopy?" He said, expectantly. 'Joopy' had one droopy ear, hence the name. "Was that you?"

Alison smiled. "Nope." She winked. "Had you going, though."

She looked him straight in the eye. "Seriously, good luck with the whole... ring thing. I'm no expert when it comes to... well, you know... but it looks beautiful. *Expensive*. If... and I stress the *if*... she says yes, I hope to God she knows what she's letting herself in for."

"Alison," Strauss said, his tone turning serious. It was so out of character that it seemed for a moment as though it were coming from another man. "I would cross deserts, oceans and mountains for that woman."

She smiled. "Let's hope you don't have to. So... are we ready to go?"

Strauss narrowed his eyes, then smiled back and turned once more toward the console. "There's still time to change your mind, you know. About the trip, I mean, not the dog."

"I'll be fine," she said with a forced smile.

She wondered if she would.

Klein and Alison had spent almost the entire previous day in each other's company as she had driven to his directions in order to find a suitable recovery site. He was beyond trusting anyone now and wanted only he and she to know exactly where this new site would be located. The others would find out, of course, but not until fifteen or so minutes before he told them to start digging and watched from the comfort of his chair.

They had talked at length about what she had really wanted from this world, more than anything, and how that had led ultimately to her volunteering to perform the duties that only a criminal facing death would even have been slightly tempted to undertake.

Alison's task, however, was to be so much different than that of the others

- they had been gaining their freedom in much the same way as she would be losing hers forever. There were simple theories of time travel, it transpired, and they must be obeyed. Just in case those theories were ever proved correct enough to become hard and fast laws. Come what may, Alison would have no option but to adhere rigidly to them.

Which was why, despite Klein's worries, she had asked to be sent back approximately two years prior to Mason's arrival. Before she did the things she had to do, she first needed time to do the things she had always *wanted* to do.

"What charge are we going with?" Strauss asked, having already positioned the arm he was now freewheeling his chair back to the computer terminal.

Alison looked straight at him. "One-nine-four," she said. Given the calculations Sherman had long-since produced onto his timeline graph, this should place her arrival toward the end of April or the beginning of May 2009.

"Last chance to change your mind and go meet Newton," Strauss joked.

"One-nine-four," Alison said again. She wasn't really in the mood for jokes. Not any more.

Strauss keyed the number in and wheeled himself back to the console. "Ready when you are."

"Okay, time to go," she said, but there was no emotion in her voice. It was just business.

She started to shake hands with Strauss but he lifted from his chair and hugged her tightly instead.

She pulled back with a smile and kissed him gently on the cheek.

"Thanks, Pete." Then she stepped backward into the airlock and pressed the button, the airtight cylinder spinning her slowly around so that she faced into the room. She quickly moved over to the mask dangling from the ceiling and placed it over her head, elastic behind her ears.

"I really can't believe I'm doing this," she said into the mask, her distorted voice coming over the speakers in Strauss' control room.

"I can't believe I'm actually going to see you naked for two frames," Strauss added with a mischievous smile, already framing her in the viewfinder of the tripod-mounted camera.

"Yeah... say 'Hi' to Rachael for me, won't you..?"

Alison moved around the room, the air tube following her every move, and brushed her hand over the Siberium sphere. She had only ever been this close on the day that Charlie had disappeared and she had never really studied its surface, beautiful as it was.

Here, she thought, embedded into the last gasp of a star's life, were the answers to so many questions that should never have been answered. It looked like a curved pool of orange-red liquid, so smooth and perfect from the laser cutting and her reflection stretched around its surface and distorted her features. She wondered how she might age in this new time. Would she age the same; faster; slower? Who knew?

She felt a strange sticky feeling in her hand, as though it was somehow being magnetised toward the surface of the sphere and she pulled back, gently brushing her fingertips with her thumb.

Strauss patiently allowed her to explore the room and prepare herself mentally; far more than he would ever have granted one of the mice and now, feeling as ready as she ever would, she turned slowly to face him, her arms by her side and took a final deep breath of the brand of air that 2043 had to offer.

She closed her eyes and nodded to him.

In those final few moments after Strauss had hit 'Orange-One' and the buzzing had started to build, she prayed to herself that the things she had assumed were correct proved to be just that.

She had spent over six hours the previous night, having returned from the recovery site with Klein, memorising each of the index cards she had written when trying to piece together the chain of events; the sequence, and now she had no choice but to commit them to that all-powerful memory with which she had been blessed. There were so many things that had to happen, and in so clear and precise an order, and she hoped that she had been blessed with the ability to recall them clearly when the time came to pull this off.

She had tried to convince herself that these events were now committed to history and that they would happen whether she played her part or not, but she had still failed to fully believe it. This world could not be all fate and destiny, she decided, there must be some kind of human interaction. Like a stage actress she had a role to play and she needed to know every one of her lines before the curtain went up. There would be no dress rehearsal and no second night if she messed up the first. So much to do, so little.... she laughed quietly to herself as the screaming sound began to resonate through the room... *time*.

The screaming reached heights of pitch that defied the laws of propagation, almost bursting her ears. She could see Strauss leaning over, headphones in place and checking the read-out. He looked to her and nodded. She paused for only a second then nodded back once more.

Time.

To go.

"Good luck," he said, and he meant it.

"You too," she offered, knowingly. She meant it too.

She saw his right hand move, he smiled ever so slightly and she knew that 'Orange-Two' had now been hit.

Right at that moment the weirdest thing happened. Time did not speed up or become some motion-blur from which she would suddenly grind to a halt in the blink of an eye. Instead, it slowed down, so much so that she could see Strauss' mouth moving at quarter speed.

Everything was so white, as though she was watching the world through a bridal veil. Perhaps even a death shroud? Paler and paler in infinite slow motion until the finer details of everything around her were lost. Then they returned, though markedly different than they had appeared before.

She could see trash cans in the lab around her and empty boxes scattered all over the place. Buildings seemed to rise to her left and her right, running away into the distance. And there seemed to be a gap. In that gap were cars, slowed to a crawl.

In less than half a second, far less than a breath, all became perfectly clear once more. The colour returned to her field of view, the shroud removed, and the cars increased to full speed, the noise of their engines echoing along the alleyway. Other noises came with them; sirens, machines and voices all merged into a weird kind of backstreet symphony.

Cold. She felt so very cold; as though she was standing in a god-damned refrigerator. The air was not still; there was wind blowing around her legs and discarded scraps of paper were blowing in and out of her line of vision. She looked down at her own body and saw that she was naked; as naked as the day she had been born. Even though, if she had just been through what she thought she had just been through, then she hadn't actually been born at all. Not yet.

"You want some lady?"

A gravely voice from behind her. Old. Slurring.

She turned quickly. An old man was slumped beside the boxes, his clothes filthy and his straggly beard clumped with dirt and grime. He did not look surprised at her instantaneous arrival, nor at her complete lack of clothing, rather he was just smiling wide, sans front teeth. He held a brown paper bag with fingerless gloves, his nails black like tar and a green glass bottle neck poking out from the top of the bag.

She should have been embarrassed that she was naked, but there were more pressing things to attend to. "What year is this?" she asked. Somehow she even managed to deliver the question without it sounding as crazy as it should have done. In spite of her clear voice she felt weak, as though some of her blood had been stolen somewhere along the way.

The tramp's toothless smile grew even wider, but only for the briefest moment. Then he leaned forward and tried to look deathly serious, one finger held resolutely in the air as though checking the direction of a non-existent breeze. Very calmly and trying his utmost not to slur any more, he said; "Who gives a damn?" and laughed like a man possessed by so much more than simple inebriation.

The sound echoed prophetically along the dismal alleyway which now surrounded her.

Strauss carefully placed the ring over the manicured nail of his left ring finger and smiled gently to himself. One more week and, one way or another, life was going to change forever.

Just one more week.

He removed a 1922 Peace Dollar from his trouser pocket; a good luck charm given to him by his grandfather many years ago, and placed it across his thumb. All he needed was for the coin to give him a sign; to tell him that his odds were currently just a little better than 50-50.

"Heads she says 'yes'. Tails..." he took a breath, "...she says..."

He daren't even say it. So he flipped instead.

Suddenly the door flew open and he span around to find Burgess, one of the security guards standing breathless in the doorway.

"We've got a problem," he said, wheezing.

Strauss narrowed his eyes. "What kind of problem."

"Cardou," Burgess offered. His face turned deathly serious. "There's been an explosion. A *big* explosion."

For a moment Strauss was frozen to the chair. Slowly, like awakening from an anaesthetic, realisation crept through his body and thawed the shock into something that felt so much worse. It tore something inside.

Only one word found an exit. "Rachael..."

He leapt to his feet and pushed past Burgess to run the full length of the corridor beyond. When Burgess had finally turned and followed, all that could be heard were panicked footsteps in the distance and the metallic rhythm of the coin still spinning on the cold hard tiles; faster and more erratic until it found itself a level and slowed to a halt.

No-one to see which side it had chosen. ·

FORTY-TWO
SUNDAY, JUNE 12, 2011.
42KM NORTH OF FORT TEJON STATE PARK, CALIFORNIA.

Twelve or so miles since we had made the turn from I-5, Sarah stopped fanning herself with the map, glanced swiftly down and then looked up again, almost triumphantly. She asked me to take the next right. Personally, I couldn't even see the next right; just the same never-ending road we'd been on for the past twenty minutes stretching infinitely ahead as though searching for the end of the world. I kept looking. And kept looking.

"Here," she said suddenly, as though the turning was staring me in the face just as critically as she was.

I slammed my size nine and stopped the car hard, the tyres skittering on the dusty road, and looked around at the barren landscape. The sum total of nothing times nothing. No trees, very little that even qualified as foliage and impossibly flat, the only hills staring darkly back from the far distance. There was a road out here, sure, but only one and it would appear that we were already on it. Then, to my right, I saw a barely visible set of tyre tracks leading off into the brush. Leading yet further into the sweltering depths of nowhere.

"You are joking?" I said. "That isn't a road, Sarah. It's a... well, it's... it's not a road, that's for sure."

She smiled. "It'll do."

I made the turn and we headed off to... somewhere. I really didn't know at this point. I daren't even guess.

"So you *really* think time travel is feasible?" I asked when the ensuing silence became a little too much to bear.

"Yes I do," she replied, forcing that smile wider.

I smiled and shook my head. There had been a great many things in this world that had been impossible and then taken a swift turn into reality. Flying. Space travel, with the possible exception of lunar landings. Me getting enthused about a case, perhaps, like I was now. Not time travel. That was something forever destined to appear under 'fiction' in just about every library on the planet.

Not unlike my wedding vows.

"There's certainly a few situations I'd like to take another look at," I said. It was just an idle comment, not really one aimed at Sarah. Not one aimed at anybody in particular.

Yet Sarah picked up on it straight away. She flicked her head toward me. "What did you say?"

I turned to face her. "Mistakes," I said, raising my voice slightly. "I was thinking I could maybe go back and correct a few."

"'Fraid not." She swigged Bud and looked away again.

"Why not?"

"You just... can't," she said, shrugging. "If it happened then it happened and if it didn't..." she turned to face me again, "then I'm really sorry, but it sure as hell ain't gonna."

"That's hardly fair," I said. And this from a man who doesn't actually believe such a thing is possible in the first place.

"I don't make the rules."

"Then who does? The great number cruncher in the sky?"

"I guess so."

"So, short of it being a spectator sport, what would be the point?" I asked.

"My thoughts exactly. No, the only point in time travel would be to change a few things."

"You just said you *can't* change things."

"No," she said firmly, "I said you can't change the *past*. Do you ever listen?"

"Only to the point where you lose me, which incidentally...."

"Okay," Sarah explained. "Let's say that time is merely a carpet, like a red carpet being rolled out for a film premiere, yeah?" I nodded. "And it rolls out at the speed of time. One second per second. We, the human race and all the little furry creatures only know what's happened in the past. We have no idea what the future holds, because it's still rolled up. Still with me?"

I pulled the bottle away from my mouth, spilling beer down my chin. "I think so."

"So, if that's the case then we have to assume that, in terms of our position on the carpet, we're walking just behind the roll, and I mean right behind it, following it forward."

"Sounds reasonable."

"So... the carpet that has already been laid has... already been laid. How it was laid cannot be altered because if one person travels back in time, there are still millions of people just behind the roll looking back at what's been laid. They have history books and/or memories that cannot be altered."

388

She looked over at me. "I'm still with you," I said. "I just don't get the 'change' thing yet, that's all."

"Okay, so let's say that one of the people just behind the roll wants to throw something over the roll so that in a short while the carpet will run over it and there'll be a lump. But he can't because this roll is huge and his angle is just way too steep."

"So he takes a few steps back, gets a better angle and throws the stone over the roll?"

Sarah nodded. "In terms of 'past affecting future' it's that kind of thing. Now the thing is you can't throw a stone into the future but you could bury one in the past that could be dug up in the future."

"And why would you want to do that?"

"Because there's a world shortage of stones," Sarah mocked. "We're talking analogies here, Nick."

"I know. What I mean is, why would you want to bury *anything* just for it to be dug up later?"

Sarah thought for a minute, breathing heavy. "Right," she said, getting herself into real 'explain it to the stupid guy' mode. "Let's say you've got a grandma who's dying and her only wish is to die wearing the first wedding ring she ever had; the one she lost fifty years ago."

"Okay," I agreed.

"Now the ring is definitely lost because it hasn't been seen even once during any of those fifty years. But you want dear old grandma to die happy so you think right, I'm gonna go back and steal that ring from her..."

"Steal it from her? Why would I do that? I mean, if I really loved her...?"

"*Because* you love her. Don't you see? The ring's gone anyway; there's nothing you can ever do to alter that. What you can do though, is become the reason it's lost. Only what you do, fifty years ago, is bury it in a place that no-one has *ever* dug up, but where you just know grandma is going to dig a hole, say, five minutes after you've gone.

"So, grandma digs a hole for her tree and, hey presto, there in the dirt is the ring she lost all those years ago. She picks it up, she slips it on and, because it still fits, she dies a very happy grandma indeed."

"So what you're saying is that you cannot change anything that has happened up to the point that you leave, but you could go back with the intention of changing something that's going to happen *after* you leave?"

"Exactly. Beyond the roll of the carpet."

"The red one?"

"Yeah."

"And, despite the fact that this makes you sound like a crazy woman, you don't feel even slightly embarrassed to voice to me that you quite honestly think it's possible?"

"Even you admitted that it might."

"Yeah, but I lied. Primarily to get you off my case."

Sarah smiled at me wryly. "Which only makes me wonder if there's anything you don't fail at."

I hoped to God - or whatever - that she was kidding.

I'm guessing that the only reason nothing else fell off the car as we spoke was because the Taurus had now, officially, run out of things to throw down in disgust. Yet it bounced and it skidded and it groaned. And hot? Jeez. The breeze that poured through the space where that window had once been was now little more than a hot fan. The kind you use to warm your toes, not cool your face.

Fifteen miles; I checked the clock; that was how far we were from the main road now. The actual road; the real one made of tarmac. According to my calculations we were less than twenty miles from the boundaries of the Mojave Native American Reservation, probably the most well-segregated site of its kind in the entire United States.

Suddenly, the track dropped and started to run across the centre of a dry lake; another huge expanse of nothing particularly exciting.

Sarah now removed the 'Magellan' from its box and inserted the battery. She pressed one of the buttons on the front and it beeped loudly. It had the look of an oversized cellphone with a backlit screen and five or six buttons at the bottom, four of which were arranged into arrows. On the screen was a crude LCD line-drawing of a map and some numbers.

Lots of numbers.

None of them made even the slightest bit of sense to me.

"So what is that thing exactly?" I asked.

The car lurched as the track dropped, seemingly to run the full width of the dry lake. Sarah nearly dropped the device, but her eyes never left the screen. "GPS," she said, almost disinterestedly. "Tells us exactly where we are on the planet."

"So what does it say now? *Who knows? Lost? Arse end of nowhere?*"

"Nope," she said, "It says *'Stop the car Detective Lambert, because Sarah would very much like to get out now…'*"

FORTY-THREE

Tuesday, August 18, 2043.
42km North of Fort Tejon State Park, California.

Save for the four men who drove through the barren environment there was nothing living or breathing within fifty miles. Eventually the light on the handset flashed intermittently and the vehicle ground to a halt, the wheels skidding softly on the uppermost layer of sandy earth.

The area was completely level for at least a mile in all directions with large red mountains rising like a protective barrier at all sides. It had been Klein's idea, through his increasing sense of paranoia, to utilise the technology available in the early part of the twenty-first century and select a site that possessed no visible landmarks whatsoever; one that required an extremely accurate set of co-ordinates in order to be located by either party.

Now, as he was wheeled down the ramp and they looked out across a beautiful California morning, the hot sun casting elongated shadows across the pale red surface of the dry lake, even Sherman smiled at the old man's ingenuity. There would be no fear of anyone having stumbled across this site at any point in the past thirty-two years.

Despite the fact that they had yet to receive confirmation that Alison had actually commenced her journey, they all had to assume that she would go successfully, that she would do what was required of her and steal the tables from Mason before burying them at the allocated location. In many ways it was almost tempting for them to start digging straight away, but they knew in their hearts that they couldn't. Alison had to be gone before the first spade made the its cut into the dry earth. This time around, every one of the four men was convinced that something very special indeed would be waiting to be rediscovered when they peeled away the surface.

Alison and Klein had spent over an hour in this very spot the previous day, after many more hours than that searching the surrounding area. Alison had brought beers along, not something Klein normally drank, although with a little persuasion he had recognised, like Alison herself, that the selection of the final site should indeed warrant some form of liquid celebration. The intense heat that filled the air around them only added to that.

Klein had sat in his chair, making full use of the shadow cast by the four-wheel-drive, and stared out across the vista as Alison opened two of the bottles and handed one over. They clinked the heavy glass together with polite smiles then Alison leaned heavily against the side of the vehicle, a baseball cap and sunglasses protecting her eyes from the glare that seemed to fill the vast open space around them.

After her first drink, with noticeable concern in her voice and because they were alone again, Alison had asked the question that had been on her mind for too long now.

"What will you do with them, Josef? Once you finally have them?"

And Klein had said nothing. Not at first. For almost a minute an eerie silence, broken only by the crackle of the engine as it cooled, filled over four square miles of empty wasteland. He had thought about his lifelong quest and the inordinate lengths he seemed to have gone to in order to attain something as precious as he believed the tables to be. He had thought about every aspect of his life; the highs and the lows and had realised, increasingly over the past few months, that what had guided his life most; indeed, what had made that life fun - on occasion - was the not knowing; the uncertainty that life had always seemed to throw his way.

"When I was a child," he said eventually, his voice full of memories older than Alison could ever hope to remember, "I read so much. Day and night.

393

I was a real bookworm."

He smiled proudly. It was his love of books, his desire for knowledge at all levels that had been so instrumental in his success, he felt.

"Fiction, but always something with a scientific bent, of course. The kind of books that took the technology we could all see around us daily and expanded further than even the best scientific minds had been able to see, to create some new and exciting world. For a time, I would be reading one of these books and I would get maybe halfway through, and suddenly the impatient child within me would take over and force me to turn to the last few pages, just to find out how it ended. I would still have to read the rest of the book, of course, because I still had no idea how events had gotten to where they were, but something would be missing. The excitement was gone. I knew the ending. Yet still, time after time, I would skip forward, knowing full well that it would ruin it all for me. In the end, I think it was when I was about fourteen, I found the strength to stop doing it."

He sent his gaze searching across the designated area, his eyes looking for a moment in time that had long gone and Alison could now see a man who knew in his heart that he was approaching the end of his life. His voice had the tone reserved for confession, for making peace with God in the hope that he would open his arms and accept you as His child in the months or weeks to come.

"Now I look back and I realise that I never really stopped at all. My entire life has been devoted to discovery, to finding out the end before we have even entered the second half of the book." He shook his head in despair. "Nothing has changed. I'm still the same impatient child I always was."

Alison looked hard at his eyes, deep-set with no glint and she could see a fear in them. She could also see what it was that he was afraid of. He ran the risk now of finding the ultimate answers to this world, and it could just be that this world's sole purpose was nothing more than a journey toward finding those answers. The moment they were held in human hands, the quest was at an end and the world would cease to have purpose. The excitement of discovery would be lost and everyone would be reading the book of the world whilst already knowing the things that had yet to come. Like Klein and the pulp paperbacks he read as a child, something would now be missing from the lives of every single person whose feet walked endlessly across the earth.

"There's still time," she said, wondering if he might rediscover the strength he had somehow found at fourteen.

He shook his head gently. "No," he said. "It's too late; it's already happening now. Even if you do not succeed in your task we still have the Siberium and we still have the technology. Mankind will simply try again. And keep trying until he gets it right. So if we don't do this then somebody else undoubtedly will. Knowledge cannot be taken. Once bestowed it is fixed. We cannot choose to erase it any more that I could choose to forget how my book ended. The instant I knew, I knew."

He looked at her with resigned serenity. "I'm only glad that my life is drawing to a close and that I don't have to be here to see what I've done."

This really was a deathbed confession, Alison thought. A man seeking forgiveness for the unstoppable he appeared to have put into place. She wondered if whoever filled his shoes when he had gone would have the balls to admit that intrinsically this whole charade was one big mistake. The likes of Strauss might, but of Haga, Kerr and undoubtedly Sherman, she could not be so sure.

Sherman had become less of a scientist with every day that had passed since his realisation that the world had an inherent structure and that the structure could, quite possibly, be controlled. Manipulated. Marketed. She had seen a look in his eyes too many times that had been more akin to selling an idea than welcoming a new dawn.

"Why are you telling me all this now?" Alison asked.

"I don't know," Klein said softly. "Guilt? Scientists can feel that, you know. Let's face it, Nobel only decreed that the major portion of his nine million dollar estate be left to the provision of annual prizes, the peace prize included, because of the guilt he felt for his invention of dynamite. He knew he could never take it back. What was done was done, but perhaps he wanted some of those around him to know that he did in fact have a conscience."

"So tell me, Josef? What are you looking for now you've found your road to Damascus?" She shrugged. "Salvation? Praise? What is it that you really want?"

Klein smiled voraciously at what he felt was Alison's extraordinarily astute turn of phrase. He had indeed suffered a conversion. He might not be ready to change his name or to found a new church, but it certainly seemed as though a somewhat imminent death had somehow served to alter his once resolute views. The conviction that seemed to have driven his life was not behind the wheel when it came to death. Somewhere along the way it had simply lost its grip.

"I want the one thing I cannot have," he replied eventually, his voice full of regret. "I want to change the past. To make it stop."

For the next five minutes two of the world's most brilliant scientists, the young and the old, sat quietly in the shade. No more words were spoken. Klein wondered to himself if, given this new 'sequential structure' that the world was known to possess, there was still a heaven.

He would find out soon enough, he mused.

Probably at the same moment his rejection slip came through.

Less than twenty-four hours after that confession, Klein stared once more across the retrieval site, his three colleagues anxiously waiting for news from Strauss. He glanced down to his open palms, his life-lines deeper than they might have been once but certainly no longer, then closed his eyes and prayed to the numbers.

Kerr and Haga were exchanging half-time small-talk whilst Sherman paced impatiently back and forth, the radio clutched firmly in his right hand. He strolled over to Klein and stood to the right of his chair without ever looking directly at him. "Do you trust her to do the right thing?" he asked.

Klein smiled. He hoped so, though not for Sherman's benefit.

"Yes I do," he replied. "I really do."

"And the explosion at Cardou? You think she...?"

"No," Klein said, shaking his head. "I think we have Mason to thank for that little gift. Miss Bond will do exactly what she is required to do, you can be assured of that."

Required, he thought. By whom? By what?

Sherman cast his employer a suspicious glance and walked away, though inside his mind he felt assured enough that things were going to plan. Who would have thought that his ex-wife's penchant for what he referred to as LCD-TV (Lowest-Common-Denominator-Television) would have resulted in him being here today to witness this? The discovery of what was probably the one set of laws that had eluded the world's best scientists. The binding laws. Through his elevation within KRT itself and the haphazard Strauss' accidental discovery of the power that Siberium could wield, Sherman was now the most senior member of the most senior team within the organisation. Add a little knowledge beyond reason and that was one hell of a stepping stone to have one's size ten Italian soles resting on.

Make no mistake, he thought, a stepping stone is all that this was. All that it had ever meant to be. Better still, he mused; a springboard. One from which David Sherman was taking one last bounce, ready to land on its surface for a final time and launch himself into the crystal clear waters of global scientific domination. Every aspect of design, manufacture and innovation would be driven by a technology which stemmed from the answers to every unwieldy problem that the desperately weakened field of physics could throw into the pot. Of course, given such technology, prices would have to be set that emphasised the sheer brilliance and speed at which advances could be made.

Computers would be faster, cars and planes would be faster and the entire advancement of technology itself would be faster. During those heady days to follow, nothing would be faster than David Sherman's meteoric rise. Nor would he have to design or manufacture anything either. He would not have to worry himself over offices or crippling overheads any more than he would need to concern himself with packaging and shipping. What he would hold would be nothing more than pure, usable, *patentable* information and he would simply have to sit back and watch as the mass of licensing royalties mounted up like no other company in history.

Even Microsoft with their clever negotiations with IBM or Apple with iOwnEverything would marvel at this new venture, having convinced themselves - and others - that the world was so much wiser now and that such a massive financial coup could never, would never, occur again.

Sherman was just forty-nine years old. Old enough to understand the concepts of business with which he would be faced whilst young enough to enjoy the rewards that such a business would offer him. Today was not Josef Klein's day, Josef was far too old and weak to appreciate such things. Today was Sherman's day. The future was his.

The radio crackled. Even digital waveless technology couldn't cut out the increasing amount of shit that seemed to infect this world's atmosphere, it seemed. Then Strauss' voice on the other end. Not excited but resigned. Like maybe he was already missing someone.

"Okay, fellas," he said. "She's gone."

"Good," Sherman said, bluntly clicking the device. He had neither the time or the inclination to exchange hollow pleasantries today.

Klein sighed heavily then nodded to Haga and Kerr whose faces were nothing if not expectant. They smiled knowingly at each other, then walked to the MPV, slid open the side door and retrieved two spades from within. Sherman followed them and removed a deep red hard-sided briefcase, padded internally, in which the tables were to be transported back to Los Angeles once recovery was complete. Given Klein's failing health and his own sense of superiority for uncovering this technology in the first instance, Sherman decided - without seeking approval - that the time was ripe for him to take charge of the scene.

He walked slowly across the flat bed of the dry lake with the GPS system in his hand, the numbers on the screen adjusting slightly with every step he took. Then he paused, double checking the final co-ordinates, reached out one of those expensive shoes of his and used the toe to indicate a crude 'X' in the thin layer of sand which had settled on the hardened earth.

"Right," he said without looking up. "Time to start digging."

FORTY-FOUR

TUESDAY, APRIL 21, 2009.

Alison banged on the door as hard as she could with the sides of her fists. Like so many doors which are hidden down back-alleys, used only in case of fire or to come out back and deposit trash, there was no outer handle with which to ease the act of burglary. She shouted at the top of her voice, naked save for the sheet of plastic bubble-wrap she had pulled from one of the trash cans now held firm around her body to form a semi-opaque barrier between herself and complete embarrassment. If anyone actually opened this door, and she prayed that they would, then they would know damn well that she was wearing nothing underneath, but she hoped that there would still be just a little something left to the imagination.

She had ruffled her hair as best she could and used a broken bottle found near the old wino to carve a thin line down her right cheek, backing up the story she had been perfecting in her mind. The tramp, who had witnessed the whole thing but was way too far gone to make head nor tail of any of it, was still a little way up the alley, mumbling in his own little world. It was only she and he, however; nobody else seemed to be coming.

She did not want to go to the end of the alley, out into the main street because there would just be too many people and too many questions. Better, she reasoned, to keep it low-key, the way such an embarrassing and personal event should indeed be treated.

After two or three minutes of solid banging, and at the point at which she had almost given up, she heard a subtle sound from inside; gentle at first. Soon it got louder; and she began to hear more clearly what it was; footsteps on a steel ladder. She banged harder, her hands already throbbing, and shouted 'Hey' over and over at the top of her voice.

She did not stop until she heard the sound of the internal bar being pressed and the catches releasing at the top and bottom of the door. It had started to rain heavily almost as soon as she had arrived and thick droplets were now clattering loudly on her impromptu clothing and running in thick streams toward the ground. Her pale brown hair had darkened dramatically and her cheek was running red with watered-down blood from the cut. But somebody was here now, she thought. Thank God.

Now, at last, she could finally start to get things sorted.

The door opened with a metallic creak and the face of an elderly Chinese woman peered inquisitively out. Like the kids in 'B-Movies' pushing open the creaking oak of a long-haunted house, her expression was undoubtedly created from an amalgamation of a senseless desire to investigate and a worry at what she might discover when she did. In her hands she held two cardboard boxes over-filled with garbage which she had undoubtedly been ready to deposit in one of the trash cans. The boxes fell to the floor, empty packaging and smaller boxes spilling out across the inner hallway. For a few moments she did nothing, simply standing like a cornered thief and staring in disbelief at the wretched, rain-soaked and very frightened young woman who was now - inexplicably - standing right outside her door.

"Help me... please," Alison said, her voice desperate and her eyes begging. "They... they tried to rape me."

Within ten minutes Alison was sitting in the warm back office of 'Mister Yang's', the door closed and the one note tune of the till playing every few minutes from the long stretch of store beyond. She drank herbal tea, cupping it in quivering hands as though it was the first drink she'd had for days whilst staring blankly at her still-naked feet.

She wore an ill-fitting tracksuit, a loan from Mrs. Yang who had opened the door, and a blue and green checked blanket was draped over her shoulders. Her hair had been towel-dried and the blood washed from her cheek, though the cut was still visible in a fine line from below her right eye to the side of her mouth. It was Mr. Yang who was back on the shop floor serving customers, no doubt also peering to the street at regular intervals to see if anyone had arrived.

"Police come soon," Mrs. Yang said reassuringly. "You want I should get you something?"

Alison huddled over her cup, the warmth flowing up and into her face and shook her head. "No... I mean, thankyou. I'm a lot better now."

She looked around the office and saw items which, whilst similar to those she used daily, were just that little bit more old fashioned in design; late museum pieces or props from some of the 'classic' shows which crowded the digital channels. She smiled. She had definitely come back but to where, to *when*, she could not yet be entirely sure. Sequencing, after all, had been plotted by Sherman and a team of unknowing theorists (with the emphasis placed firmly on *theory*) on a very loose graph. It had been based on the supposed effects of charge application and had only just become plausible as a science. It still had one hell of a long way to go before it even had a dream about becoming an exact one.

On the left hand wall of the room, above a heavy blue safe piled high with papers, was one of the free month-by-month calendars that suppliers were always so keen to dump on their clients. On the page in view was indeed the month; April, as well as the name of the company who had supplied the calendar; Ming-Chi'i, and the fact that they had been voted Los Angeles Chinese Food Distributor of the year 2006/2007. But that did not necessarily make this year 2007, did it? In fact, given that award had already been bestowed, it was far more likely that this would prove to be April 2008, making her arrival a year earlier than even she had hoped. There was no year indicated on the page and the only thing which even hinted at one was a graphical representation of an ox at the top of the page, in the area where the year might normally be expected.

Year of the ox, she thought. When the hell was the year of the ox?

Sequence

Why did it have to be a Chinese supermarket? Why not an Italian one - she spoke Italian fairly well - or at the very least a shop with a regular calendar, with regular dates.

What animal had it been when she left, she wondered? She tried to remember the beginning of that year, the fifteen day celebration held by L.A.'s rapidly expanding Chinese community not five blocks from her apartment. On the Saturday they had held a pageant replete with fifteen-man dragons and a series of floats. Nearly all the participants who had not been in costume had carried banners, but what creature had been on every damn one of them? Think, think, think.

The pig, she remembered suddenly, that was it. Because some of the revellers had even dressed as pigs. Daft looking pigs, sure, but pigs all the same. So 2043 was the pig. That would make this year... she deliberately looked blankly at her feet again, covering the fact that she was doing arithmetic in her head... 2033, 2021 or 2009. Which, considering Ming-Chi'i's award, meant that this just had to be 2009. They had obviously been pipped by another supplier in 2008, but had wisely not chosen to advertise the fact.

Which also meant that, whilst Sherman's graph had always been seen as 'estimated', it had actually been damn-near precise and had, so to speak, landed her right on the cusp of the asp. Alison Bond was sitting in an office in a Chinese supermarket in Los Angeles in April 2009 and she had two full years to do what she needed to do before she aided Mason's escape. She successfully prevented her face from demonstrating any emotion whatsoever but Christ, she thought, how cool (and so weird as to be classed as wrong) was that?

It was only as she glanced back at the calendar that she noticed April's proverb for the month. It was written across the base of the page in small black Roman letters indicative of a Chinese style: One may be in the same place two times, but even the most adventurous travellers cannot be in two places at the same time. She smiled. The creator of the sequence, it seemed, had a clearly defined sense of irony.

Mrs. Yang was still fussing like a bee gathering pollen. She was concerned for the girl, but in no way surprised to find her thrust into her midst. Neither she, her husband or indeed any of the fast-turnaround staff they employed were strangers when it came to acts of violence in the neighbourhood. In the eight years that they had owned and run the store they had been presented with twelve rape or attempted rape victims, innumerate muggings, four shootings (three fatal) and the store itself had been held up on no less than twelve separate occasions.

"They... rape you?" she asked, placing her ageing hand on Alison's arm.

"No," Alison replied. "I think... I think I fought them off. They got scared and ran." She tried her damndest to sound convincing, using carefully spaced words, a pretence that her thoughts were on darker things as she added just the right hint of pain to her voice.

"You very lucky girl," Mrs. Yang said, every ounce of genuine sympathy she felt colouring her heavy Chinese accent. "You could be killed."

Alison nodded pitifully. "Yes, I know."

"We have noodle soup." She tried to sound upbeat, to lift the girl's spirits if she could. "You want I bring some?"

Alison stared deliberately into space, then clicked herself back with near perfect timing; her expression was the kind one would have when trying to decipher a complex problem in the mind. Her eyes were focused on an area of empty space and she was very gently biting at her bottom lip. "Sorry?"

"Noodle soup. Very good. You want some?"

Alison smiled, but Mrs. Yang could see that she didn't look at all happy inside. "That would be nice."

A few minutes later Mrs. Yang handed over a polystyrene bowl of soup along with a flat-bottomed spoon. Alison blew vacantly across its surface then gently fed some into her mouth, ensuring that her hand trembled just enough to shake the soup without actually spilling it all over the floor.

She nodded and smiled that same unhappy smile. "It's good." She didn't say thankyou. People in shock never remember to say thankyou.

"Full of herb," Mrs. Yang explained. "Good to restore Yang." She took a seat next to Alison and they both waited together.

"I've been so stupid," Alison said, hanging her head low and taking deep contemplative breaths.

"Not your fault," Mrs. Yang protested. "This place very bad. Many bad peoples. You fight and that good. You show them who boss. Still... very lucky."

Mr. Yang opened the office door slightly and stuck his wide-eyed head through the gap. "Police come," he said. He smiled lamely, as though he did not know what to say, then disappeared again.

A man and a woman, both wearing LAPD uniforms and heavy black jackets entered the room.

The guy was the elder of the two, maybe late forties with a grey buzz-cut, a five o'clock shadow and ridges at the top of his nose where his sunglasses, the ones now tucked into his shirt pocket, usually resided. The woman was much younger, not much more than a girl, really. She was perhaps in her early twenties, hispanic and with a youthful glint in her eyes. She gave Alison a genuine smile as she entered the room. The guy, McInley according to his badge, barely glanced at her before turning and leaning against the wall by the door. He peered through the gap to the people in the supermarket and those passing outside the large window in the distance. He liked to watch the streets, see the people. He could spot trouble a mile off and he always kept his eyes open. Besides, he wasn't really needed on this call anyway, it was a woman to woman thing. Best let Maria handle it...

Officer Maria Esperanza crouched down in front of Alison in an effort to make eye contact. "Can you tell me what happened to you, honey?"

"There were three of them," Alison said eventually, all the while staring intensely at both nothing and nobody. As she continued with her description, her eyes kept narrowing and opening and her head turned slightly with every fresh, concocted, recollection. "White guys. In denim.

In a... car. A black car. A long one, you know? They stopped me uptown, asked for directions and then dragged me in. One had a knife. He put his hand over my mouth and held it to my throat while the others...." She started to summon all the pain she had ever felt in her life. All the suffering of her youth. "...started taking my clothes off."

She started crying.

"And where are your clothes now?"

"I don't know," Alison said, sobbing. "In the car I guess."

"So how did you come to be here? In the alley?"

"One of the guys, dark haired guy. He drove whilst the others.... whilst they... Anyway, they were driving me somewhere to... do me.. I think. They drove down here and told me to get out. I... I don't know.... I just freaked and panicked. Started screaming; yelling as loud as I could. They looked real shocked. Didn't expect it. They got in the car and drove away."

"Had you seen any of these men before?"

Alison shook her head. "No."

"And would you recognise them again? Or the car, maybe?"

"I don't know," Alison said. "It all happened so fast. It was just..." she increased the sobbing, carefully blocking out the words.

"It's alright," Maria said, placing her hand on top of Alison's in genuine sympathy. "Is there anyone we can call for you. Any relatives or friends maybe?"

Alison shook her head. "I'm... I'm from Chicago," she said, still clearly upset. "I was coming to visit my sister."

"And where does your sister live?"

"She's at Oakdene," Alison said slowly, knowing that the word would leave a dark silence in its wake and ultimately kill that particular line of enquiry.

Then Alison looked up suddenly, as though some inescapable truth had suddenly flown into her head. Which, in truth, it just had. On the polished beige floor she had seen a reflection of the clock on Mr. Yang's desk and, although reading both backwards and upside down, she could see that it read 10:15pm. They would take her to the station, probably still wearing Mrs. Yang's clothes, but what then? She would have no time to find somewhere to spend the night.

"My bag....?" she said, almost throwing the words at the female officer. "They took my bag." She looked blankly around the room, her head darting from side to side. "They have my money, my cards, my I.D, everything. I don't... I mean, I can't... I mean.... I have nowhere to stay."

"Don't you worry yourself about that," Maria said. "We can find you a place to stay until tomorrow. Longer if you need. You'll have free access to a phone. In the morning you can maybe call the bank, or home maybe, and sort something out."

Alison had to try hard to stop herself from laughing. Call the bank? She had a bank, sure, and in it was two thousand dollars in tightly rolled hundreds and three uncut diamonds worth maybe another twenty-k. It was just that her local branch had the smallest vault in the world and right at this moment in time she was sitting on it.

"In the meantime we can arrange a full examination, if you'd like," Maria continued. "Internal as well... if there's something you know that we don't?" By which she had meant whether or not these bastards'd had their grubby little paws - or worse - inside her.

Alison looked up. "No, thankyou. I mean, they didn't actually..."

Maria was nodding. She understood. "It's okay," she said gently. "Just now I'm going to have a talk with partner here, and then we'll need to take you down to the station for a full statement. I'll be with you all the time and then afterward we'll see if we can't get you fixed up, eh?"

Alison feigned relief, still staring at her feet, but didn't reply. Maria sidled over to McInley and started talking in deliberately lowered tones. Alison could not hear much of what was said, but she got the basics. There was probably very little that could be done right now. The girl was obviously very shaken by the attack but there would probably be no clear descriptions being thrown in their direction of either the car or her three assailants. Best to just take down the report and get her safe for the night.

If something came to her at a later date she could always give Officer Esperanza a call.

Alison knew just as well as they that the vast proportion of such crimes, especially in this area of town, would go unsolved. She would become what she had needed to become; a mere statistic. One that carried with it the only thing she had needed to acquire on her arrival - a truly believable explanation as to why she had suddenly appeared naked in an alleyway with no I.D. and no money.

When they had finished talking McInley shrugged, his eyes still fixed through the store's over-stocked shelves to the street outside. A group of maybe six or seven Chinese youths were grouping at the far side of the street and he wanted to see if anything stronger than Lucky's changed hands. They had a look about them and, despite the patrol car parked in clear view outside the store, they'd been hanging around just that little bit too long.

Maria returned to Alison and crouched down again, a black notepad in one hand and a pencil in the other. "Right then," she said. "I just need to take down some details. First of all, what's your name, honey?"

Alison looked up very slowly, her eyes still vacant with an award-winning combination of shock, despair and an inability to comprehend the situation she had found herself in.

She pretended to think, and think hard.

"Fiddes," she said eventually, before spelling the word out letter by letter for the young officer.

"Sarah Fiddes."

FORTY-FIVE

SUNDAY, JUNE 12, 2011.

42KM NORTH OF FORT TEJON STATE PARK, CALIFORNIA.

We were about as close to the centre of the dry lake as it was possible to be; undoubtedly the largest area of perfectly flat, mundane and featureless land I had ever seen, surrounded in the distance by the kind of mountains that seem to get farther away the faster you walk. As I pulled the car to a halt and we both climbed out, I fully expected to see some land speed record attempt come whizzing by. Truthfully, I didn't know that places like this actually existed; I thought they just made them up for television. My shirt was sticking to my skin and even the sunglasses I was wearing couldn't fully dullen the strength of the sun. The all-encompassing silence was like nothing I've ever known. More painful than the heat.

I looked across at Sarah and saw an extremely satisfied young lady; that semi-permanent knowing smile she had perfected resting with pride below the dark shades. I was starting to understand by this time that the smile would remain that way whether I asked her about it or not. Knowing, but not telling. It was as though she was building me up gently, feeding me snippets of something each time she sensed my excitement level was flagging whilst ultimately setting me up for some grand finale. Perhaps this vast area of desert was it, in which case the only feature it seemed to be missing was the word 'anticlimax' carved indelibly across it.

I placed a half-drunk bottle on the roof and, as I turned to light another Marlboro and take in the full three-sixty at the nothingness which surrounded us, I could see that she was already slinging the rucksack onto her back, completely ignoring me and walking slowly away, her eyes fixed only on the screen.

"Where the hell are you go...?" I began, but then I stopped. Instead I just grabbed the beer back and started after her.

She walked a few hundred metres from the car and then stopped suddenly, scrutinising the screen and testing the ground with the toe of an olive sneaker. Then she scored an 'X' on the ground. "Here," she said, looking up to me expectantly. "Did you bring the shovels?"

Somehow, though I'm not sure how, I managed to stay calm. Nobody had mentioned the goddamned shovels. With only the slightest look of mock-indignance, I headed all the way back to the car whilst Sarah placed the rucksack down on the ground and carefully extracted the DHL package. Then, very gently, she placed it on the ground.

I returned, handed over a shovel and starting making the first incision, the dry ground cracking audibly before sliding gently out. Soon I was creating a decent pile of earth to one side and an even greater amount of sweat inside my shirt.

"Why here?" I asked.

She started to dig alongside, expanding the hole to my right. "Why not?" she said. "Don't you think this is a good enough place?" I noticed that she had been very deliberate about not answering my direct question, and that the tone of her voice told me that she had wanted me to notice.

"As places to hide something where it will never, *ever* be found go, it's absolutely ideal," I said, "In fact, unless you start seeing fit to tell me why you've chosen to utilise a Global Positioning System to select it, rather than just picking some random spot, I'll be making the hole big enough to include a female body as well."

Sarah smiled. "But I *do* want it to be found." She paused long enough to wipe the sweat from her forehead. "Just not for about..." she tilted her head, pretending to think, "...thirty-three years or so, that's all."

The pile grew larger until the hole was more than deep enough to accept the package, still in the brown paper wrapping with the bar-coded DHL sticker emblazoned on its face.

She leaned back and sighed, then picked it up and lowered it very carefully into the darkness.

"That should do it," she said, starting to shovel the darker sand back over.

I didn't bother to help, not this time. I just leaned on my own shovel and stared, waiting for an explanation. One that, as I'm sure you will appreciate, never came.

"You told me you didn't want the tables to be found," I said eventually, trying to force the issue. "*Ever.*"

She glanced up, but didn't stop shovelling. With every fresh load the package was disappearing further out of sight.

"I don't."

"But... in the ladies room... at the airport...?" I said, trying to work this one out, "You put the tables in the package, right?"

She shrugged indifferently, still replacing the pile of earth. "Did I say that I put the tables in the package?' she said. She looked at me puzzled. "I don't actually remember saying that."

"So what's in the package?" I was getting annoyed now and it was becoming less and less fun trying to hide it.

She scooped a last shovelful of sand, tipped it down and patted with the back of the shovel to level the surface. Then kicked the spare with her feet so that it spread thin across the surrounding area.

She looked up and I could see in an instant that she was very pleased with her day's work.

Very pleased indeed.

"What's in the package," she said, looking quizzically skyward. She turned back to me and flicked her eyebrows before walking away.

"Well, it's not going to be the thing that *I* put in the package. That's for *damn* sure."

FORTY-SIX

TUESDAY, AUGUST 18, 2043.

42KM NORTH OF FORT TEJON STATE PARK, CALIFORNIA.

Haga's shovel hit first. A gentle thump, but a discernible one.

This was no rock that had been struck; this was something decidedly hollow and it sounded exactly like the one thing it was supposed to; a box.

Carefully Kerr leaned into the hole, a little under three feet deep and started to scoop out the remaining sand with his bare hands. Sherman and Klein watched in silence, though their expressions could not have been more different if they had tried.

Klein seemed worried; apprehensive almost, whilst Sherman looked eager and impatient. His right foot was tapping gently against the ground and, in the absence of anything useful to do with his hands, he was idly scratching his chin.

To Klein he held the air of a drug addict. The kind who, having been starved of a fix for days, was now watching his girlfriend heating a wrap for him to syringe into his arm. He was desperate because he wanted this so very badly. Worse; he needed it, and he needed it now.

Kerr reached in for the final time and eased his fingers to one side of the package, some of the paper tearing away as he pulled. Little by little he managed to work it free, then he lay face down on the ground and reached in with the other hand as well, even though the hole was probably only two hand-widths wider than the box itself. He almost had it when he lost his grip; the box falling a little way back down the hole.

"Careful," Sherman said angrily, sighing at the level of incompetence he felt forced to work with here. Did this dumbass truly not understand the importance of what he had momentarily held in his clumsy hands?

Slowly, the package came to the surface for a second time. Kerr placed it to one side, smoothed the loose sand from its surface and rolled onto his back. He stared into the clear blue sky and exhaled a long, deep breath.

"Open it up," Sherman said bluntly.

Klein, meanwhile, wheeled himself across the sun-hardened earth, the creases around his eyes looking like scars in a rock face. His expression was still anxious, more so the closer he came. Kerr, having rolled back over, was now kneeling in front of the box. Carefully he began to tear away the brown paper wrapping, leaving it to flicker gently in an almost imperceptible breeze.

Sherman laid his briefcase on the floor, placed the radio to one side and undid the clasps, opening it wide in readiness for acceptance of the tables. He removed something from within and rose to his feet, approaching the others from behind. Haga was now kneeling also and watching to see if Kerr would open it up to find the treasures they had all been praying would be found inside.

"This is it," Kerr said, tearing away the last of the paper and staring intently at the box.

"Open, yes?" Haga said excitedly. "Open it up."

"I don't think so," Sherman said, his voice eerily calm.

Klein looked over to see that Sherman was now, without further warning, squeezing the trigger on an automatic pistol he held in his right hand. The barrel was less than an inch from the back of Haga's unsuspecting head. There was a loud bang, one that seemed to chase itself across the desert floor and a jet of red shot forward through the man's face, pieces of his brain falling across the smooth wooden surface of the box.

Haga slumped forward like a badly inflated rubber-dolly, his body ending its life on its side with his eyes wide open, a gaping red tear now obliterating what had, until recently, been his forehead.

Kerr looked swiftly around, facing Sherman and less than four feet away. The look on his face changed in a half-breath to one of stunned shock. He barely had time to comprehend what was happening and form an expletive before the barrel was pointing straight at him.

"What the..." and the gun went off again, throwing Kerr backward on his knees so that he was again facing the sun, this time his body slowly contorting and his legs twisting in the last throes of death.

"David, what are you doing?" Klein said. He didn't actually sound as shocked as he might have done.

"What do you *think* I'm doing?" Sherman barked, turning toward his boss and pointing the gun directly at his head. "Old man." He stressed the words as though it was the worst insult one human being could possibly bestow upon another. "I'm taking what's rightfully mine."

Klein looked remarkably serene. Resigned to his fate.

"It's not yours, David. And nor is it mine. It is nobody's." He looked at the box, a pool of Haga's blood creeping slowly around its base as it waited patiently on the hard earth. "It belongs to God."

"God?" Sherman spat. "*God*? Have you forgotten already that God does not exist; that I proved once and for all that he does not exist."

Klein looked away from Sherman, across the expanse as though smelling fresh flowers on the air. He seemed too calm, too relaxed and way too happy with this turn of events.

"Then who wrote the sequence?" he asked.

Somewhere along the line Sherman, it seemed, had chosen to forget the first question he had asked himself all those years ago; indeed the first question he had put to Klein when he had entered his office laden with exciting new theories:

What if God actually existed?

"Who made you and I, David? Who made the rules?"

He was speaking now like a college professor who had just uncovered the fatal flaw in the thesis of a student for whom he held an inherent

415

dislike; complete contempt at a complete lack of understanding.

"All you uncovered, David, was the fact that God has a tangible structure in the way he works. Nothing more. You think you proved that He does not exist? Fine. Then perhaps you'd like to tell me just who it was that wrote down all the answers? The ones that you are now so desperate to claim as your own?"

"Who cares who wrote them?" Sherman said, spacing the words. "They're mine now."

"No they're not," Klein said. He half-closed his eyes and looked to the floor. "If you attempt to open that box you will be stopped." Sherman sneered. "*Stopped*, David. By a power you can only dream of possessing."

"What is this shit?" Sherman almost screamed sarcastically, his arms flailing. "Is the old man having a crisis of conscience? Does he suddenly want to bow to his knees and accept the existence of his maker because he's scared shitless that he runs the risk of actually fucking meeting him? What next, Josef? Are you going to confess your sins?"

He shook his head with contempt.

"Christ, you're all but ready to cry out to a non-existent God and beg forgiveness for proving he does not exist, and yet I'm the crazy one? Seriously, Josef, just how fucked up a concept is that to play with?"

"Somebody wrote the sequence, Dave. Soliloquise all you like, but it's the one hard fact you simply cannot escape.'

"You're forgetting what we are, Josef," Sherman said, still throwing his words with an almost ministerial sense of passion. "You've lost sight of our reason for being. We're scientists. It's our job to prove that God does not exist. And now, just as we finally achieve it, you've buckled." He scoffed. "Just like all the rest."

The more Sherman spoke, the more exasperated he became, if that were possible.

"And… and… anyway, what about *your* role in this, Professor? Until a few moments ago you were so very keen to have the answers in *your* hands, weren't you? Never too holy for your grubby little fingers until today, were they? Hell no. And now you want to sit there and... and... preach... to me about what's right and wrong? Does the word hypocrite not even figure in that tired vocabulary of yours?"

"I made the decision a long time ago," Klein said wearily. "We would take one look, that's all. We would take the merest glance at the work of God and know, once and for all, that in spite of all our science and all the false claims we've been selling about understanding this world, there is something bigger... something we will never - ever - understand. Like it or not, Dave, He exists. And when, like me, you had been shown the truth, that ultimately we still know nothing, I would go alone and bury them again. Somewhere they would never be found."

"Why would you want to go and do a stupid thing like that?"

Klein smiled to himself. "Basically to stop messed up little shitheads like you from ever getting their hands on them," he said casually. "You're merely standing on shoulders, Dave."

The worst insult a scientist could receive.

"Standing on who's shoulders, Josef? Yours? Give me a fucking break. I discovered this technology, remember? I found it and I harnessed it." He pointed to the box. "You'd spent years searching for these and what... nothing! Then bam," He slammed the hand holding the gun into his opposing palm. "I come along and I give you the means. If anybody's standing on shoulders here, Josef, it's you."

"You really are a seriously disturbed individual, aren't you Dave?"

"No, Josef, unlike you, locked in your little confessional, I see very, very clearly. And do you know what I think about your precious creator? Your all-powerful being that placed the sequence in the hands of man?" He leaned in close. "Do you know who I *really* think that person is, Josef?"

Klein shook his head wearily. "No, Dave, I don't. But I'm sure you feel extremely compelled to tell me."

"Me!" Sherman said with an evil smile. "It's me, Josef. Do you know why? Because when I know my time is over, when I see myself as the pitiful

417

wreck you are now, do you know what I'll do? I'll climb into that little room we have and I'll go back. Way, way back. And maybe, just maybe, I'll get myself an audience on a mountaintop and I'll hand over everything I have. I'll give them back, Josef. And it will start all... over... again."

To Klein this had gone way beyond simple megalomania. This was clinical psychosis in its purest form.

"Are you telling me that the tables themselves, the answers to our universe, exist... because of you? That you can have them now only because you put them into the loop when you were done with them? And now you think you're what...? God?" He shook his head. "You're crazy."

"Crazy...?" Sherman mused. "That's the second time you've used that word. If I'm not mistaken, Josef, you used that very same word to me once before, remember? When I first came into your office with the idea that this was all possible. And look at me now. Look at the wonders I have created for you. Not so fucking crazy now am I?"

"No. You're much, much worse."

"Do you know what I'm going to do now?" Sherman continued, striding purposefully back toward the box. "I'm actually going to let you cast your eyes on the one thing you have sought all this time, just before you die. I am going to prove to you, Josef - once and for all - that your precious God does not exist. I will show you that these laws are the works of man. And then, when you've realised that there really will be no divine entity waiting to accept your pathetic little ass on the other side, I will end your suffering and take full advantage of a power you said I would never have."

He pushed Haga's body out of the way with the side of his foot, the dead man's face rolling skyward with a frozen look of horror; pain carved into the grotesque fragments that remained of his face. Sherman crouched in front of the box and ran his finger gently over the surface, then placed them carefully around the lid, held his thumbs on the clasps and clicked both in perfect unison.

He looked up with a glint and, lifting the lid, said, "Behold the glory of the Lord your God...."

I hated having to repeat myself and, through use of deliberate emphasis, I think I made that pretty clear.

"Sarah... what's in the damn package?" It almost felt like I was begging.

"Well, I can't be entirely sure, but...." she said nonchalantly, leaning backward as though straining to think.

She looked straight at me and even the shades could not disguise the naughty look that was coursing through her eyes. From just above the rims of those glasses the eyebrows flicked upward for the merest instant.

Then she told me.

Offering the most deliberately forced look of mock embarrassment and shame imaginable, she rested the shovel on her shoulder like Bashful and started walking back toward the car. Not a care in the world. I was not a little surprised that she didn't choose to throw in a whistled rendition of 'Hi-Ho...' whilst she was at it.

What had she just said? Had I seriously heard her correctly, because to my ears it had sounded something like:

"I'm kind of hoping it's a rather large bomb."

★ ★ ★ ★ ★

Klein, still around six feet away, looked to Sherman, then to the box and finally to the brown paper wrapping, a small portion of which was still flapping gently from beneath Kerr's lifeless body. He smiled gently. Here was something that not even Klein had expected to see.

He was so very pleased that he had.

Clever, clever girl.

He had prayed that Alison would understand the truths he had told her only the day before. Was it the day before? Or was it years ago? Did it really matter any more? The fact was she *had* understood. She had read his fears and, better still, it seemed that she might even have shared them.

Klein knew his days were numbered. He was staring down the barrel of a gun whether Sherman was holding it or not, and being so close to death had indeed brought with it the worst fear he had ever known. He feared not only for how he had handled this situation from the start, but also for how he might handle it again now.

Which was why he had agreed to send Alison back. That way the decision would be left to her. Intuitive as Klein believed himself to be, Alison's mind was far more logical and forward thinking than his could ever hope to be.

From the start, from her childhood within NorthStar, Alison Bond had possessed an ability to plan a great many moves ahead. Better then, he reasoned, to give her two years in which to consider the situation, analyse the options and the consequences, and then make her move accordingly.

What was it that Grier had said to him so many years ago? That they had intercepted the package, contents intact, but that it had left them with a dilemma. Namely, how to get rid of the detective from whom it had been retrieved. They considered the options and came up with an answer.

They simply re-sealed the package and sent it on its way.

No Tables of Testimony inside, though. Not any more. Instead Grier and his team had installed a little surprise; one that would cure their problem of the cop's very existence on this planet once and for all. And they had gone to so much trouble to ensure that he would have no idea that he'd been tricked. They'd opened his package very carefully and that was exactly how they put it back together again.

Identical; right down to the brand of tape and the bar-coded label under which it had been travelling.

The label that was now peering at Klein from beneath his dead colleague, gently dancing its presence to the tune of a gentle breeze.

If you attempt to open that box, you will be stopped… By a power you can only dream of possessing.

Never a truer word spoken.

Alison Bond, given her unbelievably logical mind, was one very powerful young lady indeed.

She had done him proud.

Sherman flipped open the box with wonder etched into his eyes.

In an instant the wonder was gone and taking its place was a horrific realisation. His jaw dropped and his eyes opened wider than they had been in his entire life. He did not have time to scream even if he had wanted to. His world was suddenly filled with a blinding yellow light as the full force of the blast tore into he, Klein, and the bodies of the two dead men with slicing ferocity.

On its journey outward the explosion collected a layer of the loose sand and spread it in a wide ring across the dry lake as though it was again full of water and a stone had been dropped from heaven itself into its midst. One single ripple extended out from the centre of the blast, travelling almost a quarter of a mile in all directions, the MPV breaking apart in a second explosion as the wave passed through.

Then the purest silence.

Nothing living or breathing within fifty miles.

Josef Klein's final thought in this world, as he had gently closed his eyes for the final time and prepared to meet his God, was to wonder exactly what Alison had chosen to do with the tables themselves. She would know, like he, that to destroy them forever would be the worst form of sacrilege, but would she… *could* she… find the means to ensure that they would never again be uncovered by man?

God. He hoped so.

FORTY-SEVEN

Sunday, June 12, 2011.

42km North of Fort Tejon State Park, California.

"You mean to tell me I've been driving around with a... What? A bomb? In my car?"

Sarah gave me that enigmatic smile for the last time. "I hope so."

"We could have been killed."

"I knew we wouldn't."

"How exactly?"

"Do you *really* want to know what this is all about, Nick?"

Number thirty-eight in a series of forty-seven stupid questions.

"Damn right I do."

"Good," she said quietly. "Pull the car over."

We were back at the edge of the dry lake, the track rising into the mountains once more. There was no way to pull off the track so I simply stopped the car where it was and we climbed out and walked around to the back, facing the lake. The sun was low in the sky, the furthest reaches of the lake rippling in a gentle mirage but we still had a clear view across the level surface.

In the middle distance I could still make out a tiny piece of discoloured earth; the burial site.

Sarah took a few moments to herself, punctuated by deep thoughtful breaths, and finally started to explain what the hell was going on. Or, more specifically, what she hoped was going on, because even she admitted that she could not be one hundred percent certain.

The first thing I learned, the first of many, was that our package never made it to LAX. At least, not in anything like its original form. Of course Smoking Guy and Mid-Sentence had seen us go to the DHL desk, because that was what Sarah had wanted. Then they had done one of two things; either they had watched us board the flight to Paris and allowed the package to be intercepted prior to handover when we arrived to collect it in Los Angeles or, more likely, they had simply intercepted it at Caucassonne. Either way the result was the same.

They had the package in their hands for over half a day and they used that time well.

Once they had opened it up, very cautiously, they found exactly what they were looking for; the Tables of Testimony. This made them very happy indeed. So much so, in fact, that they didn't even bother to lay in wait for us when we went to collect. Of course, had they found a cuddly bear or a bottle of Vin de Table wrapped neatly inside then I'm sure that it would have been a very different story, but no... they got the tables. Which meant that Sarah and I were particularly stupid and they could now dispose of us via a far more expedient method.

Except they weren't the tables. They were good, sure, but they were also very wrong.

They were fakes.

According to Sarah, the ones in the box were much more simplistic. They were heptagonal (seven being some kind of divine Hebrew number or something) and had all manner of ancient Aramaic inscribed across only their upper surfaces. Badly, but who was to know they weren't real? It had taken her three days to design them on her computer system and form a complex conundrum. They also looked authentic enough, having been laser-etched with a roughened finish by a friend of Sarah's working at Caltech.

One could make hundreds upon hundreds of words if these tables were rotated, not unlike the originals, but there was only one true solution. Sarah had been careful to embed it so that it would take a very long time to find.

As I mentioned earlier, I think it took them about eight months in total.

It had been easier than it might sound, she said, because when you already have the solution, all you have to do is hide it in the text and then work backwards, carefully pushing that answer deeper into the puzzle at every turn.

But even though Grier and his two cohorts thought they had the real thing in their hands, getting rid of Sarah and I was still very much on their agenda. It had to be. In the great scheme of things we'd seen more than too much. In truth we'd nigh on seen it all and they couldn't allow us to live and breathe for very much longer.

But how to do it? Perhaps they'd had that bit worked out in advance or perhaps it was one of those spur of the moment flashes of genius. But genius it was; even I'm prepared to admit to that...

They placed a bomb in the box.

A bomb designed to trigger in the instant the lid was opened.

Very carefully, they re-sealed the entire package and used their contacts to feed it back into the system; sending it onward to its original destination. In this way, they would already have achieved one of their desired results – a recapturing of the tables - and then, when we arrived to collect the package and opened it up somewhere - and they really didn't care where - they would achieve result number two.

Sarah, myself and anybody standing within one hundred feet of us at that unfortunate moment, would suddenly be torn into pieces not much larger than a human fist.

Two birds; one very explosive stone.

Very clever indeed.

But then, so was Sarah. So much so that she knew all this probably before they did. In fact, that was why she had carefully selected a box with a latching lid, to make it that bit easier for them. She was able to look at the options and plan that far ahead. And this was why they now thought... assumed... that we were both dead and why they hadn't bothered to follow us into the arse end of nowhere.

They did not want to be anywhere near us.

Certainly not within a hundred feet.

"So why bury the bomb?" I asked. "And why use such precise co-ordinates?"

"Grandma's wedding ring," she said with a smile.

I thought for a few seconds, looking back across the plain to the site, barely visible.

"So you do think that somebody's going to come along and dig it up?"

She nodded without smiling. "I know damn well they are."

"When?"

She took a moment to herself.

"Not for a very long time," she said eventually, then she placed herself cross legged, beer in hand, on the elongated trunk of the car and started to explain. "Remember Josef Klein?" she began. "The guy in the picture with Grier?"

I nodded. "Balding guy?"

"That's him. When Klein was twenty-eight, the government formed a company for him; KleinWork Research Technology. They had to, because he was pretty much working solely for them at that point anyway, but it was all the kind of stuff they might need to distance themselves from should it ever get out."

"Such as?"

"Trust me," she said, "you really don't want to know the kind of shit that goes on. Anyway, the government set up accounts, grants and so on and listed themselves as a fairly prominent client of his. But they held the strings. Always. Klein ran the company as an external entity, as well as an independent profit making company, and received a high share of any profits.

"Then, one day, they sent him to investigate a chunk of metal. Nothing special to them, nothing special to him. Just something they found buried in the ground somewhere. Only it wasn't just somewhere; it was Siberia. Not too far from the point where a meteor had hit in 1907. So Josef Klein now had a piece of metal that was, for want of a better expression, out of this world."

"Space rock?"

Sarah laughed. "Not really. I mean, okay it was different to anything on earth, but only insofar as it was very dense in atomic composition, denser than anything on earth. But for a very long time that was it. It wasn't highly explosive or any kind of superconductor and nor did it have super-powers or anything. In fact, they couldn't actually think of even one use for it. It was all a bit of an anticlimax really."

"So it was just a useless chunk of rock?"

"For a long time, yes it was. Useless, metallic rock, like iron ore or bauxite. They gave it the name 'Siberium' because of where they found it, and allocated it the atomic number 120. At present, we only have a periodic table that goes as far as 104, but this was so far out of the ball-park that they needed to leave room for others in between. The material had an atomic weight of 603.498; two and a half times that of our current heaviest element; Uranium. It was so dense, in fact, that on a very minor level it exerted its own gravity."

"It's own gravity?"

She nodded. "Very minor, but you could just about feel it with your bare hand. It was only under lab analysis that they really picked up on it."

"So what then?"

"Nothing. For years. They did all the things that labs do. They super-heated it, super-cooled it, fired protons at it, magnetised it further and still it looked damn near useless. Until one day; when they decided to immerse it in a complete vacuum environment and throw immense quantities of electricity at it. That was when the fun started. Because that was the first time that they didn't like what they saw."

"What did they see?"

"They saw the walls in their lab *bend*, Nick. Solid titanium sheeting, three inches thick and covered with half-inch ceramic, bent inward whilst the charge was applied. Like rubber. Then, when the charge was released, it flipped back. Twang."

"Because it had it's own gravity?" I asked.

"Ignore gravity," she said. "That's a side issue. Gravity wouldn't bend the walls, Nick, it'd break them. They'd implode and the ceramic would just crumble inwards."

I needed a cigarette. I struggled one from my pocket and lit it, the lighter flickering in the breeze.

"So what was it?"

Sarah turned and smiled like a kid who's just opened a new present. "Time, Nick. It was time."

I coughed and dropped the cigarette. "It bent time?"

"No, Nick, it *bent* the walls. It *changed* time. Try to keep up."

"I told you about black holes, yeah? Well this... this... rock was the *core* of a black hole. Displaced by an event that probably happened thousands and thousands of light years away, probably before the earth had even been born. Sure, it had a gravitational pull already, but when electricity was applied in its natural environment, ie. a vacuum, that pull increased to unbelievable levels. The kind of pull that could pull light toward it, like a black hole."

I wished I'd listened closer to her black hole theories now. Something about a gravitational pull so strong that even light could not escape and something about Einstein telling us that time stood still at the speed of light.

Something like that.

"So..." Sarah continued, "Klein put himself a team together, because he wants to look into this some more. They performed some controlled tests, very carefully you understand, and the results were forwarded to his theorists; the people whose job it is to take the data, analyse it and come back with answers to what is and isn't theoretically possible. I mean, before they all accidentally kill themselves or something."

"And what did these theorists say?"

"They agreed that Klein's team had uncovered something extremely powerful indeed. The theoretical ability to place living tissue in a vacuum, alongside the Siberium, increase an electric charge around it and send that tissue backward through time."

"Why only living tissue?"

"Because, as part of this sequential world, the kind that Tina seems to be able to see and interact with, only living tissue, or things surrounded by living tissue, can actually be affected by time. Even if they don't realise that they do. Consequently it's impossible to send something back if, like a brick, it cannot understand what has happened to it. It has to have some comprehension of the sequence if it's going to be affected by it."

"And this is.... *time travel?*"

"Of sorts."

I laughed. "Except that it's just not possible."

"And why not?" Sarah said, turning to face me. "You've seen Sarah adjust the numbers. She told the Snickers to move from one set of co-ordinates to another. Over a period of time. Like I said, time is the fourth dimension."

She swigged more beer and wiped her mouth with the back of her hand. "According to the theorists, Klein's team would only be able to go backward. Which is fair enough, if you remember our little discussion earlier about how time is an unrolling carpet. We have to assume that we're just behind the roll, watching the sequence unravel in front of us. Which means that the things to come haven't ever happened yet."

She raised her eyebrows. "But the past is very different, isn't it? We know that's happened... we can see it. And if we can see it, we can access it."

"But we can't change it?"

"No, we can't change it. Which meant that Klein's team had succeeded in something very, very wonderful. Except that, even if they could send a human being back in time, they'd still uncovered the single most amazing and single most useless circus trick mankind would ever be able to perform."

"But you could change the future...? The things that will happen after you've gone?"

She smiled and shoved my shoulder. "So you were listening, after all?"

Listening, yeah. Understanding, no. "The wedding ring thing?"

Sarah slid away from the car, took a few steps into the brush and found a clear patch.

"Yeah," she said, "but instead of a wedding ring imagine this... I want the body of Christ. I don't have it at the moment, so if it's ever going to happen it's got to happen in my future. Which is fine. So, what I do is I put you into the vacuum, increase the charge and bang..." she gestured heavily. "I've sent you back to 32AD. When you get there you steal the body for me and bury it where it would only be found by me. Here..."

She scored an 'X' on the ground with her foot.

"And then, *after* I've sent you... I dig up this area of land and *voilà*; there it is."

"So what about me? Where am I now?"

"You, Nick, are in a place called 'fucked'. Because you can never, ever come back. You lack the technology."

"I'm stuck there?"

"'Fraid so. But that isn't the real problem. The real problem is I send you back and then I dig up this area of land and my prize isn't there..?"

"Then I failed?"

"You failed, and I *can't change* the fact that you failed... But I can still be the *reason*." She looked up at me. "Because I can send someone else back and give them a brand new task. That is… to steal the body either *before* you or *from* you, either will do. Of course, I don't tell them anything about what you had to do, because I'm paranoid."

"Of course." Made no sense to me.

"So, having already dug this patch of earth up, I tell my new guy to bury the body here…"

She used her foot to mark a new patch of earth.

"If, when I dig this patch up it's still not there, I simply keep trying until I succeed."

"And is this to do with the tables. And why they were hidden?"

"Yes. But, whilst Davies did the job he was supposed to do, he screwed up."

"Wait a minute… *who the hell is Davies?*"

"Big-style loner and nasty piece of work," she said nonchalantly. "No family and very few friends to speak of. He's also a man convicted of numerous rapes and murders and sentenced to death by lethal injection."

She smiled knowingly. Again.

"Unless, of course, he wanted to live the rest of his life free as a bird. For a price."

"The price being what? That he has to live that life in the past and he has to steal something when he gets there? You're just being ridiculous now."

"Am I?" she said. "Okay, if you don't believe it fine... just try to *imagine* it."

She looked for something and I gave in; I indicated that I'd do my best.

"Okay, so... the idea is that once he's performed his one task, his life's his own, but they make it very clear that his execution might just be a bit more drawn out if he refuses. I mean, the doses might be wrong or something. Accidentally, of course, but very slow. Very painful. But if he agrees to the task then he mustn't ignore it when he gets back there or, indeed, mess it up. Because if he does then somebody else will be sent back to choose a new location..." she pointed to the second 'X' with her foot, "...and put things right. But the first part of their task will undoubtedly be to take away all those extra years that Davies had just bought himself."

"But, and I'm speaking extremely metaphorically here, you said Davies *did* mess up."

"He did. Credit to him he stole the tables and he hid them where he was supposed to. Job done...? You'd think so, but unfortunately, somewhere along the line, it seems that Davies must have opened his mouth. Doesn't matter who to. So, this becomes the stuff of legend and travels through the ages until one day, hundreds of years after his death, somebody discovered the tables. They had no idea what to do with them, though, so they put them back. But not before they'd left some clues. They got Teniers to paint the picture and the tables were found so Klein had to send somebody back to fix the problem."

"And did it work?"

"I don't know yet."

"So, if this is actually true, and it's worth pointing out that it isn't, then how would you be in a position to know all this?"

"Because I'm not really an archaeologist, Nick," she said slowly. "I'm a scientist. In fact, I'm a damn good scientist. In truth I'm part of the team that discovered this was actually possible in the first place."

I took off my shades and narrowed my eyes. "But, surely that would mean you worked for Klein?"

The smile was lame. "Yes it would, Nick.' She looked out across the waterless lake. "And guess what? I still do."

Klein was searching France for the tables and yet Sarah had sneaked in and found them before he did. Now his men were trying to steal them back and kill us both for having them. Which could only mean that Sarah had gone out on her own. She'd tried to steal the tables for herself.

"So you double crossed your boss?"

She nodded. "Kind of, yeah."

"And what about the package? The bomb, if that's really what it is? Assuming that you did create some fake tables, how do I know that the real ones aren't buried over there." I pointed into the distance.

"Because the real ones are here, Nick."

Sarah reached into her rucksack and pulled out a large wad of tissue paper. Carefully she unravelled it to reveal the tables, shiny black surfaces glinting in the sun.

"So why bury a bomb? For what? Klein to dig up?"

She nodded.

"Why?"

"Because I think Klein wants me to kill him."

"And why do I find that very hard to believe?"

"Because you haven't lived through the things I have, that's why," she said, carefully folding the tissue back around the tables and gently placing them back into her bag.

"Okay, so tell me. Tell me what it is that you've been through," I said. "Tell me everything."

"I intend to, but I need to visit Tina first," she said, moving around to the car door. "Will you take me there?"

"Not without answers, no."

She looked at me intently. "You don't need all the answers, Nick. Not just yet. What you do need, however, is to go home and get some sleep because... no offence... you look like shit. But I promise you, if you'll drop me back at Oakdene on the way, then by tomorrow you will have every one of the answers you've been searching for."

"And how do I know I can trust you?"

She shrugged indifferently.

"You don't. All I'm asking is *will you?*"

FORTY-EIGHT

SUNDAY, JUNE 12, 2011.
RESEDA, LOS ANGELES, CALIFORNIA.

For better or worse, if that's not too ironic a statement, I still lived in the apartment I once shared with my wife and Vicki - a big old building in Reseda, just the wrong side of Hollywood.

It was not in as good condition as it was all those years ago, but it was home. It had a bed, a TV, a place to keep Jack and a freezer compartment for ice. There really wasn't a lot else I needed. Having done as requested and dropped Sarah off outside the doors of Oakdene I parked the car in front of my block but didn't bother to lock it up, given the continuing window deficiency. At some point I'd either get it fixed or try myself, but it was a not point that would be arriving tonight. I felt wrecked from the inside out and if I looked half as bad as I felt then it would be fair to say that I didn't look too good..

At the point I opened the lower door I had no idea just how much this simple fact would go in my favour.

I was tired from the heat and tired from flying and driving and flying and driving again. I'd slept on the plane, but it wasn't anything like real sleep - the kind where you're curled in your own sheets and comfortable enough to fall right into a warm place that your body's been saving a long time to buy passage to.

I checked for post but, as it was all bills or glossy leaflets offering me yet more lines of credit, I left them in the hole and climbed the bare wooden stairs, my footsteps echoing up the central well. I was so worn out from flights of the airplane kind that if there had been just one more of the stairs kind I might never have made it. Nicola, the bisexual pro in three, would have found me asleep against her door come morning; like I'd camped out early for her mid-season sale or something.

When I reached the heady heights of four I blearily pushed my key forward to place it in the lock and... the door inched open. Just a fraction. Until that moment I hadn't even noticed that the lock was broken. I opened the door wide and forced my eyes to do the same.

I didn't particularly like what I saw.

I'm not for one moment going to pretend that I'm one of those 'neat and tidy' guys, because I know you wouldn't buy it, but I do have standards. Low as those standards may be they'd been seriously compromised. The apartment looked like a train had hit it. Followed by a bomb. Then rounded off quite nicely with a small grenade. Drawers were pulled out, clothes and magazines strewn across the floor. The sofa had been up-ended and the TV unit lay in a rather unceremonious heap of shattered black plastic and glass in the far corner.

Anything that had found itself in somebody's way had been broken and anything that hadn't had been broken as well, just to be sure. At some point in the last few days my apartment had been quite seriously trashed.

Now, concealed within these low standards of mine is an annoying tendency to leave coffee cups hovering on the pile of magazines next to the sofa. And, because it's rare that I ever finish a cup before I've drifted off to the late night schedule, these cups are usually still half full. As it was with the one that was there now, only it wasn't half full any more because it too had been tipped over. Which again was not surprising. The fact that the coffee was still dripping from it, however, was. This had not happened over the past few days. This had happened today.

In fact, this was something that was probably happening...

"Now!"

A guy (Mid-Sentence, as it happened) appeared from behind the door. I only just saw the outline of his face, carved from a hunk of anger and spite-filled retribution, before his fist thundered into me and sent my whole body flying backward into the dimly-lit hallway.

I stumbled on the badly fitted hall carpet and found myself with my back thrown hard against the wall, suddenly unable to feel the floor beneath my feet. Then Smoking and Mid-Sentence both appeared in front of me. Only this time they looked a little weird, their features being pulled at odd angles. Stranger still, there was a light fitting on the wall behind them, the bulb dead.

Which I guess, if I thought about it logically, meant that I was actually lying flat on my back.

They looked around, checking the hallway. Empty. Many's the day I reasoned you could fire a gun in this place without a door sneaking open, but I was still kind of hoping that this day wouldn't be the one where they would be putting my theories to test. They grabbed a foot apiece and dragged me back over the threshold, very graciously closing the door only when my head had cleared the jamb.

"You're supposed to be dead," Mid-Sentence said, his gun

now pointing at the small area of flesh which fought for space between my eyebrows. He had a flesh-coloured plaster stretched tight across his widened nose and his voice was almost comically nasal. I'm guessing I'd hit him real good.

"Why do I get the feeling that's only temporary?" I said without irony. I sounded almost as nasal as he had.

"Probably because it is. Where's the girl?"

So now, even though I wasn't actually on my feet, I somehow had to think on them. Fast. They knew that I was still alive, despite the bomb, but they probably had no idea about Sarah. Which meant that if I could buy her some time then one of us – the one that wasn't me – might just make it to the end of the day alive. If not, they'd send someone to finish the job before she even made it down the steps at Oakdene. I just had to make it convincing. If I could.

"You packaged it, she opened it," I said, stretching the sentence as though the grief of the whole world had suddenly chosen to wrap itself around my neck. "Work it out for yourself."

His eyes narrowed inquisitively. "So how come you're still breathing?"

I took a moment. It's never good to hurry these things along; haste versus speed and all that crap. "Because she didn't want me to see what was in the package. She said it was something important."

"It was," he said, throwing me the kind of nasty smile you feel like hitting with a bat. A large bat. Perhaps even one with rusty nails hammered through. "Bagged it up myself." He narrowed his eyes. "So tell me… when you saw all the little pieces of her spreading across the ground, did it make breaking my nose worthwhile?"

I looked him straight in the eye. "The only thing that made breaking your fucking nose worthwhile," I said, "was breaking your fucking nose."

Smoking, meanwhile was on the radio, presumably to the man without whose authority he probably couldn't even take a piss. He was explaining that, 'despite their measures', I'd just managed to show up at the apartment. Then he listened. At this point I assumed that it would be more a case of how to kill me than whether or not to do it. Adhering rigidly to my ongoing record for assumption, it seemed I was wrong.

Grier had apparently hit a bit of a problem and it seemed that they might still have a use for me after all.

Like I said, I got the feeling it was temporary.

★ ★ ★ ★ ★

At about the same time, almost 8000 miles away, somebody else was discovering that a door that should have been closed was hanging wide open. Unlike mine, however, this one did not suffer the indignity of a broken lock. Why should it when they had carried with them a spare key? One that had been stolen from her bag and cut almost as soon as she had arrived on the scene, just in case.

Mme Mercelle knew that it was not like her guest to spend the whole day tucked up in her room, though she had not seen her leave at any point throughout it. Still, the girl came and went at such irregular hours that it was often hard to tell. She liked her guest house, one that she believed was the finest in Couiza, to be kept neat and tidy at all times so, assuming that her guest was out and about, she had decided that it was a good opportunity for a quick clean. Dust round; spread some fresh sheets over the bed, that kind of thing.

When she reached the door, however, and found it ajar she was a little concerned. Whether or not her guest was on the premises, here was one door that was never left unlocked. Her guest was particular about things like that. Liked to keep stuff private. So private, in fact, that she'd even ignored the existing furnishings and bought her own little drawer unit, one with her own key, and asked Mme Mercelle if she'd be kind enough not to make any attempt to open it. This, she said, was the place where she elected to keep her personal files.

Of course, Mme Mercelle had agreed without argument. After all, her guest's affairs were their own, and she was never one to snoop. She could even have used one of the existing drawer units, she had said, and Mme Mercelle would have promised faithfully never to look inside, but she had said that she would feel so much safer if she had known for sure that there was only she who had a key. A strange request, perhaps, but certainly not an unreasonable one. Besides, she was one of the best long-term guests Mme Mercelle had ever had. She was always polite, always paid her rent on time and always adhered to the rules and regulations of the pension, few and fair as those regulations were.

The room itself was small, especially with a double bed taking up so much of the available space, but it did have a corner given over to an attempt at a kitchen replete with sink, microwave and kettle, plus an en-suite bathroom with shower. Most of the wall space was taken up by an array of freshly-developed snapshots. There were larger places to stay in the town, and even some two bedroom apartments for rent on the outskirts to the south, but such places usually required longer term contracts to be signed and perhaps the girl had simply wanted to remain that little bit more flexible.

And so, if the door being open had been surprising, you can imagine how Mme Mercelle might have felt when she found the room apparently empty whilst the drawer, the *secret* drawer, remained wide open. After all, there had been no break-in, how could there have been when the door had seemingly not been forced? Her guest must simply have left in a hurry, she reasoned, presumably in the early hours of the morning because she herself had been up since seven and seen nobody coming or going. So she moved inside and pushed the drawer closed without looking inside, though from the corners of her eyes it appeared... empty.

She could not lock it, of course, but things sure looked neater now.

The drapes still drawn tight as well, she thought. She tutted and muttered to herself in French, pulling them apart to let the morning sunlight glide inward and then turned, her foot catching against something as she did. It felt soft, spongy almost, as opposed to something solid like a book or a box.

She looked down.

Seconds later, Mme Mercelle was running fast from the room, her slippers flapping down the hard stairs as she screamed as loud as she could, "Aidez moi! Aidez moi!"

Kelly Brown's body lay at the side of the bed, her eyes wide and her tongue hanging blue from her mouth. She faced the ceiling, her legs twisted and buckled but her night-shirt and pants were still in place. The sleeve of her left arm was rolled high, a leather belt tied into a tourniquet across her slender biceps and below, in the fold of her inner elbow, an empty syringe still pierced her cold flesh.

It would be clear from the autopsy that Kelly had never

injected drugs before, but impossible to say whether or not she had previously utilised other non-invasive methods. All that would clearly be ascertained was that her final dose of pure-grade heroin, administered via the syringe, had been almost instantaneously lethal. In the few seconds she was allowed, she may have been aware that she was dying, or she may not. Autopsy or no, however, the expression of pure horror on her face pretty much told that story to anyone who cared to work it out.

It had only been a slight detour for Smoking and Mid-Sentence. They had called in to see her, at Grier's express request, on their way back to Cardou with the tables they had sequestered from the DHL desk at Caucassonne. Nobody saw them enter the pension and nobody saw them leave, least of all Mme Mercelle who slept heavily in the years since her abusive husband had died.

Even if they had been seen then it would have made little difference. Along with Grier, who had requested that Klein return from Siberia and meet him in Los Angeles, they were aboard a privately chartered plane back to the United States less than an hour after Kelly's heart stopped beating.

The verdict, it seemed, would be recorded as one of *'La mort par misadventure'*.

FORTY-NINE
FRIDAY, MAY 22, 2009.
OAKDENE, LENWOOD, CALIFORNIA.

Alison Bond, or rather 'Sarah Fiddes', the name she had now adopted, pulled up outside the Gothic architecture of Oakdene in a rented Toyota compact and stepped gingerly out onto the gravel. She looked the building up and down with dismay. It was in a far worse condition than she had ever imagined; crumbling stone, flaking paint and bushes growing wildly out of control around the main entrance.

It looked in many ways as though it had simply been abandoned to the elements, though she knew it had not. Inside were over a hundred needy people, including the one she had come to see, and not one of those needs would be attended to adequately. She sighed, partly through despair and partly through a sense of apprehension. It had been a long journey to get here but that journey was over now. She was here at last. The right place at most definitely the right time.

The heavy door creaked loudly on its hinges as she pushed it open, the sound echoing through the wide entrance hall beyond and causing the large black woman behind the desk to pull her glasses down from her nose and look upward. She waited patiently as Sarah's feet clicked along the floor and then said, "Can I help you?"

"I hope so," Sarah said. "I'm here to see Tina Fiddes."

And she could see the look in the lady's eyes. Something that said that this, whilst not impossible, seemed highly improbable. Nobody ever came to visit Tina Fiddes, it seemed. Nobody ever had. But yet she was narrowing her eyes, scrutinising Sarah's face before she spoke. "Are you a relative?" she asked.

"Yes," Sarah replied. "I'm her sister."

"Her sister," the lady said, though she looked dubious. "She's in room...."

"One-one-three. Yes, I know."

"I see," the lady said. "If you like I could show you the way."

"Thankyou, that would be great.....?"

"Maggie," she said, finishing Sarah's sentence as she rose to her feet and held out her thick hand in greeting. "I'm Maggie. I'm duty supervisor today."

"Sarah," The lady responded. "Sarah Fiddes."

Maggie closed the files she was working on and locked them back into her drawer, then retrieved the key to one-one-three and they walked along the corridor.

"She's not expecting you, is she?" Maggie asked, although she already knew the answer to that one.

"Not at all."

"I don't believe we've ever had a visitor for Tina. I really didn't know she even had a sister."

"Neither did I until recently," Sarah said with a wry smile. "I came as soon as I could."

"And does she know she has a sister?"

Sarah smiled. "Not really. We've been separated almost all our lives, so we've never truly met."

"Bit of a special day today, then?"

Sarah nodded. "For us both."

They started up the steps for the second floor. "We do have a lift," Maggie explained apologetically, "but she can be a little temperamental sometimes, so we only try to use her if we've a patient in a chair."

"What's my sister like?" Sarah asked.

Having reached the top of the steps, Maggie stopped for a moment and turned. "Do you know something," she said with a proud smile, "your sister is a lovely girl. Never a moment's trouble. I mean, you know she can't speak, don't you...?" Sarah nodded. "Well, don't you go forgetting she can hear, and write if she needs to. She's very clever indeed."

"Does she seem happy?" Sarah's eyes were probing.

Maggie thought for a moment. A long enough moment for Sarah to realise that the answer was 'no' but that she had no desire to answer the question in such blunt and negative terms. "Well," she said, having thought it through, "let's just say she doesn't seem unhappy."

Sarah nodded. She understood.

They passed an elderly caretaker carrying an open tin of beige paint who nodded in tired recognition as they walked, clearly the cheapest help available, and then continued along the upper corridor, walking in silence until they reached the door to Tina's room. Maggie peered inside to check that all was well, then stepped back so that Sarah could take a look for herself.

Tina was sitting on her bed, her knees drawn up to her chin and folding a sheet of bright white paper, origami-style, into a fragile bird. Her hair was hanging loose around her ears and she had a gentle but mischievous smile carved across her face.

"She loves reading," Maggie said. "Always got that pretty nose of hers in some book or other."

"I see that the rooms are well kept," Sarah said. With the exception of the small area in which Tina was sitting now, everything was where it should be and the bed was perfectly made.

"We do our best," Maggie said, correcting, "but what you'll see in Tina's room is usually a result of Tina herself. She can't settle if the room's a mess so to be honest she tends to take care of that side of things herself."

Whilst the room was almost painfully spartan, there were approximately twenty books of varying sizes and thicknesses stacked on a low shelf in the left hand corner. Each one had been carefully arranged in ascending order of height to form an almost perfect downward slope.

"Now I must warn you," Maggie said quietly, "that she doesn't much take to strangers at first and you might think she's, well, ignoring you. It's not so much that, it's more that she needs to see somebody a good few times, and they have to be real nice to her, before she'll really let them in."

"I understand," Sarah said.

"I just didn't want you to have come all this way and feel disappointed," Maggie said. "Because she really is a lovely girl if you're prepared to put in the time."

"Thankyou," Sarah said, and she seemed to mean it in more ways than one. "Can we....?"

"Oh, yes, of course," Maggie said, sliding the key into the door and opening it wide.

Tina looked up and saw Maggie standing broad in the doorway, her smile wide and genuine. She smiled gently back but did not move to get up. She was just about to look back down to her book when she saw that Maggie was not alone. Not today. There was another person with her, a younger woman with jet black hair tied into a pony tail and black clothing. This woman was smiling gently back at her, almost knowingly.

Tina turned on the bed, laid the paper dove on the covers and slowly placed her bare feet on the cold floor. Then she lifted slowly to her feet, her eyes never leaving her guest. Sarah edged into the room and walked toward her, but Tina did not move. She remained motionless, standing at the side of the bed like an army recruit undergoing first bunk inspection.

Sarah approached, her eyes and smile full of a magnetic warmth.

"I wouldn't get too close..." Maggie began, but she was too late.

Sarah threw her arms around her sister. Again Tina did nothing. Not at first. Her face indicated that she should know what to do, but the answer would not bring itself to the fore.

446

Then, slowly, her hands started to move. They climbed around Sarah's back, three or four inches from touching, and planted themselves firmly and decisively beneath her shoulder blades, gripping tight.

The two women held each other for what seemed like an eternity.

All the time Maggie, whose only concern was Tina, watched her patient's eyes. They had been unsure at first, sceptical, but now they shone and glistened with the kind of happiness she herself had never been able to extract from the young girl. As she moved her chin above Sarah's shoulder she could see the smile; the smile of a child opening the birthday present they had prayed each and every night that they would find when they awoke the next morning.

"Does she.... Does she know who you are?" Maggie asked. How could she? Had Sarah not told her only ten minutes ago that the two girls had never actually met?

Tina was staring straight at Maggie now, thanking her with those huge brown eyes of hers for the present she had brought along with her today.

But it was Sarah's voice she heard.

"Oh yes," she said, her voice happy and gentle. "She knows who I am. Don't you pumpkin?"

And though Tina's chin was embedded firmly into her sister's shoulder, Maggie could see her nodding gently. She knew that she was nothing if not a perceptive girl and she didn't need to understand how or why Tina recognised her guest.

She just did.

Tina knew exactly who this stranger was and, if you knew Tina as well as Maggie did, you would know that, where this girl was concerned, far far stranger things had happened.

Her back to Maggie, Sarah hugged her sister tight.

They were together now and, for the next two years, that was pretty much all that mattered.

FIFTY
SUNDAY, JUNE 12, 2011.
LOS ANGELES, CALIFORNIA.

I hadn't the first idea where they had taken me.

I'd guessed for a while that we were heading toward the beach, that's certainly the direction we started in, but I lost track further en-route. The van had no windows and it became so that it was hard to tell whether we were even turning left or right, especially when there were so many other things to worry about. Things like a broken-nosed guy with a gun pointing right into the face of the guy who did it.

Secondly, there was finding a way to get out of the bigger situation alive, if at all possible.

I was guessing that darkness had fallen by the time we arrived, though again I could not be sure. Wherever it was that they had brought me, it was one of those places with an underground parking lot, empty save for the van in which we'd just arrived, and no way to see if there was still a world outside. The two men bundled me out of the back, still handcuffed, and into a lift. They pressed for floor five of eight and that was about all I ever knew.

Five was, in every sense, a building site, though I guessed it was more demolition than construction. What had once been segregated offices were now broken panels hanging loose and wires dangled limply from the ceilings. There were quite a few old office blocks near the sea front that were undergoing some kind of delayed regeneration but even at this point I was realising that, like most things today, them being here would only be temporary. Even if I made it out of here alive and managed to track this building down in the weeks to come, I knew they would be gone. They were here because it suited them to be here - like most other particles in this world - only at this particular moment in time.

I was marched roughly down what was once a corridor and into a room on the left, without windows, where Mid-Sentence pretty much threw me into a chair. Then they stood to my front - left and right - just staring and smiling in that way that people do when they're so cock sure that they've just won the game. Maybe they had, but in the van I'd been thinking fast and, on the odd occasion, I've been known to be successful where such things are concerned.

I only hoped it would be the same today.

It was quite clear, from the inescapable truth that I was still breathing, that I was of some limited use to them and unless they had already figured out that they now had some fake tables, which I doubted, my guess was that they hadn't got the first idea how to go about translating what they considered to be the real deal.

Which would explain why they'd been ransacking my apartment when I arrived home. They'd been looking for something, anything, that might help.

After a few minutes Grier marched purposefully into the room, a file tucked under his broad arm, and pulled out the opposing chair. He was a tall man, maybe one-ninety-five with a short black hair, greying at the sides. He was younger than he had appeared in the picture, maybe mid-forties. Certainly a lot younger than my tired old ass.

He took his seat, his eyes never so much as glancing in my direction, like I didn't even exist, and opened the file wide across the cheap brown laminate. I could see various documents inside as he sifted through and it looked to me as though he'd used the time it had taken us to arrive, perhaps three quarters of an hour, to put himself some notes together. I had no idea just how far reaching those notes would prove to be. Not yet.

Of the sheets I did see, many contained diagrams and figures, and quite a few were just pages of hardcopy; probably a report. I could also see that one of those reports contained a detailed chemical analysis. I hoped to God that what Sarah had told me about her fakes on the way to Oakdene, was true; that she had used a stone slab that had once been discovered buried in the floor of an Egyptian tomb.

If she had, this would mean two things; firstly that chemically her tables were of the right material composition and secondly that, in the absence of recent weathering, carbon dating would prove inconclusive (unless of course they took samples from the etched areas and they wouldn't want to go doing that for quite a while). And then I caught sight of the pictures. The close-ups of the tables that had been taken for study. The god-damn fakes.

Oh, yes; they'd bought them alright. Hook, line and all that other crap..

Grier looked upward and nodded to his cohorts who retreated to the wall behind me, then he addressed me verbally, though his eyes remained on the pages he was casually flicking through.

During his swift glance he seemed to have taken a deep look at what had been, until Mid-Sentence's intervention, one of my better features. "I like the nose," he said blankly.

"I'm trying a new look," I said, like I didn't care and like it didn't still hurt quite as much as it did. "I figured that, seeing as it looked so very fetching on your friend...?"

I could feel Mid-Sentence's daggers piercing my back.

"It seems you're a very difficult man to kill, Detective." Grier continued, disinterested. "Commendable, but ultimately quite annoying." He looked up, big bushy grey eyebrows raised for the briefest moment. "Tell me, do you know who I am?"

His expression suddenly became the same as it had been in the picture on Sarah's wall; severe. He looked me straight in the eyes, desperately trying to stare me down. For the record, he failed.

"I know your name. Is that enough?"

He smiled at me like one might smile at an interview candidate and it didn't reach his eyes; "To be going on with," then pulled out four high-quality black and white pictures of the fakes; two fronts and two reverses. He laid them on the table in such a way that they faced me. "And do you know what these are?"

I didn't even glance down at them. "You killed her, you bastard."

Play calm but look pissed off, I figured. Make them buy the lie.

"Unfortunate but necessary," he said. Nothing about his face was genuine, however, his lips were pursing toward regret simply because he asked them to. "And I'll be honest with you, Detective, in many ways it was somewhat unfortunate that we did."

"Was that an apology?" I asked.

He looked even colder than before. "I'm not in the habit of apologising for my actions, Detective. It doesn't suit my position. It just left us with... a bit of a problem, that was all."

I smiled. "And that would be what...? A puzzle you haven't the first idea how to solve, perhaps?"

He avoided the question. Had he answered he might have said it would take them 'longer' to solve, but not that it 'couldn't' be solved. I could sense that 'couldn't' was something he wouldn't care to admit existed in his vocabulary. Maybe they printed different editions of dictionaries for guys like him, deliberately omitting words such as 'cannot' and 'failure'.

I'll bet it included words like 'egotistical', though.

"We know that the girl..." he began.

"Sarah," I corrected. Give the supposedly dead a name, Grier.

He paused for a moment and smiled lamely. "Sarah... deciphered a code. The results of which are what ultimately led the pair of you directly to the place where these tables were hidden. And yes, I have to admit, she did just beat us to it..." No, I thought, she succeeded where you failed asshole. Hear that? Failed. The word does actually exist. "...because like all good codes it appeared to have a primer."

"And you've worked out a little too late that this one might have a primer as well?"

Grier sounded disinterested again now. He only wanted results so that Klein could do his thing, he didn't want to actually understand what it was he was getting.

"Something like that, but..."

"And now you want me to help you?" I interrupted. I didn't give him time to reply to my question. Like I said, I knew his name and I better knew what it was he wanted. A quick fix. "So you've killed an innocent French local; you've killed Sarah and you've very nearly killed me." I leaned purposefully forward, my neck stretching in disbelief. "And now you want my help?"

He looked straight at me with jet black eyes. No life, just death and probably lots of it. "It really would be very beneficial to your health, Detective, if you told us what you know."

I leaned back in my chair and sighed. Then I pretended to think, almost offering him an answer twice, but pulling back an instant later. Ultimately I sighed again and did the best resigned look I knew.

"Okay," I said. "I'll tell you what I know."

Grier leaned forward. Not excited, particularly, but certainly ready. "Go on."

"I know that if I don't tell you what you need to know right now I'm a dead man. I also know that the minute I tell you what you need to know, ie. right now, I'm a dead man. In fact, even though I'm sitting here passing the time of day with you right now, it's all one great big illusion. Because I get the distinct impression that, even as we speak - right now - I'm a dead man."

I leaned back. Happy with my wash.

"So you're here to bargain for your life, is that it?"

I guess that Grier liked to see people bargain for their life. In truth, I'm sure he preferred to see them beg. Either way, he looked smug. I hate smug almost as much as I hate cocky.

"I'm not here to bargain for anything quite so worthless," I said coldly. "This is, after all, your little get-together. As I recall, you invited me."

453

Grier took a deep breath and pulled another sheet from the file, a photograph. It had been at the back, the place which I hadn't realised, until now, he had carefully avoided when sifting through. He'd wanted to size me up first, that was all; to see how hard I wanted to play. And the first rule of any game like that is to always keep something in reserve and shit, had this guy kept something in reserve.

It was full colour and looked like one of those 'covert' style photos, the kind taken from the oblique angles you used to see on Candid Camera. Foreground left was what appeared to be the upright of a car windshield, indicating that the photographer was seated in his or her car at the time. Which also went some way toward explaining why the subject, a young blonde girl talking to a man dressed in a black polo neck in front of a row of shops, was completely unaware that the picture was being taken.

There was a 24hr Laundromat, a Bob's Supplies and a SonicStuff. The latter of the three looked like one of those rastafarian, pot-smoking places, its windows completely blocked out with lurid green, yellow and white vinyl graphics. Except that this wasn't a pot-smoking joint, far from it, because in the centre was a huge graphic 'S' embedded in a circle. It was that graphic which told me, without even looking as closely as I might have otherwise needed, who the young girl was. Because the 'S' stood for 'Sonics', as in SonicStuff. Green, yellow and white were their team colours.

If you don't know already, the Sonics play NBA Basketball.

And they play it in Seattle.

"You son of a bitch,' I said. I tried to sound angry but unaffected. Like this was nothing. But it wasn't, was it? This was my daughter, and somehow the bastards had tracked her down, something I'm not altogether certain that I would have been able to do at that point. "You leave her out of this."

"I'd love to," Grier said with a cold smile. "but the thing is… you might not care whether you live or die, Detective, and given the pitiful state of your existence, I find myself struggling to blame you for that. But what about this young lady? Don't tell me you're going to take her down with you? I mean, that just wouldn't be fair, now would it?"

"This is absolutely nothing to do with her," I said.

"*Was* nothing to do with her," Grier corrected. "But you see this is very, very important to me and, as such, it is to do with whoever I damn well choose. The gentleman she is speaking with - names aren't really important - is her dealer. Very small time, hardly worth bothering about really, and yet he's the kind of guy who shits bricks every time anybody so much as mentions an eight-to-ten stretch."

My daughter… my Vicki… is a drug addict. You have no idea how much that hurt; on two levels. The first was that it had taken Grier to tell me; that I hadn't actually known for myself. What kind of a father did that make me? The second, which in some ways was even worse, was that I wasn't actually surprised.

I should have been, but I wasn't, and what kind of a father did *that* make me?

Grier continued. "Currently this gentleman gets his 'shit', and I use the phrase in a purely narcotic sense you understand, from a supplier who is of great interest to the Seattle P.D. Consequently they have what you might term an 'agreement' with this gentleman. He's been known to… 'help them out' on occasion."

He leaned forward. "So I do hope for your sake, he doesn't end up giving young Vicki here some 'bad shit', don't you? That could be very nasty for her. Very nasty indeed." He shrugged. "Fatal perhaps."

"You know something?" I said, leaning as far into his face as the neutral territory of the table would allow. "You really are a cocksucking piece of crap."

FIFTY-ONE

Sunday, June 12, 2011.
Oakdene, Lenwood, California.

Sarah spoke briefly to Maggie as she entered the halls of Oakdene for the final time. She explained in no shortage of detail what was about to happen and they shared a warm embrace, then she headed upstairs to one-one-three. She did not look as happy as she normally did when she came to see her sister, and Maggie knew why. Better still, she understood. Her heart went out to them both. She wished that she could speak to Carey, but she knew that such a thought was impossible. No-one must know.

The minute Sarah was gone, Creed emerged quietly from his office and squeaked his cheap shoes across the floor in the direction of the reception desk...

★ ★ ★ ★ ★

Tina was in a world of her own that night and didn't even hear her sister enter. Her first recognition had been when the Snickers had been placed directly in front of her on the table. Then her eyes burst into life, the way that only Snickers and sisters could make them do, and they hugged.

Sarah spent a long time brushing her sister's hair, very carefully tonight because she knew what was to follow in her wake. She had worked it all out already, and it was for that reason, I learned

457

later, that she had tears in her eyes the whole time. Tina didn't know. That, Sarah figured, would have been far too upsetting for her to cope with, especially considering the other events that were waiting just over the dark horizon.

They walked in the grounds and enjoyed the sunset for a while. Quality time. As it tapered toward an end, they took a seat, at Sarah's request. With tears welling in her eyes once more, Sarah told her beloved sister the one thing that she had not wanted to hear. Ever.

"I have to go away," she said quietly. "I have to go away for a very long time. The truth is I won't be able to come visit for a while."

Then, whilst Tina stared toward another place, and not knowing if she even truly understood, Sarah had finally started crying, the tears flowing like water from a freshly squeezed sponge.

"But it's alright," she said, her voice making a poor attempt to sound upbeat. "Because I've left some money with Maggie and she's going to make sure that you get a Snickers every day."

Like that would be any form of compensation. Personally, I think Tina had seen in her sister's eyes then and there that this was no temporary goodbye. Or maybe, being the person Tina was, she had simply *felt* it. Either way, she too had tears forming. She didn't want Snickers, not half as much as she wanted her sister.

"I'm really, really sorry, Pumpkin," Sarah added. They gripped each other tight, their heads resting on each others shoulders and shared just a few more precious moments. "Because I do love you so much."

And then Tina had failed at something. But, according to Sarah, even that failure had been the most amazing gift she had ever been offered. Because her sister had, for the first time in her known life, *tried to speak*. Sarah gave her the space, but nothing came, just a fractured clicking from deep in her throat.

But she had tried.

After a while, she had closed her mouth, tight like a secret, and had instead taken hold of Sarah's hand. Lifting it slowly and gently placing it against her own heart.

"I know," Sarah had said. "And I love you too, Pumpkin. Always."

Sarah remained seated for a while longer, her sister's head nestled once more on her shoulder and together they stared out into the fall of night; watching the close of a chapter become the close of a favourite book.

She had known that this day would come, she had known it for two years now, but there was nothing that could ever have made it any easier. Of all the things Sarah had ever faced in her life, this was by far the hardest. She had arrived today feeling that she was prepared. She had been so very wrong.

Eventually she lifted her sister's head, kissed her warmly on the cheek and left her there in the grounds, tears rolling slowly down as she stared into the distance. Sarah tried desperately to hold herself together until she reached Maggie who, as requested, was now watching quietly from the weed-infested patio to the rear.

"You will, I mean...." Then the tears came again.

Maggie had taken Sarah's slender hand and engulfed it with her own, the warmth of her soul seeping in through the skin. "I'll make sure she's well taken care of," she said. "You don't go worrying yourself about that."

"Bad things are going to happen," Sarah said.

"They sure are," Maggie said, "but you always knew they would. You knew that you could not be here to help her out the other side. But I'm here, and I promise you I'll do everything I can to help her get through it."

She leaned forward and gave Sarah a motherly hug. "You better get gone," she said gently. "You have a lot of things to do."

Sarah nodded. "I'll never forget you, Maggie," she said, her eyes still wet with tears.

"Nor I you," Maggie replied. She followed it with a closed and knowing smile.

Sarah smiled, glanced back at her sister, still seated, and left.

She never saw Tina again.

★ ★ ★ ★ ★

"Miss Fiddes, could you spare me a moment?"

Sarah was almost out of the door. Almost.

"What is it Mister Creed?"

"It's a... personal matter," he had said, tiny obnoxious eyes peering out from behind his glasses. "I think we'd be better discussing it in my office."

Sarah sighed, but reluctantly accepted the invitation. Creed held the door and she walked in.

He followed and closed the door behind him. Then locked it.

"I don't think there's any need for that," Sarah said. Fairly decisively.

"It's just for privacy," he said, placing the key in his jacket pocket. But his sneering mouth had said that this kind of privacy was the wrong kind. This was not 'confidential' this was 'confident'. Overly so. He took that confidence and leaned against the edge of his desk with it. "Maggie tells us that you will not be visiting us any more. Is that correct?"

"Yes it is," Sarah had said. "But I don't really see what..."

"Well, it's just that Tina needs so much care," he had continued, his voice almost slithering. "And I'm sure you would like to make sure that she continues to get the very best."

"I've spoken with Maggie and it's all taken care of, Mister Creed. So if that's all...?"

Creed tried his best to look like he cared and failed miserably. "Oh, Maggie's excellent," he had said, his tone unwaveringly sickly, "an integral part of our staff. But, of course, it is I who runs this facility. So if you really want to make sure that your sister gets the best possible treatment, then perhaps I'm the one you should be speaking to. I mean, I can make sure she gets the best of... everything."

With every word he had taken another slow step closer until eventually he backed Sarah up against the door, his eyes full of something she had not liked one little bit. He was smiling like he was going to get something he had always wanted and she could feel and smell both his foul breath and the caustic smell of fake-brand aftershave on her face. Then he had placed his warm, sweaty palm on her left breast. Pressing, moving.

The cold wood pushed through her flimsy white vest into her back but Sarah didn't move. She just smiled, looked Creed in the eye with warmth and desire and said softly, "Really, Mister Creed. You'd do that?"

He had nodded, though his head was lowered as he carefully studied his hand running over every curve of her body, finally seeing it where he had probably pictured it in his messed up mind so many times. "Oh, yes. Yes, of course."

Maybe, because he had been looking down at that point, Creed had actually seen Sarah's knee coming up. Or maybe not. Either way he stood little chance of actually stopping it and it had done exactly what it was supposed to do; catch him full in the balls. The force was as hard at that moment as he probably was. It sent him reeling backward, staggering until he fell against his desk, where he then collapsed, clutching his crotch.

Sarah walked over, a satisfied smile melting into her face, crouched directly in front of him and very carefully spit in his face. "You are one sick little puppy, Creed," she said, her mouth curled into a vicious sneer. Then she reached inside his jacket pocket and retrieved the key for the door. "Tina will be out of here within a week, I'll make damn sure of it. You, meanwhile, can rot in hell."

For a few more moments, just to let him know she was serious, she stayed right in his face, looking at him; observing him as he held his balls and tried to get the blood to retreat from his pudgy face. Then she shook her head in disgust, despair and genuine pity. She had summed him up and the answer wasn't worth sharing with him. It wasn't good.

"You'll pay for this you bitch," he had said, still wincing.

Her reply had been simple; to the point. "I already am, Mister Creed." Then she unlocked the door and walked out of the room. "Every single day of my life."

Creed probably held those swollen balls of his for another five minutes; embarrassed and angry. All the while, along with too much blood, he would have had Sarah's words coursing through his head. *Within a week.* And that pained expression had very probably turned into one huge devious smile. *Within a week.*

Sarah had known exactly what she had just told him, and why. She had hated doing it, of course, more than anything she had wanted to hold back the words, but she could not. They were too important. If the world was ever going to be the way it needed to be, then they simply had to be spoken.

FIFTY-TWO
SUNDAY, JUNE 12, 2011.
OAKDENE, LENWOOD, CALIFORNIA.

I allowed my face to sink slowly into one that told Grier
that I knew damn well I was finished, although in some ways
I actually still felt I was winning. I had been dragged here,
rather unceremoniously, knowing that somehow I would need
to try and engineer a deal. What I could not do, however, was
let Grier know that, so I had needed to play it very unco-
operatively from the off. I have to be honest, I hadn't expected
the Vicki trick, not for a moment, but for now it was simply one
more bridge; I'd cross it as and when I could.

"Go on then, give me what you've got," I said angrily. Not
'tell me what you need', because that would be too much too
soon. This was 'tell me what you have and if I can add to it to
help Vicki I will, but no promises'. "I'm guessing that you're
prepared to make a deal, right? I mean, if you're still telling me
that Vicki and I are dead whatever, then I might as well just
keep my goddamned mouth shut. Yeah?"

"Yes, detective, we are prepared to..." he searched in that one-
track skull of his for the word, "...negotiate." Negotiate my ass.
Blackmail yes, negotiation no.

"Good, because if I'm going to give you what you want, then

you have to give me the things I want. I believe that in all good textbooks that is the true definition of a successful... *negotiation*."

Grier sighed and shook his head, because I had not said I wanted a 'thing' as in my life, but rather 'things'; as in, lots of things. "And what are these *things* you want exactly?"

I smiled contentedly. Time to play.

"Well, Grier," I said calmly. "I've been a detective for twenty three years. I've watched people's heads get blown off not three feet from my own and I've cleared up a great many more deaths than I care to describe to you now. Getting killed myself is an occupational hazard that I've so far succeeded in only narrowly avoiding. I know how the world works and I also know that Sarah Fiddes played with the biggest box of matches she could find, knowing that they might just explode in her face. Which, thanks to you, they did. Now her death might have been a risk she was prepared to face, but at the end of the day it was still unnecessary. You knew she was capable of finding these..."

I flicked one of the photos of the tables, "...and you knew she might even know how to understand them. I mean she's one of Josef Klein's top scientists, for God's sake. You shouldn't have taken her out and in my book that, my friend, classes as a very big mistake. You wanted notches on your gun and played it badly."

Grier looked puzzled. Genuinely puzzled.

"Who told you Sarah Fiddes worked for Josef Klein?" he asked.

"None of your business."

"Because Sarah Fiddes has never, *ever* worked for Josef Klein," he said.

As he spoke he looked me straight in the eye and, bullshitter as he was, I don't actually think he was lying.

But Sarah was lying. In fact, she'd lied to me. And I'd let her go, tables and all. The truth, which I really got the feeling this might just transpire to be, hurt like hell. I tried not to let it show, but what did I say about me and poker? Crap at it.

Ask Maggie.

Grier leaned forward. "Oh dear," he said quietly. "Looks to me like somebody hasn't been entirely honest with you, detective. Doesn't it?"

I looked up at him like I didn't care. "It doesn't change the deal. The only deal... if you ever want to understand what's in those tables."

He placed both his fingers under his nose, his hand covering his mouth and squinted his eyes like he was genuinely interested. Pensive. Thoughtful. Asshole.

"And this deal is...?"

I figured now was a good time break some ice and test 'Smoking' and 'Mid-Sentence'; just to see both how stupid they were and how long they'd have survived in the old west. I liked playing games sometimes, it livened up dull moments. So I reached into my pocket for my packet of cigarettes just a little too quickly and the guns flicked up. Very quick. In fact, these guys could have given Billy the Kid a run for his money. Nine out of ten for Smoking and ten for his friend. Except they'd already frisked me. Twice. And neither time had they found a weapon.

So they really were stupid.

I smiled, placed the cigarette in my mouth and lit it with the lighter I kept in the pack.

"I'd like you to do three things for me, Grier," I said, blowing smoke into the air. "The first is to assure me that both myself and my daughter get to finish our lives at a time dictated by a power far higher than you; and that we won't become another couple of your unnecessary notches." He creased his mouth, like that might be possible. At a push. "I have the answers you want and we're both aware that what I know and what I can prove are two very different things. I doubt me trying to stir trouble in the future would do me any favours and, if I keep quiet and get on with my life, I doubt that killing me would do any for you. Besides which, I have insurance."

"What kind of insurance?"

"The kind you don't want to mess with." Which, by the way, was one humdinger of a lie. "But it's nothing more than an unclaimed policy if my daughter and I stay alive." I leaned across the table, stared him right in the face. "And we both want to make that happen, don't we...?"

He sat back again, thinking it through. And I'm sure he agreed with me. I'd never be able to prove anything, and I'd be dead within a day of trying. And yet here I was offering the one thing he needed. Or rather, the one thing Klein needed. Klein, however, would probably remain unaware of the methods used to obtain it. Seeing as how Sarah was already 'dead', all I was asking for, it seemed, was for me and my daughter to avoid ending the day the same way.

"And the second thing?"

"The second is an apology," I said. "I want you to apologise to me, right here and now, for killing Sarah."

Grier laughed in disgust. "You are joking?"

"Not for a second," I said, shaking my head and dragging hard on the Marlboro. I had to make it look like I was prepared to ask for stupid things because it was a very long road from where I was now to begging, and if they thought they could have me begging I'd be truly finished. "I want you to say that you're very, very sorry you killed Sarah. That you fucked up."

He blinked his eyes slowly, giving nothing away. "You said there were three things. What's the third?"

"Well," I said, "if I'm going to give you what you need, then I want you to promise me faithfully that you'll take damn good care of it."

"Take good care of *what*?"

"You get nothing until the deal is agreed."

Grier smiled. And though he hated doing what he did next, I could see it trying to explode in his head, he did it anyway. His voice was slow and laboured, his teeth very firmly gritted, but it would do. It did what it was supposed to do; it pissed him off. "I'm really, *really* sorry we killed the girl, Detective."

And, with certain obvious conditions, I was suddenly no longer a dead man. I was very much an alive man, albeit not a particularly happy one. Probably because I knew full well that this was just one more of those *temporary* state of affairs that kept rearing their ugly heads. Still, within the space of less than an hour I had successfully negotiated the lives of three people and heard Grier apologise. And, whether he meant it or not, I'm pretty sure he felt mildly humiliated by it.

That, for me, was not a bad day all told.

We spent the next couple of hours working out the finer points of the deal and ultimately Grier let me go. By which I mean he had me bundled back into the van, driven downtown and dropped off near City Hall. I had been wherever it was I had been pretty much all night and it was almost eight in the morning by this time. I'm not even going to begin to explain how tired I was, but I wasn't going home. Not just yet.

I knew that Grier's men would come after me again, in time, I wasn't so stupid that I hadn't worked that one out, but I'd already decided that by the time they did I'd have something else up my grubby sleeve that would save my ass second time around. I hadn't figured out what that would be just yet, but the one thing they had given me was time and I was sure I'd use it to think of something.

As for Sarah, I really didn't know what form her plans were taking, but what I did know - or what I sensed to be the truth - was that she had (to quote Grier) never worked for Josef Klein. Which actually went a long way to explaining why she might have buried, of all things, a bomb. It struck me that our Sarah Fiddes might just have enjoyed her double-cross so much that she'd taken one look at me and gone for the triple.

As I'd no cellphone on me I went to the nearest payphone and rang the main desk at Oakdene. I didn't actually expect Sarah to still be there, not for a second, but I hoped Maggie was. I caught her as she was just about to finish her night shift and she pretty much told me what I had needed to know. Yes, Sarah had been in last night, which I knew because I had dropped her there myself, and yes, *she had said goodbye to her sister.* When I asked why Sarah had been saying goodbye, Maggie just said that she couldn't tell me, that it wasn't her place to do so, but that Sarah Fiddes would definitely not be visiting her sister again.

She was very clear about that.

Sarah Fiddes had lied to me, she had the tables and she had visited Oakdene with only one intention; to bid a fond farewell to the only person, besides herself, that I figured she cared about; her sister. She had promised that I would have the answers I needed today and her last words to me as she had climbed out of the car at Oakdene, when I'd asked where and when she had wanted to meet, were; '*Don't worry, Nick, I'll find you*'.

You'll forgive me if I very much doubted that. Truthfully, I doubted I'd ever see Sarah Fiddes or the tables again.

So no, even though it was early morning and I'd spent the night bargaining for my ass, I didn't go straight home.

Sorry and all that, but I so very desperately needed a cigarette.

More importantly, I needed a drink.

FIFTY-THREE

MONDAY, JUNE 13, 2011.
LOS ANGELES, CALIFORNIA.

"We don't open until ten, Nick. As well you know."

Michelle had spraygun and cloth in hand and was cleaning around the bar. I doubt she'd even realised that the door had been unlocked.

"I do know that," I said, somewhat nasally, "but to be honest I don't actually give a monkey's at this precise moment in time." I couldn't even be bothered to raise a smile. "Jack with ice, if you'd be so kind."

She placed her cloth down and edged behind the bar. "Cody will kill me if he finds out," she said, drawing Jack from the optic. "Anyway, judging by the state of your face, there's no point asking if you've a rough day, this is way too early even for you. A rough night then, I'm guessing."

I knew how rough I felt - hell, I was the one feeling it - but I could only hazard a guess at how that might have migrated into the way I looked. I had a sneaking feeling, however, that somewhere in this world Death, scythe in hand, was coming to collect some near-departed soul, all the while complaining that he felt like Detective Nick Lambert warmed up.

"The worst," I said, wearily accepting the drink. Michelle took a lingering look at my face, winced in the direction of my nose, then placed the bottle on the bar as well.

As I stared into a better space, her cloth-hand moved in broad strokes along the bar surface, trying to resuscitate the sheen.

"Want to talk about it?" she asked, stopping for a moment and looking up.

"Take a guess," I said.

She carried on cleaning.

I never wanted to talk about it, whatever 'it' might happen to be on whatever day it might happen to be. As I'm sure I'd told Michelle numerous times, that was the only reason I frequented Cody's at all; to forget about it, not to make some half-hearted drunken attempt to make sense of it. Cody's was a gloomy place, and perhaps that's why I liked it so much. Sure, it had big windows to the front but the bar was set so far back and the ceiling so low that it had the air of some darkened cave in a storm. It felt safe, my haven from the roaring seas and the swirling fish I tried to catch outside. Now that everything was over I would, at some point, have to pick up my rod again and head back out. It was no use drinking until the seas calmed, either. I'd tried that before and they never did.

I opened my wallet and threw two twenties on the bar. Michelle knew the routine better than I did; don't take the bottle back until the money runs out. Then I saw a picture in my wallet and I pulled that out as well.

Vicki, when she was about thirteen. I think. Still all long blond hair, innocent face and pigtails. Messed up, no doubt, just not yet visibly so. And who'd have thought that less than seven years later she'd be a drop-out and a junkie; her life all but ruined. I stared at the picture for a long time, wondering if there was anything I could do.

Then I figured 'why the hell should I?'

The world is a shit place, it throws shit at you and you either run away from it or it sticks to your face. She'd be fine. I knew she would because I spent a whole five minutes convincing myself of it.

Michelle walked behind me and stole the picture from my hand. "Cute kid," she said. "Yours?"

"Was," I said. Meaning she was mine and she was cute.

"What happened?"

"I did," I said, stealing the picture back and sliding it back into the wallet.

The first Jack went down in one and I poured another. I kept the bottle in my hand, scrutinising the label like it was some amazing drink, the likes of which I had never experienced before. I didn't see the words, the white on black however, I saw a face. It was Monica's, her mouth open wide and the drops of blood falling one after another and soaking into pure white sheets in a room left silent by shots; the father lying on the floor with too much of his face missing to live.

I had been starting to feel good. I had almost found a cause. I didn't have to believe it, not all of it, I just had to believe *in* it. And I had. Somehow, deep down, I had figured it might even deliver some form of reconciliation for all my failures of the past. To finally do something worthwhile by stopping the bad guys from getting some holy tables that were apparently very dangerous or something.

Save the world. Stop the flow. Cauterise the wound.

But Sarah Fiddes had lied to me, and for that I felt like shit inside. Or maybe, just maybe, I was just feeling like the stupid, gullible and ultimately worthless fool I was – the one who really should've known better. Or, at the very least, should have seen it coming. My next, and indeed most heavily favoured option, was that I should just stop thinking about it and start Jack on the road to erasing it for me again. But somehow I couldn't, it seemed to be pissing me of way too much to want to go away.

Especially after what I just done for her sister...

Sarah Fiddes spoke a lot of crap, that was a given. I mean, time travel for God's sake. Did she really expect me to buy that? Thing is... the thing that hurt most, I suppose... is that she almost had. Ridiculous as it might sound to you, me and any sane thinking person, it would have answered one or two of the bigger questions I had and explained many of the things she had said.

Like how she had known, minutes after the event, that I had been suspended for two weeks, and that it had been described as 'leave'. Not only had she known it, but she had even bought me an airline ticket, knowing that I would be able to travel to France with her that day. She had known that Wells and Rodriguez were dead, even though I had only just discovered that myself.

And she had known that they would intercept her package and replace it with a bomb. Even if I doubted that myself to begin with, Grier and his cronies had all but confirmed it for me. How could she have known that? Suspicion was bad enough but this wasn't suspicion; she had *known*. And whilst we're discussing the bomb... why the hell had she buried it for Klein to find? Because if I remember her words correctly, as we were digging the hole, I had said that it was a good place to choose if she did not want the package to ever be found and her words had been; *But I do want it to be found. Just not for about thirty-three years, that's all.*

Thirty-three years. If Klein was going to be digging this thing up, how would she know that he'd be doing it in thirty-three years? *Unless..?* No, Nick, I thought, grow up. That's just crazy Jack starting to talk.

This had all started with a stiff, as so many of my cases do. Except that this stiff was as naked as the day he was born and had Latin text rammed up his ass with Tina's name scrawled across the top. I pulled the Latin out of my pocket and looked at it again...

Rammed up his ass. Surrounded by living tissue. And Deacon's voice ringing through my head... *despite the fact that blood patterns show him as being killed in the alley, the two bullets which passed clean through him are nowhere to be found.*

What if the shots weren't fired in the alley? What if they were fired to stop him coming back, loaded with some clues as to where the tables could be found? The bullets that had passed straight through would not have been surrounded by living tissue. They would have stayed where they were.

Just how screwed up did I have to be to be even voicing this in my head?

I looked at the text again. Not at the Latin, because I still didn't fully understand what it meant, but at the note at the top; *Tina Fiddes - 113* and there was something about it that I did not like. Something I hadn't actually noticed before. I had only seen Sarah's handwriting once, and that had been when she had filled in the forms for the DHL package, but she had a real weird way of doing a capital 'F'. A big, heavy swirl.

And this was the same.

The 'F' on Fiddes, the one rammed up the guy's ass, was the same swirly 'F' that had been added to the DHL forms.

It had been written by Sarah...

But surely, again, that was just as impossible...

I stared at my glass; hard as I could and for a few brief moments I so wanted it to move. I mean, *without me touching it.* It was full of Jack Daniels' for Christ's sake and, as longings go, that just has to be my ultimate. So I stared and I longed and I wanted, my mind supposedly clear of all other thoughts. Of course, stare at it, long for it and want it as I did it never so much as moved a millimetre. It stayed exactly where it was on the bar, laughing at me. I guess I just didn't want it enough. Not anymore.

Until, of course, Cody burst through the far door, banging it heavily against the side wall. *Then* the glass moved quickly enough, but I think my hand had a lot to do with that little manoeuvre. He stopped dead in his tracks, looked at me, then slowly turned to his now-shrugging employee. "We don't open until ten, Michelle," he said. "You know that."

"And so does he," she replied, nodding in my direction. "Only today he says he doesn't give... what was it...? Ah, yes '*a monkey's*', whatever the hell that means."

Cody looked at me, shook his head and walked behind the bar. "What happened to your nose?"

"Somebody hit me," I replied. Then, with the forced smile of a never-to-be-explained in-joke, I added; "Mid-Sentence."

He nodded, but that was all. Then he leaned on the bar, inquisitive, and said, "Do you mind if I ask you something, Nick?"

"As long as it's not 'please vacate my bar'," I replied, "Sure, knock yourself out."

He smiled. "You know me, Nick. I never throw a good customer, a paying customer or indeed a desperately messed up one like yourself, out on to the street," he said. "No, this is something different altogether."

I drank some more Jack and filled the glass again; before Cody got wise and took the bottle back.

"What is it that I do for a living?" he asked.

I looked straight at him. "You're the best and most charitable bar owner in L.A.," I said, deliberately over-icing the cake.

"So I'm not Postmaster General, then?"

I narrowed my eyes. "Not that I'm aware of, no."

"Good," he said, reaching under the bar and retrieving a brown envelope. "You be sure and tell your girlfriend that for me, won't you." He smiled like he didn't really care and disappeared back out of the bar the way he had entered. I kept drinking, my hand automatically feeding my mouth like some character money box dropping in the coins. Kept drinking and kept staring. I really did not want to touch that envelope, let alone open it. Did I?

"By the way," Cody shouted back. "Said I'd to give you it because you're 'a real nice guy'. Her words. *Definitely* not mine."

I kept staring at the envelope, and that didn't move without me touching it either. All that was written on the face was '*Nick Lambert, c/o Cody's Bar*'. The words stayed in my sight even when I looked away.

In the end I picked it up. What harm could it do to pick it up? It was heavy. After turning it in my hands a few times, I somehow summoned the courage to go one step further; to tear it open and find out just how shafted I'd been.

Inside was a second envelope, along with a handwritten note: 'Told you I'd find you'.

I took another large drink, a real determined one, and tore open the second envelope, the heavy one. This one had quite a few sheets of paper inside and two items wrapped in thin cloth which I folded open with a sense of anticipation, though from the feel alone I guess I already knew what they were.

And then I saw them again, hauntingly black and glistening even in the low light that Cody's had to offer. The Tables of Testimony, a myriad tiny symbols etched and raised across all four sides and edges that would fit with perfection in numerous different combinations. I held one in each hand, turned them as slowly as I had the envelope, and smiled. Wherever Sarah was now, she had chosen to leave these with me. Which, if nothing else, demonstrated an inordinate amount of trust.

Michelle, having finished cleaning the bar, walked behind me again and peered over my shoulder at the tables. "That's a fancy set of beer mats you have there Nick, but we do have our own you know?" She smiled at her own joke before joining Cody in the back. The world, it seems, is just chock full of Philistines.

I rewrapped the tables, carefully placed them down on the bar and turned my attention to the sheets of paper. All appeared at one time to have been rolled tightly, but were now straightened flat. I spread them across the bar. Whatever this package was, it sure as hell wasn't shaping up to be the 'Dear John' I'd been so readily expecting.

With one notable exception, all the sheets were press cuttings. the first of which took be by surprise...

FORMER TRIBUNE PHOTOGRAPHER
FOUND DEAD IN FRANCE

Kelly Brown, a one-time photographer here at the Los Angeles Tribune has been found dead of a drugs overdose in a guest house in Couiza, France. Kelly, who had been covering various freelance stories in the country, including the government funded archaeological dig close to the Spanish border for which she had been granted exclusive rights, was found lying dead in her room by the guest house owner who arrived to clean her room late yesterday morning. French police say that they are not treating Kelly's death as suspicious as it appears to have been the result of an accidental overdose which, according to sources, may have been the result of the long hours she was consistently working. The owner of the Vie D'Éte Pension, Mme Glorie Mercelle, described Kelly as 'a very likeable young lady who was very considerate during her extended stay' and that 'all the guests had been extremely shaken by the tragedy'.

Kelly worked for the Tribune between 2005-2008 where she covered a great many stories, including her 'StillsAmerica' award-winning photojournalistic piece on the effects of gang rivalry in the city. Tribune Editor Jean Sampson said, "Kelly was a fantastic member of the team and a great person. She was very ambitious and I know that gaining exclusive rights for the U.S. Government work in France had meant a great deal to her. Our condolences go to her family who, like us, will greatly miss her presence."

Kelly was 28, unmarried and left no children.

There was a picture above the story, presumably a stock shot from the *Tribune* archives. Kelly, the long blond-haired girl I had met in the bar at Arques, posing with a long-lensed SLR camera. Written to the side of the picture, again in Sarah's distinctive handwriting, were the words, *Kelly never took drugs, Nick. Yet now she was dead from an overdose.* Presumably because they had discovered that she had been breaching the agreement and leaking pictures before anything had been found. Leaking them to Sarah. Sarah had told me in Arques that her friend had been caught out; Kelly just doesn't know it yet, that's all. Like Sarah, no doubt, I didn't think for one second that young Kelly Brown's lethal overdose had been accidental.

The next two cuttings were more intriguing, however. Also a little closer to home, personally speaking. They appeared to have come from a magazine, rather than a newspaper.

SECRETS OF SCIENCE FOUND
HIDDEN IN FRANCE
and
TABLES TURNED ON CARDOU SCIENTISTS

The first article detailed how a United States Archaeological team, digging at the base of Mont Cardou in the South of France, were reported to have uncovered a 'secret chamber' containing tablets of stone of 'a detailed scientific nature'.

These tables, it was claimed, appeared to have been compiled by an artisan/scientist working in the early 1600's and it was hoped that, if the theories put forward were correct, they could improve man's understanding of the world around us and aid future scientific development. A U.S. spokesman was quoted as saying that 'this individual was undoubtedly far ahead of his time and had offered modern science some exciting new avenues down which to pursue future research. We are all very excited about the find and hope it will lead to discoveries which will benefit mankind as a whole'.

The piece went on to explain that these exciting new finds were 'nearly lost to the world forever' when they were stolen by an unscrupulous member of the team and secreted out of the country via a reputable courier firm. Fortunately, the theft was uncovered swiftly and this allowed the package to be intercepted and the tables retrieved in the United States. Detailed scientific analysis of the tables was now, apparently, underway.

What a crock of shit. Tables found at Mont Cardou. Stolen by a member of the team. My guess was that had they not had to intercept them in the first place from 'a reputable courier firm' then none of this would have come out at all. It was a cover up and it wasn't funny.

Unlike the next piece; tables turned. That one I found very funny indeed.

This second piece detailed how the amazing 'Cardou Tables' had transpired, disappointingly, to be nothing more than very well-crafted fakes. Officials admitted that, whilst they had been sceptical about the find from the outset, they had nevertheless invested a great deal of time and effort deciphering their contents. They admitted to feeling an extreme sense of disappointment, but did not feel that the Tables had been faked recently. It would appear that dating techniques had been accurate but that the content was 'not what was to be expected'.

Too right it wasn't. The way Sarah explained it to me, and I'm no expert, there were approximately 2500 text routes that could be taken through the text she had carefully encoded, the vast majority of which threw up gibberish. Aramaic gibberish. Thirty-three of them, however, didn't. They threw up sequences of letters containing embedded texts, themselves quite tricky to find. The letters from the embedded texts then needed to be highlighted in the disks as a whole and a series of patterns were formed. Once these patterns were uncovered, they could be laid over the three remaining sides of the disks in turn, uncovering further texts. I'm sure it's slightly more complex than that, but you get the general idea.

The answer? Well, again, as I understand it, when the full intricacies of the code are uncovered and pieced back together, the phrase which appeared was;

FUCK YOU KLEIN.

Or something similar. Typically Sarah.

There were three other stories as well, two deaths and a suicide, but I won't bother to detail them for you here, as well as another handwritten note. And on it, in Sarah's very discernible script, were the words; 'Meet me. Coastal Path. Montalvo. 8pm. S.'

And yes, it all intrigued me. More than you could know. Because less than an hour ago I had bartered with Grier for my life and offered him a way to uncover his 'answers' over a period of time. Yet, according to the second of the two magazine articles, the code had already been deciphered.

Worse still, uncovered as a fake.

Until I read the one piece of text, visible on each of the cuttings, that I had never even thought to look at. Until now. To give you an idea of what I mean, I can tell you that Kelly Brown was already dead from her 'accidental overdose'. She had been found by the guest house owner, Mme Mercelle, this very morning and news had indeed reached the *Los Angeles Tribune*.

But not yet. This paper was dated Wednesday June 16th 2011.

The day after tomorrow...

FIFTY-FOUR
Monday, June 13, 2011.
Montalvo, North of Los Angeles, California.

Montalvo, if you've never been, is one beautiful piece of country. It lies shoulder-on to the coast a little way north of Los Angeles. This is a place where the beaches give way to cliffs and the organised world seems to have been left behind for a while. I visited an area like this, only a few further miles up the coast, when I first met my wife, Katherine. And that's the kind of place it is, generally - calm and serene; a place where lovers come to walk uninterrupted along the cliff paths and watch the sunset over the cool glass of the Pacific. And whilst Sarah and I were not lovers, and never would be, I'm sure that she recognised its other quality; seclusion. Privacy.

I'd been back to my apartment to shower and change, as you'd probably expect, but there was no point cleaning the place up. That could wait until another day. So instead I'd just stepped over my stuff as best I could and picked some clean clothes from the wide selection I found strewn across my floor.

Sarah was already waiting when I pulled into the parking area; her slender frame visible a little way along the path. Her rucksack was by her feet and was she leaning wistfully on the white steel barrier, her back turned. She was motionless, staring

483

out across the sea, the sky now tinged with hopes of a better tomorrow.

She didn't turn around, not even when I walked up beside her, she just turned her head very slightly to the side and said; "Still in the land of the living then, Nick?" Then she turned back and stared again.

Her almost deliberate lack of greeting reminded me of someone else; her sister.

I stared across the ocean with her. "Temporary visa."

She looked at me fully, probably alerted by the fact that I was now sounding like the result of some unimaginable sexual encounter between Jimmy Durante and Daisy Duck.

"He got you back then?"

I nodded; he got me back. "Where the hell have you been?"

"See a boy about a dog," she said cryptically. "Joopy; cute little thing I got from the pound." She smiled. "Never mind; it's a long story."

She turned again, closed her eyes, opened her mouth and inhaled deep, like an ex-convict savouring fresh air after a lifetime in captivity. Then she gave one long drawn exhale, as though casting out demons. "It's beautiful out here, isn't it."

"Yes it is," I said, then I smiled. Smiled at just how clever I felt I had been. "Listen, I was thinking. Wouldn't it be great if Tina could have a view like this from her window. I mean, instead of Oakdene we could maybe move her up to, say, Thousand Oaks?"

Sarah turned and placed a hand on my shoulder. "I know what you did, Nick. Thankyou." Then she kissed me gently on the cheek.

In an instant her comment had stolen my thunder, and not even the kiss could bring it back. "I think you need to start telling me just how you seem to know things before I do, don't you?"

She took a deep breath and nodded. "Yeah, I guess I do. Come on, let's walk."

We headed away from the parking lot, walking in slow silence whilst she composed herself for the task ahead and following the path as it undulated near and far to the cliff edge.

"You got the cuttings then?" she said eventually.

"That's just one of many things I think you need to explain."

"I thought it would make more sense that way," she said. "You know? Make it easier to believe."

"Was that the reason? To convince me?"

"Let's face it, it's not an easy scenario to get to grips with, is it?"

That was an understatement. "So do you want to tell me why you buried the package?"

"To stop Klein," she said. "or another guy, Sherman. I'm not sure which."

"I've been told you never worked for Klein," I said. "That you lied."

"No I didn't, Nick," she said. "Honestly."

I took a deep breath. "Go on then, Sarah. Explain it to me. If you can."

"Because the system only works with the same three co-ordinates when you adjust the fourth, ie. time, Klein has to operate it in exactly the same place as his... travellers... would arrive. So, as well as the facility he built in Los Angeles, where Yang's is now, he based another one in France, on land the

485

government already owned."

"Cardou?"

"Yeah. It's a small building, but it did the trick. And this way, those travellers he sent back really early wouldn't be stuck in the middle of nowhere; in a place that wouldn't even become the United States until long after they were dead. Plus, Cardou was close to Narbonne, which was a port even in Roman times, which ensured that they could travel around easily when they came back. Then he got them to steal things which they, in turn, had to bury in the South of France for him to dig up later."

"In Cardou?" I asked.

She smiled. "Oh no, as you well know, Klein has already led the dig in Cardou. Which meant he couldn't dig there because it had already been dug up once and nothing had been found. First rule, Nick; *you can't change history.* So he had to choose completely fresh sites. They were all close to Cardou but essentially outside of the skull perimeter. And... whilst he'd known that you and I had uncovered something, Grier had never told him exactly where we'd found it. Because they thought they'd intercepted the tables, there was no point. By the time they turned out to be fakes, he figured that we had found fakes, so he had no qualms in choosing the altar at Serres as a site. He'd no idea we'd ever been there."

"So what happened?"

"He had me do some research and I found that the tables had a Templar link. So he sent a guy called D'Almas back to 1307 and kind of 'infiltrate' them, find out what he could. Then, before he went off and lived in freedom, he left a detailed account of what he knew in one of the Serres graves. Yes, the Templars had possession of the tables, once, but they had lost them sometime around 1132. Once Klein had that information he sent Davies back prior to D'Almas, and Davies stole the tables. He became the *reason* they lost them. Then he hid them in the altar and went off to live his life a free man."

"And the tables stayed in the altar?"

"For a while, it seemed. There were rumours for centuries of something important buried in that general area, but nobody found anything. Somebody knew something, though, because they commissioned Teniers for the painting. They just didn't actually steal the tables themselves, that was all. Or, if they did, they then realised that they were too complicated for them to ever understand and placed them back, leaving a code for wiser men to follow in the years to come." She cast me a glance, looking over the top of her eyes. "And then Mason came on the scene."

"Who the hell's Mason?" I asked.

She laughed. "He's the guy on the slab, Nick. He's your naked dead guy."

"The guy with the tattoo on his ankle?"

"Prison mark. Things have changed. Now, everyone who goes to prison gets one; a kind of branding. Our unemployment level is astoundingly high and so crime requires punishment to be that bit more permanent now. Even a convict that has been released has to carry a stigma. A sign."

It was more than just a neat design. It meant something to someone. Which would have been great. It would have justified my theory, had it not all sounded like more bullshit.

And the way she had said 'now' proved it. I was talking to a woman who used the word now about events that had, in her twisted head, yet to happen. Things that wouldn't happen for....? How long?

"When is this exactly?" I asked.

"A long time away," she said. She said it quietly, subdued almost, but even so she made it sound so natural; as though she was talking about a long time ago. But she wasn't. Christ, Sarah was in a bigger world of her own than her sister. "And before you ask, Nick, nothing much has changed. There are no flying cars, no butler-robots and the world is still very much run by bastards."

"So how exactly did Mason arrive on my slab?" *Humour her, Nick. Find the flaws.*

"I sent him," she said. "I found out from the files, *your files*, that he had been here before he had even been sent and your file told me that he'd shown up dead. That's why I told you not to worry about Mason; because - technically - he wasn't even dead yet."

"You remember saying that?"

"I was tired, Nick, not dead." She sighed. "I guess this is a little weird for you?"

I laughed. "Oh, I've had worse." Like *yeah, sure I have.*

"Anyway, Klein had found a drawing of *Mason's* tattoo. And the words '*Fuck you, Klein.*'"

I smiled broadly, my head shaking in admiration of the high quality of Sarah's continued incomprehensible ingenuity. I'd heard that it was a trait of paranoid delusionals that their worlds were nothing if not very carefully constructed and very hard to disprove.

"So, on the face of it, Mason got to the tables first. Klein has no idea that he'd been way too dead to make the journey. So now he needs somebody to put it right. Someone he can really trust, and he's not sure he can trust *anyone* any more. Not when he's come *this* close."

She gestured a tiny amount with her fingers. "He thinks that after years of searching he's only one tiny step away. So, he needs someone to come back *before* Mason, be the reason the drawing was there and then to hide the tables somewhere else for him. A place that only he will know about because he's getting really paranoid now."

"And so you volunteered? Why the hell would you do that?"

"I had my reasons. He wanted me to come back much earlier; maybe twenty years before Mason, but I convinced him that as long as it was well before the date Mason actually arrived, we'd be safe. And I promised him I'd bury the tables precisely where he needed me to. Which, as you've seen, I did. It's just that when he opens the box...."

"Boom," I said, looking back toward the orange sunset. The orange of the package. The orange of an exploding bomb.

"That's the idea," she said, her voice tinged with something that bore a passing resemblance to regret. "I had to, Nick, I really did. To be honest I think he was having his own regrets anyway, that he was almost asking me to make the decision for him the day before he sent me back. Like I say, our history couldn't be changed. If you'll pardon the pun, it was already cast in stone. But our future could. I had the chance to change the things that happened immediately after I'd gone."

I turned away. I really couldn't listen to this any more. It was like Jamie, the diamond shitting king of Oakdene, and yet so much worse. At least with Jamie it had all been a game, a way to get himself out of the loop for a while, but Sarah actually believed her own words.

"Christ Almighty, Sarah. Do you have any idea just how ridiculous this sounds?"

"Yes I do." she said. Her voice was subdued. "But it is true, Nick." She turned, placed a hand on my shoulder and looked at me, pleading. "I think you know it is."

I pulled away and turned, shaking my head. "All I know is that this is a very well-constructed crock of shit. That's what I know. And you? Christ, you're a... a... mental case. You need some serious help."

"I need *your* help, Nick. What about the cuttings?" She was so calm. "You've seen the dates." And I had. I just didn't believe them, that was all. "The Tribune cutting is the day after tomorrow," she continued, "*they don't even know Kelly's dead yet.*"

"Then you made them up," I said. "Anyone with a computer can..."

"So how did I know about your naked dead guy with the Latin up his butt, long before you told me?"

I thought for a moment. "I don't know. Some big mouth inside the department probably."

"And if I never I checked your record, *after this detail had been entered*, how did I know to get you a ticket to France? How did I know that Deacon had given you two weeks leave?"

"I don't know. Probably the same way."

"And how did I *know* they'd intercept the DHL parcel? And what was in it? And that you'd be free to meet me by eight o'clock tonight."

"Three very lucky guesses," I said sarcastically. "Like knowing

I'd be at Cody's. Shit, I'll bet that was a tough call."

"No," Sarah said with a smile, "that one came from knowing you now." She could see I wasn't budging. "And come on, lucky guesses? Listen to yourself, Nick," she was almost spinning with despair, her arms flailing. "You don't want to believe me and yet you don't even believe your own alternatives."

I turned again, leaned side-on against the railings and stared directly at Sarah. She stopped dead, hoping that maybe, just maybe, I was starting to believe her. I hated to disappoint but I wasn't. *I couldn't.* Not unless I too wanted to end up sipping food through a straw at Oakdene, and how Creed would have loved that.

"You know what, Sarah? There's one thing that tells me that none of this is true;" I said, "that it's nothing more than a figment of your dangerously-skewed imagination."

"And what's that?" she asked.

"Tina," I said quietly. "If any of this was true... even one word... then how the *hell* could she be your sister?"

FIFTY-FIVE

MONDAY, JUNE 13, 2011.
OAKDENE, LENWOOD, CALIFORNIA.

Save for those low desperate moans, the kind that seemed to
permeate at all hours, the corridors at Oakdene were quiet that
night. Maggie had done the day shift, stayed for the pill-run
at six and clocked off around six-forty-five. Then she'd gone
home to the three boys, cooked some TV Dinners and they'd all
watched Regis on 'Millionaire'. Carey came in just before six,
helped Maggie sort the pills, watched the front desk whilst she
did the rounds, and settled in to read PC Format in front of the
screens until his own first run.

Creed was in his office, finalising some budget papers
apparently. I mean, sure, there was the odd scream coming
from one or two of the rooms, but nothing out of the ordinary.
According to Maggie, you get so that you don't even notice
them some nights. In every way possible it was just an average
night at the crazy house.

Until around seven-thirty, half an hour before Carey's first run
was actually due. Creed came out of his office, sidled up to the
desk and made some small talk about the latest PC laptops and
how you had to be careful because the DVD Drives always
seemed to be the first to go if you bought a cheap one.

Then Creed had told Carey that he fancied 'stretching his legs' before he headed home so he would do the round for him. Carey could have another two hours with the magazine and make the ten his first instead. *And that was real weird,* Carey had said. *Because Creed never offers to do nothin'.* Like *ever.* Tonight he had. Who knew, maybe he had just wanted to stretch his legs?

And I'm sure that Creed had cast his eye through every window, knowing that Carey might just be watching on the monitors and he wanted it to look good; genuine. But Creed also knew which cameras worked and which didn't and, this being Oakdene, quite a few fell into category number two. Including the one he so desperately needed not to be working; camera eight on the first floor.

My guess is that he had cursed Sarah Fiddes all the way around those long corridors, with nothing but the squeaky sound of his own pitiful footsteps and the memories of humiliation to keep him company. He would have remembered Sarah's face; all venom and spite and it will have burned into that sick ego that he had. Nobody spoke to Creed like that. He ran this place for Christ's sake. Every stone on the walls and every cracked tile on the floor was his. Every breath and shit taken, every emotion that was felt; they were all his. I mean, in here, Creed could be God. Shit, he was God, and both the people for whom this was home, and those who came from the outside, would just have to start realising that.

Now Jennifer Sanchez, the young Costa Rican girl, she'd lost sight of who was God.

Like Sarah, she too had rejected Creed's advances. Worse still she'd kicked and screamed and shouted and called him every name imaginable. And she'd thrown in one or two you probably couldn't. So she had needed to be reminded of the most important facet of institutional life; hierarchy – with Creed seated right at the very top. And he'd shown her too, good and proper. She had no qualms about who was boss around here any more, no sir. And even that stupid detective, Lambert, had been too slow to catch the mighty Creed off guard. Sure, he'd noticed the blood on the trophy, but Lambert was no poker player and his reaction had been written across his face long enough for Creed to quickly wipe it clean again. He'd get nothing. And there'd been others that had needed to learn. Lots of them.

Creed was God, and his mission was to spread truth and understanding amongst his chosen people.

And then, as he reached one-one-three, Creed will have remembered what Sarah had said to Maggie; that she'd no longer be able to visit. And, better still, what she'd said to Creed himself. That Tina would be out within a week. I mean, how stupid could she have been? You just don't tell somebody things like that. It's like… well, it's like laying out the red carpet, isn't it? It's like saying 'do what you like, because I won't be back checking and your time's running out'.

And that's what Creed would do. That's what any God would do. He would do exactly what he damn well liked.

Tina was on the bed, but not in it. She was reading poetry with the help of a torchlight, one of those that clips to the top of a book. Sarah had bought her that. Lovely kind Sarah, who came to visit and brushed her hair. Then, if the weather was nice, they'd take a nice walk outside and get some fresh air. And she'd even bring her a Snickers bar with lots of peanuts in it. And she'd laugh and tell her sister that she'd had the guys at Mars put some extra in, just for her.

And she'd talk to her. Properly, in one long flow. Not like the others who broke their words up into fragments. She couldn't speak, she knew that, but she could hear, for God's sake. She could hear very well as it happened. And Sarah knew that. Sarah understood.

But Sarah wasn't coming back. Sarah had to go away, that's what she had said. And Tina had wanted to be angry but she couldn't, not with Sarah, because she had seen in her eyes that she had been sad too. Genuinely sad. She wasn't leaving because she wanted to, rather that for some unknown reason she had to.

So how could she be angry? It wasn't her fault. She'd spent the first twenty-three years of her life without Sarah anyhow, and she'd been fine. Those extra two years they shared had been a bonus, that was all. A gift for being a good girl.

And it all sounded very good, very grown up, but it didn't stop the tears. She'd only been gone a few hours and now, maybe because she knew she wasn't coming back, Tina was missing her already.

And maybe the tears in her eyes caught the light as Creed looked in through the glass. Maybe they did it for him, gave him the fuel he needed. I mean, everyone knows that sadness can be sexy, don't they? Creed did. He knew why Britney Spears kept pulling that lonely child face at him on her videos. It showed innocence combined with a desire to be looked after; taken care of. And that was why he was here now and why Carey was downstairs reading up on the latest App-Creation software. Because Creed was going to do what anyone would do for one of their own. One who was hurting.

He was going to take care of her.

So he opened the door and went inside, no camera to see him.

And then he closed the door behind him, locking it just like he had for Sarah. There would be no rejection this time. In fact, this could be his fantasy. I mean, the two of them looked so god-damned alike that he could almost be *doing* Sarah, couldn't he? Only this time she wouldn't be calling him a sick bastard, she'd just lie there and take it. She might struggle, sure, but only because she wanted him to push harder, deeper and prove to her just how powerful a God he really was. He was ready now; fired up. He would not disappoint.

I guess that as Creed crossed the room Tina, her face illuminated along one side from her tiny reading light, would look even more frightened, even more sexy. Her face would be pleading to him, begging almost. But no words would come, so only Creed could decide exactly what it was she was begging for. And he would give her it.

It wouldn't last long, but it would last long enough. And, of course, there would be no screams. None whatsoever, because the beautiful Tina was mute. She couldn't scream even if she wanted to. Not that it would have stopped Creed even if she had. He was here for one thing and one thing only. He was here for what Tina's bitch sister had refused him and he wouldn't be leaving until he got it.

Besides, it's like Maggie said, even when there are screams you get so you don't even notice them some nights.

FIFTY-SIX

MONDAY, JUNE 13, 2011.

MONTALVO, NORTH OF LOS ANGELES, CALIFORNIA.

"Jesus wept."

I didn't know what else to say. If indeed I'd heard her correctly, and I was pretty sure that I had.

Sarah turned away and leaned against the railings. I didn't need to be a detective to know that she was crying.

I never saw it before. Then again, why would I? How could I? I mean, Sarah was at five years older than Tina, at least. Wasn't she? She was her *older* sister. How could she possibly be what I was now being told she was. It just plain wasn't possible.

"Your telling me that she's... she's you mother?"

Sarah's voice was laced with tears. And she was angry. Really, really angry. "I really appreciate what you did for her, Nick, really I do. Thousand Oaks was a nice touch, and she'll be very happy there, I know she will. For a while." She sobbed and looked at me long enough to say just one word. "Thankyou."

She was referring now to my 'deal' with Grier. A deal that was so simple and yet, I had figured, so very brilliant. Convince Grier that there was no need for me to die, something I could only hope he would stick to. More importantly, I needed to explain to him that it had never been Sarah who had broken the code; that she was not the important link in his chain.

It was Tina.

She was the one with the skills, the one who could see things that we could never hope to see. So why not, if he wanted to break the code, get Tina to do it? It might take her some time, but she'd manage it eventually. Probably a lot quicker than his computers because, as Sarah had told me, computers didn't think; they did what they were programmed to do and held no concept of abstract or insinuation.

As I'd told Grier, if I was going to give him what he needed, then he had to promise me faithfully that he'd take damn good care of it. Which meant taking Tina out of the living hell that was Oakdene and moving her somewhere better. Somewhere like Thousand Oaks, just along the coast. A place where the standards of hygiene and care were higher and somewhere they keep the Creed's of this world on a much tighter leash.

Oh shit, I thought. And I didn't actually mean to say the next word out loud, but I did. "Creed."

Sarah inhaled deeply. It didn't flow, rather it stuttered forth in short blunt bursts, like a bruised child. She turned away from me and all I could hear for the next minute were the sobs.

"He's probably up there now," she said, every syllable laboured. "*Raping* her." She turned to me, eyes red and cheeks now streaming with tears. "And I can't stop it, Nick," she turned and started hitting me on the chest without warning, angry. She screamed. "*I can't fucking stop it.*"

I let her hit all she wanted until eventually she ran out of strength and slowed to a stop. Then I threw my arms around her and held her close, the sobs now falling deep into my shoulder.

"We can go there now," I said. "I'll find something to take him in on. Anything. Shit, I'll make something up. I only need to keep him away for a week. Tina will be gone by then and then he can't get to her, can he?"

Sarah pulled back, aghast. "Christ, you *still* don't get it do you, Nick? Even now. I *can't* change it. Creed is my *father*, can't you see that? No matter what. If he doesn't..." calmer now, she struggled for the word, "if *it* doesn't happen then I don't exist. But I *do* exist, don't I? I'm *here*. So no matter how much I want to stop it happening, I can't. Don't you see...? There was no bomb went off in Berlin in 1939."

Meaning you can't make something happen that never happened. And I saw. It meant that whatever Sarah tried to do to stop this happening she would fail. History could not be changed. Tina was Sarah's mother and Creed was her father. She couldn't change her parents any more than I could change mine. Which is why she hated Creed so much. Why she had always hated him. She hated him because he had raped her mother; an autistic girl who was completely unable to defend herself. And yet she had faced him - repeatedly - over a two year period, knowing all along that this was going to happen. I cannot even begin to comprehend what that must have done to her.

"Jesus, I hate that man" she had said. I can bet you she had really wanted to kill him there and then; just to have done with it.

And something else she said. Something that hadn't registered with half as much force at the time as it did right now. I said it out loud. "*Sarah being at Oakdene is the only reason I can be here for her.*"

"You see?" she said. It was as though she felt that she had to defend her actions, but she didn't. Not to me. "I had to keep her there. I wanted to move her, but I couldn't. Her being there was the way it was. It was the way it happened."

"And is that why you volunteered to come back?" I asked.

"I just wanted to meet her, that's all." Still defensive. "I am really grateful about Thousand Oaks, Nick, honestly I am, but it's not for long. She died giving birth to me. I never met her. And I wanted to come back, to give her something for what she had given to me. She gave me life and I wanted to give her some back, that was all. That was why I convinced Klein to send me back two years ago rather than twenty. It gave me time to collect the things I needed, create the fakes, build a case so that you'd help when you showed up and it also gave me two years of time with my..." she turned away again, "...with my mother.'

She said the word like it was the most important in the world.

To Sarah, it probably was.

"So you always figured to sting Klein?"

"I figured I could do something for the world at the same time as I did something for me, that was all."

I nodded.

Sarah looked out over the ocean again. For a long time the only sound was the occasional low crash of the waves against the rocks below and two sets of deep, laboured breaths.

And I believed.

I know just how crazy that sounds, believe me, but I did.

I actually believed.

I'd seen Tina move the Snickers without laying a finger on it, I knew I had. And if she could change the sequence, then maybe so could others. And yes, maybe that applied to all four dimensions. It all fitted.

I hate to say it, but it all fitted. Perfectly.

Except for one thing. In many ways, the most obvious thing. Sarah had told me that Tina might be being raped even now and I still couldn't get to grips with that. Nor, I suspect, could Sarah. But if that was genuinely the case; or even if she was to be raped a month from now, it still caused one hell of a major problem. Because somehow, somewhere, Sarah Fiddes was going to be born. Within a year. And yet Sarah Fiddes was standing right here; crying gently at the side of me.

"So if you're here now, what happens to you when you're born?"

Sarah turned, wiped the tears and did what she could to smile at me.

"Oh, I've thought of everything, Nick" she said. "I really have."

For the longest time, she stared right at me. Nothing more, just one long warm smile of affection, her eyes still red. Then she laughed quietly at some private joke, and spoke again. "Do you remember the envelope I gave you when we left my house?"

"Yes," I said. "I've still got it."

"Well, I think maybe it's time you took a look inside."

At least, I *think* I still had it. We'd left Sarah's, gone to Oakdene, then I'd dropped Sarah off at the airport, then rollocked by Deacon, then...."It's still in the glove box," I said. "In the car."

Sarah smiled broadly. A proper smile. The first I'd seen since I'd arrived. "Then I suggest you go and get it," she said, twirling a silver pendant through her fingers whilst pretending to chastise.

I walked all the way back to the car, opened the glove box and pulled out the envelope. I stood, slammed the door and looked back across the roof... along the path.

★ ★ ★ ★ ★

Jonathan Lionel Creed closed the door on his way out.

And locked it again.

He had no need to smile on the outside, though it was now an inescapable feature behind his eyes. Inside his mind, however, was a beam of light that could illuminate a small city for a year, or his miserable life for ten. He calmly checked his belt and fly, straightened his back and shoulders, and started back along the intermittent lighting of the corridor; his shuffled gait squeaking away into the distance of painful memory.

Inside 113, beyond the battered brown door, Tina Fiddes lay foetal on her bed, reddened cheeks bulging like a ripened spring russet and glistening with the dew of tears. She made no sound, no sobs, but her breathing was deep. She was in shock, her body still deciding how it might ultimately react.

Creed's confident closure of the door had pushed a thin stream of air along the wall, freshly painted. This gentle wisp, perhaps a degree or two colder than the stale air which surrounded Tina herself, flowed gently and silently to the end of the room and turned along the far wall. It passed gently over her exposed legs, rose the length of her body like an invisible sheet being drawn against the night and made loose strands of hair dance above her reddened eyes.

Then it turned again, rising with added heat from her body, until it met the only shelf the room possessed.

Tina saw it from the corner of her eye. White. Quivering.

The paper dove was shifting laterally. First sideways, then

forward. Its head lifted as it skittered toward the edge of the shelf, as though it were taking a breath. There it remained, balanced precariously, until the breeze passed. Then the head fell forward and the balance shifted once again...

Tina watched it slide gracefully from the shelf and drift, spiralling to earth like a helicopter seed, and suddenly she felt a chill running along her body once more. Not a breeze, but a harsh wind cutting into her skin. For a time she felt nothing else. No pain, no fear and no consequence, yet still she knew that something, somewhere, was very wrong indeed.

It was the coldest wind she had ever felt.

She was inside, she realised. Inside the dove. Falling. Gently, in the slow-time of dreams and memories. The shelf was now gone; cold rocks having taken its place and glistening in the remaining light. They rushed past her like dark fire. Above was only red; the rich red of a sunset, clouds glowing like coals.

Somehow, though her body screamed at her to do something – anything – to stop herself from falling, she resisted the desire to spread her arms, those delicate paper wings she had crafted so carefully almost two full years ago – the day Sarah had arrived back into her life - and try to catch the breeze. She resisted the urge to fly, or to soar or to save herself. Something inside, something she could not hear or see but only sense, was telling her in soft tones that it would do her no good at all.

A part of who she was, was leaving. Her eyes filled. First a sheen, then a layer and finally small saltwater pools, the banks of her lower lids not built to withstand the rising tide. She opened her mouth...

Twice she tried and twice she failed. Then, in the darkest instant of her life, despite her recent ordeal, Tina saw who she was, why she was falling and what was coming to pass in another part of the world. The dove was leaving. The dove had been with her for two years, it might have remained on the bleak shelf all this time but it had watched over her every move within this place. The dove had cared.

The dove was leaving.

She screamed.

The mute Tina Fiddes – whose atrophic vocal chords had never managed to generate anything more than a guttural sound in her life – reached into the depths of her fragile mouth, lips still bleeding from the bite of her own teeth, and screamed long enough, and loud enough, for the whole world and its future to hear.

Creed stopped dead and turned at the sound. At the end of the corridor, four or five feet from the staircase and its flaking iron balcony, he looked back with narrowed eyes. Eyes which widened in an instant.

One by one, almost in a timed sequence, the lights above exploded. Closer and closer to Creed they came as if they were heading straight for him. Or coming straight after him.

He froze.

As each light went, it did so with a sound and a force so violent that the inverted iron trough above twisted on its heavy iron chains like a manacled man writhing to escape a burning room. Sparks and glass rained as though heaven itself was casting out those who had sinned beyond its gates.

Still closer, tearing along the corridor like an attack dog chained, starved for days then loosed on an intruder. Almost too fast to see; certainly too fast to escape. As the final light, the one directly above Creed's balding head exploded, the sound of glass and discharged sparks filled his ears and he felt warmth in his face as fragments fell like leaden rain around him. It seemed to him as though this had been the most violent explosion of all. For an instant he almost allowed himself to believe that it was deliberate.

One link. In any chain, that's all it takes for integrity to be gone.

In the long strip of Creed's dark world, amid the mayhem and the screams that filled the air like fearsome wind, one blackened iron link, the rust having eaten away at it slowly and silently for as many years as it had been in position, was all that gave.

The similarly dark metal trough which surrounded and held the fluorescent tubes, cast from the heaviest iron in the days before aluminium and lighter metals had become a part of daily life, saw its chance and broke free. It swung to earth with a frightening sense of illogical precision. Before he had time to raise a scream it struck Creed full in the face; breaking his nose and cracking his forehead cleanly. His spectacles shattered; a cold shower of glass blasting backward. Eyes that had so recently feasted on pain seen on a young woman's face suddenly took all that pain back. With interest.

He staggered backward, the cold iron railings pressing hard against his spine like a rifle.

Solid as they were, they held.

He bounced forward, collapsing to his knees as the trough found a level and remained, gently swinging to and fro from the one remaining chain. After a few seconds, the longest and most searingly painful in his life, Creed took back his breath. He remained motionless for a few more moments, gingerly touching his face and trying to comprehend his new-found darkness. Then he climbed to his feet. In the darkened corridor with only the cold blue of night beyond the window above the staircase, too high to have been cleaned but once during his tenure, he blindly stretched out a bloodied right hand. It was as though he felt some saviour might suddenly grasp it and pull him free from the inferno which filled his face, his eyes and the frenzy of fear that had become his mind.

The still air fizzed with trapped electricity; an undying force that was now searching frantically for the only drug it craved; a passage to earth. Tiny sparks flickered left and right like searching eyes. It would not settle, it *could not settle*, until its need was assuaged. Nor would it be selective. It would buy from any supplier.

Creed took an instinctive step forward, his arm grasping air like a drowning man, and the electricity leapt – literally – at the red carpet it saw laid out before it. Though his hand never came into contact with the iron or the filaments, a fierce arc of orange bridged the few remaining inches. It was so bright that even he, with eyes tight closed, saw it behind his bleeding lids and screamed as it added more coals to the fire already burning in his face.

He was thrown backwards by the bolt, his legs sliding along the floor until he felt the cold iron balcony in his back once more. Suddenly even the world itself seemed to desert him, removing itself from his feet in disgust and casting him into the deep void of space. He could not see, but he could feel that somehow the perspective of the world around him had changed. Up was no longer up, down was no longer down.

Down was where Creed was travelling. At a vast rate of knots.

He felt the sudden rush of air as it cooled the sweat of a good lay, still coating his oily skin.

The last sound his God allowed Creed to hear before the final bolt of electricity – his own spark of life – drained into the earth, was that of three vertebrae in his neck snapping like matches on the concrete floor below.

Tina stopped screaming. The wind had dropped and she was alone again, curled foetal in a room that had never before seemed so empty.

Contemplating a life that would never again seem so full.

Outside the door there was nothing left for her; nothing but gentle sounds. The hum of power craving release and the slow painful creaks of the lighting units as they swayed above a long dark corridor.

A dark place that had suddenly - inexplicably - become her life once more.

Sobbing, though to do so shamed her a little, Tina reached down and felt her stomach. Something felt different. She felt different. A dark cloud might have fallen over her in the past few minutes; a darker one might have fallen shortly after, but they were gone now and when they had lifted they had revealed the brightest light imaginable. More powerful than the sun and having the potential to illuminate even those corners which were so dark as to never have been seen. She did not need to feel sickness every time she woke or feel a rising lump behind her slender stomach. She did not need her menstrual cycle to take a well-earned rest or to feel the gentle kick of a child eager to take its first steps in the world. She knew little of such things anyway; only what she had read. She knew only one thing. Sarah might have left her forever, but she was already on her way back. Everything was going to be alright.

Even in the darkest of dreams, it seemed, magic really did happen.

★ ★ ★ ★ ★

I looked back to an empty space. An open vista where, only a few moments ago, Sarah had been standing with wide eyes accentuating her sadness and a strand of fine hair wisping on a cool evening breeze. All that remained to suggest that she had ever been there at all was her distinctive rucksack, flush against the base of the railings. I had open views both ways. There was nowhere she could possibly have gone in such a short space of time.

Except I'm lying to you now. There was one place she could have gone.

But only one.

And it was the one place I didn't want to think about, just in case I was right.

I screamed something – I don't know what – and ran as fast as I could. I think I already knew that it would be too late but I prayed so Goddamned hard that I was wrong.

All the way I begged: *Please no. Please. God. NO.*

For the same reasons I hate flying I also hate heights. They kind of go hand in hand. And I mean I really hate them, but even so I leaned as far over those damn railings as I could, looking down to the crashing waves below. The tide was not yet in and the rocks were a rich deep blue, almost black. I scoured left and right, panicking, but could see nothing but bare rock glistening in the last of the light. Every so often a wave would crash, a plume of white appearing for only a few seconds before disappearing back into the black of the ocean.

Then something happened.

One of those waves receded, and I saw something else.

It was just as white as they were but, unlike them, it did not disappear back into the sea. It stayed exactly where it was; legs together and arms spread out. I am not a religious man, never have been, and yet it reminded me of an image I had been forced to see so many times in my early life, when I had been dragged kicking and screaming to attend the draughty halls of Hardenhall Baptist.

A saviour on a cross. The moment in time when someone selfless died purely so that we all could live.

I placed my hands on the top railing, tipped my head backward and cried. Outward, upward and all around. When it was done, when I had nothing more to give, I sank and stared at my feet.

It was then that I noticed something from the corner of my eye. A light; glinting and swinging gently in the breeze which swirled below me.

A silver locket.

Carefully I unclipped it and opened it up. Inside I saw more than just a locket.

It was a watch; face white as snow, numerals black as coal.

"Even the most adventurous travellers can't be in two places at the same time, Nick..." she had once said. *"and I think you'll remember I said that."*

There were too many things to remember.

None of which I'll ever forget.

FIFTY-SEVEN

MONDAY, JUNE 20, 2011.
WILLOWBROOK CEMETERY,
3KM FROM CEDAR RIDGE, CALIFORNIA.

Only myself, the minister and two of the surliest gravediggers in living history were in attendance.

Let's face it, she was filed as a Jane Doe, and there was no-one else around to care. Not in this lifetime.

It had already been shown that there was no such person 'Sarah Fiddes' anyway, that it had been an identity that she had concocted approximately two years ago and that she had travelled on a fake passport ever since. Like her other fakes, it had been well constructed and entirely convincing. As if to somehow emphasise the feeling of loss I was carrying, and not just for myself, the world also chose to spend the entire day raining like an icy hell. I stood next to a deep hole with my collar turned high as ambiguous words were spoken about a woman the minister had never met and not even I had fully understood.

She had known before she even made the decision to come back that she would ultimately have to take her own life. Perhaps she could have waited until 23rd March, the day before her actual birth, if she had wanted to draw things out a little but I guess that she understood as well as anyone that her life had begun in earnest during those terrifying moments her mother had suffered at the hands of Creed. I can only assume that she felt that the opportunity to meet with her mother and make some attempt to shine a light through a small gap in her life was worth the sacrifice she had no option but to make.

I had spent the entire day after her death and long into the night reading the file she had so carefully compiled on my behalf. Most was handwritten and I'm guessing that long before the case was handed to me by Deacon she was laboriously writing down all the things that she knew, night after night when she returned from visiting her mother. Just so that I might one day understand.

Of course, the first thing I found in the file, although this had been whilst I leaned against my car and watched the rescue team as they hoisted her body, was the suicide note itself. The finest paper; lined envelope. Some of the things she told me did not make complete sense at first, whilst others were so clever, and so typically Sarah, as to make me smile even as I watched the body sliding into the ambulance like an old memory into a drawer.

It was an inescapable fact that Sarah had given me the envelope on the morning after we had first met, before we had even travelled to France, and yet her suicide note, her explanations and apologies for what had happened, were already committed to paper. Just in case.

As the Minister stood in the rain and spoke the words 'earth to earth, ashes to ashes, dust to dust', I smiled to myself again. Here, she had said, was where a battered old Ford will soon arrive to kick some of my dust into cloud.

She had never even met me when she wrote those words, but I guess she knew me already.

Nor had we so much as shared eye contact when she wrote; *The first was that if I ever met the man who raped my mother I would kill him without a thought. The second was that I would never again try to take my own life. This special gift. It is only now, writing a note to a man I've never met, that I realise I lied on both counts* or *Take good care of me.*

She had never even seen my face, yet still she trusted me implicitly to carry the weight of the tasks ahead. I guess it's my duty now to ensure that her trust was not misplaced.

A journey which extended way beyond ensuring that her burial was taken care of. Much, much further. Indeed one of the things I would choose to do in the years to come, although I had no idea at this point, would be to visit young Kenny Wilding. Obviously, given that he had endured nine years of incarceration before being granted parole he wasn't quite as young as he had been. Kenny, if you recall, was my genius *bomberkind* who, at nineteen, had been so very similar to Sarah in the way that he dressed and had been creating complex explosive devices in the bedroom of his ma's house that would have put Mossad to shame before spending sleepless nights testing them on neighbouring warehouses.

By the time I tracked him down to Antimony, a small cactus town in Utah, in late 2015 he had been walking the streets again (albeit dustier ones) for almost a year; and he had absolutely no desire to go back. He took one hell of a lot of convincing. In the end I had to offer him eighty thousand very good reasons, each bearing a picture of the world's most famous cherry tree lumberjack, before I could get him to even hear me out. Even then it was only when we spoke of the timers I wished to use, and the fact that they would need to have special ultra-life battery systems, that he agreed to create the things I needed.

It took him nearly four months to construct the devices and I settled in cash. Fortunately, or cleverly, Sarah had understood that life would be so much easier for me, as would the things I needed to do, had she chosen to leave me just one 'Superbowl' result. Just one: 2021 season; Cowboys to beat Redskins 38-12 long before the season had even started. Before anyone knew which teams would ultimately be facing each other across the Rosebowl.

My $3000 dollar bet, every cent I owned, at odds of 250-1 netted me $625,000 dollars, more than enough to start taking care of those I loved, the late Sarah Fiddes included.

As I said, eighty thousand went straight to Billy. In return I received two devices, both of which demonstrated the same flair for ingenuity and design for which he had garnered his brief spell of infamy almost ten years earlier. Each was about the size of four shoe boxes stacked in a two-plus-two formation and contained enough heavily focused Semtex-H to send an ultra-heated explosion straight upward through anything up to thirty feet of earth and another eighty into the sky beyond. I doubted I would need figures approaching even half that.

I did two things with those devices. First I went downtown, to the place that had been Yang's prior to the barbecue. An immense sign, back-lit, now announced to the world at large that the site had been acquired by KleinWork Research Technology 'for development of their American Corporate Head Office'. In truth, it was standing and staring at that sign two months previously that had given me the very idea in the first place. At that point the work had yet to start but by the time I returned with one of Kenny's Pandora's Boxes, the foundations were already well underway.

Under cover of night I broke through the fencing and, utilising a memory stacked full of Sarah's copious notes, located the area which would become the single storey laboratory and basement behind the main tower itself. On January 2nd 2014, in one of the deep trenches already dug in readiness for the foundations, I planted the device, setting Billy's impressive timer, in hours, for 259,800 exactly. That was precisely 10,825 days or, in other words, 29 years and 240 days. As it was almost three in the morning when I planted it, the device would detonate at precisely the same time exactly one week after Sarah had left.

Or came back. I guess you can look at it both ways, if you're of a mind.

The night watchman caught me in the damn hole, of course, his dog barking down at me from maybe fifty feet away, but neither he or 'Stinger' the German Shepherd saw exactly what I was doing. Thank that computational God I read so much about for small mercies. I made some excuse about having flung my arms out during a heated telephone exchange with my wife (what wife?) and explained how I lost a grip on my cellphone. When I clambered awkwardly out of the hole with it in my hand he seemed happy enough to buy it. He even spared the time to tell me about the plans they had for this whole area and how these KleinWork guys were 'comin hot shit.

I knew that. As indeed I knew that KRT had recently patented a lithium-screen battery which, when placed in a low-power watch, perhaps; a clock or indeed a timer, would last for anything up to a century without losing so much as a second.

That was guaranteed or you (by which I presume they meant your descendants) got your money back in full. Assuming you could still find the receipt.

KRT EverLife Batteries? Irony, it seems, knows few bounds.

I doubted my 'divisive' efforts, if you'll excuse the pun, would put an ultimate end to 'Sequence travel' or whatever it might be salient to call it, but that was not the real point anyway. My only hope was that Klein and Sherman had indeed been wiped out by Sarah's package, though neither of us would ever know for sure, and that the whole project would be thrown into comprehensive disarray. My contribution was merely to hold things back for a few more years after that, that was all. Hopefully to stop anyone coming back and putting things right.

The day after Los Angeles I took another flight to France. It was the only flight I have ever enjoyed in my life. Not many miles from Serres, as expected, I found the abandoned dig site which, in a few years, would be sequestered to become KleinWork's European Livestock Research Centre. For a while I just sat and watched the sun go down; the smell of wet grass in my nose and the leaves rustling in my ears. For a short time earth itself seemed like heaven because it suddenly felt like a much better place.

Once the cover of night had fallen I located the area that would become the lab and planted the second device.

As per my instructions, this second device would explode first; at approximately 7am on the day Sarah left. The time differences between Los Angeles and France threw me into temporary disarray but I worked it out in the end. According to Sarah's notes, I got it right on the money.

The minister's sermon came to a solemn end. Silence, bar

the rain, and he looked to me instead of God, praying that his services were no longer required. I offered an inaudible 'thankyou' and he retreated respectfully, head lowered. The gravediggers – themselves keen to get the job finished and take shelter inside – also decided to make me their god.

I made one final request. With no more than a glance I asked that they allow me a few minutes alone at the graveside before they came back to fill the hole. To bury the past.

They agreed without argument, retreating under the shelter of a tired oak a little way down the cemetery to smoke cigarettes and allow me to say my final goodbyes. I didn't cry because I knew that Sarah Fiddes would be a part of this world again soon enough. I just crouched down low, wished her well and did what exactly I needed to do.

Then I retreated to a bench which overlooked the grave itself and smoked a cigarette of my own. In truth it was the last I ever smoked even though, because of Sarah's note, I knew that the damage was already done.

Very slowly but inescapably, I was dying.

I could not change that fact, because I could not change the past. Could I, Sarah?

But could I really still change the future?

The things that will happen after I'm gone.

FIFTY-EIGHT
SUNDAY, MARCH 24, 2024.
WILLOWBROOK CEMETERY,
3KM FROM CEDAR RIDGE, CALIFORNIA.

And so... here I am again...

Almost thirteen years after Sarah was finally laid to rest, I am sitting on that same bench, trying to protect increasingly frail hands from the cold and reciting the story in my mind as I await the arrival of a very frightened and angry young girl. One who should today be celebrating her twelfth birthday, but instead has recently discovered that her mother had been raped. The pain she is feeling inside, the guilt, is so strong that she believes the only way to assuage it is to offer her own life by way of an apology.

The bench has changed to one a little more worn and uncomfortable - as has my ass - but, short of a few extra graves dotted about the place, little else has. The wind has picked up strength and it's started to rain.

I knew it would.

As Sarah told me in her note and I believe I mentioned only a moment ago, I am dying. To use her words - or were they mine first? - I have a 'terrible disease'. For years it has been eating me alive and now it's feast is.... well, you know the rest.

Lung cancer from years of smoking. When I first read those words and realised that the person described in the note, this 'ScaryBob', was actually me, it hurt to know that Sarah had chosen to inform me that I would be nigh-on dead within thirteen years.

Of course, I could not help but watch the schoolyard on occasion, just to see the young Sarah...

(Alison)

...and I'm not really surprised that I was seen as some kind of dirty old man and given such a derisive nickname by the kids. I mean, what was I really? A sallow old man with dark, critical eyes - occupational hazard - and the kind of raincoat one might reasonably expect to find the elusive Mrs. Columbo sneaking into the trash. I was a dirty old man to anyone who cared to look my way, and however far that might have extended on the outside, I can assure you that even I was never entirely convinced that my dirty beauty was just skin deep.

So, at whatever junctures life allowed me, I took a *Herald* and took a seat on one of the benches nestled within the larches that bordered The Cedar Ridge Home for Homeless Boys and Girls. I know, I call it an orphanage as well, but apparently that's not politically correct any more. In the wind or the rain and, on very infrequent occasions, the kind of sunshine that the lower-lying regions of California seem to enjoy, I sat and I read and I glanced toward the children who laughed and played in the grounds outside 'the home'. The home that was now completely administered by The NorthStar Foundation which, in turn, was a wholly operated - supposedly charitable - subdivision of KleinWork Research Technology Inc.

I'm guessing with the beauty of hindsight that every attempt

I made to look inconspicuous had, like all good chemical and biological reactions, unleashed an equal and opposite reaction. For many years I was a cop. I started in uniform and then I progressed to 'plain clothes'. Never in my chequered career was I undercover. When I was a cop, nothing I could do stopped me looking like a cop. By the time I first visited Cedar Ridge I was a tired old man in an equally tired old raincoat whose only excitement in life, whose only real drug, was staring with an almost indecent degree of excitement at a seven, eight, nine and ten year old little girl.

Consequently, I looked like...

ScaryBob.

It took a long time to get to grips with why Sarah might have chosen to tell me I was dying, to ruin the ending of my book before I had lived it, but when the answers came, I took her for the special woman she was and thanked her with every breath my already infected lungs could expunge.

In the bar in Arques, having met with the late Kelly Brown, Sarah had made me feel the way she had wanted me to feel; guilty as sin itself. She had extracted my feelings, my true feelings, regarding the deaths of Monica and her unborn child, and the spiral of my daughter's life. She summed me up in just one profound sentence...

"Sometimes, whether you like it or not, you just have to face up to the things you've done. Before it's too late."

It was because of those words, I think, that she had felt the need to remind me that my time on this earth, like hers, was limited. To tell me as best she knew how that I had to make amends for the mistakes in my life, and that I had to do it before it was too late.

I doubt that prostitution is the oldest profession on earth. I believe that it's crime, in whatever form crime can take. I also believe that crime will outlive us all. What I started to realise was that crime was not my fault. I did not create it. In fact, I did everything in my limited power to halt its progress, but I also learned that the power it can wield extends way beyond arrest. It sneaks into courtrooms and continues its task until the guilty are freed.

I would love to be able to change that, but I can't.

I didn't make it start. I sure as hell can't make it stop.

What I did create, however, despite the fact that I never once recall sitting down to plan such an event, was a human life. Vicki's life. She was walking this earth, somewhere, because of me and she, more than anything else in this world, was my responsibility. I could not change her past any more than I could change my own, but I could change her future. The life she will lead when I'm gone.

Time may well be just a number, a fourth dimension, but it is a number that counts in only one direction.

Downward.

Rapidly.

The day after Sarah's funeral I walked into Deacon's office and told him that he could keep three things; my badge, my gun and any smart-ass comments he might have thought of throwing my way. I couldn't face wasting even one more of the days I had left catching, tagging and releasing fish only for them to find a big enough hole lurking unseen at the bottom of the dragnet. Deacon was shocked, I think he had me pegged for full pension, but I don't think he was ever going to consider it a major loss to the department.

I told him what I was looking for, and what I would do when I found it. He wished me luck.

I think he might even have meant it.

The car was already packed, long before I went to the precinct, and that allowed me to head directly for the coast road, a sheet of clear plastic taped in the window to protect me from the driving rain that God, the creator of the sequence, had chosen to throw down to earth that day.

As I passed the parking lot at Montalvo I pulled Sarah's tape from the passenger footwell, the one with the 'cool music' and slammed it into the stereo. Thunder, I think she called them, and that was pretty ironic given the weather. I cranked up the volume, punched out the sheeting with my left hand and, heading for Seattle to find my daughter, let the opening track and the cleansing rain wash all over me...

> *Now you've seen the worst I can do,*
> *I don't wanna keep hurtin' you,*
> *Can you find it in yourself to forgive me?*
> *Now you know what I am,*
> *do you think you can stand it?*
> *'Cos I know that it's true...*
> *I've got history in the making with you...*

And she, by which I mean Vicki, did forgive. After a fashion and to a point. It took me three days to track her down via her rather less than forthcoming circle of 'friends'. I'd already spoken to Katherine on the phone and she had told me that she, the good dentist and Vicki had fallen out in a rather spectacular fashion and that Vicki had moved out.

That had been approximately six months previously. Katherine hadn't seen our daughter since and she doubted, given the many harsh words that were spoken that day, that she would ever want to again.

I found her living at her boyfriend's house. By which I mean her pimp. Another shit day; another shit discovery. Whilst she screamed and shouted and hurled everything she could lay her hands on at me, I beat every last ounce of crap out of her pierced little punk friend that I could. Then I dragged her, still screaming her pretty little head off out to the car. It wasn't until two full days later, sitting eating badly cooked burgers in a diner in Las Vegas, that she said her very first words to me.

When they came, they sounded like honey.

"Thanks, Dad."

'Thanks' and 'Dad'. Now I honestly never thought I'd be hearing those two words in the same sentence.

It took a good many months to fully wean her off the shit she was on. Even now I don't think I know *all* the shit she was on. She stayed with me for the next two years or so before finally getting her own place. Close enough for me to keep an eye out for her wellbeing and just far enough away.

As I sit here today, pondering, Vicki is still pierced, still beautiful and working as a social worker for pre-teens. She does a great deal of drug rehabilitation work as well, which is 'kinda cool', to use her words. I never once told her about Sarah, or the things I believed to have happened and to be true. Let's face it, it had taken me long enough to sort her head out and a story such as mine would achieve nothing short of screwing it all back up again.

Once she and I got back from our little road trip, deciding to settle a little ways out of Los Angeles in a desert-edge town by the name of Newberry Springs, I took one last trip back into the city and visited my doctor. Despite the fact that there was visibly nothing wrong with me, he was ultimately persuaded to do the tests I wanted him to do. It was odd that, when he came back with the results the following week; chronic carcinoma of the lungs at least six months old, he was surprised and I wasn't. Not at all.

I rejected all offers of chemo and radiotherapy and shrugged off his claims that without it I would be dead in less than five years. Thanks to Sarah I knew I had a few more, treatment or not. It was only then that I really looked up to the sky and thanked her for telling me that I was going to die, but not just yet.

I would use the time well.

I made peace with Vicki, I made it through to today and if I can make it just that little bit longer, which I will, then I will have done all that this world expected of me.

I can leave on a high note.

I'm not Marlon Brando, but if I was then I'd probably be filming the last scene of *Apocalypse Now* right now. I've had my other minor classics; my *Julius Caesar*, my *On The Waterfront* and my *Godfather* and I know that now I'm using the state I'm in - and the fact that I can remain in shadow - to play one last role; the one that suits.

The one that, when it's done, should close off my life in style. I could try to go on and battle in whatever style I can muster against the creeping rust which is rife within my lungs, but what's the point?

Like Sarah, I know that the time to leave is when the time is right. Besides, when you've abused your body the way I have and you're a frail and crumbling mess, trying to pretend you're Superman's dad only serves to make you look stupid.

★ ★ ★ ★ ★

And now I see her, *God's special gift to us all*, entering the graveyard through the heavy iron gates down the hill to my left, having no doubt sneaked away from the confines of Cedar Ridge. She is not crying, not that I can see anyway, but she is walking with a pace that suggests that the weight of the world might be carried on her tiny shoulders. She is as beautiful as ever; the kind of girl that friends of parents, where there are parents, say 'she's gonna break hearts someday'.

She is still wearing the uniform she described in her note and the one which, as ScaryBob, I have seen her wearing in the schoolyard on occasion. What I still could never get over, right from my very first playground visit, was and is how much she looks like her sister... her mother. Those eyes, and the hair; the exact same shade. Not a trace of the jet black dye that dominated her adulthood in my version of L.A.

Though she is upset, she does not meander left and right with no direction as the distraught so often do. She thinks she knows where she is going and, very purposefully, she heads there directly.

The twelve year old Alison Bond has dealt with more in those few years than many more fortunate souls suffer in a lifetime. As yet she has no idea where her mother's body had been buried in the weeks after she had died following the emergency midnight Caesarean in the ward of Thousand Oaks. As yet she has no idea of her mother's true name; who she was or indeed what she was. She will learn all these things in time, but for now it does not really matter. She has been to this place before with her friend Gemma and has noticed a grave which seems to be the embodiment of the things she knows about the woman who offered up her life for her.

I have visited this grave often and for the first few years I even brought flowers - orchids. Other times I brought the weather with me along with a seemingly pointless array of stories, updates and memories. At first speaking aloud in an empty graveyard seemed to be the first rung on my descent into a senility that would never be granted the opportunity to run its course. By the fourth of fifth occasion I started to realise that I was not going crazy, but it was the world around me which was spiralling out of control. From that moment on I spoke to Sarah with the kind of forced clarity usually reserved for politicians at rallies.

I have resisted all temptation to dress Sarah's grave or tend to it in any way in the years since I braved the rain following the funeral. Never did I bring a trowel and I never did I bring soapy water for the stone. I ensured at all times that the this place would continue to be what it was always destined to be....

'as far away from the neatly tended plots and marble statues as it can possibly be... alone and left fighting for itself against the world, its twenty-dollar stone crumbling at the edges whilst year after year the inscription fades beneath another layer of dirt.'

> *Hear Lies, God's special gift to us all.*
> *Those who care are those who need to know.*
> *Until He crosses our paths again.*
> *Be at peace.*

I like to think, given that it was my decision to give the twelve year old Sarah somewhere meaningful from which to find the strength to go forward - to make the most of the life that she was handed - that I am not without my own sense of irony. And yes, the miss-spelling of 'here' to 'hear' was, of course, deliberate and caused a no small degree of puzzlement from the mason when I commissioned it. No-one I had met had heard more lies throughout their life than Sarah, and no-one had been more capable of finding the truth.

Truly a special gift.

So here she is, begging forgiveness at a grave that is not her mother's but is, in truth, her own. And yes, the words on that twenty dollar stone - which actually cost eighty - could indeed have been written specifically for her, because she did care and she did need to know. I know that she will find peace, but she will do it like her sister – her mother - in her own very special way.

As yet Sarah, *Alison*, is totally unaware, as I was until after she was gone, that the real beauty of her existence is that she has absolutely no idea just how unbelievably important it actually is. Not yet. My job now is to be a friend to her, to give her the strength to keep fighting against the knowledge that has been thrust upon her and lead her instead toward a life in which she will make some attempt to put things right. She has come here today to apologise to her mother. My job is to put her back on the right road, at the end of which she would still be apologising, but she'd be doing it in person.

The world has changed a great deal over the last few years of my life. It keeps changing. In time – its similarly relentless partner - you will see for yourself what I mean. Suffice for me to say that a relentless pursuit of science is not always a good thing. Progress is not always in the right direction, 'cheaper' often costs more of the things we hold dear, and better... well, it usually isn't.

Alison understood that, but Sarah doesn't. Not yet.

I read somewhere that in the years since the world experienced the Industrial Revolution, human advancement has doubled every fifty years. From then, until now. If plotted on a graph, the line of progress would now be almost vertical. Shooting straight into the heavens.

How ironic, then, that every progressive step takes us further away.

So where is it that we are going and do we really want to go there anyway? I don't suppose it matters, given that they'll probably just carry us along whether we like it or not.

I've heard stories of people who drink 'milk', still blissfully unaware that now, in my time, it is nothing more than a shortened version of a trade-name: 'Tastes Like Milk', and has never seen a cow in its drastically extended shelf-life. The only milk remaining is the clichéd one: that of human kindness and, given that there is no profit to be gleaned from tampering with it, the shelf-life on that is as short as it always was.

I've got my cell phone, I made damn sure of that, and I'll call Sheriff Coulson before I go to meet her, but before I do I also check that I have the locket. The wind is biting cold against my hand, but somehow I manage to open the tricky clasp and see the near-perfect face inside.

For the first time since this all began, I begin to understand just how important this watch must be.

How important it must always have been.

The reason I understand this only now, so late in my day, is because for the first time I realise just how heavily degraded the outer casing has become, having been exposed to the elements over and over again. Yet nowhere in that history that cannot be changed is there a record of this watch ever being made.

I have been born - true - and very soon it seems I will die. Sarah has also been born, and yes she will die, albeit in a completely different time in readiness to be born again. Now there's a mindfuck loop to get your head around; *for me it always starts…* I stopped trying a long time ago.

Nevertheless, Sarah has been born and Sarah will die. Yet this seemingly insignificant piece of jewellery has passed from Sarah to me and I will soon be handing it back. She will carry it with her and keep it safe only to leave it hanging from the railings when she is gone. Over and over this process will repeat.

Maybe until the end of time itself.

So where the hell did it come from?

Until the end of time itself. So maybe, strange as it sounds, it's true after all. Maybe this watch has been sent into our loop by some higher power, just to remind us that *if the seconds ever stopped counting, so would those of the world around us.*

That sounds about right. I'll remember to tell her that.

I place the locket back in my pocket and look to my constant companion, Sarah's letter, just one more time. With a broad, knowing smile. Then I lift my head to see this beautiful, hurting child as she falls desperately to her knees.

This is no suicide note; it never has been. Quite simply, it is Sarah Fiddes' personal instruction manual to Nick Lambert for the things which must - and will - happen today. Prepared as I might finally be, I find I cannot wait another second. The time is now. *My* time is now, and I must go to meet her. My hands are trembling, but not from the cold. As I believe I mentioned before, this is the kind of feverish excitement that has eluded me all my life and, I mean to enjoy it to the full before I go.

With the call to the Sheriff's Office complete I amble down the path and, whilst I make no attempt to tread quietly, she does not hear me approach, so wrapped is she in her grief. I can hear every one of her hopeless sobs the closer I get.

I stand behind her for a moment and take a deep breath in readiness for the task ahead. Then I speak the words she told me I would speak.

"Are you alright, young lady?"

She does not hear me, and didn't I know that would be the case?, so I crouch down and ask her for a second time, expanding. In a few minutes we will both be seated on the bench from which I have just walked, talking as though we have been friends for years (and in many ways we have) as I await the arrival of Coulson's Dodge, the one with the smudged 'D'.

As we talk, I wonder to myself if Sarah ever gave serious thought to what would happen to the tables after she was gone; what I would choose to do with them. Did she ever realise that, because she had expressed a desire that they should *never* be found, that I might seek out and choose the perfect place? Or did she simply... trust me?

Again, I used my time well, I feel. Whilst the diggers smoked cigarettes in the rain, I removed a package wrapped in cloth from my inside pocket, took one last glance, added a wry smile and lowered it gently into Sarah's grave

Minutes later the men returned and started shovelling the heavy soil back over, the cheap wooden coffin disappearing into the spirit of the earth. How long it remains there will, as ever, be dictated by a power far greater than you or I.

Émile Zola once wrote, and I'm quoting directly here: *'If you shut up the truth and bury it under the ground it will but grow, and gather itself such explosive power that the day it bursts through, it will blow up everything in its way'.*

You may choose to believe that I made this whole story up, but if that's the case then I must warn you that you are crediting me with far more creative intelligence than I deserve. As a free and rational thinking individual, choosing to believe that none of this ever happened is indeed your prerogative, but trust me...

It will.

Some of it already has.

★ ★ ★ ★ ★

I am sixty-two years old, I am cold and I will be a darn sight colder in the not too distant future. I'm sure as hell gonna struggle to shake hands with sixty-three. And yes, I may be dying, but that's not to say that I am unhappy. I found a purpose, and I suppose that by expounding everything that has happened – good and bad – to you, I feel that little bit cleaner.

I have nothing left to hide.

In the meantime, whilst I await the guy with the keys to the downstairs gate, I am crouched beside a beautiful young girl, one who is begging forgiveness at her own grave and who is about to take the first tentative steps on a journey to find and steal back sacred tablets of stone, supposedly handed down from God himself. If they are what mankind believes them to be – and like all true religious icons, they make no claims of their own – then those tables hold the kind of coded knowledge that mankind should never, ever be allowed to possess.

And yet, as she begs, that knowledge is buried approximately four feet beneath Sarah's very own shoes.

The ones she normally keeps so clean

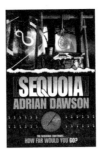

THE SEQUENCE CONTINUES...
ADRIAN DAWSON
[SEQUOIA]
SPRING 2012

There were always going to be consequences...

Peter Strauss had no idea just how devastating and
far reaching those consequences would be...

In 1645, at the height of the Witchfinder General's tyrannical campaign
through England, Rachael Garland is brutally tortured then tried,
convicted and hung as witch; her body dumped in a well. Almost four
hundred years later, all that remains of her existence are shattered bones
and a wooden crucifix laid on her body; the sequoia crucifix that Peter
Strauss had personally given to Rachael... on March 22nd 2040.

Strauss has just one week before all hell breaks loose. One week to
decide whether he should try to save the future of mankind or the
woman he loves. He knows that not one moment in history can
be changed and that ultimately Rachael Garland will have to die.

If he's clever, he can make it part of the plan.

**If you could travel back in time, knowing you could
not change the past... just how far would you go?**

READ THE OPENING CHAPTER OF
[SEQUOIA] ON THE FOLLOWING PAGES...

To be published by Last Passage
in Paperback and all ebook Formats.
buy the paperback and get the ebook for free

isbn: 978-0-9565770-9-2

PROLOGUE

AUGUST 1ST 1645.
MANNINGTREE, ESSEX, ENGLAND.

"Stretch the bitch! Stretch her neck!"

The ears were the first to wake; scooping the full horror of the screams, taunts and jeers and sending them to a brain which almost begged the eyes to follow suit.

"She conjures with dark spirits..."

The chorus of baying, of which her voice had long been one of the more vocal members, echoed through a head that felt all too empty and remote. It formed a pounding beat, more powerful even than the drummers heralding the victorious not two months past as they took the proud march back from Naseby. Their heads had been held high to catch every scent of victory the air might carry. Her head, by contrast, fell limp; her body denying her the strength required to lift it.

"Don't touch her. She lay with satan..."

The cries and cheers now forcing their way inside her mind were not those of victory, but it certainly carried an air of imminent triumph. Indeed, on previous occasions such as these, victory itself had felt hollow by comparison; a vacuum, if such a heretical, godless thing could exist. The end result was

2

always the same; one more malefactor swaying limply from the hemp as the wind blew away the cheers as quickly as it had the life of the damned. The lives of the crowd, meanwhile, the jeerers and the cheerers, the screamers and the shriekers, just... carried on. No searing light from above congratulating them on their godly deed and no wind of change to cool their still-sweating skin.

Which could only mean one thing... there were more... and they were hiding in plain sight. More to watch, more to search, more to prick, more to swim and more to judge.

More, inevitably, to hang.

It felt so right; wholesome, pure and glorious.

And yet, this time, so very, very wrong.

Eventually her eyes got word and started to open. Gently at first, as even the first strains of daylight cut like shards. Slowly, the shapes came into view; a sea of colour turbulently riding a dark storm. Bodies pushed hard against each other as they fought to get close enough to convince themselves that this was all their doing, that they alone had saved the world from the darkness which crept through its midst as the end of days drew ever closer.

She had seen it so many times, and she loved it. She *lived* for it. It had become a part of who she was. Some would scream, some would prod and some would throw their dunny buckets and cackle loudly but she... she was a spitter. And she knew, just *knew*, that one day her pious spittle would do what the law – save for the treason of killing one's husband – would no longer permit: it would burn the flesh of the heretics and make them scream right back at her.

As the half-opened eyes began to focus and the raging sea

formed into a jostling crowd, she could see for the first time why things had felt so wrong this time. Every venomous eye was present, casting judgment as surely as they once cast stones. Mary Parkin; washer woman with whom she had jostled shoulders many times of late; Martha Saunders to whom she had given a piglet not a year past; and the saturnine John Cutler who had long suspected that the scurrilous Anne West had borne the cause of his son's excruciating death, but was not blessed with enough of God's strength to prosecute.

All were there, crammed in the still air and sharp shadows of late summer sun, to reap their share of the glory and carry it righteously home. The only eyes that were missing were hers, and these others were not casting hatred *with* her, as they had done many times before; they were casting it *at* her.

As she was pushed through waves of bodies like flotsam on a ferocious tide, she felt a harsh metallic rub against her ankles and heard the tell-tale rattle of manacles. They impeded her stride, though she felt her stride was not much of her doing anyway, and caused her to stumble with alarming regularity. Each time she was heaved near-upright by rough hands and pushed once more into the squall. No pause for breath.

She felt as wretched and weak as they saw her and, as sensation began to slither through the rest of her body, she realised that she was not, as times before, being jostled herself. There was pain, but not the mangle-squeeze of days gone by. What she felt instead were a thousand pins cutting into her throat – a scarf of thorns – and a full-length poking; harsh, violent, ceaseless prodding which ran a random course from the tender flesh of her thighs to the unforgiving bones in her shoulders.

Those who prodded only ever did so with a hastily acquired

4

branch or a 'skill-carved' walk-stick, never with flesh or finger. Evil was, after all, that most vile of diseases; more consuming than tuberculosis and more disgusting than the pox. Worse still, one might not even know one had caught such an ague. There would be no ring of roses, no blood in the sputum and no rasping cough to keep the household awake throughout the victim's final days.

Evil was imperceptible in form. It hid its dark infection in the shadows of the mind, slowly stripping away the love for ones neighbour on which puritan beliefs were founded. There was only one cure for such evil and that was to send it back to the depths from which it had risen; something that could only be achieved by destroying the vessel in which it had sailed.

Love thy neighbour, certainly, but only if thy neighbour was pure of heart and clean of soul.

Lay waste the flotilla of evil.

In an irony that she could barely find space in her frantic mind to perceive, she prayed that this was some mistake. Or, perhaps, it was a trial of faith that her God; the true God who scorned the lavish iconography of the King, was allowing her to see before he lifted her to his bosom and thanked her for her resolve. As she thought such thoughts, never daring to truly believe them, the shackles from her ankles seemed to fall away and her feet did indeed begin to lift from the earth. She felt as though she were floating toward heaven itself. She wanted to stretch out her arms, as the Lord had done, and await God's embrace but there was no strength to be found in her blood.

It did not take long for her to realise that she was wrong...

This was no lift of glory. She could feel from the force thrust upon, around and about her that her body was not being raised as one might elevate a conqueror, but rather as one might elevate the conquered. She had seen heads sliced clean from the lower vessel, crimson still pouring from their necks as they were paraded into the village from a nearby skirmish. They were held high for all to see, violently thrown from side to side with unabated anger; vile icons held aloft as such.

And that was how it felt. How *she* felt.

She could see the full extent of the crowd as her head fell limply to one side. They filled the square and, in the distance, had climbed aboard every wall, barrel and pillar in order to get the clearest possible view of her imminent demise. All arms were raised in anger; all eyes creased in disgust.

Within a few seconds, those who had dared to raise her removed their hands and she was on her feet again; higher now. She felt something solid below her feet, a bar perhaps, on which her heels were perched, but with her body still weak it offered no support. It seemed as though all the fear she felt – all that she had ever known – had risen from her belly and gathered in her throat, its volume impairing even her ability to breathe. When she tried to speak, and then to cry out, nothing came.

Something had gone wrong. Terribly wrong. She was not supposed to be here. There had been a mistake. This was not how or when she was destined to meet her God, but the hatred in the eyes of those screaming and spitting up at her told her in an instant that they knew or cared little. Only one man might know and – if, please God, he were here – he might be her one chance at salvation.

She mustered all the force her body might allow and slowly raised her head; the thorns cutting deep and strands of matted red hair sticking to eyes already darkened from the filth which clung like blackened scabs to her face. As she narrowed her eyes to focus, the mists in her head not yet cleared, she took on the appearance the crowd had long expected: evil coming to the fore as she, in their eyes, scoured their faces and seethingly condemned every soul among them.

Eventually she found her prize: Matthew, the man whose word was as close to God as many of the lesser villagers might ever come, standing in the distance. Matthew did not try and he did not condemn; that was for those who filled his purse. Matthew merely confirmed what they had all suspected and, by his confirmation, sent the wretched to a fitting end. Accordingly, he stood on the periphery of the crowd, slightly raised (though she could not see how, a small barrel was often his device of choice) and watched. As he too scoured the crowd, a gentle smirk carving an arc through a shortened beard, fate intervened and their eyes crossed paths. Again she tried to speak and again she failed, so she pleaded to him with her eyes; begging with all that she found. She expected him to see the error in an instant, to spot the good amongst the foul as surely as he spotted the malevolent among the gracious, but he did not.

Instead, the smirk grew wider.

Once the ladder was kicked, so would his purse.

She opened her mouth, cracked lips sticky with the most unholy concoction of blood, saliva and thrown excrement and took a deep rasping inward breath. When it was released, it would form just one word; *his* name in *her* voice and... if his eyes could not know who she was... then his ears surely would. Like Matthew the Apostle he would spread the word and she - the blessed - would be saved. A raised hand and a stern word would bring a halt to proceedings, his unerring authority still riding with him, and she would be lowered - gently - back to earth.

She would meet her God another day.

As the inward air started to slow and her lungs were filled so tightly that she thought her chest might burst, she prepared to scream. Suddenly, as if to listen, the crowd fell silent...

"Matth..."

And she fell. Not all the way to earth, but far enough for the tight hemp she now felt around her neck to pull tighter still, crushing the thorns into her throat, gripping her windpipe in its fist and stopping the word before it even dared cut the air.

She moved her feet, unsure if it was by twitch or by design, and found nothing below them. She was neither on earth nor in heaven but caught in that realm which lies between; the realm inhabited by bats at night and by ravens by day.

The ladder was gone. With it, her chance of life.

Seconds turned to minutes and minutes to what seemed like hours. Her breath grew weaker and her body weaker still.

As the crowd slowly started to cheer once more, she did not even feel the cold relief of hands tugging at her ankles; family or friends desperately trying to shorten the suffering of those they loved. She had no-one in this world because no-one knew who she was. To them, she was a stranger from another place; a usurper. When they looked at her now they saw someone - something - they did not, and could not, comprehend.

No-one here really knew why the sun rose. As such, they feared that it might never rise again. No-one understood why the rains came in spring and gave new life to crops, so they fretted that every drop they felt might be the last. If one does not understand, then it is wise to fear and such men and women as know this do not wish to live their lives afraid. Instead, they seek to remove those who will not conform, banish the unclean and wage war against the agents of satan.

Kill what you are afraid to understand.

Stand and cheer as the life they carried is hung to dry in the midday sun.

With one final rasping breath, she closed her eyes.

★ ★ ★ ★ ★

When Old Lady Partridge - Milly - had ceased to breathe some years ago and then returned within the hour to her children, there had been many in Lawford who had sought to swim her, as such a reawakening was surely the work of dark spirits. This was, of course, in the days before swimming was outlawed (though you could still find it practiced if you had a mind to look) and a good many years before the authoritative Judgment of Hopkins and Stearne had ridden into town.

Milly, they said, was a witch and must be proven as such. In a precursor to Hopkins' own techniques, a jury of matrons was assembled and they ventured to her cottage on the outskirts of town. There they would watch and walk her for as many days as it took to gather the 'Tokens of Tryall' that would ultimately condemn her to the gallows.

It was only when Old Mil' had recounted her tale, and told with new found life and no shortage of detail how she had spent those minutes 'in clear dream of a light, some distance away but calling her name', that the villagers began to change their views. Of course, until the day she died, dropping like fresh-hewn wheat in the field as she worked, Milly was never treated the same. She was different, perhaps, and to be feared for that alone but the question had ceased to be about whether she should be feared for being an agent of evil... or rather feared for being an agent of God himself.

If Milly were indeed a malevolent soul, then why had heaven itself brought her to its gates? Why had it beckoned her into its fold and then, more strangely, sent her back to the toil which had ultimately keeled her skyward again? Had her piety, which until that point had never been questioned, been rewarded by heaven granting her a new position; overseer of living souls?

From that day forth, not one in the village spoke ill of Old Milly Partridge and even after her second, more permanent, demise her name became one with Divine Retribution. From 'mind thy chatter' to 'eat your pottage', all were bolstered now with 'lest Old Mil' come back to reap you'. For Old Mil' had glanced the truth of death. She had seen heaven calling - a bright white light, the brightest she had ever seen, nestling at the end of a long dark tunnel and gently calling her forth...

That's what heaven looked like.

★ ★ ★ ★ ★

Which was why, when she finally awoke, the woman whose grave - had she been offered the dignity of one - would have been marked "Rachael Garland" (the very reason the villagers of Lawford and Mistley had felt it so apt to adorn her with a garland of thistles) believed that she too now saw heaven.

The gallows might have taken her breath but, as was so often the case (especially where there were none to tug the ankles), it had not fully taken her life. That usually came later, often in a shallow grave below the gallows themselves or behind the gaol, and usually held down by a stake or a rock to prevent the unholy rising again come Judgment Day. A day which, in all their hearts, loomed ever closer.

"Open up your eyes."

As sticky eyelids peeled apart one more time than she had ever thought they would, she saw ahead of her the sight that Old Mil' herself must have seen as she lay swaddled in her bedclothes. A long, round, dark tunnel which stretched toward a distant, powerful light; the brightest she had ever seen.

All the while her name was being called to her, not in a thousand harsh tones as it had been in the square, but in the gentle lilt of melody; a minstrel singing a psalm direct into her heart. Over and over, as clear as day and an instruction to open her eyes. This was not a melody she recognised, though she had seen most of the touring minstrels at the fairs and been sung many a song by beggars looking for pennies. Nevertheless, it was a beautiful, ethereal tune; a serene breeze crossing over the Stour on a warm summer day and caressing her face with soft, harmonious fingers.

The words contained within told her that the sun was up, that the sky was blue. This was, they said, a brand new day and she was now a part of everything.

She could feel searing pain, and yet she felt assuaged to it. Her body seemed as though it were cushioned; perhaps resting on soft velvet as she made preparation for her final journey.

When a dark human-esque shape came into view at the farthest reaches of the tunnel, presumably St. Peter himself, the light around his frame was so bright that he seemed to glow, his form suffused with holy divinity. The melodic words came to a halt and, in a crisp clear voice, he said:

"You forgot something..."

She could see a slender arm outstretched; a glimmer and then suddenly something was falling toward her. As it fell it seemed to waver as though dancing on the breeze. Closer and closer it came until it landed firm but light; dead centre on her chest. It took all the strength she could muster, and hurt more like hell than heaven, but she reached across and clumsily took it in her bleeding hand.

A solitary crucifix, rough-carved from a dark wood. She could just make out an inscription, and feel the ridges with her thumb, but the blinding light beyond would not permit her to read it.

She smiled, albeit lamely. Her faith was being returned, she decided. She had allowed the flame of hope to dwindle at the gallows and God, rather than punish her, had seen the piety of her existence. He had brought her soul, like Old Mil's, to the gates of heaven itself. Now, her faith rekindled, he would surely lift her aloft to join her fallen kin.

As she wriggled, pain tearing through every bone, and turned her head, her left cheek pressed against something soft and slightly warm. She struggled more, pushing into the softness with her elbows and turning further to see what it might be. The light was poor but when she finally realised; she screamed. With her throat long-since crushed, what crept forth and echoed before her, however, was more akin to the desperate rasp of a dying animal spending its final hours locked in a trap.

She craned, looked to her right and saw more. Then down to her feet; more still. They were everywhere. She wanted to kick out, to push them away, but her legs refused to move. She could see her feet in the gloom, but they could not see her and they resolutely ignored her commands. As she tried, the darkest pain she had ever felt was beginning to make itself known in her lower reaches of spine.

[Sequoia]

Not velvet. Bodies. She was laid upon layer after layer of bodies. How many she did not care to count, but some were fresh enough to be warm whilst others wore the torn blue of ragged flesh and had maggots where once they might once have had eyes. Some had only the last gasps of hair to show that they were once a living thing.

She looked back to heaven, to her waiting Saint, confused. No melody now and no words, just another shape, smaller this time, creeping into the halo of light. She saw it falter for the briefest moment and then tumble; a breeze pressing her face as though some unstoppable force were hurtling toward her.

Finally, she opened her eyes.

Not only to the world, but also to the truth of who she was, of where she was and of where it was she might be going.

The last thing she saw, in that brief glimmer of realisation before her face was shattered and her skull crushed near-flat, was the sharp cut of the stone from the edge of the well picking up speed. It bounced awkwardly from the dank sides, spinning wildly as it caught the rough-hewn boundary of a sixty-three foot descent. Eventually, it filled her field of view.

When it stole the last of the light, it did so forever.

Had she been alive to hear him leave, she would have heard her Saint one more time; the melody dancing through the wind.

Cheerier this time.

This was indeed a brand new day.

He would make it last an eternity.

ALSO BY ADRIAN DAWSON:

THE NUMBER ONE BESTSELLER
ADRIAN DAWSON
CODEX

"A classy, compelling and intelligent thriller." - The Bookbag

"It's refreshing in a blockbuster thriller such as Codex that one doesn't have to put one's intelligence on the back burner." – Crimetime

When Jack Bernstein's prodigal daughter Lara is killed as a result of the bombing of flight 320, the chess grandmaster is completely unaware that the flight was downed for one reason... to ensure that his daughter never made it home.

Having been summoned via a strangely coded message to a meeting with a man referring to himself only as 'Simon', Jack is made aware that his daughter was leaving a lot more than her new life behind. She was also leaving a secret... one that has been building for centuries and one which a global group of corporations will stop at nothing to protect. It soon becomes apparent that Lara Bernstein's new life was no accident. Lara was selected to become part of an ever-expanding belief and her selection was a direct result of her father's company's near-perfection of the one thing they need - true artificial intelligence, computer systems capable of cracking the most complex codal system known to man.

Slowly, Jack Bernstein is being drawn into a global game of chess in which he has been an unwitting pawn for over a decade. To keep him in the game they have already killed his wife and now his daughter. When the game is over, they will kill a whole lot more unless Jack can find the one thing he never dreamed existed...

PUBLISHED BY LAST PASSAGE
AVAILABLE IN PAPERBACK AND ALL EBOOK FORMATS.
BUY THE PAPERBACK AND GET THE EBOOK FOR FREE

ISBN: 978-0-9565770-0-9